MOM SQUAD

A SWEET, SMALL TOWN ROMANTIC COMEDY

KACI LANE

For all the mamas out there struggling to juggle it all.
Know that you ARE enough and you're NOT alone.
I see you, boo!

MOM SQUAD

CHAPTER 1

Aniston

"Aniston! I told you to stop eating crack."

I blink until Morgan comes into focus. She's standing over me, hands on her hips, like Captain Marvel about to throw down some bad guys.

But in this scenario, the bad guy is me. My crime? OD-ing on cookie crack.

Yep. Of all the family recipes my mom left behind, the one I chose to learn consists of four ingredients. Two of those being sugar.

I roll onto my side and moan. Like an addict, I reach for the pan of decadent homemade dessert, but Morgan squeezes me between her feet, immobilizing me from reaching farther.

She's got a good sixty pounds or so on me, and I'm coming off a sugar high. "Move your foot, or I'll puke." My tight-as-a-tick stomach can only take so much before it blows.

Morgan moves one foot the slightest bit so I can breathe, then bends at the waist. In one fell swoop, she snatches me up by the arm and grabs the pan of cookie crack with her other hand. Raising four kids with minuscule help from her cheating ex has made her scrappy.

When we were growing up, she was much more like my sister. A poised Southern belle who wouldn't hurt a flea. Now she'd be my number-one draft pick for any type of backyard ball or in case I need an alibi or wingman—eh, wingwoman—to help me bury a body.

I slide from underneath her and adjust the T-shirt I'm wearing. Even though it's so old and faded, you can see straight through it, pulling it down to cover my Thursday panties at least gives me the illusion of decency. And by Thursday panties, I mean that they say Thursday on the rear and that I've had them on since Thursday.

Today is Sunday. Not that I'm counting.

The first thing I did after my sister and brother-in-law's funeral was treat my niece and nephew to a nice, long road trip that ended at Disney World. In the time we've been back at their home, I can't seem to function.

Morgan gives me her best mom stare as I hoist myself onto the edge of the bed. "I'm worried about you, Aniston." She pinches off a corner of what's left of the cookie and slides it into her mouth.

"I thought you were on a diet."

She rolls her eyes and laughs around a mouthful of cookie dough. "I'm at least forty pounds overweight and carried four kids full term. I'm always 'on a diet.'" She accents the words with air quotes. "Besides, this is your one-woman intervention. Don't try and flip the script on me."

Busted. I smirk and fold my gangly legs under me. "I'll be fine." I glance around the guest bedroom, wishing that were true.

It's worthy of a *Southern Living* center spread, with a comfy queen-sized bed and peaceful view to the property below. But with the woman who put so much love into making this place a home no longer here, it feels like the most hospitable prison cell imaginable.

"It's just being here. Back in Apple Cart. In *their* house."

"I know." Morgan sighs and breaks off a larger piece of crack as her eyes mist. "I see her in every room." She sniffles, then glances back at me. "And I see her in you."

I raise my eyebrows high enough to hurt my head.

Morgan shakes her head. "Not now, not like this." She points a finger at me and scowls. I stare at her chipped purple nail polish to keep from letting the scowl intimidate me.

"It's just hard, you know?" My voice cracks. I try and convince myself it's from eating too much cookie and not because I'm on the verge of crying—again.

Morgan sits beside me and sets the crack pan on the opposite side of her. "Absolutely. Raising kids is hard, especially alone." She pats my knee. "I can't even begin to put myself in your place. One minute you're the cool, traveling aunt who blows through during the holidays with one-of-a-kind souvenirs, and the next you're signing custody papers after a tragedy."

That summary is all it takes for my vision to blur. I dab at the corners of my eyes with my fingertips. Morgan gives my knee a gentle squeeze. "I'm not gonna lie to you, Aniston. It will be hard. But you're gonna make it, and I will be here to help you along the way."

I bite my bottom lip to keep it from quivering and give her a slight nod. She smiles and wraps me in a hug. We both cry for a minute, mourning the loss of my sister. Yet again.

As we pull apart, I glance behind her at the pan. She snatches it up and stands before I can even think about trying to steal it. "No more crack!"

I sigh. "How do you do that?"

"I have a theory that God gives you an extra set of eyes with every child, and I'm a mom of four." Morgan points two fingers to her eyes, then to me. "I'm watching you, Aniston Wilson."

I laugh, and my shoulders ache, proving how worn my body is from lack of sleep and proper nutrition. Some nights I have to lie in my RV to sleep. Not so much out of habit as out of not wanting to stay in Jennifer's house.

Both my parents were dead by the time I finished college, so when I came home, I came here. Being ten years older than me, Jennifer was like my mom and sister all rolled into one. I had the best of both worlds with her. We didn't always see eye to eye, but she loved me unconditionally, as I did her.

We'd talked before about me raising the kids if something were to ever happen to both her and Luke. I gladly accepted the honor of stepping up to the task. Deep down, I never anticipated it becoming a reality.

I'm like a third-string quarterback. I studied the playbook now and again and had a good relationship with the other players. However, I never thought the first and second string would go down at the same time, leaving me to carry the game. And every game from now on, or at least until all the players reach legal adulthood.

I blow out a large puff of air and blink. Wow. Morgan doesn't blink back. She's like some sort of eagle-eyed mom robot. "Morgan, I appreciate you helping me."

Her expression softens at my compliment. Score! I really did mean it. Even if I said it to get rid of her RBF.

She sets the cake pan on the dresser. "Why don't you and the kids come to my house for supper tonight?"

"Are you not tired of my kids? You had them last night and this morning at church."

"Nope. I love cooking for people, and you guys are like family."

I smile. Morgan is like family, and she's a great cook. I remember when she'd bring something to Jennifer's holiday parties or summer grill outs. I've survived on cereal and sugary treats since parking the RV last week. My body needs some Southern soul food.

"What can I bring?"

Morgan's cheeks shake like she's fighting off a laugh. She straightens her face and nods at the pan. "The rest of this will be fine."

I wrinkle my nose at it. Only a third of the cookie cake is left. The rest of the pan is scattered crumbs and scrapes from where I forked my way through most of it last night and today.

"I'll be checking to see how much is in there tonight too. Come at six."

I nod. "Yes, ma'am."

Morgan smooths out her shirt and heads for the door. She turns and narrows her eyes at me. "Please shower and put on some pants . . . or shorts. Anything, really."

I salute her, and she shakes her head before walking out and closing the bedroom door behind her. One more deep breath to compose myself, then I'm on my feet and reaching for the cake pan. Not to eat it, but to safely put it away until tonight.

After one last peek at my kryptonite, I take the lid from the floor and cover the pan. I start out of the room, but first circle back for a pair of shorts. Best not to scar my seven-year-old nephew with a front-row view to my Thursday panties.

My athletic shorts fit a little snug around the waist after the cookie binge, so I slide the waistband a little lower. Probably for the best, as my shorts now show beneath the oversized shirt I've slept in the last few nights. It's also a good thing I'm so small chested, since this sports bra's elastic is about as taut as a piece of yarn.

I emerge from my lair and hope my niece and nephew can't smell the "I cried and ate crack all night" practically leaking from my pores.

Who am I kidding? They're smart. My best hope is that they choose not to bring it up and embarrass me further.

On my way to the kitchen, the doorbell rings. I start to yell for someone to get it, but decide I've been enough of a diva for one decade. The least I can do is open the front door. It's probably Morgan forgetting something. I pass the kitchen and answer the front door.

"Hey, Mor—" My eyes meet a broad chest in a snug T-shirt and follow it to broad shoulders and a handsome face.

Between my self-induced low blood sugar and realizing what I must look like to him with greasy hair mounted on my head and a see-through shirt/nightgown, I have to steady myself from falling. One hand on the door frame and one hand holding the pan, I manage to whisper, "You're not Morgan."

"No, I'm Easton, your neighbor from the carriage house." He holds out a hand, and I realize he's offering it for me to shake. I let go of the door frame to grasp his hand, but start to fall forward. He catches me and steadies me against the door.

"Thanks." My cheeks are on fire. Either I'm having an unnatural allergic reaction due to cookie crack OD, or I'm blushing. I swallow as he hands me a box.

"This was left at my place by mistake. It's addressed to Aniston Wilson, and I know that was . . ." He shakes his head. "Or is Jennifer's sister."

I nod. "That's me." I take the box and exchange it for the cake pan. Why, I'm not sure, but he takes it when I shove it at his Marvel-hero-worthy chest. "Well thanks, neighbor." I turn and go inside, then slam the door and collapse against it.

Immediately, I regret shutting the door on him. However, in my recent life as a nomad, not once did a handsome man come knocking on my RV. And no amount of romance novels or fairy-tale movies could prepare me for how to react to this IRL. Especially when I look like a homeless hippie.

I lick the corner of my mouth. Make that a homeless hippie with dried cream cheese frosting on her face.

Welcome home, Ani, welcome home.

Easton

I'm cemented on my new landlord's front porch. Luke and Jennifer spoke of Aniston often, but meeting her for the first time made me want to learn more. I've heard plenty of stories about her traveling and living in an RV. No doubt the pink one parked in the yard.

I always pictured a woman similar to the ones climbing a mountain in a protein powder ad. Not someone so . . . casual? Even without a stitch of makeup and what I think might be frosting on her face, she's beautiful. And a little frazzled.

Snapping out of my statue state, I crane my head to peer inside the windowpane beside her front door. I catch a glimpse of her darting down a hallway and disappearing into a room.

Either I caught her off guard or she's really busy. My eyes drop to the pan in my hand. Curiosity gets the best of me, and I open the lid. Beneath is a slathering of crumbs on one end and a thick sheet of chocolate chip cookie on the other. I doubt she meant to give me a half-eaten dessert, especially since I surprised her.

I start to set it on a small table beside a potted plant and leave. Then Luke's dog comes up. Well, I guess it's the family dog, since Luke no longer lives here. My stomach pits at the reminder of Luke and Jennifer's plane crash. They weren't that much older than me when they died in an instant when his personal plane malfunctioned. Something so tragic happening to someone you know well, who's close to your age, really puts things in perspective.

Like how the single, attractive sister now lives across the pasture from your carriage house.

I slap my forehead. Stop it, Easton. This woman just lost her sister and her whole lifestyle changed in a blink. She doesn't need the neighbor across her pasture pining for her.

And it's not exactly like I'm in the market for a relationship right now anyway. *Or am I?*

I sneak a glance in the window again. Nobody. Balancing the pan in one hand, I reach for the doorbell, then pull back. She clearly doesn't want or need to be disturbed. Given the moppy state of her honey hair, maybe she's in the shower?

Great. Now I'm imagining her in the shower. I decide it's time to walk back home. The dog nudges me, reminding me that I need to find a higher altitude to set the pan. I'm no veterinarian, but as a people doctor, and someone with basic knowledge for an animal's livelihood, I know not to put chocolate in reach of a canine.

I try the windowsill, but it's too narrow. Sighing, I make the split-second decision to take it home. There isn't that much left. I'll just dump it out, wash the pan, and return it later clean and fresh. Then Aniston will be clean and fresh as well. After her shower . . . or whatever she's doing in the back of the house.

I rub the dog behind his ears, then start down the driveway, cake pan in hand. In an effort to remove Aniston from my brain, and the thought of her possibly taking a shower, I try and remember the dog's name. I'm sure it's on his collar, but I'm not going back to check.

If she catches me on the porch again or peering in a window after this long, I'll have to move. Which would suck. Rental houses in Apple Cart are far and few between unless they're in town. And I didn't move to the country to not live in the country.

The small carriage house on the edge of the Stevens family's field is perfect for me. I have everything I need in addition to a full field and fish pond for my view. Peace and quiet, with a nice couple and sweet kids as my only neighbors.

That was, until the nice couple was replaced by a tall woman with intriguing blue eyes. I didn't see that one coming. And from her reaction, she didn't see me coming either.

Grass swishes against my jeans, reminding me that I'll need to cut the hay before long. Luke graciously shared his tractor with me whenever I wanted to do something to improve the place, mainly out of my own desire to be back on a John Deere.

Some of my favorite childhood memories growing up took place on my grandpa's farm in Tuscaloosa. My family lived in a neighborhood, but I always wanted to live "out" like my grandparents when I grew up. Joining the rural-doctor program in med school made perfect sense to me. Become a small-town doctor so I could do what I love all the time. Practice medicine, then come home to a peaceful country setting.

The only thing I didn't intend on was every person in Apple Cart trying to set me up. It's like they can't accept that I'm fine living the bachelor life for now. Or at least I thought I was.

Something about Aniston has me reconsidering my relationship status. Maybe it's because even despite her disheveled appearance, her natural beauty made me catch my breath. Then she wavered between hospitality and annoyance, offering the most entertainment I've had since I wandered into the General Store for the first time.

I cringe. Those clown figurines by the cash register still haunt my dreams after long nights at the ER. Needless to say,

I've only gone back once for a new pair of boots, and avoided direct eye contact with the register.

I open my front door, and the air conditioning hits me like a ton of bricks. Even though I consider myself in good physical shape, we're at the time of year where walking a few feet in direct sunlight will make sweat roll down your back. Gotta love Alabama.

I shut the door behind me and bask in the cool space. The great thing about living in a tiny house is that it cools off quickly. I walk to the kitchen and step on the trash can pedal to open the lid.

Just as I'm about to dump the remainder of the cookie in the trash, I stop. I pull a piece off the end that looks like it has claw marks. Hopefully that was from a fork and not the dog. The dog looked well, so I'm optimistic.

As soon as the gooey moistness hits my tongue, my eyes roll back in my head. When I bite into the creamy middle, I decide this may be the best dessert I've ever tasted.

I take my foot off the trash can and walk to the table with the pan. I'll clean the pan and return it after it's empty, like planned. I'm just not going to empty it the way I had planned.

CHAPTER 2

Aniston

I massage my scalp for at least the third time, because my hair is *that* dirty and because I've lost count.

Jennifer and Luke had mentioned renting the carriage house to a new doctor in town. It never occurred to me that the new doctor also meant a young doctor, and a very attractive one to boot.

I step back from the hot water and fan my face. Either I've stood in the shower too long, or the doc has me hot. Probably both. But I can't help it that my RV isn't equipped with enough hot water for a decently long shower . . . or that I never stay in one place long enough to daydream about the possibility of a relationship.

But I'm back in Apple Cart, and my main residence has an address instead of wheels.

That's it, I'm getting out. This steam is getting to my head. Making me a bit crazy.

My life now consists of two goals, neither of which

include a romantic relationship. Most importantly, give Willow and Carter a good, stable life, and raise them to adulthood. Secondly, somehow manage to keep my travel vlog engaging while living in a tiny, rural town that offers zero attractions.

I laugh as I reach for a towel and dry off. Marketing Apple Cart as a travel destination would make for a funny vlog. Paul's General Store could double as a museum of sorts with all the antique junk. I keep waiting for it to show up on an episode of *American Pickers*. There's Double Drive, the mini golf, go-kart, and paintball place. Visitors could stay just across the county line at Quality Inn, which also houses a Mexican restaurant and a liquor store. Of course, anyone wanting to really golf would first need to check if the county golf course is in operation or if it's covered in cattle. The apple orchard is by far the most positive landmark in our community.

Yeah . . . my vlog is good as gone once I'm finished uploading all the clips from my road trip with the kids.

I sigh and wrap a towel around my head. Then I grab another to wrap around my body so I can go across the hall and change in my room.

Willow told me to stay in the master suite, but I can't. Not yet. It's bad enough living under the same roof where my sister made her home. I don't sleep well as it is. Trying to sleep in her and Luke's old room would make me a total basket case.

If it weren't for the kids needing as much stability as possible, I'd sell the place in a heartbeat and find us a new home. One just as nice, but with much less land to manage and no hot doctors lurking around the porch.

That's not fair. I doubt he was lurking around. He meant well bringing the package. It just caught me off guard.

I find some clean underwear, a pair of khaki shorts, and a tank top, then shut my door for privacy. Despite all the changes in my life, living with other people has been the biggest adjustment.

Our first night together on the road trip, I ripped off my pajama shirt and started to change in the middle of the RV. Willow said something before I took off anything else, reminding me that they were there too. I went in the bathroom before changing the rest of the way. Thankfully before Carter noticed.

No more walking around in my panties and T-shirt only or peeing with the bathroom door open. I don't want my niece and nephew grossed out or weirded out because I've somehow made it to age twenty-six living like a pirate. Except that my ship is a used RV, and I've yet to find any buried treasure.

I open my makeup bag and practice swiping on just enough coverage to look presentable. My makeup habits tend to go extreme—as in nonexistent or camera ready for a vlog intro. I need to find a balance between the two for life as a normal adult functioning in everyday society.

Something I've never done before.

One semester abroad in college, and I never went back. I worked my way around half the world doing odds and ends, sharing my stories online. Eventually, I got enough followers on social media to become an influencer. That led to Instagram reels and video stories, which led to a monetized video channel.

At that point, I bought the RV and decided I could actually make a living doing what I loved. I'd travel the US and share every hidden gem our great nation has to offer. It helped that it didn't take much to support a single woman willing to live off of gas station coffee and peanut butter sandwiches. But after a few years, I actually made good money.

I shake out my hair and comb through the tangles before drying it. Then I fluff it over my shoulders and examine my makeup. Much better. Funny how much difference a shower and a little paint on the old barn can make.

I step into my favorite pair of sandals and bounce down the staircase. "Kids, it's time to go to Morgan's."

Carter pops his head in the back door, dripping wet from the pool. Willow emerges from the living room, where she was reading a book. "Dry off before coming in," she tells her younger brother as she folds down a page and shuts the book cover.

I cringe a little inside. Dog-eared pages are one of my pet peeves. I make a mental note to buy that girl a few cute bookmarks.

Carter trots in with a Spider-Man towel around his shoulders. He's still wearing goggles pushed up on his forehead. I pull them off, activating his front cowlick. I attempt to smooth it down with my fingertips. Even dripping wet, it rears its ugly head. More like adorable head, but still disobedient.

He'll likely chop his hair short by middle school to hide it, but I like it. The look fits his laid-back, outdoors-loving personality.

Willow puts a hand on Carter's shoulder and steers him toward the stairs. "Come on, Carter. You need to change, and I need shoes."

Although I haven't spent a lot of time around kids, especially other than these kids, I suspect she's more mature than most twelve-year-olds. I can only hope she'll stay levelheaded.

Jennifer and I lost our mom to cancer when I was eleven. Middle school started my wild streak. Jennifer was starting college and Daddy didn't know how to handle me. I'd like to think I can at least be less naive with these two if they ever try to follow in my wayward footsteps. I'd also like to think I'll be a suitable parent for them since I've turned the straight and narrow.

That's not to say I didn't take a lot of bumpy back roads to get to where I am today—both metaphorically and literally.

Loud footsteps interrupt my thoughts as the two minors in question trample down the wooden staircase. Carter is wearing jeans, boots, and a T-shirt that reads, "Fishing is life." Oh, son, if only it were that simple. Willow is wearing her same athletic shorts and tank top with black tennis shoes and a high ponytail. She looks straight out of cheer camp, which thankfully took place before I took guardianship. Unlike Jennifer, I did not participate in cheerleading or any other team sport.

At least I was smart, book- and street-wise. I managed to make A honor roll throughout high school without showing up half the time. Now, that takes some skill.

"Let's go see what Morgan's cooking." I lead us out the front door.

As if right on cue, my stomach growls. Our last covered dish of sympathy meals rotted in the refrigerator during our road trip, so I'm due for some home cooking to bless my heart —and stomach.

Branches scrape the top of my RV as I pull under the large oak tree in Morgan's yard. In my effort to avoid parking in the grass or driveway, I didn't consider low tree branches.

Would it have made more sense to drive my sister's minivan or even my brother-in-law's truck? Yep.

Am I ready for that? Nope.

Clearly, I have a lot of work to do. I glance at Willow in the passenger seat. My throat catches. I can only imagine what these babies must be going through if it's this tough on me.

I kill the engine and open the door. It catches on something, and I realize I've stopped too close to the tree trunk.

"Stay in," I say to Carter, who's trying to climb out the back. I crank the RV and back up a few feet, seething when the branches make another fingernails-on-chalkboard noise. At least the RV's too tall for anyone to see the damage.

I turn the key and open my door. "Okay, clear out." Both kids barrel out, and I follow, slamming the heavy door behind me.

Morgan's yard practically screams, "I have four kids of varying ages." Everything from sports equipment and play-houses to bicycles and skateboards adorn her front lawn. Yet another reason I needed to avoid parking on the grass.

Sofia meets us on the porch. She's in the swing fanning herself dramatically with one of those battery-powered hand fans. She's ten and a total diva. Also a bit annoying, if you ask me. After thirty minutes with all of Morgan's kids, I get why Willow relates more to Isabella, who's fifteen.

We hear a scream and Andrew runs from behind the house in his underwear. His older brother, Ethan, is chasing him with a massive Nerf gun.

"Hi, Willow." Ethan lowers his weapon and blushes when he sees my niece.

I bite back a laugh. She's pretty and already has signs of being built like a brick house just like her mama. I'm lankier, which is why I avoid trampolines and bouncy houses at all costs. Lightweight and long limbs don't mix well with bounc-ing, and I always end up folded like a pretzel.

Morgan opens the door before I can knock. She takes the dish towel in her hand and tosses it over one shoulder like a butler in a kid's movie. "Come on in." She opens the door wider and shakes her head. "Why did you drive your house?"

I arch a brow. "Vacation home . . . now. I don't want to drive their things, you know that."

Morgan frowns. "You about took out my favorite shade tree's shadiest branch."

"I think I suffered the most damage on that one."

She shakes her head again, making me feel like a kid caught with the candy jar. I need her to give me a tutorial on effective mom glares one day, just in case my kids ever act up. However, five minutes on Morgan's property has me praising Jesus for the kids I inherited.

Carter mixes in with Andrew, who's a year younger than him, and they wander toward the back. Willow follows me inside, then peels off toward the living room when she spots Isabella watching TV.

I follow Morgan to the kitchen, where Brooke and her son are standing by the sink. Timothy's eyes light up when he sees me. "Is Carter here?"

I nod. "He's outside."

Timothy grins, showing a few missing teeth, and rushes toward the back door.

"Play safe," Brooke calls.

Morgan and I give one another a knowing look. Timothy is about to enter the battlefield. Good thing Carter is there to protect him from the wilds of Morgan's boys.

I haven't been around Timothy much, but I can sense Brooke is a little overprotective. The boy could use a little toughening up, in my opinion. Maybe a good five minutes with Andrew in a bounce house.

Now that I'm the sole parent of my niece and nephew, I have a little more empathy for Brooke. As far as I know, Timothy's father was never in the picture. Brooke has never mentioned him, and neither has Morgan, which is saying something. I refer to him as Bruno since nobody ever talks about him.

"Good to see you, Aniston." Brooke smiles, and I'm instantly reminded of the dental billboard up Highway 280.

She's my age and was the cliché all-American girl in high school. Straight As, head cheerleader, sweet as tea, and dated a baseball star. Petite, with soft brown hair and doe eyes.

Everyone loved her. Except for the few who hated her because there was literally nothing about her to hate.

"Hi, Brooke. Good to see you too."

She grins wider, which I didn't think was possible, then turns her attention back to a Crockpot full of macaroni and cheese. My stomach growls when she stirs it. I sit at the kitchen counter to try and muffle the one-woman drum line performing behind my ribcage.

Morgan crosses the kitchen and opens the oven.

"Do you need help with anything?" I ask.

She shakes her head as she lifts a pan of pork from the oven. "Nah, but thanks. Just the crack."

"Crack?"

"Yeah, you said you were bringing the rest."

I slap my forehead. "Shoot. I gave it to the neighbor. The Dr. Easton guy."

Brooke turns to me, her eyes widening. "Dr. West?"

"Oh." Morgan sets the pan down on the stovetop and gives me her gossipy face.

"Not like that." I roll my eyes. "Wait, the dude's name is Easton West?"

Both of them nod, and I laugh before continuing. "The doorbell rang, and I thought it was you coming back. I had the pan in my hand to take to the kitchen but went to the door first. He was standing there with a package for me. I grabbed it and handed him the crack out of impulse."

Morgan bursts out laughing. "What a welcome."

Brooke scrunches her forehead. "Wait, when you guys say crack . . ."

"Cookie crack," Morgan and I answer in unison.

"Ohhh, that stuff is awesome," Brooke answers.

"Yeah, and we could've had some tonight." Morgan narrows her eyes at me as she removes her oven mitts in an intimidating way. If we were nineteenth century British women, she'd be removing her carriage gloves to perhaps slap me.

Just in case, I take a step back and send a silent thanks upstairs that the oven mitts are heavily padded.

A large boom on the side of the house startles us. "Excuse me," Morgan says as she slams the oven mitts on the counter and marches toward the back door.

She opens the screen door to the backyard and yells something to her boys about how she's told them a hundred times not to throw baseballs toward the house. There's a little back and forth before Morgan lets the screen door slam behind her as she heads back to the oven.

"So, back to Dr. Goodbody," Morgan announces. "What did ya think of him?"

I shrug. "I don't know. I mean, Luke and Jennifer said they were renting the carriage house to a doctor."

"Oh, so they told you about him?"

I roll my eyes. "Not like that. They just said the renter was a doctor. I was actually surprised he looked so young."

"And handsome?" Brooke raises her eyebrows.

I waver my head. "I mean, yeah, what I saw. I really was just looking at the package."

"Oh, honey, he's the whole package," Morgan sneers.

I blow out a puff of air. "That's enough, y'all."

Brooke straightens, but Morgan unsuccessfully hides another laugh. I try not to make eye contact with her as she moves the food to the island in front of me. My mouth waters at the loaded mashed potatoes, barbecue, and macaroni and cheese. Cookie crack really would be the perfect ending to this meal, but my awkwardness got in the way. I'll blame it on my sugar crash.

Morgan grins, and I brace myself for whatever sly comment she's about to say. Before she can open her mouth, Brooke yells, "Watch out!"

I turn to a baseball flying by my head. I lean back, stumbling off the bar stool as the ball lands smack in the center of the pulled pork.

Morgan snatches it from the meat and glares at the new hole in the screen door. "Andrew, Ethan!" She marches across the wood floor and jerks open the door. She tosses the ball out. "You're both grounded. Get in here and fix your plates."

Brooke and I exchange glances across the kitchen. Morgan pulls a paper plate from the stack on the counter and fills it with meat from where the ball fell. She covers it with tinfoil and writes "Buster" on top with a Sharpie.

"Uh, is that Buster as in our dog?"

"Yep. Can't let it go to waste. I'll put this in a doggy bag for y'all. No pun intended." She winks, then drops the tongs from the meat in the sink and puts a new pair in the pan as if the ball never landed there.

Kids start filing in from outside and the living room. Everyone else makes plates while I hang back. Even Brooke fixes her plate and allows Timothy to make his as if the ball never landed in the meat.

After everyone else clears out, I grab a plate and add a heaping pile of potatoes and macaroni but avoid the meat. I just can't. I'm not to the point of parenthood where I can forsake basic hygiene. After living on the road for half a decade, I still find eating baseball-leather meat a bit barbaric.

Andrew is still in his Spider-Man underwear. Morgan finally notices and tells him to go put on clothes. He hops on a hoverboard and zips down the hallway.

We gather around the large dining room table off the kitchen and listen as Timothy prays. He recites the "God is great" prayer we all learned in Sunday school as little kids.

Midway through the familiar prayer, the sound of Andrew's hoverboard zips past. As soon as Timothy mutters "amen," we all lift our heads to Andrew beside Morgan. He is wearing shorts, but still no shirt.

"Mama, I peed on the hoverboard for the first time!"

"You what?" Morgan's eyes are the size of half-dollars.

"I drove up to the toilet on the hoverboard and peed without even getting off."

"In the toilet?"

"Well, yeah." He frowns at Morgan, clearly confused.

Morgan puts a hand to her chest. "Oh, thank God. Sit down and eat."

I make eye contact with Willow, and we both snicker. Morgan shakes her head and looks around the table. "School starts next week, and I, for one, can't wait."

My stomach pits at the reminder of school starting. I've enjoyed staying holed up with Willow and Carter, not having to venture out in Apple Cart aside from the occasional grocery store run.

Morgan may be ready for school to start, but I'm not.

CHAPTER 3

Easton

Another exciting day in Apple Cart.

Most of my colleagues would laugh at my patients' worries, but I oddly enjoy it. I'll take small-town ailments over big-city crime-related injuries and massive car wrecks any day.

Today's highlights consisted of Mason Magill trying to convince me to take a look at one of his chickens, followed by a little girl in need of rash medication after she picked her mom a bouquet with poison oak for the "flower leaves."

I might not be in a medical tower trying to cure cancer, but I enjoy the human aspect of helping people with everyday life so much more. Even if Mason tried to put up a bit of a fight when we charged him a copay for the chicken checkup.

As I turn down the gravel drive leading to my house, I'm reminded of the main reason I like life in Apple Cart so much. The peace and quiet. No more going home to a noisy apartment with pavement instead of grass or even a suburban home where the streetlights dim the stars.

Out here, it's just me and nature. Well, and the Stevenses' house across the pond and pasture. I glance that way as I park my truck in front of the carriage house.

Funny how I always managed to block out the fact that their house was in view. Maybe because the white farmhouse is more of a picturesque painting than an eyesore. Aside from taking my rent money to Luke, I didn't go there often.

We both had Venmo, but neither of us offered to pay that way. I think on a subconscious level, I enjoyed a small amount of neighborly contact. I try and tell myself that's why I rang the doorbell when delivering Aniston's package rather than simply leaving it by the door. Delivery people ring the bell too, right?

It's just an added bonus that the package came from Victoria's Secret and I had a bit of curiosity as to what the person who ordered it looked like. I'm only human, right?

And despite having no short-term plans to find someone, I can't deny that I'm still a single man.

I go inside, the door creaking against the dead silence. After setting my briefcase and keys on the kitchen counter, I change from my slacks and button-down into my preferred jeans and boots.

I need to cut the hay around the big house today. Yesterday, I cut my side of the pond, which means I should finish the entire field by dark.

My stomach knots as I'm reminded how Luke won't be around to teach Carter to drive the tractor, which now belongs to him. I should teach him, but he's only seven. Which brings up another question. Will I still be in the carriage house when he is old enough to learn?

Ideally, I'd buy my own place, right?

I run my hand over my hair and shake my head. No use

getting ahead of myself. Besides, this house is perfect for just me.

I pop in my earbuds to try and drown out my thoughts. They're getting too deep for an evening on the tractor, which is supposed to be my relaxing time of day.

The humidity swells when I step outside the comforts of my air conditioner. I pull on a pair of sunglasses and tread across the fresh-cut hay to the pole barn, where Luke's tractor stays parked.

After the accident, their lawyer had a talk with me about how everything went to the children. Aniston was the only sibling of either and was granted custody, per their will. The lawyer agreed it was a good gesture from me to offer to help keep the place up with no man around for the foreseeable future. I was happy to volunteer, as I know Luke would do the same for me.

Although we weren't super close, I thought a lot of Luke, Jennifer, and their kids. They'd always been kind and hospitable to me.

I climb in the cab and cut on the air. Thank the Lord for an air-conditioned tractor. My grandpa never had one. Once retired, he liked to brag how he toughed it out in the heat, which I find unnecessary with modern technology.

Kenny Chesney blasts through my headphones to drown the sound of the motor as I circle the pond toward the big house. Once I reach the place I stopped the day before, I lower the cutting deck and begin.

Something about minimal movement calms me. Circling a pasture slowly, holding a fishing pole, walking in the woods. The tractor is by far my favorite.

When I get closer to the house, I notice someone out by the pool. I continue cutting, not paying much attention once I realize it's Carter. That boy can swim better than most adults.

Then I start cutting beside the patio that leads to the pool and notice Aniston, standing under the covered porch beside the pool—in a hot-pink bikini. I stop for a second and watch, more to see what she's doing than what she's wearing. Or if I'm being honest, a little of both.

She's holding a phone and talking. Then she turns toward me, and I jerk the tractor back in gear. I try and catch a glimpse of her from the corner of my eye, but I'm now past the pool. I continue cutting that patch of grass, then move toward the front.

The only spot that remains is where both her RV and Luke's truck are parked in the grass. Without giving it a second thought, I park and get out. I walk around to the pool, where she's videoing the swimming pool and backyard with her phone.

I step behind her, trying my best not to focus on the fact that she's wearing near nothing, and clear my throat. She jumps.

"Aniston, do you mind moving your RV and the truck into the drive? I'm trying to cut all this tall grass to bale it and get it out of your way."

She glances down at herself and leaps toward the patio table, snatching a towel and wrapping it around her. "Uh, sure."

Her face is flushed, whether from embarrassment or the sun, I'm not sure. I can say, however, that she has nothing to be embarrassed about. At least from my point of view.

Without another word, she marches toward the front of the house. I follow. She turns suddenly, bumping into my chest. Flinching, she grips her towel tighter. "I need the keys."

"No worries," I say, a little lost for words. In my defense, it's not every day that a half-naked woman bumps into me. Or any day, for that matter.

She dips her head and hurries into the house, gripping the towel where she tucked it tightly. I rock on my heels, wondering if I should've left the grass to grow up around

Luke's truck. Another month of growth might be worth the embarrassment I've caused us both.

Aniston returns with two sets of keys and Willow. She's still barefoot, with the towel wrapped under her arms. It hangs just above her knees, exposing half of her long, slim legs. I turn away when her eyes meet mine. The last thing I need is for her to think I'm ogling her.

"Why don't you go get your tractor ready? I got this." Her tone is super authoritative for someone who could blow over in a strong summer breeze. She'll make a great mom with that voice.

"All right."

I scratch the back of my head and round the house toward my tractor. When I enter the driveway, the RV is already parked and the truck is backing up. I move closer to find Aniston standing in the driveway directing what has to be Willow driving Luke's F-250. This is not good.

Before I can park the tractor and make it down the steps, Luke's side-view mirror flies off toward the edge of the house. Both girls scream as the truck jerks into park.

I rush over to the driver's side to find Willow, wide eyed and pale. Her door is too close to the edge of the garage to open it, so she rolls down the window. "I'm so sorry, Aunt Ani. I didn't—"

Aniston hops in the passenger seat and calms her. "Shhh, it's okay. It's all my fault. I should've never asked you to drive it. Don't worry about it."

I wait an awkward moment for them to hug and shed a few nervous tears. Then I say, "Would you like me to straighten it up and pull it inside?"

"Yes," they answer in unison, a little too enthusiastically.

I wait as both women crawl out of the passenger seat, then I climb in that way. As I back up and drive in correctly, I can't for the life of me understand why Aniston wouldn't just park the truck herself after moving her RV. It's not like she's afraid to drive something big. She came here in her house.

I decide it's best not to question it. Aniston meets me at the door with the side-view mirror in her hand. Her towel has slipped a little below her swimsuit top, but I don't dare mention it.

"Thanks for parking the truck."

"You're welcome." I give her a slight smile, then head back to the tractor.

It takes one short drag across the patch of grass to finish. I resist the urge to peek over and see if Aniston waited outside any longer—and if her towel continued its journey downward.

Instead, I drive to the tractor shed and call it a day. For once, my life after work was even more exciting than my day at the clinic.

Aniston

To say I'm a ball of nerves would be an understatement. Leave it to me to pick the exact moment Dr. Hotness decides to cut hay around the house for my swimsuit shoot.

It's bad enough that the package was supposed to meet me in Mexico so I could "test" the Victoria's Secret bikini in Cancun. Well, that trip never happened. Instead, a handsome stranger delivered it when they forwarded it to the slightly wrong address.

A poolside photoshoot was all I could manage. Unless, of course, I floated the stream by Broken Bridge in an inner tube like the rest of Apple Cart. No thanks. Not my crowd.

Now I'll have a tractor noise in the background of my video, along with a broken mirror on Luke's truck. Not to mention a shook up twelve-year-old girl who I forced to drive.

I swallow hard and knock on Willow's door. "It's me." As I wait for her to open up, I readjust my towel, which has now crept toward my hips. She opens the door slowly and rubs her splotchy eyes.

I step past her, and she closes the door behind us before sucking in a breath. "Aunt Ani, I'm so sorry."

"No." I wrap my arms around her small frame. "It's my fault. I never should've made you drive."

"I ruined my daddy's truck," she mumbles into my shoulder.

I pull her back and wipe a wayward tear drizzling down her cheek. "No, baby, you didn't. It's only a mirror. I should've drove." I drop my arms and sit on the edge of her bed. "I just can't."

She frowns. I'm sure she gets why I can't drive it, but I continue anyway. "It's hard for me to be the places and do the things your mama and daddy did."

"Like live in this house?"

I fidget with the frayed edge of my towel before nodding slowly and facing her. "Yeah. That's why I can't sleep in the main bedroom even though you and Carter told me to."

She nods and plops down beside me. "It's okay."

I sigh. "It is, but it isn't. I'm the adult and I have to do things sometimes, even if they make me feel bad, to protect you two. Like drive the truck."

"I almost had it, if the mirror wasn't so big."

I pat her knee and chuckle. "You're too sweet—and mature. Sometimes I feel like you should have custody of me."

She laughs with me for a moment. There's a hint of sadness behind it, revealing she's under just as much stress as me. If not more. Now that I think about it, this is the first time I recall her laughing since we returned from traveling.

Shame on me for not noticing sooner.

I've been so wrapped up in my own worries that I haven't even considered how they feel about going back to school. Instead of coming home to their parents, they'll come home to me and Buster. When they're doing some sort of sport or activity and look into the crowd, they'll see me sitting in the stands, not their parents. What a letdown.

"Willow, I promise to be a better parent to you two."

She wrinkles her forehead as much as a preteen with baby-soft skin can. "You are."

I shake my head. "I don't know the first thing about raising kids. I never even had my own dog. I had a pet hermit crab once and killed it. The thing got out of its container, and must've crawled into the laundry basket. I found it the next day beat apart in the dryer."

Her expression morphs into a mixture of concern and grossed out, so I abandon my Hermie example.

"For whatever reason, your parents asked me to be your godmother, and I accepted. Not because I thought I'd do an awesome job, but because I love you two so much."

"We love you too."

"I know you do, sweetie." I wrap my arm around her and give her a quick squeeze.

She sighs. "We should've just asked Dr. West to move the truck."

"Agreed. To be fair, I wasn't expecting anyone to move the truck today." Or ever, as far as I'm concerned. I'd prefer to throw a tarp over it and save it for Carter nine years later. Not the most sensible solution, but it made sense to my irrational mind at the time.

Even more so, I didn't expect Easton to barge in on my bikini review. At least my legs were shaved and my hair was in a cute braid. A big improvement from the first time he saw me, for sure.

"He'll help you with things if you ask, you know." Willow gives me a parenting glare.

She's way too big for her britches, but not in a cocky way. It still doesn't help my ego that she's giving me advice on men.

"There's no need to bother the neighbor. I mean, he's already cutting the grass."

"He won't mind. He told me and Carter so at the funeral."

"Really?" I barely squeak out my response. I don't like being reminded of the "F" word. It was the worst day of my life, as I'm sure it was theirs too. Still, how thoughtful of Easton to say that.

"Yeah. He said he'll do all the stuff Daddy normally did whenever we need him."

I lift my chin, debating whether to stand up for feminism or run across the pasture and hand him a list of things that need fixing. Starting with me.

Best not get into that right now.

"That's very thoughtful of him."

Willow smiles. "He's a good man."

Something in the way she says that reverses our roles once again. I'm like a twelve-year-old having a talk about her first crush.

My cheeks heat up and I clutch my towel. How silly of me. I don't have a crush on Easton.

Do I?

CHAPTER 4

Easton

Even though it was in no way my fault, the broken mirror on Luke's truck has bothered me all day. It might indirectly be some my fault since I asked Aniston to move the truck. But I never intended for her to pass the buck to a middle schooler.

Regardless, guilt convinced me stop by the hardware supply store for some epoxy to reattach the mirror.

With any luck, it just popped out of socket. If not, I may need the glue. I've also got plenty of tools in the back of my truck to screw back loose parts.

The sun has almost set when I turn onto Aniston's drive. I'll knock on the door and explain my intentions. But I get out of my truck and notice the mirror lying at the edge of the garage, right where it popped off. Hmm . . . I bet it would be a nice surprise if I just fixed it and didn't say a word.

I pick it up and examine the damage. One side is a little broken. I get the glue and start to work on it in the driveway.

The sun lowers behind Aniston's house, so I grab my head-lamp from my toolbox.

With a hands-free light, I work on applying the glue and holding the mirror just right for it to dry. Luckily, it snapped at a place where she can still bend it in if the glue dries like I plan.

I'm standing there minding my own business when I hear a door open. With both my hands still on the mirror, I duck. I'm afraid to free up a hand to turn off my light, since the glue needs a few more minutes to dry. I try to bury my head under my arm, but the light still shines in the dark garage.

My heart rate spikes as I hear footsteps. So much for this being a surprise. I prepare a greeting for whomever it is. However, my monologue is useless when I'm hit over the head with a stick.

"Ouch," I moan as I raise my head.

"Dr. West?" Aniston gasps and drops the broom she's holding. "What are you doing?"

She's wearing a T-shirt better sized for a college linebacker than a thin woman, and some sort of weird fuzzy slippers.

"I'm fixing the mirror on the truck."

Her eyes narrow on my hands. "Oh, well thanks. But why didn't you tell me?"

Good question. "I wanted it to be a surprise."

She shrugs and giggles. "It was."

"I'll say." I wince at my throbbing head.

"Why are you holding it like that?"

"To let it dry. I had to glue a piece together."

"Ohhh." She leans her head to get a closer look. Her light blue eyes shine in my spotlight. She backs up a few feet and switches on the garage light.

"Thanks," I mutter as I blink to adjust my vision.

After walking back to me, she cocks her head. "Why are you dressed like a mining foreman?"

I laugh. "I needed a hands-free light. This thing is way more helpful than propping up a flashlight."

"I can see that."

We stand in silence for a few seconds before I slowly release my grip on the mirror. "There. Good as new—almost."

She grins. "Thanks."

"You're welcome." I reach up and turn off my headlamp, feeling like a super dork for leaving it on this long. "You have a nice night." I nod and turn toward my own truck.

"Hey."

"Yeah?"

"Have you eaten yet?"

My lips kick up. Maybe she's going to offer me more cookie or invite me in. "No, I haven't."

"I have some pizza left over if you want some."

I grin wider. "Thanks." I abandon my truck and follow her inside.

"Just a minute. I'm going to put on some pants." She disappears upstairs.

My neck heats up at the realization that she wasn't wearing pants before. Of course, her shirt could pass for a church-appropriate dress length. Still, the idea of her inviting me in wearing only a shirt makes my mouth dry.

I swallow to try and dissolve the lump building in my throat and scan the room to keep my mind off dehydration. Willow's and Carter's photos cover the refrigerator, and most everything is sleek steel and white except for a bright blue coffee maker in the corner.

Footsteps call my attention back to the foyer, where Aniston is coming in a pair of sweatpants, a better-fitting shirt, and some flip-flops. She passes me and opens the refrigerator.

"I hope you like pepperoni."

"Of course, it's a classic."

"And Quick Stop pizza," she adds, smiling.

"My first choice in Apple Cart."

She laughs at my corny comment, as it's the only choice in Apple Cart aside from a frozen pizza made at home.

I glance around as she puts several pieces on a plate and pops them in the microwave. I swallow harder. "Could I have some water?"

"Sure." She grabs a bottle and sets it on the counter. I sit on a stool in front of it.

It's quiet in here. Almost as quiet as my place.

"Are the kids already asleep?" I wouldn't think so, but then again, I don't live with kids to know their habits.

"Not unless Morgan slipped them some melatonin."

"Morgan?"

"Yeah, they're hanging out over there on their last night school free." The microwave beeps and Aniston pulls my pizza from the microwave and sets it in front of me.

"Thanks." My pulse picks up as she leans toward my face. Her hands lift toward my forehead. For a moment, I wonder if she's going for my hair, but then she gently pulls the head-lamp from around my forehead.

"You don't need this to eat pizza in the house." She smirks and sets it beside me.

I chuckle as my neck flares again, which is a sure sign I'm also blushing. That's happened a few times around her. Maybe I should stop shaving to cover up any blushing.

Our eyes lock, and I study her face. My grandma always said eyes tell a person's story. Aniston's are full of emotions. Adventure, curiosity, and a hint of sadness. Maybe a little fear too.

Before I can get totally lost in analyzing her stare, she spins around and opens the refrigerator again. "Want anything besides water? We have Coke, water, Sprite, tea, milk, juice boxes, Gatorade." She turns back and arches a brow my way.

I blink to bring myself out of the trance, hypnotized by her crystal eyes. Then I drink what's left of my bottle. Thanks to her, my throat's still on fire. I make a mental reminder to never eat Mexican around her. "Could I get another water?"

She slams a bottle of water in front of me with the force of a Western saloon owner. "Here you go." Then she sits beside me with a Gatorade.

I take a bite of my pizza as she grunts beside me. I turn to find her wrestling with the lid of her bottle. Without saying a word, I reach over and put my hand on hers. I cup my fingers around her tiny fist and squeeze as I twist the bottle open.

"Thanks." Now it's her turn to blush. Whether from embarrassment of not being able to open her own drink or from my touch, I'm not sure.

I'd like to think it's the latter, since my own heart is beating faster. She takes a large sip, and my eyes trail toward her mouth. A few red drops of liquid rest on her top lip, and it takes all the restraint I have not to wipe them off. It takes even more restraint when she licks her lips.

I turn my attention toward the paper plate of pizza in front of me. Gas station pizza. The perfect mood killer.

Not knowing what to say, I bring up the mirror. "Sorry again about the mirror on the truck."

She sighs. "Sorry about whacking you with a broom handle."

I laugh. "I'll be fine. At least I know you can protect yourself."

She smiles. "I've had a lot of time on my own."

I nod. "Me too." Ugh, I hope that didn't make me sound weird.

"I can pay you for the mirror supplies, and for cutting my grass." She starts to stand, as if she's going to get money.

"No, not necessary."

"Are you sure?"

"Positive. I want to help take care of you guys. It's what Luke would do for me. What any good neighbor would do."

"But we're not your responsibility."

"Says who?" I raise a brow.

Aniston looks around nervously, obviously shocked by my challenge. "You're not even kin to us."

"I'm your neighbor. The Bible says to take care of your neighbor and of widows and orphans."

She twists her lips, as if trying to come up with a rebuttal. "I'm not a widow."

I shrug. "But you're now taking care of orphans, so you're doing your part too. Let me do mine."

One corner of her mouth cocks into a sad smile. "Jennifer used to say it takes a village."

"I've always heard that too."

"Do you want kids?"

I choke on the water I'm drinking and reach for a napkin. There isn't one, so I do my best to gargle it back down. Aniston starts beating my upper back. She's surprisingly strong. At last, I catch my breath.

"Sorry, I didn't mean to put you on the spot like that."

I clear my throat. "It's fine. I like kids, you know, I just . . ." I sigh. How do I explain that I'm one of those perfectionists who wants all his ducks in a row before considering a stable relationship? "I've been busy on my career first. Medical school and all."

She nods. "I hear ya. Kids take up a lot of time."

"Yeah." I smile at her as she throws back her Gatorade like a burly man chugging beer after a stressful day at work. "Do you work?"

She lowers her drink and turns to me. "I run a vlog."

"Blog?"

"No vlog." She over-pronounces the first part.

"That's a word?"

She nods. "It's like a blog, but with a video instead of typed article."

"Oh, cool. What's it called?"

She smiles. "We Be Trippin'."

My eyes bug as a marijuana leaf pops into my mind. I'm afraid to ask for details.

She smirks at my reaction and clarifies. "A travel vlog."

I let out a breath as she continues, relieved it's that kind of tripping.

"But now that I'm in Apple Cart, I've had to get a bit creative." I continue eating pizza as Aniston twists toward me, her knees bumping into my thigh. "So when you were on the tractor and I was by the pool, I was doing this review of my swimsuit. It was supposed to be in Cancun, but I'm here, so I worked with what I had."

She sure did . . . I mentally scold myself for that thought. This poor woman is trying to work, and I'm daydreaming of her in a bikini.

"Anyway, I have a lot of footage from where the kids and I traveled right after . . ." Her voice trails off before mentioning Luke and Jennifer's funeral. "I've got to do a lot with that, then I'm not sure what I'll post."

"I'm sure you'll come up with something." I grin more at her than what I just said. This is the first time I've heard the word "vlog," and I'm not sure she can run a travel site from Apple Cart.

Which means eventually she will leave Apple Cart. Maybe not until the kids grow up, but I don't foresee her sticking around here forever.

Before I can ask her anything more, the front door opens and voices fill the house. Morgan comes in the kitchen.

"Oh, what do we have here?" She makes a not-so-subtle matchmaker face at us both.

"Did you give my kids melatonin?"

"Of course not, Aniston." Morgan bats her eyes to try and

look innocent. "What kind of mother do you think I am? I only give melatonin to my own kids."

Aniston rolls her eyes. "Were they good?"

"Your kids? Always."

"Thanks for letting them hang out."

"Anytime."

Aniston turns to me as she stands. "It's their last night of freedom before school."

I nod. "Well, I better get going anyway. Thanks again for the pizza."

"You're welcome. Good night." She smiles shyly as I pick up my headlamp.

"Good seeing you again, Morgan," I say.

"You too," Morgan calls in a flirty tone as I exit the direction I came and drive home.

Aniston

"Backpacks!" Wow, the last time I yelled that, I was leading a group of hikers around Yellowstone. Not the same as screaming it upstairs to my kids.

My kids. The thought of that causes my stomach to buckle. I'm in charge today. On the first day back to school.

Suddenly nauseated, I sit on the bottom step of the staircase. Willow passes me with her backpack on one arm and a small purse on the other. Carter comes barreling down the stairs a few seconds later with his camouflage backpack bouncing on his shoulders.

"Carter, where are your shoes?" Willow asks.

"Oh yeah." He runs back up and returns a minute later

wearing tennis shoes. Thank God for Willow keeping him in check.

I stand, clutching my stomach. "We need to eat and then leave early. Morgan said the first day is a train wreck."

Willow's eyes widen. "You have no idea."

Just what I didn't need to hear. I wrap my other hand around my stomach.

We all migrate to the kitchen, where I've made eggs and toast. I still haven't mastered bacon, and I decided not to try it on a morning like this.

Easton would run to our rescue at the first sign of a smoke signal. Then again . . . maybe I should've cooked bacon?

"Aunt Ani?" Carter tugs at my shirt, snapping me out of imagining Easton bursting though the kitchen wall with that dorky headlamp.

"Huh?"

"Did you pack my lunch?"

My eyes widen.

"I did," Willow calls. She brings a camouflage lunchbox over and drops it in his backpack.

"Thank you, Willow," I say.

"You're welcome."

"Okay, eat, and we can go."

Everyone fixes a plate. We eat in silence, then all take our drinks to the car—or RV. Carter starts toward the van, but I motion for him to follow me to the RV. He and Willow exchange a funny look, but follow me inside.

I set my Sprite in the cup holder, and off we go toward the school. Neither kid says a word on the ride there, and I'm not sure if it's from nerves or sleep deprivation. Maybe both, like me.

When I pull up to the middle school, a long line of vehicles curves into the main road. At last, Willow speaks. "You need to go down to the end and get in line."

"By the Dollar General?"

"Yes, ma'am."

I shake my head and drive a good country mile to the end of the line. Someone honks as we turn behind the car last in line. I guess they're not used to RVs turning on a dime in the middle of town.

"There's a lot of people here."

"It gets better after the first week," Willow comments. "A lot of people start riding the bus then."

I open my mouth to ask if they will be bus riders, but refrain. My sister wouldn't dare make her babies ride a hot, bumpy bus, and I know it. I could change that, but these kids have had enough change for a lifetime. Best get used to long lines.

After inching along, we come to a standstill beneath the only traffic light in town. I glance at Carter to find him nodding off. His head droops, but he jerks it back when his chin hits his neck. Willow stares out the window at her new school. I'd give about anything right now to read her mind.

Is she excited? Nervous? A mixture of both?

Another honk jerks me out of my daze. I sigh and pull up, closing the maybe two feet of asphalt between me and the car in front of me.

We're now within spitting distance of the middle school. That is, for anyone with a huge lung compacity and perfect aim. But still, we're close enough that even I'm nervous.

Middle school sucks. I wouldn't trade places with Willow for a million bucks.

Once we make it to the front of the building, I smile back at her. "Good luck today."

"Thanks," she mutters through a forced smile.

Of course this would be the time for the passenger door to stick. She tugs at the handle until we hear another honk from behind. I turn my head, ready to give the car behind us a piece of my mind.

Then my eyes lock on Willow's, which are sending me a

silent cry for help. "Go out back," I say, motioning toward the rear, where Carter is drifting off again.

She crawls to the living area and creaks open the door. A few girls near the entrance laugh when she barrels out, almost tripping over the running board. I bite my bottom lip to keep from yelling obscenities at the modern-day mean girls. I do, however, stick my tongue out at the rearview mirror when the car honks yet again.

Then I gas it out of there—as much as one can when stuck in bumper-to-bumper traffic.

The good news is that with all the honking and Willow climbing over him, Carter is now wide awake. I glance back at him blinking his eyes. Poor little buddy. Second grade isn't middle school, but a first day of anything is tough.

Kind of like a first day of parenting or being back in Apple Cart.

I grip the wheel tighter and veer on the main road. The elementary school is maybe a mile away, which is the only convenient part about this morning so far.

My nerves unravel the slightest bit when I notice the honking car turns in the opposite direction. I make a mental note of the vehicle so I can try to avoid it whenever possible.

As the elementary school comes into view, I notice a dozen or so people in reflective jackets mingling among orange cones. Is this the school or a construction site?

We make it to the drive in front of the school, and a police officer steps in front of the RV and holds up a hand. Sweat beads on my head as I roll down the window. He drops his hand and comes to my door.

"Officer, I didn't do anything to make that car honk. We just had a stuck door—"

He interrupts as if I'm not even talking. "Pull up to lane three when these cars clear out."

I nod as if that makes perfect sense. It doesn't.

Bless Carter for sticking his head beside me and directing

me to lane three. I had no idea a car line could be a four-lane .
. . or have traffic jams.

"So I just follow the car in front of me?"

He nods. "Unless someone in the traffic patrol signals you
to stop."

"Oh."

For the next ten minutes, we start and stop until we're
near the entrance to the school. Out of nowhere, a tall, thin
woman in a reflective vest steps in front of the RV. I slam on
the brakes to not hit her. Her hair is pulled into a high ponytail so tightly that her eyebrows look permanently raised. Or
maybe it's Botox. Either way, she does not look happy to
see me.

She marches to my door, and I roll down my window.
Before I can introduce myself, she starts talking.

"You cannot drive that land barge in here."

I turn to my right, where an older Cadillac is pulling a
boat in lane four, then turn back to her. "What about that
guy?"

"It's not the length of the vehicle. It's the width. You won't
fit when we merge to the drop-off zone. He purposely pulls
his boat with his car to fit in our lanes." She points a manicured nail toward a row of cones.

I exhale through my nose, halfway expecting smoke to
flare out my nostrils. I'm surrounded by other vehicles on all
four sides. "What do you want me to do?"

"When I signal, you pull out of the line and go park."

"Okay."

She steps back and pulls a whistle from beneath the
neck of her vest. Like a drum major, she marches back-
ward while whistling and waving her hands. The cars to
my right stall, allowing me to pull in front of them. I
weave around and head out of line toward a nearby
parking lot. The cars shuffle back into place as seamlessly
as a synchronized swimming team. I'm like the new kid in

a karate class full of black belts, and this car line is kicking my tail.

Carter doesn't say a word as I find a place to park. "Okay, you got everything?"

"Yes, ma'am." He lifts his lunch box with one hand and shrugs his backpack over one shoulder with the other. He squirms in his seat and stares toward the building.

"Do you want me to go in with you?"

He shrugs. "You don't have to."

My lips curve into a slight smile. "I will." I turn off the ignition and follow Carter outside. We've made it halfway through the parking lot when the woman with the tight pony-tail and super scowl walks up to me.

"You can't park there." She points to the RV.

"You told me to park. I purposely found a place between two small cars so I'd fit."

"It's not the size this time. That parking spot is assigned."

"Okay . . . I didn't know that."

"You didn't see the sign?"

I shake my head.

"You need to move."

I cross my arms so I won't accidentally punch this chick, because I'm certain she's a triple-striped black belt in car line. "The keys are in it. You're welcome to move it to a place where you approve."

Her jaw drops, as if she can't believe I just asked her to move it. I wrap an arm around Carter's shoulder and continue toward the school. When we reach the catwalk, I glance back to her picking up a wooden stake in front of the RV. A hundred bucks says it's the sign I didn't see. Oh well.

"Hey, you made it." Morgan greets us at the door.

I sigh dramatically. "I haven't made it yet. We've had a few hiccups with the RV. Some woman with a high ponytail is making me move it. I left her with the keys."

Morgan's mouth morphs into a mischievous grin that

would rival the Cheshire Cat in *Alice in Wonderland*. "You made her move it?"

"Not made, but I told her she could."

Morgan bursts out laughing. "That's got to be Georgia." She shakes her head, then stops in front of the office window and scribbles on some notes with a pen. "Here." Morgan slaps a name tag above my boob with the word "Visitor" printed at the top. "I signed you in, so we're free to go."

I scan the congested lobby of adults and kids shuffling about. People taking photos and filling out paperwork, signing visitor passes and straightening their kids' clothing. A sudden fear comes over me when I realize Georgia wasn't with a kid. "Hang on, so is Georgia a teacher?"

Morgan snorts. "She wishes. She's head of the PTSO."

"What's that stand for?"

"Parent-Teacher-Student Organization. Your sister was president before . . ." Morgan's voice trails off and she swallows. "Anyway, Georgia was happy to step in and pick up the slack. That woman's some kind of power hungry."

Morgan shuffles her kids toward the edge of the hallway and leads us through the crowd like a Disney tour guide. "We'll take the boys first, since they're in the same hallway."

Sofia stops and pops one hand on her hip. "Mama, I can take myself. I'm not a little kid anymore."

Morgan narrows her eyes at her daughter. "Fine, but I'm stopping by on my way out to get your first-day photo."

Sophia sighs. "Yes, ma'am." Then she skips down the opposite hallway.

"Preteens." Morgan shakes her head.

"Wait, is first-day pictures a thing?"

"Yeah. I mean, most of us do it."

I groan. "I didn't take a photo of Willow, and I didn't bring my phone in to take one of Carter."

Morgan pats my shoulder. "Calm down. Middle schoolers don't care. I had to sneak one of my older kids inhaling waffles this morning. And I can take one of Carter with his teacher, then text it to you."

"Thank you." I smile with relief, relaxing my shoulders for the first time since I entered the car line. All these drop-offs have me feeling like a fish jumping from one shark pond to another. I now have an extra level of empathy for the plot of *Nemo*.

"Ah, here we are, boys." Morgan stops in front of a room with a young, pretty teacher. She introduces herself as Mrs. Haynes, and Morgan snaps a photo of her with Andrew.

After a few hugs shared between Morgan and her son, we cross the hall. If Andrew's teacher is like a fairy-tale princess, Carter's would be the weird old woman who lives in the forest and tempts him with some earthy soup.

Not that she looks evil, but she looks like . . . well, like she could cook a mean pot of soup. Preferably in a cast-iron kettle.

She stares up at me through thick-rimmed glasses, her hair in short gray curls around her face. "I'm Mrs. Pebbleton."

I greet her and shake her hand. She smiles sweetly, promoting her to the princess's grandma in my mind rather than the soup-cooking cat lady.

Morgan takes a photo of Carter with his teacher. Then, I give him a side hug. I'm new at this and don't understand the protocol on initiating hugs in public. At what age does it become embarrassing? Is it more embarrassing since I'm his aunt and not his mom? These are some of the many questions that make me wish there were a book on *Getting Custody of Your Niece and Nephew for Dummies*. No such book exists. I've googled it.

I follow Morgan down the hall like a lost puppy, which isn't too far-fetched. Along the way to Sophia's classroom, she points to people and tells me about them.

"That's Maribelle Daniels. Her husband works on an oil

rig off the Gulf. She has twin boys Carter's age, Charlie and Jack, so she may be a big help."

I nod and smile at the woman rushing past us, holding hands with two young boys. She smiles back tiredly. I fight the urge to salute her. Then it hits me. "Wait, her kids are named Charlie Daniels and Jack Daniels?"

Morgan snorts. "Yep." She stops in front of a doorway and waves at Sophia. "Just a moment." Sophia stands and walks toward her teacher as Morgan enters the classroom. Morgan snaps a quick photo and leaves. No hug or words exchanged between Sophia and her mother. I'm curious if this is more of an age thing or a Sophia thing. I swear, school is such a social study for me. Social study . . . like social studies. I'll remember that if I ever do stand-up.

Morgan and I exit the building through the back. I can't tell if she's upset or mad, but this time I'm one hundred percent sure it's Sophia. I keep silent until we pass a woman in a tight leopard skirt, with heels higher than Georgia's eyebrows. She has a baby on her hip and another little one in a stroller.

I crane my head to watch her priss around the gym. "Who's that?"

Morgan snaps out of her funk and smirks. "That's TikTok Tami."

"*TikTok* Tami?"

Morgan grins. "She has quite the following."

I lift my chin, my brain churning. "What kind of videos?"

Morgan raises one brow. "What kind do you think?"

My eyes widen. "Oh."

She laughs. "I would walk you to your car, er RV, but I don't know—" Morgan's words cut off and she shakes her head. "The devil went down to Georgia, I see."

I frown, then follow her gaze. Parked beside a row of dumpsters is my RV. "At least we found it." I laugh nervously, trying to hide my hurt and stress.

Morgan wraps an arm around my shoulder and starts walking me toward the RV. A trash truck beats us there and starts unloading the bins. We stand several yards back and watch as a stream of liquid leaks onto the top of my RV. I hold my breath to mask the smell and keep from screaming.

Then I mentally debate that whole homeschooling thing again.

CHAPTER 5

Aniston

I don't make it home until almost ten after dropping off the kids. Before going home, I stopped at the self-serve car wash by the Quick Stop.

It wasn't easy reaching the top of the RV with a water hose. Between the wall and the wind, I'm pretty sure some of the trash liquid backwashed on me. I sniff the ends of my hair. Make that definitely sure.

I would take a shower, but I'd rather edit some video footage before having to pick up the kids. My preloaded videos on the vlog stop sometime next week. I like to work ahead, and need to get some of our trip footage edited ASAP.

A tinge of fear swirls inside me. How will I be able to keep a travel vlog successful when I don't travel? Best use every second of our journey and make it count.

I sigh and plug the camera into my computer. Yes, I still use an actual camera and not my phone for videos. Oddly enough, I take photos with my phone. It makes more sense. I also video short snippets with my phone, but like to keep the camera rolling in the background. Some of my most shared posts have come from the GoPro cam.

The first scene is of Willow jumping into the ocean. Her face goes from sad to shock when a wave hits her in the back. Then she laughs. I smile at the memory and vow to do everything in my power to create as many happy times for these kids as I can.

Beach scenes transition into sightseeing, and then our time at Disney. How I enjoyed seeing Disney from their point of view. I watch every bit of the first storage card and rewatch some of my favorite parts. Reliving our trip together is like a healing balm after the day I've had in the car line.

My phone dings and I check it. Two fifty-seven. Two fifty-seven!

I jump up and rush to the door. School ends at three, and I live a good fifteen minutes out. I rush back to grab my phone and purse, then hop in the RV. Remembering the drama it caused me this morning, I climb out and take the truck instead. I race down the driveway, gravel slinging behind me.

Despite my NASCAR-worthy performance, I make it there at twenty after three. The car line has transitioned from a booming metropolis to a ghost town, with only a few vehicles in the lane nearest the school.

As I get closer, I see the drivers getting out and going inside the school. The door is guarded by none other than Georgia. She'd make the perfect bridge troll if she weren't so pretty.

Unsure of what to do—like I've been all day—I park behind the last car and get out. I take the keys with me in case anyone gets the urge to move Luke's truck near the dumpsters.

Georgia greets me at the door with her pointy-browed scowl. I nod and follow the parent in front of me to the window at the office. Maybe Georgia caught a good whiff of my garbage-juice hair gel.

The man in front of me initials by a name on a clipboard, and a teacher calls for his kid on the radio. Simple enough. After he moves from the window, I scan the pages on the clipboard for Carter's name or mine, or possibly Luke's and Jennifer's names. Even Willow and Buster aren't on there.

I flip back to the front page and straighten as a chill comes over me. I slowly turn my head to Georgia standing behind me. Flinching, I jump back and knock the clipboard off the counter.

When I reach for it, she beats me to it. Georgia slides it back across the counter and stares at me. "He's not on here, because he's not registered for after-school care."

"What's after-school care?"

She shakes her head and sighs. "Anyone here after three is checked into the after-school program. It's for kids whose parents work later." She scans me up and down like I'm front and center stage in a pageant, and she's the judge. "And clearly you haven't been to work."

I puff up my flat chest like an animal in the wild trying to appear defensive. "I do work. I work remote. In fact, I was late because I was working so long."

Well, sort of working. More like taking a stroll down memory lane. But Super Troll doesn't need to know that.

"Well, you'll need to sign him up for after-school care if this is a common occurrence."

"Can I please just start with getting him today?"

She reaches through the office window and grabs a different clipboard, then shoves it toward me. "You need to go ahead and register him for after-school care and pay the registration fee of ten dollars, plus the eight dollars for today."

I pull my phone from my shorts pocket and glance at the screen. "Eight dollars for thirty minutes?"

She nods. "It's a set fee, not by the minute."

"Okay." I pat my pockets and look back at the truck, trying to remember what's in my wallet. Then I turn back to Georgia. "Do you take Venmo?"

"No, but we do have a scanner for all major credit cards."

I narrow my eyes and click the pen attached to the clipboard. Might as well start filling out the form before scrounging up money. The first page is simple enough, with contact info. It's the next page that gets me. Medical conditions and allergies? Vaccinations? Blood type?

"Problem?" Georgia purrs like a conniving cat.

I raise my head to her arched brows. One is more pointed, like a baby caterpillar in downward dog. I let the pages fall from my hands and set the clipboard on the counter. "Let me go find a card."

A wave of doubt splashes me in the face as I exit the school. I walk slowly to the truck and retrieve my wallet, contemplating how I'll make it through knowing so little about my kids. *My* kids. For better or worse, they're now mine.

When I return to the school door, it's locked. I knock on the glass, but nobody is close enough to hear me. Georgia makes eye contact with me and points toward the wall. Why she doesn't just march her skinny self over a few feet and open the door is beyond me.

Finally, I notice a button on the wall and press it. A buzzer sounds, and then I hear the door click. I push, and it opens. I enter, letting it slam behind me.

"Here." I hold out my check card, clutching it a little tighter when she reaches for it. Do I really want this woman to have access to my bank account?

Georgia finagles the card from my death grip and disappears behind the office opening. As soon as she does, the teacher with the radio comes up to me.

"Who's your child?"

"Uh." I'm a little gun-shy at this point. Will she charge me admission for standing here so long? However, she doesn't carry the same condescending glare as Georgia. In fact, quite the opposite. Her face is honest, and maybe a little tired. "Carter. Carter Stevens."

She nods, then lifts her radio. "Carter Stevens, your guardian is here."

I smile and mouth a silent "thank you" to her as Georgia trots around front.

She hands my check card back, as well as the clipboard. "You left some information incomplete."

I swallow, my neck heating with tension. "I need to check a few details before filling everything out."

"We need this vital information before he can be accepted to after-school care."

I suck in a breath, trying to center myself. I've climbed countless mountains, and none have made me as nervous as talking with this woman. "I understand, but the only reason I even registered him was to pick him up today. I—"

Before I can finish my plea or Georgia can butt in with a response, Carter walks up. We both stare at him.

His eyes widen. "Is everything okay?"

"Yes, sweetie." Guilt bubbles in my stomach at the thought of him thinking something might actually be wrong. I pat him on the back with my free hand, then move my hand to turn the page on the clipboard. "Do you know if you have any allergies?"

"I don't."

I smile and check "none." Carter knows his blood type and when he had his last shots. He even knows his Social Security number.

"I have all the phone numbers for my parents too," he says, before realizing those are no longer needed. I exchange looks with the teacher who radioed him in, before we both turn to Georgia. A lump slides down her thin throat. She stares at the ground.

I flip back to the first page and hold out the paperwork. "If that's all you need, we'll be leaving now. I have a middle schooler to pick up as well."

Georgia says nothing and continues staring at her feet. I hand the clipboard to the teacher and wrap an arm around Carter's shoulder, then lead him to the truck.

"Where's the RV?"

"At home, as it should be."

Carter smiles up at me, and I give his shoulder a gentle squeeze before releasing him. As we climb in the truck, an older, candy-apple-red Mustang pulls in front of us and screeches to a stop. TikTok Tami hops out, yawning widely. She's dressed in fuzzy SpongeBob pajama pants, a tank top, and Uggs. She stretches and heads for the school doors.

Not the least bit surprised after the day I've had, I back out and head for the middle school. *Dear God, please let this pickup go better than the last.*

One silver lining to all this school stress is that it's been great for my prayer life. I've gone from praying maybe a few times a week to a few times an hour today!

After we pick up Willow, I'll take these babies home for a nice, relaxing evening in the pool. I can't imagine they'd have homework on the first day, right?

When we reach the entrance to the middle school, there are several kids under the catwalk. Willow perks up when she notices her dad's truck. I smile at her as she climbs in the front seat.

"Sorry I'm a few minutes late." I decide not to bring up why.

"That's okay."

"How was it?"

She nods. "Not as bad as I thought it might be."

"Great." Not a stellar report, but anything not negative is a positive for today.

"Oh, there is one thing." She reaches in her binder and pulls out a sheet of paper.

My pulse kicks up a notch. *Please don't be another after-school form.*

"I got this from Coach. I need my physical for volleyball turned in by tomorrow."

I slant my eyes toward the paper she's holding, then back to the road.

"I normally get my physical at the school, but they did it while we were at Disney. Sorry, I forgot until now."

"No, that's fine. We'll figure something out."

So much for that relaxing evening I had planned for us.

Easton

"Eleven. Twelve." My voice grows breathier with every count. I grip the pull-up bar tighter for unlucky thirteen, when the doorbell interrupts me.

Most likely it's a package delivery, since nobody ever comes to my house, especially not at night. I ignore the ding and knock out a few more reps to make it to fifteen, then drop. There, my last set is complete.

The doorbell rings again. Strange.

I rush to the door, not bothering to put on a shirt. In a small town, it could be someone needing emergency medical help. Even though we have an ER at the hospital, Apple Cart folks are a little old school. Most of the older generation would think nothing of dropping in on the doctor at home.

I open the door, expecting Paul or any woman over sixty. Instead, I find Aniston and the kids. My chest flushes when Aniston's eyes flicker to it. I shrink back to hide behind the open door. Partly to not make her uncomfortable, and partly so I won't get too excited about her reaction to me shirtless.

"Hey, neighbors. What's up?"

What's up? What am I, a fraternity brother? Not exactly how I wanted to greet my neighbor, but too late now.

The heat in my chest travels to my head. "Come in." I open the door wider, then continue into the living room and grab my shirt from a nearby chair.

"We need a favor," Aniston says as I tug my shirt over my sweaty trunk.

"What is it?"

She fans a piece of paper. "Willow needs a physical turned in by tomorrow in order to resume practices and play in the first volleyball game coming up."

"I'll need it for cheer too. That game's just not as soon," Willow adds.

I scratch my head and glance around my bachelor pad. "Why don't y'all have a seat, and I can get my bag."

"Thank you!" Aniston squeezes my bicep, and I watch the tension leave her face. Maybe it transferred to me since her grip on my muscle has me a bit flustered.

I'm really glad I just worked out.

The kids sit on my couch and Aniston stands awkwardly by the fireplace while I disappear into the hallway. I use the tiny spare bedroom as my home office space, and keep a few items on hand, one of those being an old-school doctor's bag.

I pause before heading back to the living room and stop in the bathroom between my bedroom and office. Not wanting to take any chances, I spritz some deodorant on my armpits. Then I finger comb my hair in the mirror before grabbing the bag and meeting the others.

Aniston now stands beside the bookcase, staring at the

one photo in my home. It's a family photo of my parents with me and my sister's family. She turns when I enter the room.

"Is this your parents?" Aniston lifts the photo from the shelf.

"Yeah, and my sister, brother-in-law, and nieces."

"Cute." She grins at my sister's twin daughters, then returns the photo to its spot.

I set my bag on the coffee table and pull out a few things I know I'll need.

Aniston walks over and holds out the paper. "Here."

I take it from her, allowing my hand to brush her slim fingers. She's wearing neon nail polish that's terribly chipped. "Thanks." When I lift my head, she's standing within a few inches of my face. I clear my throat. "Let me get a pen."

Instead of retreating to my office again, I step into the kitchen. I keep at least one pen near the refrigerator at all times to jot down groceries. The first thing I notice is Aniston's cookie pan shoved back on the far counter.

I grab it, along with my favorite pen. One of the small perks to being a doctor is all the nice pens. Pharmaceutical reps spare no expense when it comes to dishing out top-of-the-line office supplies.

When I return, Aniston is scanning the spines of my books. Willow and Carter sit patiently on the couch. I set the pan beside my bag on the coffee table. "Here's your pan back."

Aniston spins around and smiles. "Thanks. Did you like it?"

I grin. "It was great. Thanks for the treat."

Her lips stretch into a nervous smirk. "Next time, maybe I can give you the whole pan."

I laugh. "I think that's about all my stomach could handle. For the record, you're the first to ever give me a third of a cake."

Carter speaks for the first time since they got here. "That's because she ate the rest of it in her room."

Aniston's eyes grow big and she blushes. I burst out a deep belly laugh, and even Willow laughs.

Aniston crosses her arms and stares at Carter. "I'll have you know that it's not that uncommon in Apple Cart to receive a half-eaten dessert as a gift."

"Oh?" I'm now intrigued, as I am by most things in Apple Cart County.

"Yeah. People brought over all kinds of food when my mom died. One lady had hosted a baby shower earlier that day, and when she heard about Mama, brought us the rest of the cake."

I raise my brows. "That's a little extreme."

"Oh, that's nothing." She snickers. "Another time, a neighbor brought over half a watermelon because he didn't want the rest and didn't want it to go to waste."

"Like sliced watermelon?"

She shakes her head. "Just cut in half."

I shrug. "Let's get Willow taken care of." I pat the chair next to me. "Have a seat."

Willow crosses the small space and sits. I go through the motions of checking her vitals, making notes on all the necessary lines. Blood pressure, pulse, etc. Once we're done, I have her follow me into the bathroom to weigh her on my scale.

"Slip off your shoes first." I record her weight and am starting back into the main room when she gets my attention.

"Dr. West?"

"Yes?"

One side of her mouth ticks up. "What do you think of my aunt?"

I pause in the doorway. Where is she going with this? "Your aunt?"

Whenever I'm at a loss for words, I resort to repeating

what the other person said. I've done so since childhood, and have found this practice helpful as a doctor in rural Alabama.

You hooked your own ear fishing? You thought poison oak was cannabis? You want me to castrate your pet pig?

"Yeah, Aunt Ani?"

I shrug. "She's a nice woman. I can tell she really cares about you and your brother."

"She's pretty too."

I scratch the side of my head, more out of nervous energy than to satisfy an itch. Willow's lips curves into a grin when I don't respond. By not responding, I'm sure she knows I agree.

"Leave your shoes off and we'll go get your height."

As Willow bends to pick up her shoes, I make my escape to the living room before she can interrogate me further. Carter is slumped back on the couch, either tired, bored, or both. Aniston has moved from snooping at my books to checking out my DVD collection. Since I stream all new movies, most are old—and a little embarrassing.

I grab a tape measure from my bag and roll it out. It goes to eight feet and almost hits the wall of the tiny living area when it uncurls. "Okay, Carter, could I get your help?"

"Yes, sir."

I help Carter hold the end of the tape measure against her heel. "Okay, Willow, stand straight and still, with your head level."

She straightens her shoulders and stiffens. I pull the tape up to her scalp and note the height, then write it down. "Carter, do you mind rolling that up for me?"

He nods and starts rolling up the white measuring tape. I sign and date the bottom of Willow's form and hand it to Aniston. "She's all set. Healthy girl."

"Thanks." Aniston halfway smiles, and our eyes lock. We stare at each other just long enough for me to worry I'm being weird.

I drop my gaze and take a step back. "Is that all y'all

need?" I raise my eyes too soon and catch a glimpse of Willow trying to hide a smile. I quickly turn my attention to Aniston, which I'm sure only feeds Willow's assumptions.

"We're good. Thank you, Dr. West."

Aniston says my name as if she's trying to keep things more formal between us. But it doesn't get much less formal than coming to my house at night for a physical while I'm doing pull-ups shirtless.

"Call me Easton." I keep my eyes on Aniston, not wanting to catch Willow's expression. In my defense, any kind, small-town human being would ask their new neighbor of the same age bracket to call them by their first name.

"Easton," Aniston repeats slowly. Heat rises up my neck and tickles behind my ears at the sweetness in how she says my name.

"If y'all need anything else, let me know."

Aniston blushes slightly and turns toward the door. I cross the room and open it for them. The kids exit, but she stops in the doorway and turns back to me. We're now inches apart, and I can smell my Axe body spray kick into overdrive as I begin to sweat.

"I'll let you know if we need anything else."

I nod and smile as she steps onto the small porch and follows her kids to the truck. Then I shut the door and selfishly hope she needs something else real soon.

CHAPTER 6

Aniston

"Call me Easton." I mutter the words under my breath as I flip another pancake.

I'm certain I've called him Easton before, but Dr. West seemed appropriate last night, since we were there on official health reasons. Even if he did answer the door shirtless and sweaty.

I reach for a nearby potholder and fan my face. It's getting hot in here, and I don't think the oven is to blame. Oven. *Oh, shoot!*

I stuff my hand in the potholder and open the oven door. The bacon sizzles in the pan, seconds from being burnt. I pull out the pan and set it on the stove top beside my pancake skillet. Maybe the kids like their bacon extra crispy.

After all the mishaps of yesterday, I decided to wake up early, dress nicely, and cook a reputable breakfast. No tossing snacks over the back seat on the way to school. At least not today.

No sooner than I scrape the last of the pancake batter into the skillet, I hear footsteps. I turn to find Carter standing in the kitchen doorway, dressed for school. However, he still needs to comb his hair.

"I knew I smelled bacon."

I grin. "I'm afraid it's a little too well done."

"That's fine." He offers me a sympathetic face, which backfires and makes me feel even worse about my lack of cooking skills.

"Help yourself." I pull some plates from the cabinet by my head, then continue tending to the final pancake.

Pancakes are a great metaphor for most things in life. The first one always comes out a little wonky, but by half-a-dozen tries, I can make at least one worthy of appearing on Paula Deen's blog.

Carter picks up a plate and selects a pancake and some bacon. I carry the skillet and spatula to the sink. A cloud of smoke forms around my head when I run water into the pan. It reminds me of the smoke whenever Aladdin rubs the Genie's lamp. What I wouldn't give for a good genie lamp right now.

What would I wish for? *Make Georgia disappear? Make the car line disappear? Make me stop thinking about my hot doctor neighbor?*

I wince at that last wish. How simple it would be to snap my fingers and go back to before I met Easton West. To not have his perfect face float up in the back of my mind at random times.

Of course, if I could go back in time, I'd go back and do something to save my sister and brother-in-law. But this isn't a Disney movie, it's Apple Cart. There's no going back in time or turning Georgia into a pumpkin.

Something wet hits my stomach, and I realize I've had the water running the whole time. I hurriedly turn off the knob and lift the skillet by the handle. It had covered the drain, causing the sink to fill up. It didn't overflow, but it did wet me enough to require a partial wardrobe change.

"Do you need anything, Carter?"

He crunches his bacon and shakes his head.

I hold my shirt out from my stomach and head for my bedroom. Willow passes me on the way. "I made breakfast," I call behind my back.

"Thanks," she answers without stopping.

Once I'm in my room, I pull off the wet blouse and thumb through my closet for another one. This was my best option for dressing sophisticated yet approachable. Like a woman from an Ann Taylor ad. Now I'm stuck with choices that make me resemble a woman from Banana Republic . . . or Banana Ball. And thanks to my travel vlog lifestyle, I have way more of the latter.

I find a cotton shirt that would pair better with slacks than leggings and toss it on. Then I check my appearance in the mirror. Cute top, pencil pants—a tiny bit too snug from recent lifestyle (and diet) changes—and black heels. Perfect.

Even better, I have freshly combed and straightened hair, which no longer reeks of trash juice. The one good, right thing I did yesterday was take a shower before going to Easton's house.

I reenter the kitchen to Willow packing a lunch for Carter. Bless her heart. That's the one thing I forgot to do. At least until I think of something else I forgot to do.

"You look nice. Are you going someplace today?"

"Thanks." I smile at Willow. "Just taking you kids to school."

She narrows her eyes skeptically before lowering them and stabbing a piece of pancake.

I focus on the other kid. "Carter, please brush your hair."

"I did."

I raise one eyebrow, then decide not to challenge his state-ment. Maybe that's the best a seven-year-old boy can do. I hurry upstairs to the bathroom I use and grab some tangle spray and a comb. He doesn't protest when I come back and start pawing at his hair, then comb it flat.

"There." I stand in front of him and examine my work. I'm no hairstylist. I tussle it a bit to take away some of the glued-on affect. "Okay, y'all ready?"

"Yes, ma'am." Willow stands and carries her plate to the sink. It's empty, and so is Carter's. A calm satisfaction runs through me at the thought of making a meal everyone ate. Good thing I pulled that bacon from the oven when I did.

The kids gather their belongings as I snatch my purse and lead us through the garage. "Let's take the truck."

They climb in, looking relieved that I didn't make them take the RV to school. It's not only cumbersome to drive through the car line, but probably embarrassing as well. It sure embarrassed me when I had to spray trash droppings off the top.

I fasten my seat belt and check my teeth in the rearview mirror before backing out of the garage. Good. No bacon remains. I've got to do some serious damage control to make up for running around late with trashy hair.

We ride to school in peaceful silence and slide in line. Leaving fifteen minutes sooner buys us a spot closer to the school instead of in the ditch by Dollar General. After a few minutes of stop and go, we're in line to drop off Willow. "Do you need me to take your physical inside?"

She cocks her head as if I'm crazy. "No, I'll drop it by the office."

"Okay." I give her my best motherly smile as she climbs out and shuts the door. "Have a good day."

"Stay out of trouble," she calls, smirking back at me.

"Trouble?" I huff as I exit the line.

By some small miracle, we make it onto the road without anyone honking. The policeman greets us, and I now understand that by holding up two fingers, he means lane two and not "peace."

I fall in line behind the Cadillac with the boat and look at Carter through the mirror. "Hand me your folder."

"What folder?"

"The one with all that information stuff in it."

His eyes widen. "Did we forget to fill something out?"

"Nope." I grin.

How could we? I triple checked everything during our family dinner of Jack's takeout, right before we dropped in on Easton unannounced.

Carter unzips his backpack and hands me the red folder with his name on the front.

"Thanks." I set it in my lap and drive closer to the back of the boat.

"What are you going to do with it?"

"Turn it into the office. I want to make sure everything is right."

Carter looks confused, but shrugs. "Okay." He stares out the window as we approach the line of cones.

Georgia is front and center, waving her fingers at cars. I'd like to wave a finger at her . . . but only one.

I squint to make sure she is holding up three at me. It's hard to tell when she keeps shaking her hand back and forth. Before she gives me whiplash, I make the decision to veer into line three. This must be correct because she doesn't knock on my window or blow her whistle.

We inch toward the entrance, watching various teachers open car doors. A chubby kid hobbles out of the Cadillac and stops by the boat to grab his backpack. Strange, but so is the whole car line experience.

It's our turn to merge by the door, and I stop for Carter to get out. "Have a good day."

"You too, Aunt Ani." He grins and hops out.

Once the teacher shuts his door, I follow the car in front of me and reenter the road. I straighten the papers in my lap and smile to myself. Georgia is waiting for me to mess up again. I just know it.

Well, today I'm prepared.

I drive as far as necessary to find a suitable parking space void of signs—or trash bins. Then I park and lock the truck. Luckily, I didn't have to park too far away, since the temperature is already rising.

By the time I make it to the front door, sweat beads on my hairline. I take my time ringing the bell and glance around to make sure Georgia catches a glimpse of me before I enter.

Sure enough, she hands her stop sign to another safety-vest fashionista and follows me inside.

I go through the motions of signing my name like Morgan did for us yesterday, then get the secretary's attention. "Miss, I have my nephew's paperwork."

She sticks a hand through the window and receives the stack. After thumbing through, she wrinkles her brow. "Thanks. You can put these in his backpack next time. It's not necessary to come up here."

I nod, a tad bit defeated when I hear Georgia make a nasally sound behind me. "Thanks," I say through a forced smile.

"You're welcome. I'll pass these on to the room mom."

"Room mom?" That's a new one I haven't heard before.

"Yes, the mother in charge of organizing all events and special activities in his class."

"I'm Carson's room mom," Georgia says. I cringe, as she's close enough for me to feel her breath on the back of my neck.

I jerk my head around and take a step back. "I thought your son was in a different class?"

"He is."

I glance at the office for backup, but the secretary is already away from the window, filing papers.

"Any room without a room mom defaults to the PTSO president, who as of June fourth is me."

My skin crawls at the mention of that date out loud. That's the day my world changed forever, and we all know what happened to make this vixen president.

I choose to ignore that fact and take a second to center myself before responding. "If nobody volunteered, I'll do it."

Georgia's eyes lift, raising her brows and hairline until she looks bald in the front. Well, except for that tight and tall ponytail poking up. Her hairdo is one big bow away from a cheer competition.

"What? Is that not allowed since I'm not his birth parent?"

Her mouth twitches as if it's fidgeting for words. I smirk, enjoying this a little too much.

"That would be good," a voice calls from behind me. I turn around to find my new friend, the secretary, smiling. I really should learn this woman's name.

I raise a brow back at Georgia, whose face is a cocktail of shock and sour—with a hint of lime to pucker her pout. "It's a little late. School's already started."

"We've only been in a day. I think it'll be fine," a male voice calls out.

I watch Georgia's face whiten before I turn back to Principal Dingle. Real name, I swear.

He gives me a nod of approval. "Your sister did a great job at this school. I, for one, would love to have you on board."

Georgia steps beside me. From the corner of my eye, I watch her mouth drop as she stares at the office. Then she reaches over and puts a hand on my arm.

Her hand is tiny and cold like a baby salamander. I shiver at the thought of her slime transferring to me.

"Now, we wouldn't want to overburden Miss Wilson with all these recent challenges." She drags out the word "challenges" as if she's challenging me. Maybe she is.

I tighten my muscles until the salamander slides off. Principal Dingle frowns at Georgia. "If she has any questions, it will be your place to help her."

Georgia snaps her head to me and grins mischievously. "Let me get the paperwork."

Oh great. More paperwork. New beads of sweat form on my forehead as I try and remember my own blood type.

Georgia brushes past me and trots into the office like a show pony. She returns with a binder thicker than a Southern woman's recipe Rolodex. I swallow audibly when she thrusts it toward my midsection.

My hands shake as I grab the edges of the binder. Georgia flips open the front cover. Then out of nowhere, she produces a pen, clicks it, and drops it on the page like a proverbial mic drop.

"Sign your name if you're willing to commit to the responsibilities listed in this binder. Of course . . ." She glances back at the office, then smirks at me. "We all understand if you want to read through first before your sign."

Everything in my logical brain screams that I shouldn't sign this before reading it. But it's kind of like my friends who have bought homes. They swear that after a few pages, you just trust the process and keep signing your name.

And I can't look weak in front of Georgia.

I pick up the pen and scribble my signature on the line at the bottom, not even taking the time to read the first page. Then I hand her the pen. She smiles like a cartoon villain as she snatches the page I signed from the binder and closes the cover.

I smile toward the office. "Have a good day, Mr. Dingle."

"You too." His glasses frames raise on his thin cheeks as he smiles.

Once his perfectly combed, graying dark hair disappears behind a filing cabinet, I turn and start out the door. I can't resist glancing back at Georgia, who's still standing between the door and office, watching me leave. Her lips curve, and the silver pen catches the sunlight as I open the door.

"The Devil Went Down to Georgia" plays in the back of my mind as I exit the building.

By the time I reach the truck, my forearms have buckled beneath the weight of the massive binder. I toss it on the passenger seat and grimace at the cutesy schoolhouse cartoon on the front. I'm afraid I really just made a deal with the devil.

Easton

"And here's another one on the Facebook." Mrs. Maudy's shaky finger scrolls through her photo albums.

"Yes, ma'am." I give my polite smile that conveys respect for elders, even though my patience is wearing thin.

She came in for dizzy spells, but seems way more concerned with showing me photos of her great niece.

"The divorce wasn't her fault, you know. She caught him with the cleaning lady. And they didn't have kids yet, so no baggage there."

I keep my head down, trying to appear like I'm listening best I can without actually making eye contact. The last thing I want is to encourage this conversation.

"Okay, Mrs. Maudy, here's your prescription." I rip a page off my notepad. "You can drop this by the pharmacy on your way out. Please take it as prescribed, and don't just save it for a rainy day."

As she stands slowly, I cradle her elbow with my hand to

help her up. She shuffles toward the door. "You know, my dizziness only acts up when it rains."

I shake my head. "Doctor's orders."

"If you consider Claire, I'll take my meds."

I sigh as she holds up her phone and grins. "I'll consider her."

"Great. Then I'm off to the pharmacy." Mrs. Maudy shuffles down the hallway leading toward the main hospital area.

I shake my head and go back to my office. When I first moved to Apple Cart, I actually went on a date or two. Nothing panned out, as my mind was more on work and making a life here.

Now all I do is think about Aniston.

She's nothing like the women I've dated before. They were less sporadic, more poised and settled. More like me. Maybe that's why I'm so attracted to Aniston all of a sudden. She's nothing like me.

I check my messages for a few minutes before the nurse pops her head in my door. "Dr. West, you have someone in room two when you're ready."

"Thanks." I stand and straighten my tie as I prepare to meet my next patient.

Every case in Apple Cart is an adventure. Especially since I never know if the person is wanting care for themselves or an animal. We really need a vet closer to town.

I'm prepared for another older person ready to fix me up with a relative or someone smuggling a farm animal in for a shot. What I'm not prepared for is . . .

"Georgia?"

"Easton."

This is new. I shut the door behind me and widen my eyes. She looks perfectly healthy and, to my knowledge, her family has always gone into the city for doctor's visits.

"What's bothering you?"

She sighs laboriously and slumps her shoulders before

pinching the bridge of her nose. "I've been having these migraines lately."

"Hmm." I shine my light at her pupils and massage her temples. "Does that hurt?"

"It actually helps," she giggles.

"What about here?" I put pressure points where her sinuses might affect her head.

"Still fine."

I step back and put my light in my pocket. "Any nausea?"

"No."

"When did your headaches start?"

"Oh I don't know, maybe around a few days ago."

I make a note on my pad. Most likely, these are stress-induced headaches.

"So, I met your new neighbor."

My hand stops midsentence. And there it is. The real reason Georgia came in—to gossip.

I continue writing, choosing not to acknowledge her comment.

"She seems a little lost, you know."

"Do you have a headache right now?" *Because I sure do!*

"I did a little earlier. Right after I saw Aniston. Poor thing, seemed so lost. Bless her heart. Have you noticed anything unusual about her?"

My insides heat up and I get the primal urge to defend Aniston, even though I barely know her. But I do know Georgia.

"No, I haven't."

Georgia clinches her unnaturally white teeth. "Bless her heart, my head's hurting just thinking about her. She's so scatterbrained, don't you think?"

"No, I never got that from her." *Maybe from you.*

I make a mental note to add Georgia's husband to my prayer list. He's undoubtedly the one dealing with recurring migraines.

"I guess living like a nomad for years will do that to a person."

I refuse to dignify that dig with a response. Georgia is constantly throwing out bait, hoping someone will bite so she can reel them in.

The first time I met her was at a golf tournament our dads played in. I was in middle school and she was in early college. She showed up with her now husband on her arm. Even as a naive thirteen-year-old boy, I could sense her showing off for her date by putting others down in the process—her friends, parents, whoever would play along.

Ever since that first encounter, I never cared for her. The day I found out her family lived in Apple Cart, I cringed. Of course, she's too good for the Pig and most other local establishments. She mainly stays at the school.

Poor Aniston has to deal with her there.

Georgia sighs, likely impatient with waiting on me to respond. Too bad she didn't hold her breath. She stares at me with sad eyes. "I guess Aniston can't help it. She just isn't like us."

"Us?"

"Yeah, you and me."

I frown. On what planet am I like Georgia? "You mean since we're both from Tuscaloosa?"

She shrugs. "No, we're, you know, better than how she conducts herself."

Something inside me snaps. I wad up the paper in front of me, where I'd planned on writing her a prescription. It's clear she only came in to meddle. I'll make sure she leaves with no medicine and still gets charged a copay.

"Georgia, if your head is bothering you, it's probably because you spend too much time at the school worrying over pointless things. And as for Aniston, I've found her to be nothing but concerned with the well-being of the kids entrusted to her. She's a caring woman and should be none of your concern."

Georgia opens her mouth to respond, but I tug her arm until she stands and lead her to the door. I open it and wait for her to leave.

She blinks at me, stunned at my response. "What about my headache?"

"Stay home from school and take an Advil."

As soon as she steps outside the door, I close it and lean against the handle in case she tries to return. A little extreme, but so is Georgia.

After I hear her footsteps down the hallway, I slide down the door and take a deep breath. I'd rather do the Heimlich on a hen than deal with Georgia. There's no telling what she's put Aniston through this week. I need to do something extra nice for her and the kids.

Another minute passes before I stand and peek out the door. The coast is clear, so I retreat to my office.

As I'm checking my email, Aniston wanders into my mind again. I can't begin to imagine what she's going through.

I've never been great with reading feelings or showing compassion. Bedside manner is something I've really had to develop as a doctor, and I'm still not great. My last girlfriend broke things off because I was "too mechanical and not passionate enough."

That stung.

Last I heard, she married a counselor. Sounds about right.

A loner at heart, I may not be the best with other people. But I get the urge that Aniston and the kids need my help. Sure, they have people in town like Morgan who can do whatever they need. But when it comes to family, they have no one. Plus, I'm literally within spitting distance of them.

On some small level, Aniston needs me. And on a slightly higher level, I want her.

Aniston

My stomach growls, and I check the time on my laptop. It's close to one, so I should be hungry, especially since I'm waking up much earlier than before.

I save my progress and head for the kitchen to find some lunch. Today, I managed to actually work instead of scroll through memory lane. That means I should be on time to pick up the kids too.

As soon as we get past this first week of school, I plan on taking them with me to the store. I also need to look up some simple recipes on Pinterest. We can't live off takeout and Morgan forever. Unless Morgan offers, of course. I wonder how many times I could make bacon and pancakes before they complained.

I settle on a peanut butter sandwich and some pretzels. When I take my plate to the table, the room-mom folder catches my attention. The bright red cover with colorful cartoon prints is hard to miss among muted neutrals.

For a few minutes, I eat my sandwich and try my best to ignore it. Just like I do whenever I'm sitting across a restaurant from someone with a really crazy haircut. Does it call my attention? Yes. Does it need my attention? No.

However, this particular crazy haircut needs my attention. I chug half a can of Diet Coke to muster up courage, then slide the folder in front of me.

I never made it past the first signature page until now. A table of contents glares up at me. It runs for two pages. Most of the novels I read don't have this many chapters.

It's sectioned off by seasons of the year, as well as by special days.

Hat days, parades, holiday parties, hundredth day of school. Why would you count the days of school? My mind flickers to a teacher drawing a hundredth tick mark with chalk in the corner of the board. Not unlike a prisoner marking his days in the pen. Depressing, if you ask me.

There are pages dedicated to the teacher and administrators, with all their likes and dislikes. More pages have information for all the students in the class. Carter's entry has my sister's phone number listed, so I'm assuming she filled it out earlier.

All of this material is either really helpful or really unnecessary, in my opinion. I don't understand why there are so many special days. Friday should be special because it's the last day of the week. That's it. Dressing like your favorite celebrity will not make a Monday morning better. Trust me, I've tried.

I cringe at the memory of my Carrie Underwood days. Nobody should wear that much fringe on a daily basis. Some things are better left for the limelight.

Every section of the binder has instructions for what I need to do in every event. While I appreciate the *Room Mom for Dummies* additions, having this many details makes my skin itch. Since Georgia took the time to include all of this, anything I don't do will likely be held against me. After all, she has my signature.

I down the rest of my drink and wipe my mouth with the back of my hand. Before I panic, I best call Morgan. She said to call her if I had a problem instead of indulging in cookie crack.

My phone is across the kitchen, plugged into the charger on the counter. A perfect excuse to get away from the folder.

I dart across the room quicker than a cat on a hot tin roof. I grab my phone and find Morgan's contact. The cartoon kids on the front of the folder smile at me as I wait for Morgan to answer. Even though they're meant to look cute and fun, they creep me out. They give me the same vibes most people get from clowns. I drop my gaze and hold my breath while the phone continues ringing.

"Piggly Wiggly, this is Morgan."

I hold the phone back and wrinkle my nose. It's not a local extension. "Uh, did I call the store?"

Morgan laughs. "Sorry, Aniston. This is my cell. Just got confused."

"Oh." I laugh nervously, as if the fake cartoon kids are holding me hostage and this is my one phone call. "If you're at work, I can call back."

"Nope, I can talk." A scanner beeps in the background. "That'll be thirty-two fifty-seven."

"What?"

"Not you, Mr. Peterman's food. What you need?"

I shake my head as I hear a cash register open. "Have you ever been a room mom?"

"Once." After a pause she says, "Here's your change. Have a nice day."

I wait for her to clarify if the once was meant for me or a customer.

"Sorry. I've gotten in trouble for talking instead of doing my job before, so I've learned to multitask. So, room mom. Done it once to help out your sister. It's a lot of work. Why?"

I bite my bottom lip. Morgan is the ultimate juggler of things. If she thinks it's a lot of work . . . "Uh, I kinda signed up to be it for Carter's class."

"Kinda or did?"

"Did."

"Oh lawd, child!" Morgan cackles like a hen.

"What?"

"Price check on turnip greens. I need a price check on greens."

I hold the phone away from my ear and wince. The intercom beeps, and I wait another beat before holding the phone closer. Now it's just the scanner, which I can handle.

"Why would you do something like that? With Georgia in charge?"

I shrug before realizing Morgan can't see me. "I dunno. I wanted to impress everyone at the school and do something nice for Carter."

"Then you bring cupcakes. Heck, we've got some on sale right now. I'm looking at them." The scanner beeps. "Do you still want this?"

"No, but I'm stuck."

"Oh, not you, Aniston. I'm asking Velda about the turnip greens. Keep talking, I'm listening."

I roll my eyes and continue, even though cookie dough would've lifted my spirits by now. "I signed this piece of paper saying I'll be room mom."

Morgan cackles again. "You're screwed."

"Apparently." I imagine Georgia drilling screws into a voodoo-doll version of me. My muscles twitch at such a vivid nightmare.

"Hey, Velda needs help with the card reader. Don't jump off a ledge or anything. I get off at two. I'll get your kids from school and help you out this evening."

"Thank you! I'm finally getting work done."

"Sure thing, hon. I'm gonna add you to my prayer list too."

"You're the best, Morgan."

"You know it."

After the phone clicks, I sigh. The kids on the folder don't look quite as creepy as before. Even though I'm sure the information beneath them is even more terrifying since I know Morgan's stance on room mom.

"It's all for Carter." Maybe if I say it audibly, my decision will make some sense.

Nope. I'm still crazy.

I pick up my plate and try to ignore the folder beside it. Time to take this lunch elsewhere before those characters make me vomit.

I may be crazy, but at least I get to avoid the car line today.

CHAPTER 7

Easton

As soon as we closed the clinic doors, I headed for my truck. There are a few hours of daylight left for me to move hay.

After dealing with Georgia and a few other crazy characters, it's safe to say I need some John Deere therapy.

For a small town with hardly any crime, there's a lot of gunpowder-related injuries. I've dealt with a few cases of people getting too close to targets or making homemade bombs, but today marked a first.

A guy burned his arm while moving a giant balloon filled with colored gunpowder for his brother and sister-in-law's gender-reveal party tomorrow. He'd planned for the couple to shoot the balloon with a bow and arrow. Unfortunately, he held the balloon a little too close to a pitchfork when trying to hide it in their family's barn.

He'll eventually heal up, though I warned him that the hair may never grow back on his forearms.

I trade my slacks for Wranglers and nice boots for work

boots, then head to the kitchen for some water. Mason Magill wants some hay for his cows, so I need to move all his bales by the road. Whatever is left, I plan on donating to the town golf course . . . which currently has cows on it.

Quite a change from the golf courses in Tuscaloosa, but golf is more seasonal in Apple Cart. The mayor said it's more feasible to raise cattle when it's blazing hot outside and during football season.

I down a bottle of water and grab another for the tractor. When I step onto the porch, a dark cloud blossoms in the distance. It's supposed to rain later tonight, which gives me more reason to get right to work.

Inside the tractor, I enjoy a small bubble of comfort from the heat. The air-conditioning and radio help me relax almost instantly. Since my encounter with Georgia earlier, I've worried about Aniston.

I can only imagine what Georgia has said to her so far. That woman can make anyone doubt themselves—including me. For a minute after she left, I regretted not prescribing a migraine medication in case she really wasn't faking. Even though I have no doubt she was.

Speaking of Aniston, it would take less time to pull Mason's hay from their end of the property, since it's closest to the road. I turn toward the big house and slip on my cap to shade my eyes.

The wind blows through some oak trees around the pond as I cross into Aniston's territory. I stop near her driveway and spear a bale of hay, then drive toward our mailboxes. There's a worn path where the mail carrier stops and turns around every day, which is perfect for stacking Mason's hay.

I continue doing so with a few more bales as I whistle along to the Thomas Rhett song on the radio. Soon, I have all the bales except for a few right around the house.

The sun dances between the tree branches outlining the property as I drive toward the house. A sudden breeze shifts the leaves, hiding the sun. Although it's plenty bright, a rainstorm could strike at any moment. That's part of Southern summers.

When I turn toward the house, I notice Aniston out by the pool. After a moment, she looks up from a stack of papers strewn in front of her on a lawn chair. I wave, and she waves back before gazing down at the papers.

I stab another bale and drive toward the end of the road, then repeat the process. As I'm going for my third bale by the backyard, a huge gust of wind blows in front of me. Loose hay pieces fly past my windshield, and I hear a squeal, followed by what I think is an obscenity.

I stop the tractor and turn toward the noise, which is Aniston, scrambling after papers swirling like a tiny tornado. Her eyes widen as they head for the pool.

My chivalrous instincts kick in, and I hop down from the tractor and dart toward the pool. The papers scatter. One flitters over the water, and Aniston reaches for it. She misses and falls in after it. She bobs up, no problem, but more papers blow that way.

Before I can think, I'm standing in the pool, boots and all, grabbing flying papers like a ten-year-old would lightning bugs.

Some papers make it unscathed, while others land in the water. I do my best to separate the dry from the wet in my hands, but I'm not too successful.

Once they're all in our care, we stare at each other. She blinks water droplets from her soaked eyelashes. I can't tell whether it's pool water or tears. Maybe both.

I hold my hands higher and shake my fists. "Some are still dry." I grin as she lets out a defeated laugh.

"Thanks," she whispers.

I take a step closer to her, and I'm not sure why. In some subconscious way, I'm drawn to her. Even now, when we're dressed down and soaking wet. With her hands fisted around dripping papers, she takes a step toward me. We're now inches apart, staring at each other, holding wet papers.

Crazy as we must look, I want to stand like this for a while longer. Actually, I want to toss the stupid papers and wrap my arms around her and carry her out of the pool. But this isn't a Marvel movie, and I'd be no hero at all if I soaked the few papers I saved.

"Well, aren't you two a sight for sore eyes."

We turn our heads to Morgan, all four of her kids, and both of Aniston's standing by the steps, staring at us. Morgan wiggles her eyebrows at Aniston and laughs. "Maybe we should come back later. I'd hate to interrupt whatever kind of party this is."

Aniston blushes and starts toward the steps. "Dr. West—" She glances back at me, and I smile. She returns my smile before turning back to Morgan. "Uh, Easton, was kind enough to try and save my papers when a windstorm blew up."

"Yes, how kind of Easton." Morgan drags my name out and winks at Aniston.

Now I'm the one blushing. Or maybe that's just the heat of the lowering sun reflecting off the water. Either way, I'm suddenly aware that I'm still standing in the center of the pool with my arms raised. I follow Aniston's lead and march up the steps of the shallow end.

My boots weigh about as much as one of the hay bales. I glance around for a place to put the papers so I can free my hands to dump the water from my boots.

"What are these?" Morgan frowns at the papers we're holding.

Aniston sighs and drops her arms by her sides. "They are, or were, the sheets of information about Carter's class. I was organizing them to make copies tomorrow morning so I could make folders for the parents."

Morgan shakes her head. "Oh, honey."

Aniston nods. "Yeah, like you said earlier, I'm screwed."

"Let me see those." Morgan makes a grabby motion with her hand. I give her the papers I'm holding and gladly take off my boots. "Willow, go get them some towels."

"Yes, ma'am." Willow and Morgan's oldest daughter disappear into the house.

The younger kids have already scattered, and I find Andrew climbing toward the cab of my tractor. "Hey, don't get in there."

I race after him in my sock feet and catch him by the shirt-tail before he makes it to the cab.

"I just want to drive."

"How about you can ride with me to finish taking this last bale to the end of the road?"

"Cool!"

I hang out the door and yell at Morgan, "Andrew can help me move this last bale to the road if you're fine with it."

She waves an arm. "Fine by me. Put that kid to work!"

I climb in and direct Andrew to the buddy seat. "Don't touch anything."

He folds his arms and pouts, but does as he's told. I watch Morgan wrap a towel around Aniston and lead her toward the house as we fork the last bale for Mason.

Funny how I beat the rain and still got soaking wet.

Aniston

Drying off and changing into clean clothes lifts my mood. At least until I make it to the kitchen and spot the soiled papers strewn across the countertop. If only drying them were as easy as drying myself.

Easton stands barefoot by the door to the patio, a towel wrapped around his wet jeans. I'm a little surprised to see he's still wearing his shirt . . . and maybe a little disappointed too.

I step outside and find him on the phone. Great, he will probably think I came out here to eavesdrop. I walk toward the one pot of flowers that somehow managed to stay alive while we traveled for almost a month and act like I'm checking them. A stupid way to try and look occupied, but it beats standing behind Easton on the phone.

Once he says "bye" to whoever's on the other end of the line, I inch toward the door as casual as I can.

"Hey, I see you got dry," he says.

My eyes land on his wet chest. The shirt outlines his abs. I blink and force my gaze to his face, which isn't a bad view either. "Yeah." I nod to his phone. "I'm surprised your phone isn't ruined."

He lifts it and laughs. "Luckily, it was on the dash of the tractor. I don't like driving with a phone in my pocket. Gets in the way."

I notice the tractor still parked on the edge of our yard. "Do you need to go finish your work?"

"No. That was Bradley on the phone. He wanted to know when to pick up the hay for the golf course. I can get it tomorrow. Mason Magill is getting all I moved today for his place."

I twist my lips and survey the property surrounding both our houses. "Maybe we should get a cow. Would be a lot less work for you."

He smiles, and my cheeks heat up when I realize I said *we*. Why did I say we? Sharing a cow is a big deal. Only couples share a cow.

"It would take more than one cow to keep all this mowed.

Besides, I'd need to make some fences before we got cows, and that's even more work."

My insides flip when he uses the word *we* too. Does this mean he's open to owning a cow with me one day?

When Easton waves a hand in front of my face, I realize I've been daydreaming about joint cow ownership. I blink and giggle nervously. "I guess you're right. Want to come inside?"

He fans his hand down his torso to point out his wetness. "You sure?"

"It's cooler in there. And it's not like Carter doesn't come in dripping all the time anyway."

"Thanks." His smile widens, and my legs tingle the slightest bit when I walk inside.

Easton follows me with his phone in hand. Smart. I would've shoved it in my wet pocket by now without thinking.

Willow and Morgan are crowded around the countertop, working on the papers. Willow holds my hair dryer to one, and Morgan peels apart a few that stuck together. It's one wet mess.

I hold up one beside Willow, which she's apparently blown already. It's stiff as a board and the writing is splotchy. I slant my eyes and hold it closer before dropping it back on the counter and sighing.

"We can barely read these. How am I supposed to make copies of them? I could retype it all first, but not when I can't read it."

I groan as Morgan thumbs through the stack in her hand. "I have a lot of these at home from my kids' room moms. We can copy mine and just type the ones specific to Carter's class."

I perk up at the possibility of lessening my work even one percent. Then my thought bubble deflates when I spot a rogue sheet filled out by a parent. "How am I supposed to figure out these, though?" I twist the page so everyone can see the water stains covering up the address and phone number.

"Do you know the names?" Easton asks.

I shuffle through the papers in front of me. "Uh, most are here. Some are messed up."

I slide a page his way, and he picks it up. Our hands brush slightly, sending a tingle up my arm. I cross my arms so nobody notices the sudden goose bumps.

"I'm sure a lot of these people have been to the clinic or hospital. As long as I have either a name, address, email, or phone number, I can log into the system and look them up."

Before I can respond, Morgan blurts out, "All right. So Aniston can go with Easton and work on these while I cook supper for everyone."

I turn to Easton, who smiles. Apparently, he's fine with this arrangement.

Morgan opens the refrigerator, then slams it shut. "It looks like we'll be eating at my house."

"Yeah, I meant to go by the store today."

"Uh-huh," Morgan grunts. Even her grunts are sarcastic.

"Kids," she yells in her best mom voice. My kids and hers file into the kitchen. Willow sets down the hair dryer. "Isabella can help me cook while Willow and Ethan make sure everyone has done any homework they might have."

As if they're under a trance, all the kids file in line and follow Morgan out the back door. None of them hesitate or say a word, even Andrew. Man, I envy that kind of power. I can't even overcome my newfound fear of red folders.

The back door closes after the last kid leaves, and I'm alone with Easton once again. We stand in mutual silence for a moment as I stare at the door. When I look back at him, he asks, "Ready to get to work?"

I nod. "Let me get some shoes." I slip into a pair of flip-flops I keep by the front door.

Before I can make it back to the kitchen, Easton meets me in the hallway with the papers. "I have a copier too."

"Great." I giggle a little and bite the inside of my mouth to make myself stop. I'm certain he thinks I'm the biggest dork by now, and giggling will only add to that persona.

I pass him and continue toward the back door. He follows me out. Before I can turn toward the garage, he says, "You can ride with me in the tractor if you want."

Okay. So despite growing up in Apple Cart, I haven't ridden a lot of tractors. There was once in the Christmas parade as a child, then again on Hick Day during homecoming week in high school. The first was because my friend was riding it too, and the latter was to try and impress the boy driving it. I guess I'm easily influenced.

Of course, I have no problem following a soaked Easton into the cab of this John Deere and sitting beside him on a tiny fold-down seat.

He cranks the engine and off we go toward his house. We ride in silence as I gander at all the bells and whistles on the tractor. The two I'd ridden before didn't have fancy screens and buttons, or even a cab. They were old-school Apple-Cart style.

My brother-in-law was a tech-savvy pilot, so it doesn't surprise me that he'd own a tractor of this scale.

Easton parks it close to the house and turns off the engine. "I would say ladies first, but I'm by the door."

"That's fine." I smile as he jumps down, ignoring the steps.

I take my time, placing my flip-flops on every small step until I'm safely on the ground. Easton grins at me. My cheeks flush when I realize he waited to make sure I landed safely.

We go inside, and he leads me down the hallway to a small room set up as an office. He sets the stack of papers on the desk.

"If you don't mind, I'm going to take a quick shower and

change. You can sort through these, and I'll log us in when I get out."

"Go ahead."

"Thanks." He grins again, and my heart skips a beat or two.

I lower my gaze to the papers and keep it there until he's out of the room. *Keep it together, Aniston. In one month's time, you've gained two kids, a dog, a house, and about six pounds. The last thing you need is to add a man to the mix.*

My inner critic threatens to ground myself from sweets and pool time, but the less logical part of me is contemplating falling for Easton because he keeps such a neat desk. I could use a little order like this in my life.

Instead of organizing papers like I'm supposed to do, I spend the next little bit snooping around his desk. I'm literally smelling of a fancy fountain pen when his voice startles me.

"Hey."

My fingers tremble at getting caught being creepy. I drop the pen and jerk my head toward the door, where Easton is wearing clean gym clothes and smells, for lack of a better word, delicious. *Forget the pen, let me take a whiff of his man scent.* I'm not sure what kind of concoction he's wearing, but it's intoxicating, to say the least.

"Did you have a chance to sort out the papers?"

Oh shoot, the papers. I glance at the pile under my hand, which I haven't bothered to move. "Uh, sort of."

His grin lets me know I've been caught lying as well. I pick up the pile and start shuffling through as he walks past me and sits in the desk chair. "It's fine, we can figure it out as we go."

He's now directly in front of my nose, shooting man scents my way. I replay the talk in my head about how my life makes it impossible to have a relationship. This used to work well when I moved around constantly and lived in a one-room RV. But now I have a big house with an actual address. Uh-oh, better come up with a new talk.

"I'm in the system." Easton's voice drags me out of my inner debate. "Hand me a page with missing contact info."

I thumb through and find a page with the phone number blotched. Easton takes it from me, and I try to ignore the way his arm flexes when he bends it.

"Let's get a template started for these forms." He opens a spreadsheet and types categories for us to fill in. "Do you need allergy information too?"

"Allergy?"

He looks up, and I swallow. There's a faint golden line around his pupils that fades into the brown of his eyes.

"Yeah, like if a kid has food allergies. That way when you bring them snacks, you'll know."

"Oh right. Good idea."

He nods and goes back to typing. I swallow again, as if it will make the heat rising in my chest dissipate. The heat only increases, so I shuffle the papers to feign busyness.

We work like this a few more minutes, with me handing him papers in silence. When the heat reaches my ears, I decide to make small talk to fill my mind with something other than man scents and biceps. Wow, I'm so shallow.

"So . . . what brought you to Apple Cart?" *Real smooth, Aniston.*

"I was part of a rural medical program and had wanted to live in a small town."

"Really?" As someone who grew up in a small town, I can't see for the life of me why anyone would choose this.

"Yeah. My grandparents had a farm and lived on the outskirts of Tuscaloosa. I liked the rural feel of it. I grew up in the suburbs and went to a big school. Everyone had their corners of town depending on where they lived or worked or attended school. College felt even more isolated into small groups. I loved the idea of living where everyone would know each other."

I laugh. "Well, that's definitely Apple Cart. Sometimes the older population knows what I'm doing before I do."

He laughs. It's contagious, making me laugh so hard that I buckle at my waist and close my eyes. When I open them, his face is tilted a few inches from mine.

My heart races as he licks the corner of his mouth. Why would he do that? What does that mean? Is it some kind of signal? A mating call I don't know about?

I've spent so much time alone on the road, I have no idea if a guy is hitting on me or dealing with chapped lips.

Despite everything that makes sense, I would welcome a kiss from Easton. In fact, I might just encourage a kiss from him. With that notion, I lean an inch closer.

The corners of his mouth upturn into a slight smile. I close my eyes. Either he will take the bait and kiss me, or he will turn back to the computer screen. No matter what, I'm too chicken to watch.

I'm jerked out of my waiting state when my butt cheek vibrates. No, it's not his hand on my butt, but my phone in my pocket. It rings loudly, vibrating again. I straighten and pull it from my shorts pocket.

Sure enough, by the time I open my eyes and answer, Easton is back to pecking away on the computer. The moment is over.

"Hi, Morgan."

"You sound disappointed. Are y'all able to get the info?"

"Yeah, we are. I'm just tired."

"Well, I hope you're hungry too. I'm at your place with supper. It's not much, but the kids already have a plate if y'all want to come and eat."

"Thank you. Be there in a sec." I hang up on Morgan and slide the phone in my pocket.

"That was Morgan. She's at my house with food. We can go eat."

"Perfect timing. I just typed up the last of the contact information sheets."

"Yeah, perfect timing," I say through gritted teeth.

But maybe it is. I can brush off Easton's smiles and smells. Yet I'm quite certain there would be no coming back from kissing him.

CHAPTER 8

Aniston

It was close to ten when we finished the papers last night. Easton even ran to the Dollar Store to purchase folders before they closed while Morgan and I made copies. As if I needed more reasons to like him.

I blot another layer of concealer under my eyes to try and cover up the lack-of-sleep circles. Even though I've had everything possible working against me, thanks to Morgan and Easton, my folders are finished.

Take that, red folder! I scowl in my makeup mirror at the cartoon kids on the room-mom binder. It's on the center of my bed, making itself at home. I may as well embrace the madness and accept my fate.

Thanks to my friends, I'm one step ahead—at least for today.

I finish my makeup and slip into my black heels. I'm wearing a pencil skirt and sleeveless blouse worthy of a young professional. That's the look I'm going for to redeem my earlier appearances. I also want to make a good impression on Carter's teacher when I drop off these folders.

By the time I make it downstairs in my heels, the kids are in the kitchen. I smile at their willingness to wake up on time. Then I see the time on the microwave.

I gasp. "Kids, we better leave . . . like now."

Willow turns around from wiping peanut butter on a slice of bread. "As soon as I make Carter's sandwich for his lunch."

I slap my forehead. Poor Carter. I always forget to make his lunch. Heck, most days I forget to make my own lunch.

"Thanks, Willow." I grab some Gatorades from the refrigerator and Pop-Tarts from the pantry to eat in the car. Why Jennifer thought they'd be better off with me than Morgan or any number of God-fearing old people in this town is beyond me.

Willow packs Carter's lunch, and they gather their bags. I arm up the folders and dump them into a reusable grocery bag so I can juggle the Gatorades and Pop-Tarts.

One by one, we file out of the house. Carter stops in the garage to feed Buster. He still beats me inside the truck thanks to my heels and thigh-hugging skirt combo.

Maybe one day, I'll forgo my superstitions for common sense and take the minivan.

Gravel slings as I peel out of the driveway with a Pop-Tart between my teeth. I manage to buckle my seat belt by the time we hit the main road. The kids are silent, whether from stuffing their faces or terror from my driving, I'm not sure.

By the time we reach Dollar General, traffic is backed up at least a mile. I curse under my breath and chug some red Gatorade to hide my mouth in case Carter can read my lips in the rearview mirror. Again, I'm by far the least logical choice for raising kids.

We sit in the usual stop-and-go traffic, all eating and

drinking in silence. When I turn in at the middle school, my eyes widen. I have that nagging feeling I forgot something.

"Willow, do you have any practices today?"

"Yes, ma'am. Cheer is last period, but volleyball is right after school."

"What time does it end?"

"Four thirty."

"Okay." I nod, making a mental note to make a real note of that ASAP.

We drop her off and say our goodbyes, then hightail it toward the elementary school. Well, hightail is a strong verb, since traffic comes to a standstill at least half-a-dozen times in a one-mile stretch.

I'm still amazed at how I can make it out of game-day traffic from Bryant-Denny Stadium quicker than I can drop off two kids for school.

Since we're running behind, I take Carter through the line before finding a place to park. Then, as if the heavens opened up and smiled on me, I spot an empty parking place right beside the school.

Maybe my luck is changing.

Hold. That. Thought.

A Lexus SUV pulls up behind me and stops. I may have found a good place to park, but it looks like I'll be here a while.

Before I can open my door, Georgia hops out of the SUV and bounces toward me. My whole body quivers like a poodle when the vet comes in.

She beats on the window, and I roll it down. First, I lean back to ensure her fist doesn't fall in my face.

Her green eyes glow as they narrow on me. I avoid direct eye contact in case she has the power to put me in some sort of trance. Those aren't normal human eyes. They're better suited for a cat—or maybe the bad guy in a Western.

"You're in my spot."

"You have a spot?"

She huffs. "Did you not see the word 'President' painted across the asphalt?"

"Yeah, but I didn't think the president would be visiting Apple Cart Elementary on a random Friday." I snort, and her eyes narrow even more. They're now little slits, like snake eyes. I lean back farther, afraid the predator is preparing to bite.

"President of the PTSO, not the US."

"My mistake. It wasn't specified."

"I need you to move."

I glance in my rearview mirror at the pearly barge parked behind my truck. "I can't move until you move."

She huffs. "Fine. Give me five."

"I'll give you five," I mutter under my breath.

"What was that?" Georgia snaps her head around.

"I said, 'You have a nice ride.'" I grin nervously.

She half-smirks, her eyes even more suspicious than before. Without saying another word, she climbs in her SUV and backs up barely enough for me to pull the truck out. If I accidentally scratch the pearly-white nose of her car with the side of this truck, that's on her.

Just short of a miracle, I somehow manage to back out unscathed. Now that the car line has dissipated, I manage to pull into the road with ease. Georgia wastes no time swooping in her spot.

I roll my eyes and search for a new place to park. One that isn't near the dumpster.

There's a long stretch of flat roadside where nobody has parked across from the school. That should do. I pull over and put the truck in park.

This time, a man in a hardhat comes to my window. He's a big, burly guy with sweat beading in his beard, yet a lot less intimidating than Georgia.

"Ma'am, I'm afraid you can't park in this ditch. We're running a water line." He points a gloved hand ahead of me.

Sure enough, a man on heavy machinery is digging a trench a few yards ahead of where I've parked.

"I think there are some parking spaces back toward the middle school."

"Thanks." I nod and back into the road once again.

When I do find a legitimate parking spot, it's a country mile from the elementary school. Minor setback. I've got this.

I emerge from the truck with my bag of folders and straighten my skirt. A few feet of walking confirms that I chose the most uncomfortable shoes I own. Why is it that the cutest things are often the least comfortable?

The sun beats down, making each step more painful than the last. Either it's my imagination, or a buzzard is circling overhead. A line of sweat falls down my lower back beneath my skirt. Gross.

At last, the elementary school comes into view. Or maybe it's a mirage, as I'm a bit dehydrated now. I lick my lips and hope for the best.

When I make it to the front of the school, a guy on a lawn mower passes, blowing grass clippings my way. Some stick to my sweaty calves, proving this isn't a mirage.

I bend best I can in my pencil skirt and dust off the grass remnants before stepping onto the walkway and pushing the door button.

The door unlocks and I step into glorious air-conditioning. I close my eyes and give myself a moment to suck it in. When I open them, the secretary gives me a sympathetic face, and Georgia grins from her post by the doorway as she sorts snacks.

I resist the urge to grab a snack for myself. Those high-fructose juice boxes might contribute to my dehydration. Plus, I'd rather die than ingest anything Georgia touched. Too risky.

I sign in and let the secretary know I'm going to Carter's class to pass out folders. She nods and continues giving me a "bless your heart" look. I'm sure it's warranted, but it does nothing for my staggering self-esteem.

On my way toward his classroom, I spot a water fountain. Only it's one of those newer kinds that refill water bottles instead of using a spout for your mouth. After a quick peek over my shoulder to make sure the hallway is clear, I hold my head under the spout and push the button.

Major fail. Instead of hydrating myself, I waterboard myself. Now my face is wet, and I choked up more than I swallowed. Coughing, I take a step back and see my reflection in a mirror on a nearby wall. The mirror is surrounded by fake vines and reads, "See how much I've grown."

I have to bend down to get a glimpse of my face, since I've apparently grown above the mirror. And what stares back at me scares me. My face is blotted red with water droplets from either the fountain or sweat, possibly both. There are drops of water on my blouse from the fountain drip and pit stains under my arms from the sweat. The only silver lining is the dark lining of my skirt doesn't show the sweat lines trickling down my panties. Thank God for that.

After the sheer shock of my appearance wears off, I go into fix-it mode. I dart around the hallway like a lost puppy until my eyes land on a lost-and-found bin by the library door with a bulky sweater on top. I hold it up, and it looks like it would fit me. Not to profile—it resembles something an elderly librarian would wear, or maybe a grandma in a Hallmark movie.

Regardless, it beats pit stains and water splotches. I shrug my arms into the heavy red knitting and button it to my collar. It's a bit too *Little House on the Prairie* facing a blizzard compared to my bottom half, but it'll have to do. I don't think I can squeeze into that tiny pink jean jacket or the Under

Armor hoodie. Everything else is lone socks and school supplies.

I sigh and pick up my bag of folders as if I meant to wear this atrocity to school with my pencil skirt. Confidence is key in this situation. Despite the blisters forming on my toes, I strut toward Carter's room with a fake smile plastered on my face.

Mrs. Pebbleton greets me at the door and adjusts her thick glasses. She cranes her neck to my face, as she barely reaches my shoulder when I'm in heels.

"Welcome, Miss Wilson. I like your sweater."

My cheeks flush. "Oh, this old thing?" I half-laugh since it smells like it fell from an attic full of cat fur.

"Yes. I had one just like it, but misplaced it sometime last spring."

"Oh." My eyes widen at the realization that I'm likely wearing Mrs. Pebbleton's sweater.

She adjusts her glasses again and focuses on the bag. "Are these ready for the parents?"

"Yes, ma'am."

"Great, do you have a minute, dear?"

"Sure." I smile as if she's judging me for a beauty pageant. This is no beauty contest—thank God!—but I'm certain she's judging me.

"If you don't mind, could you put some take-home sheets in the pockets for me and then stuff them in the backpacks before you go?"

"Certainly." My insides warm almost as much as my skin. I'm needed by someone other than the kids and the dog. That hasn't happened in a long time, and it tickles something warm and fuzzy inside of me.

"Great. Follow me." She shuffles to the back of the room, near a kitchenette area with a sink and cabinets.

I sneak a peek at Carter, who is sitting quietly, completing a worksheet. I fight the urge to wave or even smile, as I don't want to embarrass him. Nobody wants to get teased at the lunch table for their crazy aunt showing up in a hooker skirt and grandma sweater. Maybe I could pass this look as sexy librarian? Nah, not the time or place for that.

"Miss Wilson—"

"Please, call me Aniston."

Mrs. Pebbleton grins up at me. "Okay, Aniston, these papers are announcements from the office. This stack is their work to send home, and this final stack is from the PTSO."

I nod at the bulging stacks of papers, thankful I'm not by a pool. Although, I'd gladly give my RV to soak my sore feet in a cool pool right now.

"Let me know if you have any questions."

"Yes, ma'am." I nod again, then fan back a lock of sweaty hair that landed across my face.

Mrs. Pebbleton saunters toward the front of the room and announces something about reading time. I lick the tip of my finger and start thumbing through the first stack to divide the papers by kid.

Halfway through the work pile, my hand shakes. It's burning up in this corner of hell—I mean, the classroom. I stand and fan my face before realizing how ridiculous I'm being. I unbutton the arctic-knit sweater and slide it down my arms.

As I'm reaching to pull it off, I notice two things. My blouse now has red stains thanks to sweating in this bulky sweater, and the name "N. Pebbleton" is sewn inside. Well, there's no denying that.

I have two choices: to look like a blotchy sweater stealer or continue sweating it out and prove my innocence. I choose the latter. One second to catch the air coming from the window unit nearby, then I stuff myself back in the sweater. Not that the window unit is doing much good, considering it's higher than my head and stuffed behind a stack of art supplies.

I settle for rolling up the bulky sleeves and continue work-ing. By the time I make it to the last pile, my vision blurs. I close my eyes and swallow the dry lump in my throat. When I stand to reach for the stack of folders to file everything, my knees buckle. I go down like a linebacker, hitting my head on the cabinet door.

Then, everything goes black.

Easton

The lines on the monitor climb up and down like a hiking trail. I take a sip of my black coffee and watch Aniston sleep.

Brooke alerted me as soon as they brought her into the emergency room. She overheated and passed out at the elementary school, then whacked her head on the way down.

Her CT scans showed no brain injury, but she was dehy-drated and overheated. The weirdest part was the ambulance driver saying she had on a bulky knit sweater. No wonder she overheated.

Her eyelids twitch like she's dreaming. I take another sip of coffee and lean closer to her. What I wouldn't give to go inside her head and read her mind. Her bottom lip trembles slightly, then she sighs.

Without thinking, I set my coffee cup on the table beside her bed and reach for her hand. It's warm and small, and I wrap my much larger hand around it. Her forehead wrinkles, and I fight the urge to smooth her brow and kiss it. Instead, I give her hand a gentle squeeze.

To my surprise, she squeezes back. Then her eyelids flutter open. She makes a mousy whimper before spotting my hand in hers. Her eyebrows point together and she jerks her head toward me.

"Hello." I smile, and Aniston recoils, pulling her hand from mine. "I didn't mean to scare you."

She sits up and stares at the IV cord strung in her arm and then at the heart-rate monitor. "What happened?"

I sigh. "You're fine, but you passed out."

"Passed out?" She rubs the back of her head and grimaces. "I remember hitting something."

"The story I heard is you hit a filing cabinet at school when you fainted."

"Were you my doctor?"

I shake my head. "No, Dr. Newhart was in the ER today. Brooke had to do some scans for you and let me know you were here. I came over as soon once my last appointment ended."

"Oh." Aniston lays her head on the pillow and closes her eyes, then pops them open. "Wait, what exactly did Brooke do to me?"

I laugh. "Nothing to be afraid of. Just a CT scan. A normal procedure for anyone who passed out and hit their head."

She leans over and fists a handful of my shirt. "Why would you let her do that to me?"

I shrug. "It really wasn't my call, Aniston."

She tugs me closer and sighs dramatically as her heart rate spikes on the graph. "This is going to cost me a fortune. I don't have health insurance!" Aniston releases my shirt and falls back onto her pillow.

I hesitate a moment, then place my hand on her shoulder. "It's going to be fine. We'll work something out. What matters is that you're okay."

She covers her face and shakes her head. My shoulders slump like I've put a rack of weights across them. Medical bills are no joke. The last thing I want her to worry about is how she will pay for all this.

I reach over and rub her slim shoulder. "Aniston, it'll be okay, I promise. You're fine. They just wanted to make sure since you passed out."

She drops her hands and turns to me. "I just got too hot. That's all."

I wish that was all. "We took some blood and noticed a lot of cortisol."

"What's that?" Her nose wrinkles.

"It's a stress-induced hormone. I'm sure you got too hot, but being stressed probably pushed you over the edge."

"Stressed." Her eyes widen and she scans the room like a squirrel frantically observing the road before deciding which way to run. "I'm not stressed."

"It's okay." I give her shoulder a gentle squeeze before dropping my hand. "You've taken on a lot in the last month or so. You need to make sure and take care of yourself. How are you eating and sleeping?"

A nervous laugh squeaks out of her. She leans her head back and sighs. "I'm eating plenty and sleeping plenty. Maybe not in the conventional sense of eating a balanced diet or sleeping all through the night, but I make it work."

I frown and give her my best "I call BS" stare. The one I've perfected since coming to Apple Cart. Aniston is acting no different than a seventy-year-old farmer who neglects to take his vitamins.

She looks my way and twists her lips. "Truth is, I eat junk a lot lately. And it's hard to sleep in Jennifer's house knowing she's not there."

"I get that. I can't imagine what you're dealing with, but neglecting your health will only make things harder for you and the kids."

"The kids." She twists her upper body, tangling herself in the IV and heart-monitor cords.

"Whoa. Hang on. Let me help you." I stand and lean over her, untangling the cords slowly and steadily. It's a delicate balance between actually making progress on the mess and not touching her. My fingers tingle as they brush across her waist on the last tug. "Sorry."

"It's okay." She blushes.

I sit back in my chair and fold my hands. In all my years in the medical field, I've never been turned on by someone in a hospital gown. Of course, I've never known Aniston until now either.

"Carter saw you pass out, so he knows what's going on. Brooke called the middle school to tell Willow. Then she called Morgan and told her to take care of them after school."

Aniston cranes her neck and stares at the clock across the room. "How long are they keeping me here?"

"Tonight." When her face whitens, I press my palm on her arm. "Don't worry about anything. Not the kids, the dog, the money. For once, Aniston, worry about you. We've got this."

She closes her eyes and rests her head on the pillow. "I feel like such a failure."

"Why?" My voice is a mixture of accusation and confusion. Part of me wants to scold her for saying so, and the other part is surprised she said it. Between what I know about her life before now and the way she's stepping up to take care of the kids, how could she call herself a failure?

She pops her eyes open and arches a brow my way. "Do you know why I overheated?"

"You got too hot and dehydrated when you were overstressed."

"Yeah, but I got too hot and dehydrated because I can't adult."

I bite back a laugh and force a serious face. "What makes you say that?"

Aniston rolls her eyes. "I was all sweaty from walking to the school. I practically drowned my face trying to use the fancy water fountain. Then I grabbed that knitted sweater from the lost-and-found bin to cover my wet blouse and pit stains."

My mouth is now numb from biting back laughter.

"I tried to take it off when I overheated, then noticed it had stained my shirt . . . and that it had Carter's teacher's name inside."

Despite my best efforts, I burst out laughing.

Aniston points the finger wearing her oxygen monitor toward me. "See, I'm laughable to real adults."

My body tenses. The last thing I meant was to beat her down further. "No, you're not. You're just funny."

"Funny?"

"Yeah. If something like that happened to someone in a movie, wouldn't you laugh?"

"Maybe." She shrugs. "Sure, but this is my life."

"Which is why you need to take care of yourself."

Aniston crosses her arms, this time with caution as she watches the cords. "I've spent all my life until now only caring about myself. Now it's time I live for my niece and nephew."

My nerves loosen a bit at her vulnerability. I admire her wanting to put the kids first, but she needs some life balance. I lick my lips and mull over how to say that without coming off like a pushy doctor.

"When I first started med school, all I did was study and go to class and work at the local hospital. I ate, drank, and slept medical stuff—literally. I was so determined to keep my scholarship and prove myself that my grades started slipping and I almost burned out before I really got started. I drove my girlfriend away too."

Aniston's pupils dilate when I say "girlfriend." I choose to believe her reaction was out of jealousy and curiosity rather than the crappy lighting in this room.

"Anyway, I don't think I'd be working in the medical field today had I not learned to balance my life better."

"Would you still have your girlfriend?"

I perk up. Maybe she is jealous, or at least curious, about my love life. "I don't know." That's an honest answer.

Roxanne doesn't cross my mind much. I haven't seen her since college. She never wanted me to work as much as I did, then or now.

"Do you miss her?"

My mouth parts and I'm unable to answer for a moment. I didn't expect this question, especially from Aniston. "I haven't really thought about it—or her—in years."

"Then I guess the answer is no." Her lips curve slightly, and some of the color returns to her cheeks.

"I guess you're right." I lean closer to her, and our eyes lock for a second. I've never been smooth with women or one to use lines. But I almost say I haven't thought of any other woman since she answered the door that day.

I guess it's not technically a pickup line if it's true. However, I'm not the type to try and schmooze my stressed-out neighbor while she's lying in a hospital bed.

Aniston wiggles, trying to sit up. The cords bind her when she pushes herself with her hands. I tug gently at a cord, then allow my hand to linger beside her when it's untangled.

She turns toward me. "Thanks."

"You're welcome." My voice is hoarse, and I swallow a dry lump. I start to take a sip of my coffee, but choose to stay in the moment. Her eyes narrow on my lips, and my heart beats faster.

What would she do if I tried to kiss her? I scoot an inch closer and lower my eyes to her lips. Her mouth parts slightly. Is she about to say something, or is she anticipating a kiss?

"How are we doing, Miss Wilson?" an older woman's voice calls from behind us.

I flinch as Aniston's eyes leave my face for the door. "Good."

"Great. I need to change out your bedpan."

"Oh." She blushes and darts her eyes at me before staring at her lap.

I stand and push my chair against the wall. "I'll come check on you later tonight after work."

"Thanks, Dr. West."

I nod at Aniston, then at the nurse. "Take care of her, Regina."

"Yes sir, Doc." Regina smiles and waits by Aniston's feet while I exit the room.

I close the door behind me and head toward my office on the other end of the building. Last night, Morgan ran in before I could read the mood between us. Today, we were interrupted by a bedpan.

Maybe it's just not in the cards for me to kiss my neighbor.

CHAPTER 9

Aniston

Sometime after eating Jell-O and watching a rerun of *Seinfeld*, I dozed off. Maybe it's the medications or not having Jennifer's house haunt me, but I slept deeper than I have in months. Like to an unconscious level of rest.

It takes my leg shaking furiously to wake me. My eyes blink open to a hand on my thigh, and I'm a bit disappointed to realize it's a woman's hand.

Yes, I had hopes of sleeping until Easton returned. Though I doubt I'll admit that to him—or anyone else.

Instead, I follow the hand to Morgan's face. Before I can wipe the drool from my cheek, she has her arms around me in a bear hug. "I'm so glad you're okay!"

I clear my throat, and she releases me. "They told you I'd be fine, right?"

Morgan dabs at a tear in the corner of her eye. "Yeah, but I had to see for myself. The kids are here."

"Oh, send them in."

Morgan nods her head enthusiastically, then goes to the door. She sticks her head in the hallway and says something I can't make out from across the room. When she opens the door wider, Willow and Carter enter.

Carter's face fills with concern when he sees my IV. At least the heart-rate monitor and oxygen cords are gone. "It's okay, kids." I put on a brave face. Even though I know I'll be physically fine, sometimes I question my mental state.

Willow is dressed in her volleyball practice clothes. She crosses the room. "Do you need us to do anything at home?"

Sweet girl. I grab her hand. "Feed Buster is all. According to Easton, I'm busting out of this joint tomorrow."

She smiles. Carter eases his way toward my bed. "Is it okay if I hug you?"

"Of course, sweetie!" I hold my arms wide. He lays his head against me and carefully places his hands on my shoulders.

The door cracks, and we all turn. "Knock, knock." Brooke opens the door wider and pops her head in the room. "I'm about to leave, but I have some clothes you can wear in case that gown's getting a little drafty. Also, my mom is meeting me at the school to drive your truck to your house."

I slap my forehead. "The truck. I totally forgot about it. I hope it hasn't been towed."

She and Morgan exchange a look. "Where exactly did you park it?" Morgan asks.

"Close to the middle school, near the catwalk to the football stadium."

Morgan fans a hand my way. "You're good. Now, a few weeks from now when games start, that might get some people riled up."

I stroke Carter's short hair, then give him a gentle squeeze before releasing him. "You two make Morgan behave tonight."

Morgan snorts. "More like make my kids behave. I'm

hoping they rub off on Andrew some." She turns to Brooke. "Good idea with the clothes. I hadn't thought to bring her some."

Brooke grins. "They're scrubs from my locker. A little short, I'm sure, but they're clean and comfy." She sets the crimson-colored folded set on the foot of my bed.

"Thank you. As someone who tosses covers in her sleep, I appreciate the extra covering."

She smiles. "I figured you would."

Next to the kids and the medical expenses, my biggest worry is lack of decency in this place. All dignity vanished when the nurse waltzed in to change my bedpan while Easton and I were sharing a moment. At least, in my mind we were.

Morgan frowns at Willow. "I guess I could've stopped by your place and got her some clothes."

"It's fine." I smile. "You're a huge help." I glance at Brooke, then back at Morgan. "I appreciate you both more than you know."

Morgan pats my leg over the covers. "No problem. That's what we do. Us single Southern mamas gotta stick together."

Brooke says nothing, just smiles and nods like she successfully answered a tie-breaking question in a pageant interview.

"You guys are the best." I open my arms and motion for them to come closer. I've never been a natural hugger, so I'm not sure what's gotten into me today.

Within seconds, they're on me like white on rice. Brooke's perfume and Morgan's Bath & Body Works concoction sift up my nose. The mixture is a welcome change from the usual sterile and sickness blend of this hospital.

Our bonding time is interrupted by a loud knock at the door. My friends pull back, and all eyes go to the door. "It's probably the bedpan person," I say, mainly to myself. She has impeccable timing.

Willow pulls the door open to Easton. My eyes widen, and

I subconsciously start smoothing out my hair. Not like anyone should expect me to have any style other than bedhead, since I'm confined to a hospital room.

"Sorry to interrupt." He grins shyly over an armload of Tupperware and books.

Morgan and Brooke part like the Red Sea, clearing a path for Easton to approach me. Morgan smirks. "It looks like you're in good hands. I better go do mom duty."

Brooke smiles and adds, "And I best go meet Mama and drive the truck back."

I give them my best "I know what y'all are implying" look. Except I don't know *exactly* what they're implying. Is Easton here to stay? I drop my gaze to the stack of books he's setting on the table. There's a biography about Ronald Reagan, a book on farming, and some weird sci-fi novel. Either Easton thinks I should broaden my horizons, or he plans on staying a while.

"Do you need anything else before we leave?" Brooke asks.

I reach behind the odd stack of literature and pull out the red sweater folded on the side table. "Could one of you return this to Mrs. Pebbleton?"

Brooke scrunches her brow in confusion. "Yeah?"

Easton gives me a confused face as well. "Is that the sweater you were wearing when you fainted?"

My face heats up. "Uh, yeah."

Morgan turns from the door. "You borrowed Mrs. Pebbleton's sweater?"

"I did before I knew it was hers."

Brooke shakes her head. "I'm confused."

Aren't we all. I take a deep breath and try to ignore the flush of embarrassment that has spread from my face to my chest.

"I got it from the lost-and-found box."

Now even the kids are blinking at me like I'm crazy. But I

kinda am. With everyone waiting on an explanation, I continue. "I got hot walking in the heat in heels, then got water all over my shirt from the water fountain. Oh, and I already had pit stains on my blouse from sweating. So I grabbed the first adult clothing I saw to cover up my mess."

Easton gives me a sly smile, and my face flushes. Something about having shared this embarrassment with him before the others feels dangerously intimate.

"And how do you know this is Mrs. Pebbleton's?" Willow asks, now invested in the case.

I turn back to my audience, diffusing the intimate bubble I've created around Easton and me. "She complimented it and said she lost one like it earlier. Then I spotted this." I flip the sweater and point to the name tag.

The group collectively nods and "ahhs."

Brooke takes the sweater and smiles, as if this isn't the dumbest thing I've ever done. Okay, so maybe not the dumbest, but pretty darn close. "I'll drop it off tomorrow and tell her what happened."

I reach out and yell, "No!"

Brooke's eyes widen. She resembles a cute cartoon bunny eyeing a giant carrot.

"But you wanted to return it, right?"

"Yeah, but she can't know I know it's hers. Then she'll think I stole it."

Morgan rubs her chin. "Good point." She takes the sweater from Brooke. "Tell you what, I'll plant this on top of the lost-and-found pile with her name showing."

"Genius." I nod approvingly.

Brooke's jaw drops, then slowly closes into a mesmerized smile. She's clearly as impressed as I am.

Morgan drapes the sweater over her arm and winks. "You are welcome." Then she leaves with my kids on her heels. Brooke smiles wider, if that's even possible, then follows them out.

Leaving me alone with Easton, yet again.

I wiggle in the bed, trying to adjust my gown discreetly. Easton sets the Tupperware dish and a water bottle big enough to hydrate a football team by the books. Then he pulls out the chair by my bed and sits.

"I hope you don't mind. I offered to stay with you tonight since your friends have the kids."

My mouth goes dry, and I'm suddenly at a loss for words. I didn't expect anyone to stay the night with me. I, of all people, am comfortable without anyone. Besides, the bedpan people are great about checking on me around the clock. I expect one to pop in any minute.

Easton puts his hands on the chair arms and starts to stand. "That is, if you want me to stay."

That's a loaded question, and one I'm not sure I know the answer to.

"Of course." Now my voice decides to work?

"Good." He relaxes in his seat, and my skin tingles from my scalp to my feet.

Do I want to spend more time with Easton? More time *alone* with Easton? Duh. However, I'd prefer to do so when I'm not lying here like death warmed over.

"How are you feeling?"

"Good." I gesture toward the IV monitor. "They removed some of my cords."

"I see." He untangles the cord looped around my arm, brushing my side when he does. My skin gets that tingly sensation down the path his hand made. "Can I help you with anything?"

I giggle nervously. My mind should not be on kissing him right now. He's simply a kind neighbor offering to keep me company while I'm staying in the hospital. This is as about as far from a romantic scene as I can imagine. Yet my mind went there.

I continue to laugh for a few more seconds, then

remember the clothing by my feet. "Actually, could you open the bathroom door? Brooke brought me some clothes, and I'd like to put them on."

"Yeah." He stands and pulls back my covers.

Thank God, I shaved my legs last night. That's the only upside to my appearance right now.

"Here." Easton offers his hand. I take it and stand. "Hang on." He reaches out and pulls the IV bag from the stand with his other hand.

I use my free hand to clinch the gown tightly behind my back. I'm not sure how secure those ties are, and I don't care to show off whatever day of the week panties I'm wearing.

With Easton by my side and a death grip on my cotton gown, we cross the small room to the bathroom door. He opens it, then reaches back and gets the scrubs from the edge of the bed.

He turns toward me, sending his fresh man scent my way. It's even more refreshing than the mixture of my two friends engulfing me in a huge hug. I suck in air through my nostrils.

"You okay?"

I stop my sniffer and open my eyes, not realizing I had closed them until now. Pretty pathetic. My cheeks flush when I see him staring at me, holding the scrubs to my face.

"Oh yes, I'm fine. Just allergies," I lie. Most likely on both accounts, as it's not allergies, and people who sniff guys in hospitals are clearly not fine.

I take hold of the scrubs with the hand not white knuckled around my gown. The corners of his lips lift into a closed-mouth smile, and I notice that he's shaved since he was here earlier.

Was that out of routine for him, or for me?

My stomach twitches as I pass him and step into the bathroom. I start to shut the door.

"Wait," Easton says as he catches the door. "Set this on the side of the tub."

"Good thinking." I take the bag of fluids and drop the back of my gown to shut the door. Then I shake out my hand.

Mountain climbers hanging on the side of a cliff don't have anything on me gripping that gown. For good reason too, as it all but falls off when I let go. I unsnap the sleeve for the IV arm and shake it to the ground, then balance the bag of medicine on the edge of the tub like Dr. Goodbody ordered.

My skin-colored bra is slightly stained from the sweater as well. What kind of wool was that thing made of anyway?

I shake my head and sit on the toilet seat, close to the bag. Although short as expected, Brooke's pants slide on easily. Perhaps I get a little too cocky after that because I go right into looping the shirt over my head.

My head goes in fine, as does one arm. The arm hooked to the IV is another story. I don't want to drop the bag, so I decide to try and thread it through.

I get on my knees on the floor and start threading the cord through the armhole. When I get to the bag, I can't figure out how to fit both my arm and the bag through the sleeve.

"Everything all right, Aniston?"

I start to sweat. No, it's not all right, but how do I respond to that? "Yeah, I'll be out in a second."

I hold the bag with my sleeved hand and pull my arm back through the shirt slowly. Now I'm back to where I started. Great.

"Are you decent?"

Before I can answer, the door creaks open the slightest bit. Easton's hand slides behind the door and pushes it open farther. He tiptoes closer with his eyes closed. Well, isn't that adorable.

"I don't want to impose, but I want to make sure you're not hurt."

I bite my bottom lip to keep from laughing or saying "awww" audibly. I'm not sure what's cuter—that he's concerned about my well-being, or that he's afraid to look.

"You can open your eyes. There's nothing you don't need to see." Except for maybe me kneeling on the bathroom floor, holding an IV bag, with my arm folded inside my shirt.

Easton opens his eyes. "Oh wow."

Yeah . . . That response says it all. It's as bad as I imagined.

"I think if you put the bag in first, then you can put your arm inside." He gestures toward the bag. "May I?"

"Be my guest." He helps me get back on the toilet and I sit in awkward silence as Easton takes the bag from my hand and pulls out my sleeve.

He gently squishes the bag through the sleeve of my shirt and lifts the bottom of my shirt to pull it through the other side. I'm petrified, except for sucking in my stomach when he lifts my shirt.

Although he spotted me videoing a bikini influencer ad by the pool, I've eaten a lot of cookie crack since then, and I'm now hunched on a toilet seat. Not my best look by far.

When he lowers my shirt, our eyes meet. "I didn't see anything." He shakes his head, and his next words come out squeaky and rushed. "Not that I was trying to, but if I had seen something, I wouldn't think anything. I see things all the time as a doctor."

I burst out laughing, and Easton blushes. "It's fine. I appreciate your help."

"You're welcome." He smiles, and his blush starts to fade.

I ease myself from the toilet seat, and he holds the bag while I stand. That's when I realize I never put my arm in the sleeve. "Oh, my arm."

"Here." Easton sets the IV bag on the sink and holds my sleeve out. I wiggle my arm until my hand is near the opening.

"Wait." He grabs the bag, which is close to falling to the floor.

As I thread my hand and then my arm through the sleeve,

he moves the bag closer to my side. By the time my arm is through the sleeve, he's within an inch of me.

We lock eyes for a second, then my head starts to spin. "I need air."

"On it." He moves over so I can exit and assists me to the bed, holding the IV bag.

Once I'm back in my spot, he hooks the bag to the bar. I sigh. In a way, I'm glad Carter watched me faint, so he wouldn't worry as much. No kid wants to hear his parent—or guardian—is in the hospital. Kids freak out.

"Something wrong?"

I turn to Easton. For a split second, I forgot he was here. Good thing I remembered before digging out the wedgie I'm getting from Brooke's pants.

"Hospitals remind me of Jennifer and Luke. Thinking of them makes me wish it had been me instead of them."

Easton's face pales. "Aniston, how could you ever say that?"

I shrug. "They had kids to raise, and a home. I was living on my own like a drifter. I didn't even have a dog. Life would be easier if it were me."

My body tenses, and I can't believe I unleashed my biggest secret to Easton. The one that's haunted me ever since my sister and brother-in-law's accident.

Before I can say anything else, Easton grabs both my hands. "God left you here for a reason."

That comment stings, as I've pretty much blamed God a lot lately for taking my sister and Luke in their prime and making my niece and nephew orphans in the process. However, it's what he says next that really hits my heart.

"You are super important to a lot of people, and those kids need you. I need you."

"What?"

He squeezes my hands tighter. "You've brought a lot of happiness to my life lately just by being you."

Easton leans closers, and I study the yellowish outline in his brown eyes. I start to close my own eyes, anticipating a kiss. Again, not the best time or setting, but I'll take what I can get.

As I lick my lips in anticipation, I hear, "Good news, Miss Wilson, you can lose the bedpan."

I open my eyes to the bedpan nazi reaching for the pan by my feet. Such impeccable timing.

Easton

My butt throbs as I turn in the chair/bed in Aniston's hospital room. We had some great conversation until she started snoring around midnight. After that, I tossed and turned, replaying the moment I almost kissed her in my mind.

I got the sense she wanted me to kiss her as much as I wanted to. Then Regina barged in for the bedpan. Probably for the best. Even though I'm here as a friend rather than doctor, I'm still a doctor at this facility. Getting caught kissing a patient wouldn't sit well for me.

A loud beep outside the window makes it impossible to fall back asleep. I open my eyes, then stand and stretch. We're right beside the dumpsters, and the garbage truck is here . . . at seven a.m.

Aniston is still snoring away. I should've snagged some of the Tylenol PM pills when the nurse made rounds last night. Not that it would've mattered much in this uncomfortable chair, with my brain full of Aniston moments.

I shouldn't be falling for this woman, but I can't help myself. She's so unlike anyone I've ever dated or known.

Given her situation, I decided that she needed me. The more I get to know her, I'm convinced I need her too.

Everyone could use a little Aniston in their life.

I convert my bed back into a chair and yawn. Thank God it's Saturday, and I'm not working the ER this weekend. I rock in the chair and watch Aniston drool on her pillow. The garbage truck beeps one last time before I hear it drive away. As I attempt to close my eyes and rest, the door opens.

"Hello," a different nurse greets me. I'm sure Regina is off shift now since she stopped by about forty-seven times overnight.

"Hi," I greet her. This nurse, I don't recognize. She must not ever work the ER.

"I need to get Miss Wilson's vitals before we release her."

I glance at Aniston, who's oblivious to anything going on or anyone in the room—including me. A few kids wearing scrubs with the Apple Cart Community College logo on them step into the room.

"Is it okay if these interns watch?"

I glance at Aniston, who's out like a boxer after taking a beating. "I guess so."

"Great." The nurse smiles at me, then the students, before she motions for them to step closer.

They circle around the bed. The nurse, who's now close enough for me to read "Trudy" on her name tag, wraps a blood-pressure cuff around Aniston's arm.

When it tightens, her eyes pop open. She darts her eyes between the three interns, then to the nurse, then me. Aniston sits up and gasps.

"Am I dying?"

I try not to laugh.

Trudy strokes her arm. "No, sweetie. I'm checking your vitals before we discharge you."

"Oh." Aniston's mouth slaps shut and her face reddens.

I fight back another laugh as Trudy continues her routine

and explains everything she does in detail to the students. She acts as if she doesn't know who I am either, which makes this more fun. As an Apple Cart citizen rather than Dr. West, I can sit back and watch in amusement.

Aniston wakes up a little more with every step of the process. She yawns and pulls her hair to one shoulder when Trudy announces all is well.

"The doctor will be by in a minute to discharge you."

"Thanks." Aniston smiles sleepily, then plops her head back on the pillow once the gang of nurses leaves. She rubs her palms down her face, then turns to me. "You stayed all night?"

I yawn and nod. "Yeah."

"Thank you," she whispers.

I shrug, trying to downplay everything. "I spend the night in hospitals all the time."

"Well, I don't. I can't wait to sleep in my own bed." Aniston rubs the back of her hand, where Trudy replaced the IV needle with a giant Band-Aid. She faces me again. "I don't see how you do this all time."

"Do what?" I hope she doesn't assume I make a habit of staying with women in the hospital overnight, because I don't.

"All this medical stuff. The blood, the needles, the bedpans." She scrunches her nose at the word "bedpans," and I laugh.

"Doctors don't deal with bedpans, so that helps." I continue as she laughs. "But you get used to anything. Besides, other than the ER, I mainly deal with everyday sickness and pains."

"True." Aniston grins, then stares at the ceiling.

She closes her eyes, and I wiggle in the chair in an attempt to get comfortable. No such luck. My butt is bruised like I've ridden up a four-mile mountain on a banana-seat bicycle. Now I'm looking forward to my bed too.

After a few minutes of silence, there's a knock at the door. "Come in," Aniston answers without opening her eyes.

Dr. Newhart walks in. Unlike me, he works on the hospital side full time. Sometimes he even goes to the hospital in Tuscaloosa to deliver babies.

One of the many oddities of small-town hospitals is that some of them don't offer certain services. For instance, babies aren't delivered at Health Cross Medical Center in Apple Cart. Some women still see Dr. Newhart here for their OB-GYN appointments, but give birth in Tuscaloosa. Even stranger to me is that he doesn't specialize in gynecology. It's just one of the services he offers.

That's one service I've chosen not to offer. Pregnant women are unpredictable, and I stick my foot in my mouth enough as it is. Not everyone's cut out to deal with hormones. Perhaps that's why I've steered clear of marriage so far.

"Easton."

"Hi, Doc."

He turns to Aniston after greeting me and touches her arm. She opens her eyes. "Aniston, everything looks great. We're going to release you."

This perks her up. "Great." She pushes herself off the bed and starts to stand.

Dr. Newhart laughs and holds up a clipboard. "I need you to sign some papers first."

She clicks the pen and starts signing like a pop star after a concert. I gather her purse and clothing from the day before, then my belongings. While I fit them all into a reusable bag from the closet, one of Trudy's male students rolls a wheelchair in the room.

Dr. Newhart shakes my hand and tells Aniston to take it easy. "Yes, sir." She nods as he leaves the room.

"Okay, Miss Wilson, let me help you." The student guides Aniston into the wheelchair. She wrinkles her forehead at me as if she doesn't need assistance.

"Thank you. I'll get her from here," I say.

"Okay, have a nice day." He takes the clipboard of paper-work from the side table where Aniston set it and leaves.

I shove the cotton bag on one wheelchair handle and Aniston's purse on the other, then push her into the hallway.

"Why am I in a wheelchair? I thought they said I'm fine."

"You are. This is how they discharge just about everyone."

"Weird." Aniston folds her hands in her lap and keeps quiet until we reach the revolving door. She lets out a slight "oomph" when I wheel her over the threshold going into the door and again getting out onto the concrete. "And they think riding in a wheelchair is better for someone recovering?"

"Pushing patients isn't really something doctors do much of either."

"Right . . ."

I wheel her to the side of the building where I parked near the ER. She stares down at her bare feet and wiggles her toes. "Where are my shoes?"

I reach in the bag and pull out a pair of high heels.

She frowns. "I forgot I wasn't wearing my usual flip-flops."

Without thinking, I hoist her in my arms. She shrieks, then holds on around my neck. I carry her the few feet to my truck and unlock the door. I set her gently in the passenger seat. Aniston drops her shoes on the floorboard and blinks at me.

"I'm going to get our things and push this wheelchair inside. Be right back."

"Okay."

I shut her door, then rush to my side of the truck and crank it. The last thing I need is her overheating again. She smiles at me when air hits her face. I return the smile and slam my door to tend to the rogue wheelchair.

A few minutes later, I return to Aniston relaxed in the air, with her feet kicked up. I climb in and set her purse on the console between us, then buckle my seat belt. Despite snoring like a logger sawing power poles, I don't think she rested well either. She comes to attention when I shut my door. Then she moves her feet to the floor and buckles her seat belt.

I back out of the parking lot and turn to Aniston. "Maybe we should call Morgan and let her know we're busting out of here."

"Good idea." She rummages through her purse, pulling out odds and ends and laying them on the console. It's like Mary Poppins's bag, except the contents are all wadded up receipts, gum wrappers, and pens rather than actual useful things like floor lamps.

She finds her phone by the time I turn onto the main road and dumps everything else back inside. "I'll text. Morgan has a strict policy about calling before ten on Saturday."

With four kids, I find it hard to believe Morgan gets peace and quiet until ten, but I admire her ambition. Aniston drops her phone into her purse and closes her eyes. We ride in silence until I turn down the gravel road leading to our houses.

"I see the truck made it home safe and sound."

Aniston sits up straight and looks out her window. "Well, Brooke's a much better driver than me, growing up driving apple trucks and all."

I narrow my eyes. "You've driven an RV around for the past several years."

"Eh, not the same."

I cock my head, not understanding how a truck can be harder to drive than an actual residence.

"Ah, home sweet home," Aniston mutters as we park in her driveway. She bends down and slips on her heels.

I gather the rest of her things and get out. She walks across the pavement in her heels and Brooke's short scrubs. I laugh when she's not looking. I've seen her walk outside barefoot before, so I don't understand why she put her shoes on now.

As we step inside the garage, Buster greets us, pawing at Aniston's pant leg.

"Hey, boy." She pets his head and turns to me. "Can you hand me my purse?"

I hand it over, and she goes through the same process of digging things out to find what she needs. With no console to set everything aside, she holds papers and pens under her chin and between her fingers until she's located her keys. Then everything goes back inside that bottomless pit of a purse.

Aniston unlocks the door, and I follow her inside. She sniffs the air. "I really should buy a new candle."

"It smells fine to me." And it does. Kind of a mixture of chocolate and burnt pizza crust. I've smelled much worse.

We stand there a few seconds as she sniffs the air, then her stomach growls. Aniston covers it with her hand. I halfway expect my stomach to give it a sympathy growl, as I haven't eaten since finishing a container of watermelon I took to the hospital. I get enough hospital cafeteria food during the work week, and I didn't want to eat anything substantial in front of Aniston since they had her on mainly a Jell-O and chicken broth diet.

"Why don't you have a seat in the living room while I cook us something to eat?"

"Thanks." She half-grins, still holding her stomach with one hand and her purse with the other. Then she retreats to the living room.

I rummage through the refrigerator and find eggs and bacon. Then I dig in the cabinets for some pans. Aniston's cell phone rings, and I hear her answer.

"Hey, Morgan. Yeah, he's in there cooking breakfast."

I stop clanking the pans to hear more. After a minute, she says, "No, you dork. Not like that."

I continue the pan clanking to cover my laugh. Aniston talks a few more minutes while I lay bacon in a pan. The talking is soon replaced by the sound of the recliner legs popping out.

As she relaxes, I cook. A part of me delights in cooking for her a little too much. I don't mind cooking, but it seems pointless for one person. Having someone to cook for makes more sense. Maybe I just like helping people, or maybe I just like helping *her*.

Speaking of people, the door opens, and Willow and Carter walk inside. Morgan follows them with Andrew. He runs to the counter and reaches for my stack of fresh bacon.

Morgan smacks his hand. "Andrew, you just ate."

"Powered donuts from the store," he murmurs under his breath.

"I made plenty," I insist.

Morgan points a finger to Andrew. "One piece, then we'll get out of these people's hair."

Aniston comes in from the living room, and Morgan wraps her in a bear hug. "How are you?" she mutters against Aniston.

Once Aniston is free, she answers. "Really good. Just hungry. Thanks for taking care of the kids."

"No problem, honey. We had a great time. I took them to the Wisteria Waffle House and then we watched movies." She pats Aniston on the head, then waves to everyone. "I'm going home to see what mess the others have made while we were gone. Y'all behave." With that last line, she winks at Aniston.

Aniston scowls and sits at the bar. Carter climbs on the stool beside her. "Aunt Ani, why are you wearing those fancy shoes?"

She snorts and kicks off her heels. "Long story, but it's all I had."

I smile as she dangles her long legs, with Brooke's pants falling somewhere between her calf and ankle.

Willow takes the third stool and whispers toward me, "Will she be okay?"

"Oh yeah, full recovery. Y'all need to make her relax more so she'll stay recovered."

Both the kids turn to their aunt, who raises her hands. "I rest plenty."

I clear my throat and rake the eggs on a plate. "I made plenty, so you kids can eat too, unless, of course, you've already eaten with Morgan."

Carter sighs. "She had powdered donuts or Fruit Loops, so I just drank a juice box."

"True," Willow adds.

I nod. "All right, fix a plate, then."

Five minutes later, our plates are filled with bacon and eggs and biscuits. I say a quick prayer and try not to pay any attention to how much this scenario feels like a family. Like my family.

The family I occasionally long for but have given up in favor of my career.

When I open my eyes, Aniston is already biting into a biscuit. "Wow!"

"You like them?"

"Like them?" She wipes a crumb from her mouth and sucks it off her finger. "You made these from my kitchen?"

"Yeah." I grin.

"With what?"

"Flour, Crisco, and some milk. I normally use buttermilk, but your milk was going out of date, so basically the same thing."

At the words "out of date," Carter spits a bite of biscuit onto his napkin. We all laugh until he joins us.

Yeah, this could totally be my dysfunctional dream family.

CHAPTER 10

Aniston

This is the best I've felt on a Monday morning since I spent three months in Wyoming. Of course, I'm about to face the hustle and bustle of a full school week, but all the rest I got over the weekend did my body good.

I slant my eyes toward the pill case Easton fixed for me and get instant grandma vibes. He brought me a case filled with vitamins and supplements he recommended I take for a while to get my strength back. Then he refused to let me pay him for them.

That still doesn't come close to him cleaning up everything after he cooked on Saturday, then taking Carter fishing at the pond so I could relax. Carter commented that he'd missed fishing and used to go all the time with his dad. I'm pretty sure that had something to do with Easton taking him.

My heart almost exploded when Easton wrapped his arm around Carter's shoulder and led him away to get fishing poles. Just when I thought him washing dishes was the ultimate turn on.

How can one man be handsome, a doctor, good with kids, and super helpful around the house? He can't be *that* perfect. He must be hiding some unusual flaw, like an addiction to murder mystery shows or a large collection of toenail clippings.

Ugh. That sure popped my fantasy bubble.

I throw the pills into my mouth and chug my water. Easton also supplied me with a giant water bottle, insisting that I drink four full bottles a day to stay hydrated. I've peed more the last day and a half than I have the last few months combined.

Willow comes in the kitchen, dressed but yawning.

"Morning," I say.

"Good morning." She rests her elbows on the kitchen counter.

"I made breakfast." I smirk and push a box her way.

She opens the lid and laughs. Brooke brought by a box of muffins and donuts yesterday on her way home from church. We ate a good bit last night while watching a movie, but there's enough left to not resort to Pop-Tarts until I make it to the store. I used to laugh at Jennifer making a big deal out of driving to the next county to Walmart. Now, I get it.

Willow takes a bite of her blueberry muffin and studies me. "You look pretty."

I do a twirl, then roll my eyes. "You're just used to me looking like death lately."

She laughs. "No, that's a cute outfit."

I stare down at my newish jeans and top. "Thanks, I have a meeting at school today." I stuff half a donut in my mouth and chew.

"Careful with your sugar intake," Willow scolds.

"Yes, Mother."

She frowns. "Remember what the doctor said."

I pick the glaze off the top of the other half before taking another bite.

She pats my arm like I'm a child. "Better, but still room for improvement."

"How did you get so responsible?"

"Maybe by being the oldest child."

I lick my fingers in hopes that some of the glaze stayed on them. "That makes a lot of sense."

We both laugh, and Carter slogs in. He's dressed, but his hair is a mess. He gets the last donut and sits at the counter.

"Carter, we need to comb your hair and then leave."

"I don't mind it like this."

I start to say how he's a reflection of me and my lack of parenting skills. I can't have him rolling up with both donut crust and messy hair. One's bad enough. Instead, I go to the bathroom and return with a brush.

I tame his mane best I can, then set his lunch box in front of him. "Tada! I remembered."

"Thanks."

I pat him on the head, then brush down the part I tousled. "Okay, everyone to the truck."

We file out the door to the garage. Carter stops to feed Buster, and we climb in the truck. I sling my purse onto the console and check my teeth for donut debris. My stomach knots at the notion of Georgia nitpicking any little flaw in my system.

Nobody specified the dress code for this meeting, so I tried to play somewhere in between slouch and trying too hard. I may or may not have looked up "energetic, cute mom clothes" on Pinterest during our movie time last night.

Once my teeth are picked and licked clean, I back out of the garage and head down the driveway. Both the kids quietly finish their breakfast and blink sleepily at the window.

I reach for the water bottle between my legs, a little

annoyed that it won't fit in a cup holder. At least it has an industrial-grade lid. The last thing I need is more water stains on my clothes, especially in places that can be mistaken for pee.

The car line is about as half as congested as last week. "Wow." I check the time to make sure I'm not much earlier—or later—than planned. Nope, perfect timing. "What happened to all the cars?" I ask the kids as we swoop into the middle school drop-off area.

"All the bus riders have started riding the bus by now."

"Ah." I grin at Willow and ease in line. We wait a few minutes before she's at the door. "Have a good day."

"You too. Be healthy."

I raise my massive jug of water and wink. Willow shakes her head and shuts the front door. I know what she really meant is don't go back home and eat the rest of the muffins.

Carter stares out the window, still blinking like a baby puppy opening its eyes for the first time. We go through the motions of the elementary car line. Georgia stands by the door in her reflective vest. I chug my water and pretend it has something much stronger inside.

Why does good health have to taste so bad?

"Bye, sweetie. Have a good day."

"Bye." Carter half-grins and climbs out.

I watch as he enters the building beside Georgia, then study her for a minute. She's wearing capris, but I can't tell what kind of top with that stupid vest. The car behind me honks, bringing my attention back to the line.

I step on the gas pedal, scaring the teacher a few feet away. Shooting her an apologetic face, I drive off in search of a decent parking place for my meeting. There are a few spots close to the gym, where we're supposed to meet.

Other than the honking, this day has gone well so far. It's scaring me a little. Maybe all those late-night infomercials about how getting in better shape makes everything in life run smoother have some underlying truth to them.

It doesn't take me long to park and walk to the gym. Somehow, Georgia has beat me there and is standing at the entrance. She's still wearing her vest, but now has on a sundress and chunky sandals. What happened to the capri pants? Am I underdressed? How did she change so fast?

I stare down at my jeans, then notice the two women close to Georgia, also wearing sundresses. This is like the grown-up Alabama version of *Mean Girls*. One of them hands me a program.

I half-smile at her. Georgia opens her mouth to say something to me, when, of all people, TikTok Tami comes around the corner. Although her shirt is loose and flowy, she's wearing a red leather skirt so tight that it brings a whole new meaning to "fits like a glove." She could endorse Isotoner with that outfit, except for the dagger tattoo peeking out on her thigh. I swallow, praying I never land on her bad side.

Georgia turns from me to Tami. "What are you doing here? This meeting is for room moms only."

I slip past them as Tami explains something about wanting to meet with Coach. If I spot him on the way in, I'll try and send a warning signal. Not that he wouldn't see that fire-engine-red patch of leather coming from a mile away. I sincerely hope Tami doesn't wander near Mason Magill's place. His bull would have a heyday with that.

While Georgia's focus is on Tami, I sneak inside. I'm relieved to see a few more people wearing jeans, and one in pajama pants. That woman is my hero.

After scanning the chairs, I zero in on the most stressed-out-looking woman. Well, besides the one in her pajamas, who's in a lone chair pulled behind the back row, sending "nobody sit by me" vibes.

I sit in the empty seat beside the stressed mom and recognize her from the first day of school. "Hi, you're Maribelle, right?"

She smiles and extends a hand. "Yes. And you are?"

I shake her hand. "Aniston Wilson. Jennifer's sister, and I'm friends with Morgan."

"Oh, Carter's aunt?"

"That's right."

She drops her hand and folds it in her lap. "Nice to meet you, and welcome."

"Thanks." I glance down at the folded paper in my hand.

Those same creepy cartoon kids stare up at me. But that's not the scariest part. Underneath them, in cliché Comic Sans font, are the words "Room Mom August Meeting." That implies there will be another meeting not in August. I sigh loud enough for Maribelle to turn to me.

"Have you done this before?" I ask.

She nods. "It's my third year."

My eyes bug. "For real?"

"Yeah. In pre-K, my twins were in two different classes and it was a nightmare. Keeping up with all the things that were the same, then different for the same grade. I told your sister I'd be a room mom if she could sway the principal to put them in the same class from now on."

"That's kinda genius."

Maribelle perks up and blushes. "Thanks." Then her face goes flat as she nods toward the gym entrance. "I just hope Georgia keeps the PTSO's end of the bargain when they pick rooms next year."

As if that were her cue, Georgia marches across the gym floor, ponytail swishing. She must've never watched *Mean Girls* because she wears ponytails way too often.

The two attractive minions follow her from a safe distance and take a seat in the front row. Georgia stops beneath the basketball hoop, and I notice she's shed her vest. When and where, I'm not sure. Maybe she's a magician . . . or a witch.

I alternate between actually listening and zoning out as Georgia welcomes everyone and introduces the two women with her. Both stand, turn, wave, and smile when she does. I've only watched a few pageants in my day, but that's exactly how the judges react when introduced. I can't remember their names, so I nickname them Gretchen and Karen for now. They're some kind of PTSO officers.

Bless their hearts.

"Now, if you'll open your agenda," Georgia announces after introducing her entourage.

Everyone around me unfolds the paper, so I do the same. There's a leaf cartoon with the words "Fall Festival" in bold at the top. Then a numbered list with words like "food" and "entertainment."

"The Fall Festival is one of our biggest fundraisers and is only two months away. That's why I need all you ladies here to help."

A snore roars behind me. I crane my neck to see pajama mama dozing off. I'm so jealous. She's my spirit animal.

"Now, we have a lot of details to cover and—"

TikTok Tami makes a loud entrance, with her spiky boots clacking the gym floor as she wanders out from around the office area. Georgia clamps her mouth shut and stares at Tami.

"May we help you?" Georgia manages for her words to come out clipped yet cheerful. I'm slightly impressed.

Tami smacks her gum and scratches the back of her head. The bangles on her arm clank as she does. "Coach isn't in his office. Do you know where I might could find him?"

Georgia plasters on a fake smile. "He's on the playground with the kids." She turns from Tami to us. "They're using the new playground equipment that was purchased with money from last year's Fall Festival."

Tami turns and exits. Georgia continues speaking louder until her footsteps, or bangles, or gum, are no longer heard.

"I have Hannah and Austyn in charge of food. Maribelle and Lillian in charge of games." Georgia continues reading down her list. She names everyone in the building except me.

I'm halfway wondering if this is some sort of ambush. Then I relax and count my blessings that I wasn't called to be over something. Maribelle must misread my sigh of relief because she raises her hand.

When Georgia raises an eyebrow her way, she says, "You didn't assign Aniston to a committee."

Gee, thanks. Just when I'd handpicked you to be my room-mom bestie. Oh well.

A mischievous smile crosses Georgia's face. "I apologize. With Aniston's recent hospital scare, I didn't fully expect her to show up today."

Well played, Georgia, well played. I cross my arms and stay silent.

"Aniston, you can be my personal assistant for this event."

I almost swallow my tongue. She. Did. Not.

Maribelle pats my knee and lets out a whimper like I'm about to go to war. Maybe I am.

Well, if I'm going to war, I may as well charge the battle field full force. I put on my own fake smile and listen intently as Georgia goes over her ideas for the festival. Anytime she says something ridiculous, I raise my hand.

For the food, she suggests caterers. I raise my hand.

"Yes, Aniston?"

"Don't events like this usually have food trucks? We could invite local places like Big Butts and Mary's that people already like. They can pay a fee to park or split profits."

People start to nod and mutter in agreement. Georgia narrows her eyes, but has Gretchen make a note.

When entertainment comes up, she mentions hiring a band. My hand shoots up. She ignores me this time, so I speak up as soon as she stops talking to take a breath.

"Or get this, we could have a talent show and let local entertainment pay to play, sing, dance, or whatever."

This suggestion wins me a small applause. I settle back in my folding chair and hold my head high.

Georgia mentions a few more things, then quickly wraps up the meeting. Karen hands her a small floral gavel, which she beats against a table beside her before calling, "Meeting adjourned." As everyone starts standing and shuffling out of rows, she adds, "Check the GroupMe app for the next meeting date."

I slide out behind Maribelle. "You were great in there," she comments once we're outside.

"Thanks, I'm normally not so vocal. I don't know what got into me."

"Whatever it is, we need that around here."

I grin. "Thanks."

"See you later."

"You too. Nice to formally meet you."

She smiles and heads for a minivan. I retreat to my truck, a patch of red blinding me in the sunlight. It's Tami following behind Coach, who is speed walking away from her. Poor man.

I climb in the truck and drive home, both elated and exhausted from my banter with Georgia. I'm also a little nervous. I may talk a big game, but I've never gone head to head with a bully before. My usually tactic is flight over fight.

During my drive, I toss around ideas for a blog on my last travels. How can I wrap up where we went and make it sound more exciting than before?

By the time I reach the garage, I've got nothing. That is, about travel. Instead, my mind is filled with the reactions of all the women when Georgia and I went at it about the festival. Suddenly, I have an idea for a new vlog. One that I'm sure all moms of school-aged kids can relate to.

Easton

Ever since cooking breakfast for Aniston in her home, then sharing it with her and the kids, a nagging itch for family life has lingered in the back of my mind. One I haven't had since I dated Roxanne.

So far, I've managed to push down any lingering thoughts. Until tonight.

I invited Aniston and the kids to dinner in Tuscaloosa to celebrate them surviving the beginning of school and Aniston's hospital stay. My treat. She wasn't too keen on me footing the bill, but eventually agreed.

I straighten my tie and ring her doorbell. Buster barks from the other side. A few seconds later, Carter opens the door.

"Hi, Dr. Easton."

I smile down at him. "Hey, Carter." I'd told him he didn't have to call me Dr. West since we're neighbors and now friends. He could call me Easton. However, he insisted on using either mister or doctor since I'm his elder. He'll make a great Southern gentleman.

My eyes raise to Aniston standing a few feet back, putting on earrings. She's in a bright blue dress with her hair pulled back in loose curls. My mouth drops as I fish my brain for a compliment that won't come out lame or creepy.

"You look great." So I'm not the best with words, but at least they're appropriate.

"Thanks." She grins, then turns toward the staircase. "Willow!"

"Coming!" Willow's voice echoes from upstairs.

Aniston takes a step closer to me. "You clean up nice too." Then her eyes fall on my chest. "Oh crap, does Carter need to wear a tie?"

I laugh. "No, he looks very handsome. We may all be a bit overdressed, but I wanted to celebrate big."

Aniston lifts her head, and our eyes lock. I sense a jolt of electricity between us. It fizzles a bit when Willow bounces behind her and taps her on the shoulder.

She's holding two pairs of dress shoes. "Aunt Ani, which pair?"

Aniston taps her lips with her fingertip. I'd love to be that finger. "Hmm, the silver."

"Okay." Willow sets the pink pair by the wall and slips on her silver shoes.

Carter pets Buster as we file out the front door and into my truck. Aniston opens her own door before I can get to it. One more reminder that I'm out with everyone and not on a date with her.

On the way, Aniston controls the radio, with input from both kids. They argue a few times over which station to leave it on, and she turns it to something totally random each time they do. That results in us eventually leaving it on bluegrass.

Since nobody likes it, I turn down the volume and we start talking. If I'd have known that's what it takes to get the kids talking about their week, I'd have programmed bluegrass as my first saved station earlier.

Until recently, I haven't been around either kid for more than a few minutes at a time. When I took Carter fishing, he stayed quiet for a while. Eventually, he talked about fishing with his dad.

I'm a physical physician and not a psychiatrist, but anyone with decent people skills knows socializing can help you heal from a loss.

Willow sounds pretty busy between school, volleyball, and cheer. Carter's biggest dilemma so far is deciding whether he should try lunchroom food. What I wouldn't give for that to be my biggest worry.

Instead, I'm analyzing everything about Apple Cart and the practice Dr. Deerman built to try and decide if I want to stay and take it over when he retires. And it's getting harder and harder to keep Aniston out of that equation, even though she has no idea that I've developed feelings for her.

We pull up to the restaurant and park to the side. It's a new upscale place a buddy of mine started last year.

Carter stares up at the tall, skinny building. "Cool. This place is tall."

I laugh. "Four levels. That's why it's so narrow."

We enter through the heavy wooden door. It's cool and dark inside. A huge contrast from the heat outdoors. Everything is wooden and navy, with a few decorative nautical pieces. They specialize in seafood, but have stuff like nuggets and macaroni for kids. I wasn't sure how picky the kids are, but assume we're safe with that.

I step up to the podium made to look like the helm of a ship. "Reservations for Easton West. Party of four."

"Yes, sir." The young woman smiles and stacks four menus.

We follow her up all three staircases until we're at the top. She seats us by a large window overlooking Lake Tuscaloosa.

"Mr. Rodgers wanted to give you the best view. Your server will be with you in a minute."

"Thanks."

Aniston plops down beside me and kicks her shoes off under the table. "Remind me to quit wearing heels."

"Okay," I laugh.

"Who's Mr. Rodgers?" Carter asks.

"My friend John, who owns this restaurant."

Carter's eyes grow wide. "He cooks the food here?"

"No, he just owns it. He hired a real chef to cook all his food."

"Oh." Carter raises his eyes to the ceiling for a moment. "I wish I could hire a chef to cook all my meals."

"So do I," Aniston adds. Then she sips the water in front of her. "Easton, do you know where the restroom is?"

I point behind us. "There's one to the back of the room near the staircase."

"Thanks." She stands, placing her hand on my shoulder when she does. Her touch warms my body, and I let out a small sigh.

Aniston walks a few steps before Willow whispers, "Aunt Ani."

She turns her head to Willow, who's pointing at her feet. "Oh, thanks." Aniston tiptoes back to the table and slips into her shoes before going to the restroom.

Carter laughs. "Do you think those old people across the room saw her barefoot?"

I study the older couple at the only other occupied table on this floor. They're focused on their plates and raise their forks at snail-like speed. "Nah. But what's it matter if they did?"

Carter laughs a little louder, and Willow and I join him. Aniston comes back to us laughing.

"What's so funny?"

"Nothing," I say, then wink at the kids.

Aniston shoots me a sideways glance. "Uh-huh." She pulls out her chair and flaps her napkin in her lap as she sits.

I feel her foot brush against my leg as she takes off her shoes again. Such an accidental, minor movement shouldn't turn me on, but it does. She didn't mean to brush against my leg, but the damage is done. I reach for my own water and stare at the kids to try and kill the vibe. That actually makes it worse, as my mind whispers, *they could use a male role model in their life.*

In all practicality, I could still be a male role model for them and not date their aunt. Yet I prefer the package deal.

I slant my eyes at Aniston. The sunlight shines on her blondish hair, highlighting her silhouette. And what a package it is.

"Hi, I'm Brandi. Are you guys ready to order?"

I dart my eyes to the left, where a different young woman stands with a pen and pad in hand. I haven't even opened my menu. "You guys go ahead if you know what you want."

I flop it open and scan for steaks. That's always my fail-safe. By the time Aniston has ordered the salmon dish, I've decided on filet mignon. I add fried green tomatoes as an appetizer and hand Brandi my menu.

This is one dish I can't discuss with John. He argues that fried green tomatoes started up north, even though they're such a Southern dish. He once showed me some articles on the history of the food, and I countered that the movie titled *Fried Green Tomatoes* was set in Alabama.

"This is nice. I've been wanting a reason to wear this dress," Aniston comments.

"Too fancy for PTSO meetings?"

She rolls her eyes as I smirk. "Unless you're an officer, I suppose."

I nod. "You should come to church with me sometime and wear it."

Her expression flattens, and I immediately regret my words. During her hospital stay, she confessed to being mad at God a lot over her sister's and Luke's deaths. I don't want her to think I'm pushy or judgmental.

"Or I can take you out again sometime."

Her lips curve. "That would be nice."

I sip my water and take that as a small win. I'll wait until later to clarify that I meant only her, and not my little makeshift pretend family.

The waitress brings our fried green tomatoes, and Carter offers to bless the food. My heart pings when he mentions getting to eat dinner with Dr. Easton.

Everyone gets a tomato and we start eating. Our main dishes arrive shortly after. We spend the next half hour eating, talking, and laughing. When we're almost done, John walks up.

"Easton." He extends his hand. I take it and stand, giving him one of those one-armed side hugs us men do.

I sit, and he puts his hands on his hips. "Introduce me to your family."

My neck heats up, as I'm not sure how to respond to that. Aniston beats me to it by extending her hand. "I'm Aniston, and this is my niece and nephew, Willow and Carter. We're Easton's neighbors."

John shakes her hand, and his eyes widen at the word "neighbors." "Nice to meet you. I'm Easton's college buddy, John."

"You have a lovely place." Aniston smiles.

"Thanks." John snaps his fingers and points to me. "Say, how about dessert on me?"

I open my mouth to say I'm full, but the kids start thanking him.

"Great. I'll send up some of our best."

I sneak a peek out the window behind Aniston. "Can you make those to-go?"

"Sure. If we ever both get a free day, we need to golf soon."

"Absolutely," I say.

John pats my shoulder, then heads toward the stairs. A few minutes later, Brandi returns with our check and the dessert boxes.

When she leaves, I open the check to see that John paid for our entire dinner. I shake my head.

"What's wrong?" Aniston asks. I turn the book for her to see. "Well, how generous of him."

"I'll leave Brandi an extra-large tip and make sure to take him golfing soon."

She grins. "Good idea."

I scribble in a large tip and sign my name, then pick up the paper bag filled with desserts. "Who wants to go to the park?"

Carter raises his arm.

"Let's go."

We wait for Aniston to slip on her shoes once more, then go to the truck. I drive us to a nice park a few miles from the restaurant.

"Wow, that's the biggest slide without water I've ever seen." Carter's face lights up as I park near the play area.

"Yeah, it's fairly new. The cool part is you have to climb that ropes course to get to the top."

"Whoa." Carter jumps out and runs toward the ropes.

Aniston wrinkles her nose at Willow. "Sorry you're wearing a dress."

Willow pulls up her skirt. "It's fine, I have shorts on under it."

Aniston shrugs. "Smart girl. I do not."

We laugh and exit the truck to catch up with Carter. He's halfway up the ropes course when we get to it. Aniston and I set the desserts on a nearby picnic table for us to eat after everyone tires of sliding.

"That does look fun," Aniston comments as Carter emerges from the metal tunnel.

"Want to try it?"

She balks at me. "My feet already have blisters."

"Then do it barefoot. Just pretend you're walking to the restroom." I laugh and she purses her lips.

She narrows her eyes. "Besides, unlike my intelligent niece, I am not wearing shorts."

"I promise not to look."

She narrows her eyes even more, then smirks as she kicks off her heels. "You go first just in case."

"Then how will I know you're not looking at my butt?"

"You won't." She raises an eyebrow.

That's all I need to hear to roll up my sleeves and start climbing.

I work out a lot, but I haven't done something of this nature since running in a ninja race for a hospital charity in medical school.

Miss Travel Explorer is ahead of me in no time. I try and stay to the side of her so I don't see up her skirt. She beats me to the top in record time. An evil laugh echoes from inside the slide.

I stick my head inside. "Made it."

She giggles this time and pulls me into the slide. We tumble down together, crammed inside the hot metal tube. It was clearly not made for two people, especially two adult-sized people.

I wrap my arm around her waist to try and straighten us after hitting my knee on the side a few times. This thing is slicker than a buttered biscuit pan. Maybe because of my slacks and her satin dress.

We make it to the bottom, where it levels out, then stop. Our feet hang out, a tangled mess. The rest of our bodies are still inside, with barely enough light coming through for me to make out the shape of her face.

I rest my other hand on her cheek. "Are you okay?"

"Yeah, you?" Her voice is breathy, and I can't tell if it's from the tension between us or from crashing down the slide.

I lean an inch closer so I can no longer see her face. But I'm now close enough to feel her breath against my neck. The salmon she ate doesn't leave such a romantic flavor in the air, but I still want to kiss her. Maybe we should've eaten the cheesecakes before sliding?

As I tilt my head to kiss her, something squeezes my leg.

"Are you two alive?" Carter's voice is loud and in front of us.

I snap my head forward to him bent inside the slide. "Yes, Carter, we're alive."

I feel more alive than ever before. Even if Carter just blocked my move.

"Why don't you get out, buddy, so we can climb out."

"Okay." Carter backs up, and I drop my hand from Aniston's face. She scoots out in front of me, and I hang back another second, sucking in the smothering air.

If I can't have a taste of Aniston, white chocolate cheesecake will have to do for now.

CHAPTER 11

Aniston

Easton eases his truck onto our driveway and kills the engine. Not ready for the night to end, I sit still for a moment before slipping into my shoes.

This wasn't a date. It was friends and neighbors going to dinner. Easton had insisted he treat us, which made it feel a little like a date. But his friend ended up footing the bill, and we had two underage chaperones the whole night.

However, had we not have had those chaperones, I would've totally kissed him on the slide. Then again, had we not have had the kids with us, I seriously doubt Easton and I would've climbed a ropes course in our Sunday best and slid down a massive playground slide.

Buster saunters toward the garage, and the motion light flicks on. The kids open their doors, and I begrudgingly do the same.

Carter pets Buster, and Willow holds up the remaining to-go plates when he sniffs the air. Easton gets out and steps beside me as we make our way to the front. When we climb the porch steps, his hand lands on the small of my back. A few of his fingers brush against the bare skin where my dress is open.

I flinch and he moves his hand. Crap. I didn't mean to send a distress signal. My movement was due to surprise, not disgust. Oh well, I'm way out of practice when it comes to men . . . and apparently living in actual houses, since I can't find my key.

While I'm still rummaging through my purse, Willow lifts a pot of dead flowers and holds up a key. She unlocks the front door and puts it back.

"Thanks."

"You're welcome," she says before going inside with Carter behind her.

They shut the door, leaving me alone with Easton on the front porch. I sip my Styrofoam cup of water, making a slurping sound when I suck down all but the ice.

Easton grins. I sling my purse back on my shoulder and glance around the porch. When my eyes land on the flower pot, I laugh nervously. "I didn't know that was there."

Easton arches an eyebrow. "The key or the flowers?"

The gray, broken stems stick out like a sore thumb. "Uh, both?"

Easton laughs so hard, his eyes crinkle at the corners. I watch his handsome face and debate stepping closer so hopefully he'll make a move. Then I get caught up in my anxious awkwardness and his contagious laughter and start laughing too.

When we finally stop laughing, I take a deep breath. My stomach expands, and so do my eyes. I sincerely hope that's not what I think it is. Just in case, I cross my legs.

"We should do this again."

"Totally," I say like I'm in an eighties teen movie. I'm so lame.

Easton stands closer to me, and I take a step back. When I do, a light stream trickles between my legs.

Dear God, no! I know laugh peeing is a thing, but I only thought that was possible after birthing kids. Or at least not until one's thirties.

I clamp my legs together and back toward the door like a ballerina stuck in whatever position is the legs-together thing. Easton, either oblivious to the fact that I just peed myself or oddly unfazed by it, leans toward me.

I cannot let him kiss me with a stream of pee between my knees. That is not the first kiss memory I want.

"Thanks again for going. I had a great time with y'all." He dips his head, and I turn mine.

I plant a peck on his cheek before he can reach my mouth. "Same to you. Night-night."

With that, I open the door and back inside. I shut it behind me and drop my purse and cup. Then I march stiff-legged toward the half-bath off the kitchen.

Not caring to shut the door, I jump on the toilet and pee to my heart's content.

"Aunt Ani?"

You've got to be kidding me. Carter is standing outside the open door. First peeing myself, now a kid coming in the bathroom while I'm on the toilet. I'm officially a parent now, huh?

Technically, he's still in the hallway and I should've shut the door, but still . . .

Dang it, Easton! If he hadn't have gotten me on this "drink billions of gallons of water a day" kick, he could be having the kiss of his life right now.

"Carter, honey, I'm peeing right now." My voice is lathered on thick with sarcasm—another sign I've embraced this mom thing full force.

"Sorry, I just wanted to see if Easton said if he's going to come to my Career Day at school."

I sigh. "You can ask him again tomorrow."

"Okay." He wanders down the hall toward the living room, and I finish my business.

I step into the hallway to Willow staring at me from the living room couch. "Aunt Ani?"

"Yes?" I say, again sarcastic.

"If you decide to date Easton, we're cool with that."

I shake my head. "Where is all this coming from?"

They both shrug. I point toward the stairs. "Time for bed."

Without saying another word, they stand in silence and trudge toward the stairs. I stay planted with my legs stuck together—more by actual stickiness than choice this time. I best change too.

I pick up my purse and cup and follow them upstairs. "Brush your teeth."

"Yes, ma'am," they answer unenthusiastically before heading for the bathroom they share.

I head for my bedroom and peel off my panties. When my dress falls to the floor, I notice a small line on the back. Great, a pee stain. After sliding in the park and dropping a piece of cheesecake on my chest, I'd debated whether to take it to the dry cleaners. Now I have no choice but to take it.

Or do I?

No, I'm taking it. This warrants a trip to town. I wrap a bathrobe around myself and go to the bathroom beside the guest bedroom. A shower can't fix everything, but it can clean pee.

As I stand under the warm stream of water that fortunately isn't coming from me, something clicks. An idea for my vlog. A local travel article. I could write about the new Lakeside Landing restaurant and the park where we played. I even have a video of the kids climbing the slide before we did.

I hurry out of the shower, dry off, and wrap a towel

around my head. Then I throw on my bathrobe and hurry to my laptop.

For the next half hour, I write about our local adventure. I add in links to the restaurant and park area, then find photos from the restaurant's website. It's almost midnight when I'm done editing the footage of the kids sliding and making everything look presentable.

This will make the perfect segue post after chronicling my adventures with Willow and Carter before we came home. I yawn widely and hit publish before setting my computer on the floor and climbing under my covers.

My career is back. All thanks to Easton and our little adventure.

Aniston

An annoying melody grows louder and louder. I reach for the extra pillow and shove it over my face. It plays again, and I recognize it as my ringtone.

I push my hands on the mattress and raise my head, cobra style. The towel I forgot was on my head untwists and falls to the bed. I yawn and snatch my phone from the bedside table.

Morgan.

"Hello?" My voice is somewhere between dreamlike and hungover. That pretty much describes my current state, as this is the best sleep I've had in months.

Unless, of course, you count my night in the hospital. I don't, since I was heavily medicated at the time.

I pat my knotted hair and recall falling asleep after my late-night vlog binge.

"Aniston, did you know you're trending?"

"Huh?"

"Your video blog post thingy. It's being shared all over Facebook, and I just saw it posted to Pinterest."

I blink. What in the . . . I stare at the clock on the table. Ten-thirty. I posted that less than twelve hours ago, in the middle of the night for most people. How could it have caught on this fast?

"Morgan, shouldn't you be in church right now?"

"I am."

"Then why are you calling me?" *Seriously, woman. You need Jesus and I need sleep!*

"I've already been to service and all. I'm helping out in the nursery."

"And they let you call?"

"Eh, it's newborns. All they do is go to the bathroom and sleep."

Sounds a lot like my life lately. I shake my head and massage my temples. "So my vlog is viral, as in tons of shares and likes, and all that?"

"Yep. It's good too. Really good. My favorite part is where you said you have PTSO PTSD." Morgan snorts.

"PTSO PTSD? I never mentioned the PTSO—ohhh."

My hands numb and my chest tingles. Not the good tingle that comes from Easton, but the panicky kind that happens when I get bit by some exotic animal in the wild or my parachute doesn't pull on the first try or I see Georgia in the car line. I jerk my head toward my computer, sitting innocently on the floor.

I swallow to clear the lump in my throat. "Uh, Morgan, could you tell me the name of that vlog?"

"Yeah. I mean you wrote or made it, but you call it 'Starting School for Mommy Dummies.' Pretty original, if you ask me. Most people are hash-tagging it PTSO PTSD, though. You should really trademark that."

I wipe my hand down my face, but I can barely feel it thanks to the numbness. "No, no no!"

"Yes, yes, yes! Girl, you are brilliant."

"No, Morgan, you don't understand." My voice squeaks. "I never meant to post that. I meant to post the one about 'Family Fun in T-town.'"

"Oh, that one's up too. I think it had like ten views or something."

I slap my forehead, jarring my hand. Once the numbness subsides, I unplug my computer and head for the bathroom. Because I, of course, have to pee. Then I sit on the toilet and refresh the laptop screen.

"Are you still there?"

"Yeah, Morgan. You've got kids, I've got stuff, we'll talk soon."

She says something else, but I'm already hanging up the phone. I set it on the side of the sink and check my vlog.

Perfect. Both videos went live together. I had left the PTSO meeting post in my drafts, never intending to post it. Some people journal their frustrations. I record mine . . . and apparently post them for the world to see.

Thanks to my sophisticated SEO descriptions, all the right —or wrong—people saw this and shared it. I click on the analytics page of my site. My jaw drops when I see more than a million views. It took me months to get that many on even my most popular posts. How can ranting about mom duties outrank backpacking in some of the most scenic parts of the country?

This world really is pathetic. We're just a Gatorade garden away from *Idiocracy*.

When I click on the page that shows how many ads are attached to where my vlog was shown and how many clicks I've gotten, dollar signs blur my vision. I could make a lot of money off this mistake.

I click on the Tuscaloosa vlog about the park and restaurant. Ha, Morgan was wrong. It now has fourteen views. I sigh loudly. And to think that I tagged that one so well before publishing it.

With a few more clicks, I check my social media pages. People have not only shared my post, but also visited my accounts to follow me and tag me in their stories. That's about the best free marketing I can get.

I go back to my website and hover over the edit button beside the viral post. Everything sensible says I should delete this. Everything except for my bank account that's starting to look like the dead flowers on the porch.

The kids are set for life, thanks to their parents' life insurance. But I'm not touching a dime of that. Just because the house and their college is now secure, doesn't mean I don't need to also earn a living. And I've about earned a quarter year's worth of my normal salary overnight.

I drop my hand and set the computer on the floor. I can't do it.

Despite how embarrassed I am about this post and how much I want to delete it, the people have spoken. According to a few of the comments I read on YouTube and Facebook, I'm not the only one with PTSO PTSD. There are other women out there dealing with their own Georgia, who I thankfully didn't specify by name in the vlog. They need me to preach to the choir about school stress.

They need this post.

Almost as much as I do.

CHAPTER 12

Easton

"Hi." Aniston smiles at me through the open door. "Thanks so much."

"No problem."

Aniston turns her head toward her living room. "Carter, mind Easton. I'll be back soon and bring food with me." She steps onto the porch and looks at me. "Would you like anything to eat?"

I shrug. "I'll be fine."

She swats my chest with her hand. "No, I'm bringing you something, so you best tell me what you want."

I grin. Her voice and mannerisms are playful, which is refreshing after her abrupt exit Saturday night. With so many conflicting signals, I'm not sure which way to turn my dial. Do I crank up the heat and go for her? Or do I cool it off and shrink back to the neighborly man who cuts her hay and occasionally babysits for food?

She stares at me with raised brows, and I realize I haven't responded. "I like anything besides boiled okra."

Aniston laughs. "I think I can work with that." She smiles wider, then bounces down the porch steps and heads for her truck.

I puff out my cheeks and try not to read too much into her actions. I'm here to watch Carter while Aniston goes to some volleyball parent meeting about games and then picks up Willow from her practices. She called around lunch to ask if I could hang out with Carter for a few hours after work.

"Hey, buddy."

Carter lifts his head from the book in his lap. "Hey, Dr. Easton."

I start to correct him on the "doctor" part but decide it's no use. The kid is too polite. Better that than the alternative. "What are you reading?"

He holds up the book so I can see the cover. "*Fly Guy.*"

I lift my chin. That bug looks vaguely familiar. I think we have a book with it on the cover in the office waiting area.

"Would you want to maybe take a break and go fishing?"

Carter's eyes light up. "Can I? The teacher said I need to read this three times."

"How many times have you read it?"

"Two."

"Tell you what. It doesn't look too thick. Why don't you bring it along and read it while I get our poles ready."

"Yeah." Carter hops off the couch and rushes to the door. He shoves the book in the crook of his arm and slips on his sneakers by the entryway. "Ready."

"Okay." I pat him on the back as we exit the house and climb in my truck.

In a few minutes, we're in the shed beside the carriage house collecting our supplies. "I don't have a lot of bait, so I may need you to catch a few crickets. That is, if you're up to it."

"That sounds awesome."

I thought he might like that. I spotted a lot of them while weed-eating the other day. "Hang on." I reach on a shelf and pull down an old canning jar, then poke a few holes in the lid with my pocket knife. It doesn't much matter that our bait can breathe, but I figure a little boy will find live bait even cooler than dead. I know I would at that age.

"There." I hand the jar to Carter.

"Thanks." He bends down and immediately starts scouring the ground for crickets.

I kick a tarp off a piece of equipment and about a dozen crickets jump from underneath. Carter goes wild with excitement, and I laugh.

Once the jar is half full of crickets and the other supplies are in the truck bed, I open my door. Carter stands at the passenger side and stares through the open window. His head is barely above the door.

"Dr. Easton, can I ride in the bed?"

"Sure, we're not going far at all. Hop in."

He smiles and circles to the back. I wait until he's fully inside and situated before I back out and drive the few yards to the pond.

After we park, Carter climbs out and comes to the truck door. His eyes land on the fly book. "I'll go ahead and read and get it over with so I can fish."

I laugh. "Okay."

He grabs the book with the hand that isn't holding his cricket jar and finds a place on the bank. I carry the poles and tackle box and sit beside him.

"I don't think I told you this the other day, but my favorite place to fish was my grandpa's farm when I was your age."

"Your grandpa has a farm?"

"Had. He passed away."

Carter stares at the ground and picks a blade of grass. My

jaw twitches, and I wish the conversation hadn't taken this turn. I stand and cast my pole, then bend down beside him.

"Is he in heaven with my parents?"

A piece of my heart chips off when I try and even imagine the pain this boy feels. I swallow and answer, "Yeah, he is." I feign busyness with my reel to try and not seem too upset.

"I like to look at the clouds sometimes and imagine my mom and dad up there watching us."

I squint at the sky under the bill of my ball cap and nod. "I believe they're watching." Even though I say it to console Carter, I truly do believe it.

He casts his pole, then sits back beside me and reels a little. We sit in peaceful silence for a moment, or at least to me. I hope what I said has given him a bit a peace.

When my mind starts to wander back on fond memories of my grandpa, a small hand grabs my forearm.

"Dr. Easton?"

"Yeah?" I turn to Carter.

"If you want to date my aunt, like without me and my sister around, I'm okay with that."

"You are?" The corners of my mouth turn up at this unexpected change in conversation.

"Yes, sir. I wanted to tell you when the girls weren't around. You know, man to man."

"Man to man." I grin and hold out my hand. Carter drops his from my arm and shakes my hand firmly.

Then he jerks it back to reel in his line when the end of the pole bows. We both stand as he reels fast as his little arms can manage.

A big catfish emerges from the water, and Carter yells. I cheer with him and step closer to the edge of the water to get it off the line. Carter's face is full of childhood joy.

"Want to get it off the hook?"

He nods like an overachieving bobblehead doll. I bring the end of the pole to him and let him take the reins. As soon as he removes the hook, the fish wiggles hard enough to fall from his grip. It lands on the ground—right on top of the open library book.

Carter stares up at me with a terrified face. "Oh no."

I lift the fish with one hand and the book with the other. There's a slimy stain across the pages.

"Don't worry about it. I'll explain everything when I come by Wednesday for Career Day." I wink at Carter, and the color returns to his face. "What do ya think? Keep him or toss him back?"

"Uh . . ." Carter cocks his head and studies the fish. "I would say keep him, but Aunt Ani is bringing me back a cheeseburger, so we're good."

I toss the fish into the water and call out, "It's your lucky day."

Cater watches as it splashes under the water with a few bubbles. We fish about another half hour, then head toward their place. He reads the fly book when we're back in the house and the pages have dried.

I'm in the kitchen pouring us both a glass of lemonade when the door opens. Aniston and Willow enter with to-go bags.

"Who's in the mood for Mary's?" Aniston calls out.

Carter rushes to the kitchen sink and starts washing his hands.

"Wow, he must've worked up a hunger. What did you guys do?"

"Fish, read. That's all."

"Fish? Willow, we should've let them feed us."

Carter stretches his hands about twice as wide as the length of the catfish he caught. "We caught a huge fish, first thing. I caught it. Then we caught some brim. We could've fed us, but I told Dr. Easton to toss them back since you were buying me a cheeseburger."

Willow and Aniston laugh as they unpack the food.

Aniston sets a box in front of me.

"Thanks." I open up a steak sandwich and curly fries. She made a wise choice.

We gather around the kitchen table and eat, while the kids share bits and pieces about their new school year.

Aniston sips from the jug of water I gave her and appears less stressed than a week ago. I'd like to think I had something to do with that, even though I'm sure her health scare deserves full credit.

When we finish eating, the kids clean up the kitchen. Rather, they throw away all the wrappers and boxes. I tell them good night and start toward the door.

Aniston stands, still nursing her jug of water. "I'll walk you out."

We step onto the porch, and she shuts the door behind us. I shove my hands in my pockets and sway awkwardly. Do I head for my truck, stand with her a minute, or just continue being weird?

I haven't had such a strong connection with anyone in so long that I'm reverting back to middle school. Most women I've dated over the past few years were blind dates, or at least setups, by mutual friends or townspeople who wanted to find someone for the single doctor. Regardless of how pretty or successful they were, none of them ignited a flame in me like Aniston.

She's started a fire inside me that I can't put out, no matter how hard I try. All the metaphorical water and dirt I toss to try and stop her flame flickering in my brain won't work.

"That was sweet of you to take him fishing."

"No problem. I enjoyed it too."

She presses her lips together in a slight smile, then scratches the side of her head. "Listen, Easton, about Saturday night."

I raise a hand. "No need to explain. I expected nothing from you, and I'm sorry if you thought—"

Before I can say another word, she stands on her toes and kisses me. My eyes widen, then close as I relax.

Just when the shock turns to enjoyment, she pulls back. My stomach flares like she's doused the inner flame with kerosene. My lips curve, remembering the feel of her soft lips against them.

If I react this way to a simple kiss, I can't wait to *really* kiss her.

Aniston bites her bottom lip and blushes slightly, which I find endearing. I reach for her hand, and she takes mine. Together, we walk to my truck.

I drop her hand to open my door. She stares at the ground and fidgets with the lid on her water bottle.

"Everything okay?" I hope that wasn't a pity kiss.

She raises her eyes sheepishly and sighs. "I have a confession."

"You didn't really want to kiss me." As I tell my youngest patients, better to rip off the Band-Aid first thing.

"No, no, no." She shakes her head. "I actually wanted to kiss Saturday night."

"Oh?" She could've fooled me. Every time I inched closer, she backed up like I had a contagious disease.

Aniston scratches her neck with her free hand, then fidgets with the bottle top again. "When we laughed really hard, I—" She squints her eyes and winces before finishing her statement. "Peed a little."

I blink. This is not what I expected to hear. "You peed?"

She slaps her forehead and turns three shades brighter. "Ugh. It's soooo embarrassing. I never should've said anything."

"That's all?"

She wipes her hand down her face and gives me a shocked expression. "That's all? I peed on myself. Something toddlers do at random or tiny dogs when their owners come home."

I laugh.

"It's not funny!" She lifts the jug of water, which I can see is half empty thanks to the clear plastic. "It's all this water you make me drink now."

I laugh harder and she shoves my shoulder. "Stop laughing. It's not funny."

But it is. Even she laughs when she says the word "funny."

"Aniston, I'm a doctor. I've seen it all, and it's totally normal for someone who is properly hydrated to need to pee."

She rolls her eyes. "It's embarrassing. I'm in the nicest dress I own, we'd had an awesome evening, and I flood my panties."

My side throbs from all the laughing. Now I'm leaning on the truck to keep from falling. I haven't laughed this hard since someone brought a pregnant possum into the office and wanted us to do a sonogram.

"Please stop laughing."

"I'm trying," I say, sucking in a breath.

Aniston stares at me and pokes out her bottom lip as I cough out a little laugh. Despite working with bodily fluids more than I'd like, this might make a great excuse to never date some woman again.

However, this is not some woman. This is Aniston, and I find her honesty endearing.

As she stares up at me with a pout, I drop my face toward hers. "No more laughing," I whisper.

Then I close the space between us and kiss her like I've wanted to since the day she opened the door holding a pan of cookie cake.

After a few seconds, she kisses me back. The water bottle hits the ground with a thud, and she wraps her arms around my neck. We stand in the moonlight, embracing.

For once, we can enjoy the moment without a kid or

Morgan or a nurse interrupting. Instead, Buster comes by and starts rubbing against our legs while he licks the spilled water off the driveway.

We pull apart enough to look down and laugh at him. Then I pet his head. "Sorry, I didn't mean to laugh."

Aniston narrows her eyes. "Ha-ha."

"Good night, neighbor."

"Good night." Aniston smiles at me once more before bending to pick up her bottle.

I climb in my truck and head for my place as she waves and walks toward her front door.

I can honestly say that's the best payment for babysitting I've ever received.

Aniston

I slap another sheet on the copier and blow a loose strand of hair out of my view. It took all of ten minutes for me to realize that the title "Georgia's personal assistant" is PC terminology for modern-day slavery.

The copier lights up when I close the lid, and brightly colored papers shoot out the side. I was instructed to color code each individual form so that parents receiving more than one wouldn't get confused.

I rotate my head to try and soothe the crick in my neck. It doesn't help. At least I can sit down after this batch and start sorting.

Before August, I had no idea how much paperwork revolved around school. If I had the money, I'd hire a part-time paralegal to help.

A minute later, the light dims and the last few papers land on top of the stack. I collect the pink sheets and take them to the table at the edge of the copy room.

Georgia left specific instructions on where to send what papers. Everyone gets a paper announcing the upcoming festival. Different grades get different papers saying what they should donate and what booths parents can help work. Then there's the call for entertainment and the talent show sign-up sheet. I smile with satisfaction that she implemented my idea.

For the next hour, I sort papers by color and grade. I count off the right amount of each by grade and then divide them by classes so each teacher will get the correct amount. My head is swimming with more numbers than Rain Man's by the time everything is in the proper stack.

I start with the kindergarten classes, delivering the papers to each teacher. When I turn the corner by the library to go collect more from the copy room, I peek at the lost-and-found box. Mrs. Pebbleton's sweater is folded on top, with her name prominently displayed.

A tinge of guilt tugs at me as I worry she'll never notice it. I start to sniff it to make sure Morgan washed it before putting it back, but I've done enough weird things at this school—most of them involving that very sweater.

I imagine school security footage somewhere in which I'm the main actress. With that, I shake my head and continue to the copy room, empty handed.

By the time I make it to Carter's class, the parents helping with Career Day are seated in the back. I greet the ones I know as I pass and take the papers to Mrs. Pebbleton's desk.

A man dressed like an overgrown child athlete stands at the front of the class. If I'm hearing correctly, he's explaining how he refurbishes mobile homes he buys at auctions.

Just when I thought vlogging was a unique career.

I tune out trailer flipper and stare at Easton. My heart

melts when he grins at me from his child-sized chair, which makes his long legs resemble a cricket's. A stethoscope hangs around the collar of his white doctor's coat. I rarely see him wear a coat. He looks so professional.

How I'd love to pull him in by the stethoscope strings and kiss him. Every second of our make-out session in the driveway replays in my mind like a highlight reel. For a moment, I forget I'm at school. I'm dancing with Easton in our hayfield, not a care in the world . . .

Then I hear my name from the doorway.

I turn to find Georgia waving me toward the door. I want to hide under Mrs. Pebbleton's desk, but Georgia has some sort of weird power over me. My feet turn toward the door and start that way.

Easton brushes his hand against mine as I pass, and I curl a finger around his. That gives me a temporary confidence boost to literally face my demon.

I exit the room with the few papers I have left and face Georgia.

She raises a brow and nods at the stack resting in the crease of my arm. "You're still passing out papers?"

"This is the last hallway." Of *this* building. I don't mention that I haven't made it to the upper grades yet. If it wouldn't have taken so darn long to sort them per her instructions . . .

"Well, I'll get Mindy to handle that when she comes in."

"Mindy?" I say this to myself more than Georgia, in an attempt to jog my memory.

"My PTSO secretary."

"Oh," I say as the image of Gretchen pops in my head. Her real name is Mindy.

Georgia walks so fast, I have to stretch my legs fully to keep her pace. We turn toward the office as she explains, "I need you for something more important."

"So I'm being promoted?" I mean this sarcastically, but her smile indicates she didn't take it that way.

"You're already my assistant. There is no greater position in the PTSO." She smirks, then adds, "Other than mine."

I follow her into the office. "These positions. Do we get any say in what role we have?" I can't help but feel like I drew the shortest straw in the bushel.

"I appoint them." Georgia's smirk widens, not unlike the cartoon version of the Grinch when he's plotting to steal presents.

I narrow my eyes, studying her face to try and decipher her next move. It's hard to read behind all the Botox and fake eyelashes.

"Appointments were mentioned near the end of your room-mom manual. Did you not read the fine print in the back?"

I grin nervously. Considering most of mine fell in the pool and the other half is covered in chocolate stains or drool from where I dozed off, I'd say there's a good chance I didn't get to that part.

"Maybe it slipped my mind," I lie through my teeth. More like slipped in my pool.

Georgia raises her brows and smooths out her ponytail. "Now that you're up to speed on your role, I need your help in the gym."

I nod. "Okay."

She crosses the office and pulls a large roll of plastic from behind a filing cabinet. "We need to hang a banner, and I heard you're good with climbing."

A cocky smile sneaks across my face. Did Georgia Jenkins compliment me? "I am."

"Good." She marches past me out of the office, and I follow. We're back to power walking like geriatric couples at the mall.

We make it to the gym in record time. Georgia steps into the coach's office and returns with two massive rolls of Gorilla tape looped on her thin forearm.

"See that space above the bleachers?" She points a pale pink nail toward the north wall.

"Yep."

"I need you to climb up there and put this sign up." She drops her finger and holds the sign with both hands. With one swift shake, it unrolls across the floor.

My head follows the motion until it finally ends at half court. "That's a long sign."

She lets go of the end and pats my shoulder. "You can handle it."

"By myself?"

Georgia nods. "Unless you think you need some help."

Something fierce churns in my stomach like I've eaten Indian food after midnight. My competitive spirit resurrects, and I start rolling up the sign.

Challenge accepted.

Georgia starts toward the exit as I climb the bleachers to the top. I'm almost there when she calls, "I almost forgot."

I turn and she holds up a roll of tape. I reach out a hand for her to bring it to me. Instead, her lazy butt tosses it like a Frisbee. And she's not a good aim.

I clutch my chest as the tape falls to the bleacher in front of me. I'm bowed over in pain, but I swear I catch a glimpse of her smiling on the way out.

Instead of apologizing or simply saying "my bad" like a decent human should, she says, "Don't waste my tape."

The gym door shuts audibly, and I'm left holding my boob with one hand and the sign with the other. How dare her. I barely have any boobs to begin with. I can't afford to lose one. Maybe I'll get lucky and it will swell. Eh, but then they won't be even.

Ugh. I moan with pain and sit on the bleachers to rest a moment. When I set the sign in front of me, it rolls all the way to the floor. Of course it does. I drop my head in my hands and moan louder.

"Rough day?"

Is that? I lift my face to Easton standing by the door, the sun shining behind his brown hair. He literally looks like a savior coming to my rescue.

I stand and sigh. "Georgia wants me to hang this massive sign across the top all by myself."

He laughs and shakes his head. "I'll help you before I go back to work."

I grin and fold my arms under my sore chest. It wouldn't be appropriate to grab it in front of Easton. I've already sent enough mixed signals.

He gathers the sign, rolling it up at record speed, then climbs the bleachers two at a time.

"How'd Career Day go?" I ask once he's standing beside me.

"Good. I went after the woman who milks goats to make soap and queso."

I raise my chin. "Tough act to follow."

"I'll say. She brought samples." He holds the stethoscope up from his collar. "And I thought this would be cool."

I laugh. "You did great, I'm sure."

Laughing agitates my upper rib cage beneath the injury. I seethe.

"Are you all right?"

I nod with clenched teeth. "Eh, I will be. Georgia's not much of an aim. She hit me with a roll of tape." I lift the roll, which is thicker than most training wheels. "Either that or she's a really good aim." I snarl at the tape.

Easton frowns. "Want me to look at where you're hurt?"

My mouth goes dry and I let out a squeaky laugh. "Uh, I think it's fine." I cross my arms tightly over my chest. I'd best keep this injury to myself.

"Good. Then let's get this thing hung. Does it go across here?" He points at the wall in front of us.

"Yeah. I guess just center it."

Easton stretches the sign and then lifts the first corner to the wall. "Can you hand me some tape?"

"Sure." I pull a generous amount of tape for one corner and delight in ripping it off with my bare hands.

Some people meditate, some go to counseling—I waste Georgia's tape. Best therapy I can think of.

We continue until only a little tape is left and the sign is more than stable against the block wall. Then Easton and I take a step down and survey our work.

"Good job." He holds up a hand, and I high-five it.

We walk down the bleachers together and out the front door. "Thanks for your help. Not just with the sign, but with Career Day too. It meant a lot to Carter for you to come."

One side of his mouth curls. "I wanted to come for him." He kisses my forehead gently. "And for you."

I smile, then groan. "I best return to my duties."

He nods and backs onto the walkway. I wave as he turns to walk toward the parking lot. He salutes me like a dork, but it makes me laugh.

I head toward the main building, looking for loose posters where I can waste the rest of Georgia's tape on my way to the copy room. It's the least I can do after she tape-attacked my boob.

CHAPTER 13

Aniston

"Wee-pees!" I shake my head at yet more terminology I have to learn in Toybowl football.

The overgrown ballplayer man who talked up repossessed-mobile-home restoration on Career Day is apparently the coach for the football team.

Morgan must read the confusion on my face because she explains. "Wee-pees is a play on pee-wees. That's the younger team. He's calling second string that because he's frustrated with how they're performing."

I shake my head. "Makes me glad my child is cheering."

Morgan laughs. "You should see him in baseball."

"He coaches that too?"

She rolls her eyes. "Some years. He's been banned a few times, then rolls off probation and comes back."

"He just seems so—"

"Crazy and arrogant?" Morgan finishes my thought.

I waver my head. "I was gonna go with passionate and intense, but tomato, tomoto."

She laughs.

I focus on the cheerleaders. Willow is adorable in her uniform, and pretty impressive. "Willow's good at this."

Morgan smiles. "Yeah, your sister really encouraged her in gymnastics and volleyball. She's shaped into a great little athlete."

I sit a little taller, proud of my girl. Then a hint of guilt washes over me as I realize I never attended any of the kids' events until they became my kids. Maybe I'll be a better parent than aunt. Of course, that shouldn't be hard since I've set the bar about knee high to a grasshopper.

Brooke stands by the sidelines with another woman in an identical tank top. She bobs her head and points to the girls, cuing them when to pick one another up. After the cheer ends, she claps enthusiastically.

"Brooke is great with those cheerleaders."

"Yeah, she should've had a girl," Morgan comments.

I bite my bottom lip and watch Brooke for another moment. "Do you think she'll ever get married or have any more kids?"

Morgan shakes her head. "I never talk to her about it. All I know is that Timothy's dad was someone she was with in college, and he's not in their lives. I think she's still heartbroken over the whole thing."

I slump my shoulders and focus on the game, sorry I asked about Brooke. If anyone deserves a good relationship, it's her. She's always so upbeat and helpful.

Morgan leans against my ear and whispers, "Just between us, I think she never got over Nathan."

Nathan. "Wait, you mean the Nate the Great baseball guy?"

A few people in front of us turn when I say his name.

They scan the crowd before turning back with disappointed looks that he's not here.

"Shhh," Morgan scolds. "Yes, that Nate. Remember, they were thick as thieves in high school?"

"Yeah." I remember. I've always known Brooke was a good person, but she earned a lot of eye rolls from me in high school.

She was the head cheerleader, happy go lucky, teachers' pet type. I was the one who snuck wine coolers under the bleachers and skipped school more than I care to admit. Naturally, I blamed it on my mom's untimely death. As an adult, I realize I was jealous of kids like Brooke who had it all together. My mom dying early was a pitiful excuse for me to butt heads with my dad and rebel.

That's why I'm so mad about Jennifer dying. She was very Brooke-like. Brooke, but a decade older. Brooke 1.0. I can run myself ragged and never be half the parent she was to these kids.

My eyes start to water as I observe Willow doing a perfect toe touch. "Can you keep an eye on Carter while I go to the restroom?"

"Yeah," Morgan answers with a mouthful of nachos.

He's with Andrew beside the fence in front of us, building something out of grass clippings and dirt.

I rush down the bleachers, muttering "excuse me" on the way. I make a beeline to the restroom, sighing with relief when I find an empty stall.

After blowing my nose full force and dabbing the corners of my eyes, I laugh. Not because the idea of me floundering as a parent is funny. But the idea of parents floundering in general is funny to me.

In particular when it comes to sports.

There are enough people in those stands to start an impressive flash mob. All to watch a bunch of twelve-year-olds play ball. Brooke's out there channeling a reality TV dance judge, smiling and critiquing with enthusiasm. Meanwhile, Trailer Trader is simultaneously pulling Gatorade bottles from his back pocket, drinking from one and spitting tobacco in the other.

I wish that for the half-time entertainment, he'd confuse the two.

This is the kind of stuff parents deal with that nobody talks about. Sweating our shorts off on metal bleachers. Everyone jealously eyeing the old lady who had enough foresight to sit near an outlet and bring a blow fan. People like Morgan with multiple kids opening up tabs at the concession stand. Me escaping to the bathroom for a moment of solitude to get myself together.

I laugh louder and pull my phone from my back pocket. Why is it that all my best ideas come on the toilet?

I open my video recorder and zoom in on my face. However, I make sure to specify that I'm in a bathroom stall at a Toybowl football game. That makes for the perfect backdrop for this vlog.

Fifteen minutes later, my butt is sore from the ceramic toilet seat and my video is complete. I emerge from the restroom and wash my hands.

I hear the toilet beside me flush, and Mindy walks out. She gives me a sideways glance that communicates she recognizes me. I half-smile at her.

It's hard to read whether she's for or against me. Probably depends how loyal she is to Georgia's reign.

There are no more paper towels in the holder, or anywhere else. I wipe my hands down my shorts and exit the restroom.

Time to watch the rest of this game and get more ideas for my travel turned mommy-rant vlog.

I make my way to Morgan, who is running her finger through the nacho cheese tray. She sucks the last string of orange goo from her fingertip and turns to me. "Everything come out okay?"

I glance at my phone before returning it to my back pocket. "Excellent."

Easton

I rub my eyes and note the time on my Apple Watch. No wonder I'm hungry. I've skipped lunch and it's close to five. I shut the filing cabinet drawer and decide to call it a day.

I rarely go to the hospital on a Saturday unless I'm working the ER. Correction: I never go on a Saturday unless I'm in the ER. Today was a rare occasion, since the office manager is on vacation and I needed to organize some files.

Could this have waited for her to get back? Absolutely. But I wanted a mindless distraction from Aniston.

It didn't work.

Even though we're kind of on the same page for feelings, I don't want to get ahead of myself. A more accurate way to put it would be we're now reading the same book. However, I'm not sure if she's as far along in the story as me.

I daydream about making things official and one day joining her little family. For all I know, she could be stuck on the page soiled by fish slime. Not that our love story is *Fly Guy*, but whatever.

The last thing I want is to pressure her into moving too quickly.

After straightening a few rogue folders left on the desk, I exit the office, locking the door behind me. I drop the keys in the pocket of my gym shorts and go to my truck.

My stomach growls like a bear in heat, or at least what I assume a bear in heat might sound like. Luckily, none of the

Apple Cart residents have brought a bear in to see me. After my stomach growls again, I turn in at Mary's Diner.

The parking lot is already pretty full. Maybe this isn't a good idea. Hunger overpowers common sense, and I pull to the side and park. Besides, it shouldn't take any longer than going home and having to cook.

I open the door to the sound of voices and forks clinking against plates. Most of the people are dressed in Apple Cart Armadillos red. Some of the kids are sweaty or in cheer uniforms. Then it hits me that football has started.

A waitress passes me with a tray of food. "Hello, Dr. West."

"Hey." I nod and smile on my way to counter. Mary is behind it, with a bandana draped over her hair. The bandana matches her apron, minus the grease stains.

She fans her face with a paper menu as she rings up a customer. After counting back the guy's change, she spots me.

"Hey, sugar."

"Hey, Mary. Can I get something to-go?"

"Why, of course." She shuts the cash register door and props her other hand on her hip. "What you want?"

She hands me the menu she used to fan her face a moment earlier. I scan it quickly and decide on a steak dinner with potato.

Mary runs my card through the slot, and I type in my PIN. "Why don't you find a seat, and I'll have one of the girls bring it out when it's ready."

"Thanks." I make sure to add a generous tip and take my card.

"There's a few empty seats at that table." Mary cocks her head toward the back.

I see Aniston, Brooke, Morgan, and some of the older kids sitting together. The younger ones are at a table behind them. I narrow my eyes at Mary. I've heard she's quite the match-maker around town.

Her grin grows wider, revealing the gap between her teeth. I nod and head for the back as she laughs and greets the next customer.

So much for keeping my mind off Aniston tonight.

Before I make it across the room, Morgan spots me. "Dr. West, what a pleasant surprise." She elbows Aniston beside her. Morgan isn't one for subtlety.

Aniston looks my way while biting into a cheese stick. Her hand freezes, and the string of cheese between her mouth and hand loops down like melting wax.

I freeze too and debate turning the other way. Then Morgan yells, "Come, join us."

As I walk in slow motion toward their table, Aniston picks up the droopy cheese and stuffs it in her mouth. She reaches for a napkin, but before she can grab it, Morgan starts shuffling people around the table. She has Willow go to the other side, then Brooke and Aniston move down, leaving the seat between her and Aniston empty.

When I'm a few feet away, she pats the chair and says, "We have an empty seat waiting on you."

Subtlety is not in her vocabulary.

My temperature rises a few notches as I pull out the chair between Aniston and Morgan. "Good evening, ladies."

Aniston smirks. Morgan laughs and says, "Well, not too good. The Wisteria Mudcats just beat the panties off us. But how's your day been, Doc?"

I shrug. "I can't complain." I cut my eyes to Aniston, who continues chewing her cheese stick, only not stringing it out so wide after biting into it.

We sit silent for a moment, then a waitress comes toward us with a box. That must be my steak dinner. "Dr. West, your order is ready."

I push back my chair to stand, but a hand grips mine. Either it's Aniston, or Morgan has wrapped around me to make sure I stay put. I drop my face and see that Aniston has my hand.

"You can eat with us. If you want, that is."

I lift my eyes to her and grin, then continue pulling out my chair. I meet the waitress and thank her. "And do you mind bringing me some silverware, and a sweet tea?"

She smiles. "Not at all."

"Thanks." When I turn toward the table, Aniston blushes.

I sit back in the hot seat and open my box. For once, Morgan doesn't say a word. Probably because I'm doing what she wanted all along, eating with them.

"Cheese stick?" Aniston offers.

I laugh. "I'm good." I tilt my box her way. "Steak?"

She shakes her head and grins. "I'm good."

She squeezes my knee under the table, and I almost choke. Why did I want to keep my mind off her again?

Now that I'm right where she wants me, Morgan backs off and focuses on her fries. We have a nice meal, with only half a dozen or so interruptions of her yelling behind us at Andrew. I wish she'd turn her head the other direction when she yells, but I guess that's a small price to pay for Aniston beside me.

The waitress brings their checks and I hand her a five to cover my tea. Brooke is the first to pay and leave, likely because she only has one child—the most well-behaved one. It takes Morgan a minute or so to gather her group. I sit with Carter and Willow while Aniston pays for their meals, then walk the three of them to their truck.

Both the kids get in, and Aniston stands with her door open. "Sorry about Morgan. I have no control over her."

"Nobody does, not even Morgan."

Aniston laughs. "I guess what I mean is I'm sorry we ruined your peaceful dinner."

I shake my head. "You didn't ruin it. I would've just ate in front of the TV and watched reruns of *The Office*."

"That sounds perfect." Aniston sighs.

"Maybe we can do that sometime."

She smiles shyly. Willow and Carter crane their heads to see me through the open door. Clearly snooping, but I don't mind.

"Unless you have a game next Saturday, you could be my date for this hospital benefit banquet thing I have to attend."

"Oh." Aniston gives me a playful grin, then holds up her finger. She turns to Willow. "Where is your game Saturday?"

"She'll go. I'll watch the kids." Morgan's voice is so close, it tickles the hairs on the back of my neck.

I turn to her staring at me with a toothpick between her teeth. She picks at the back of her teeth, then adds, "I'll be at the game anyway. Y'all go on, have a good time at the ball or dance or whatever it is."

Aniston lifts the corners of her mouth. "You don't mind?"

Morgan shakes her head. "On one condition. If a good-looking single man ever asks me out for a fancy, kid-free night, you have to take my kids."

"Deal." Aniston laughs.

I want to laugh too, but I'm not sure how Morgan will react. I never can tell when she's joking or serious.

"It's a date, then." I smile one last time at Aniston, then back away so she can get in the truck.

My face heats up when I notice everyone staring at us. The kids and Morgan, of course, but also Brooke, who I thought had left by now. She's giving me a thumbs-up. Mary is doing some kind of weird victory dance from the diner window. And is that Paul? He's holding a to-go box and clapping the top of it. When I make eye contact, he salutes me.

Yep, that's my cue to leave.

CHAPTER 14

Aniston

I stand in front of the dresser mirror, holding up two dresses. One is a black shift dress I wore to Jennifer's funeral. The other is the blue dress I peed on a few weeks back. Both have since been dry-cleaned, but the memories didn't wash away.

Groaning, I drop both dresses and throw myself face first into my mattress. I need a fairy godmother.

Either I groaned way louder than I thought, or my silent wish has been granted from above, because I hear Willow's sweet voice behind me.

"Aunt Ani, are you okay?"

I raise my head and twist toward the doorway. She's standing just inside my room with her arms crossed. "You made a panicky sound."

I laugh out a new noise that makes me sound a little psychotic. "At the risk of sounding cliché, I don't know what to wear."

Willow stares down at the two dresses wadded on the

floor. She picks them up by the hangers and examines each. "Both of these are really pretty."

"I know, but I don't like the black one because I wore it . . ." I stop. She knows when I wore it. No use saying it aloud.

Willow licks her lips and nods, then takes a deep breath. She definitely knows. "What about the blue one? It's really pretty on you."

Because I peed on it right before Easton tried to kiss me, then ran in the house. Then told him about it later.

"He's already seen me in it," is the excuse I give to Willow.

She wavers her head. "I get that." Her eyes scan the ceiling. She's either thinking of something or checking out the spiderweb I've been meaning to knock down.

Her eyes bug as she stares back at me. "I have the perfect dress."

I raise up to sitting. "You do?"

"Yes, come with me." Willow drapes the dresses across the bed and reaches her hand to me.

I take it and let her lead me downstairs. When we come to her parents' bedroom, I plant my feet like a dog outside the veterinarian's office.

Willow opens the door and tugs my hand. I stare into the empty room and refuse to budge.

"What's wrong?"

I pull my hand out of hers. "What's wrong?" I lift my arms and balk. "We can't go in there."

"Why not?" Willow wrinkles her brow.

"It's their room."

She bites her bottom lip. "It was their room, but they're not here anymore."

I blink back a tear and cross my arms in protest. "It's still not right."

Willow shakes her head, her own eyes tearing up. "This is our house. Mama would want you to go in here."

I close my eyes, sending a slow stream of tears down my face. "How do you know?"

"I just know. She always said if anything happened to her, she wanted us to go on and live full lives. She left you here with us, to take care of us. You can go in here. This is your room now."

I swallow hard and try to ignore the water pooling in my eyes. My next words come out in a whisper. "It doesn't bother you to go in there?"

Willow shakes her head slowly. "No, because I know they're in heaven. Sometimes I sneak in here when you're not around."

"Really?"

She nods, then drops her gaze as if embarrassed to admit it. "I just want to feel a part of her world again."

I throw my arms around Willow and sob into her small shoulder. She wraps her arms around me tightly and sighs. "Mama would want us to not be sad."

"I know," I squeak.

"I get sad too, but sometimes it's like I still feel her with me in our house, especially this room."

I pull back and wipe my face with the back of my hand. "And that doesn't bother you?"

She shrugs. "It kinda makes me happy knowing her memory is all over this place."

Willow glances back into the room, then smiles back at me. My jaw drops when I consider the contrast. Feeling them in this house keeps me up at night worrying. For her, it's a comfort. And maybe, just maybe, since I know it's a comfort to her, it can comfort me now too.

Willow takes my hand in hers and raises her eyebrows. This time I don't fight her when she pulls me into the room.

I expected to come in here one day, but not so soon. When I did, I anticipated it feeling dull, dark, and depressing.

Instead, it's peaceful.

The sun glistens through the thin blue curtains. Their antique bed is covered in a blue-and-yellow floral bedspread with matching throw pillows. Perfectly made, and I'm certain Jennifer was the last one to make it. She never left the house without making her bed.

A few dust particles dance in the sunlight from lack of life in this room. Otherwise, there's no other indication that it's been void of occupants for months.

Willow crosses the room and disappears into the walk-in closet. She returns with a lavender dress, my sister's favorite color.

I swallow the knot in my throat as I imagine Jennifer wearing it someplace with Luke. A wedding, business trip, fancy dinner. I picture her laughing and dancing, the pastel color complementing her eyes.

Then I cock my head and consider Jennifer was a good several inches shorter than me, and with more curves. "Willow, are you sure this will fit me?"

She grins. "If it's meant to be, it will fit."

I'm a little freaked out by her wise words. If this were a movie, she'd so be the older weird person who comes out of nowhere to fix up the struggling main character. But in the real world, I guess beggars for fairy godmothers can't be choosers.

I take the dress from her. "Only one way to find out, I guess."

Willow smiles as I go into the adjoined master bathroom and shut the door. I slip off my shorts and tank top and try on the dress. To my utter shock, it fits.

I turn around and peek over my shoulder into the full-length mirror on the door. Maybe my extra height but lack of booty in comparison to my sister evened out the length. Who knows?

"Is it on?" Willow calls from outside the door.

I open it to find her right in front of me, bouncing on her

toes. "What do ya think?" I do a slow turn like a department store model.

Willow's smile covers her whole face. "You look amazing! Mama would love this."

I clear my throat to beat back tears. Willow passes me and opens a closet door. "She has all kinds of jewelry too."

A large jewelry box about four feet tall is shoved behind a shelf of scarves and purses. Jennifer was quite the fashionista. I never cared too much about clothes and jewelry. I was too busy trying to not fit in when I was younger to care. Then the older I got, the more I considered the practicality of traveling with minimal belongings—wardrobe included.

Willow squats and opens a side door on the box. Numerous necklaces hang from small hooks. She unravels a silver chain with shiny purple stones and hands it to me. "Put this on. I'll find the matching earrings."

I do as my fairy godmother commands, while she rummages through the top drawers. A few minutes later, she hands me some purple stone earrings set in silver. They hang about an inch and dangle delicately from my ears.

"Perfect." Willow beams as we stare into the mirror at my reflection. "Oh, and she has all kinds of hair and makeup stuff if you need it."

"Great." Strange how I've transitioned from mournful to excited. The combination of Willow's joy and my desperation for a makeover must be why.

"There's some good shampoo in here too."

I stop moving lipstick around in a drawer and shoot Willow a look. "What does that mean?"

She blushes. "Nothing. I'll let you get ready." She bows out, leaving me in the middle of the bathroom.

I pull the hair tie out of my messy bun and run my fingers through the fallen tangles. She does have a point. A good shower couldn't hurt. I need to shave my legs anyway.

After carefully hanging the dress on the bathroom door, I

tiptoe to the bedroom door and shut it. Just in case Carter decides to wander in out of curiosity. Kids are a lot like cats. They meander in any opening just because they can.

Then I shut and lock the bathroom door behind me before shedding my underwear. I find a towel and scan the selection of bath products. There's also a small shelf dedicated to facial creams. That might come in handy.

Hmm . . . I catch a glimpse of my face close up in a makeup mirror. I have peach fuzz? I wipe the side of my jaw and scrunch my nose.

I've never zoomed in on my own face this close. But Easton has when he kissed me. Ugh, what if he felt it on my face? Gross. I need to do something about this.

I grab the most highfalutin facial cream I can find. "Apply gently. Leave on five to ten minutes, then wash off." I read a few more lines, then decide to put it on before hopping into the shower.

My plan is in place by the time the water warms. I'll shower and let the facial stuff set while I shave and shampoo. Once I'm done with all that, I can turn around and rinse my face. All the nasty little hairs will fall down the drain, and I can forget about having a face like a pubescent boy.

The steam engulfs me when I step into the hot shower and close the door. I've always been a fan of super-hot showers.

Halfway into shaving my legs, my face itches. Not like a tickle, but more like the sensation of falling headfirst into an ant bed. The bottle said itching is to be expected. Oh well. The price to pay for beauty, huh?

I finish my shower, then turn around and let the water hit my face. I seethe as the hot stream beads on my steamy face. The only other time my skin stung this badly was when we got caught on four-wheelers in a rainstorm.

As soon as my face is free of cream, I cut the water and start to wring out my hair. Then I turn it back on and wash my hands thoroughly to remove any remaining cream. Just in case, I wipe my hands down my face to check if it all rinsed away.

I've heard horror stories on the internet about people pranking others with Nair in a shampoo bottle. That's not the hair I want rid of.

Once I'm certain the hair on my head is safe, I wrap a towel around it and step out of the shower. I grab some of Jennifer's expensive body lotion and hum as I apply it to my arms and legs.

When the fog fades from the big mirror, I catch my reflection and squint my eyes for a better look. The fog doesn't clear as quickly as I want, and panic sets in as a red circle stares back at me. I rip the towel from my head and wipe down the mirror.

Holy moly! I look like a prize-winning tomato.

Aniston

By the time Morgan arrives to pick up the kids, my face is covered with multiple layers of Jennifer's best concealer. I could easily pass for a lady of the night. Even worse, the redness is still shining through. So maybe a lady of the night who spent too much of her day out in the sun.

The only upside is no peach fuzz whatsoever remains on my face.

"Aniston, I'm here." Her voice echoes down the hallway.

I'm in front of the unforgiving magnifying makeup mirror, trying to even out the makeup over my cheeks. All I've accomplished is making my face resemble red clay.

In between cursing myself—and the mirror—I hear footsteps across the hardwood floor. I freeze for a moment. *Please don't be Carter. I'm not ready to explain what some of those words mean.*

Instead, it's Morgan. "I can get go ahead and get the kids if you want."

I lift my head and face the bathroom doorway. Morgan's eyebrows almost meet her hairline when she sees my face. It's obviously as bad as I thought.

"Whoa, tiger. Easy on the bronzer." She blinks as if resetting her face before she comes in the bathroom.

I sigh and shove the mirror to the back of the counter. "I give up." I drop my head in my hands, not caring if I smudge my face. What's it matter at this point?

Morgan pats my shoulder. "It's fine. I'm not the best with makeup either."

I shake my head before lifting it. "It's not that. I used this skin cream, it made me all red, and I tried to cover it up. But that didn't work so I kept trying to cover it up."

"I see that." Morgan frowns into the big mirror in front of us.

I throw up my hands. "I can't go to a doctor banquet looking like this."

Morgan taps her finger on her lip, then her eyes widen like a light bulb is going off in her head. She snaps her fingers. "I got it."

"What?"

She pulls me from the vanity chair. "You need professional help."

I laugh. "Well, I'm sure of that, but right now I need a makeover."

"Exactly."

Without saying another word, Morgan pulls me out of the bathroom wearing my ratty shirt and shorts, with my hair and face done up like a Broadway star. One who apparently wants the people in the very back to see every detail of her makeup.

She only slows down long enough for me to slip on my flip-flops as she piles the kids in her van. I sit in the front and try not to think of where she might be taking me. Wherever it is, my look isn't appropriate. I'm party on the bottom and business on the top. It's the kind of business I look like that worries me.

Morgan texts something on her phone after we turn on the main road.

"Morgan, do you think that's safe?"

She drops her phone in her lap and ignores me. Willow sits in the seat behind me, holding my dress and shoes. I take that as a sign we're not coming back to the house.

Morgan picks up her phone and texts something else. I brace myself in case I need to take the wheel, or in case Jesus decides to take it and we all crash into eternity.

We peel into the parking lot beside Cut and Dry Salon. There's a "Closed" sign on the door, but one car in the parking lot. Morgan cuts the engine and makes everyone get out. I follow the group to a side door, where Morgan knocks three times loudly.

It opens, and Adrianne Reynolds, the owner, sticks her head out. "Come in."

Adrianne's sister is married to Morgan's brother. That may not make them sisters-in-law, but they're something like that.

In Apple Cart, everyone is related. And if you're not related to someone, give it about a decade or two and you will be. In a town this small with a lot of big families, it's inevitable.

Once the last kid is through the door, Adrianne locks it behind us. A weird rush comes over me like I've entered a last-century speakeasy.

Adrianne leads us to a station in the back and puffs out her cheeks. "Y'all can't let anyone know I was here."

I scrunch my nose. "I thought this was your salon."

"It is, but I'm only open one Saturday a month, and this isn't it. When I started closing on Saturdays, a lot of the older women got mad. They had to move their standing weekly appointments to other days."

I shrug. "Okay, you weren't here." I cock my head toward Morgan, who's sitting at the station beside us, rocking back and forth. "But why are we here?"

Morgan steeples her fingers and grins mischievously. "If anyone can fix whatever you've got going on . . ." She purses her lips and swirls her finger in the direction of my face before finishing her thought. "It's Adrianne."

"Thanks." Adrianne beams. She pats the seat in front of her, and I sit.

She spins me toward the mirror and leans forward, twisting her lips. "Hmm, allergic reaction to your makeup?"

"Nope. High-dollar hair remover gone bad."

"Ouch." Adrianne wrinkles her nose and bends her head around to examine my face closer. "How's it feel now?"

"Uh, a little hot, but not as tender." Or maybe its numb from me rubbing so much concealer on it.

Adrianne opens a drawer under the large mirror and pulls out a black leather bag. She unzips the top. Clanking noises fill the otherwise quiet room while she rummages through the contents.

The boys have disappeared into the parking lot with an empty Coke bottle they declared would work as a football. Morgan's youngest daughter sits with her legs crossed and thumbs through a style magazine unlike a normal ten-year-old girl. At least what I assume a normal one acts like. That leaves Morgan, Isabella, and Willow staring in silence at Adrianne and me. I bet they're pondering how she'll pull this off, too.

Adrianne pulls out a few bottles from her bag, a brush, and a sponge. Then she grabs a pack of makeup wipes from the counter and tosses them in my lap. "First we need to undo the damage that's been done."

I stare at the pack of wipes like it's a ticking time bomb.

"Don't worry. These are hypoallergenic and nontoxic. Not cheap Walmart or DG wipes. They shouldn't hurt."

I glance up and lift the corners of my mouth. It's as if she read my mind. "Thanks."

After four—maybe five—wipes, every layer of makeup is gone. All that's left is my fire-engine-red face.

"Whoa, girl. That had to hurt!" Adrianne's eyes bug as she gently runs a manicured finger across my forehead. "Did you leave it on too long?"

"I don't think so. I only had it on while I jumped in the shower. Maybe five minutes?"

"The shower?" She chews on the end of her nail.

"Yeah."

"Was it hot in there?"

"Well yeah, steamy."

She shakes her head and grins. "Ah, you steamed your face."

"Steamed my face?"

"Yeah. Sometimes chemicals in highly effective creams react to different temperatures."

I cup my hands around my cheeks and moan. "I have a big date like . . ." I turn and check the clock on the wall. "Soon, very soon."

"Girl, I got you." Adrianne starts shaking one of the bottles she pulled from the bag.

Maybe if she shakes it enough, a magic genie will pop out and fix my face.

A magic genie doesn't come out, but some form of skin-colored liquid does. Skin colored as in the color my skin should be.

She dabs a few dots on a sponge and pushes my hair off my forehead with her free hand. Then she gently brushes the sponge across my forehead, cheeks, and the rest of my face.

"That feels—"

"Normal?" Adrianne leans back and cocks a grin.

"Yeah."

She dabs a little more on the sponge and completes my foundation, then moves back so I can see. "It's not cakey, and only one coat will do you."

"Wow." I tilt my chin up and then to the side, examining her work.

"Now relax, and I'll finish you up."

I rest my shoulders against the back of the chair and close my eyes. Adrianne moves from one part of my face to the next, outlining my eyes, brushing my cheeks, glossing my lips. Then she steps back and smiles into the mirror. Morgan and the girls stop chatting and stare too. I open my eyes and blink to make sure I'm not dreaming.

I look good. Real good. "You're my fairy godmother." I just thought it was Willow.

Adrianne props a hand on her hip and smiles even wider. "You're welcome." She runs a hand over my hair. "Let me touch this up some too."

"If you're offering." I wiggle in the chair, then settle in while she recurls some of my strands and pulls my hair up on one side.

In high school, she was a majorette and always had that pageant-perfect appearance. A decade ago I gave her eye rolls; now I'd give her my kidney if she asked.

Morgan stands as Adrianne drapes a few locks of my hair over one shoulder. "See, Aniston? I told you she could fix you."

I suck in air, then breathe it out slowly. What are the odds Morgan also has someone who can fix my school-mom problems? Eh, one miracle a day is more than enough for me to expect.

Willow stands and holds out the dress and shoes. "Cinderella."

"Thank you, my dear." I take them.

Morgan leads me toward a door, opens it, and gestures wildly. I smirk and go into the single-stall bathroom.

I shut the door and shake off my ratty shoes and shorts, then slip on the dress. Once I zip it, I smooth out the skirt and check my appearance in the mirror above the toilet.

Not bad. Not bad at all.

When I open the door, four heads turn and four mouths drop. I put one foot in front of the other and walk to the center of the salon. Even Sophia puts down her magazine in favor of my fashion.

"Think he'll like it?" I crinkle my top lip.

All of them start jabbering with excitement, then Morgan rushes toward me. "He called while you were changing. I answered your phone and told him to just pick you up here." She waves a hand dismissively, as if she didn't just answer my phone and ask him to walk into a scene straight out of *Steel Magnolias*. "No need to thank me."

I lift my chin. "Don't worry, I wasn't."

CHAPTER 15

Easton

Picking up my date at the hair salon makes me feel like a teenager going to prom. Though Aniston didn't need to go through such trouble, I'm flattered she put this much into getting ready for me. Or is it because the invitation stated formal attire, to an event with the word "ball" in it?

I'll pretend it's because of me.

My daydreaming of Aniston is halted when I slam on my brakes in front of the salon. Morgan's youngest kid stands in the road, arms high in anticipation of catching a football.

The football turns out to be a twenty-liter bottle, which he doesn't catch. He pouts. However, if he knew how close I was to flattening him, he wouldn't be pouting. I park at the front of the lot and get out.

"Andrew?"

He twists his head toward me, not saying a word.

"Son, you shouldn't be in the road. I could've run over you." *Son?* When did I become my dad?

His eyebrows squish together, then he nods. Maybe he's weirded out that I called him "son" like a sixty-year-old man who's annoyed someone walked through his tomato plants. I'm a little weirded out by it too.

Morgan answered Aniston's phone when I called to check if she was ready. She gave me specific instructions to go to the side door and knock three times.

I decide to have some fun with this to get her back for being so bossy. The side door is heavy metal, so I beat on it loudly. "Morgan!" Then I repeat my welcome two more times, Sheldon Cooper style.

About the time I'm saying her name just under a yell, the door bursts open. "You rang?" Morgan answers through clinched teeth.

"Just knocking three times like I was told." I smirk.

She comes back with something sassy, but I don't pay enough attention to hear the words. My eyes have found Aniston, who sits in a dryer chair beside Willow. She notices me too, then stands.

A few weeks ago, she wore this blue dress that drove me crazy. Every time I spot that shade of blue, Aniston in that dress pops into my head. It has become my new favorite color. Until now, as my new favorite color is the purple of her current dress.

Is there any color that this woman won't make my favorite? Probably not.

We walk toward one another and meet in the middle of the room. "You look gorgeous," I tell her.

Audible "awwws" fill the room, and my face warms at the realization of an audience. Aniston smiles at me, and I take her hand. Without saying anything more, I lead her to the front door.

It won't open. I start to unlock it, and Adrianne and Morgan simultaneously scream, "No!"

I turn around and frown. "What?"

"I don't want people to think I'm open today," Adrianne whisper-yells. Like she didn't just scream loud enough for everyone across the street in the General Store to hear. Or maybe all the way to the Pig.

I drop my hand from the door and lead Aniston to the side door. Carter breaks from the mob of boys and jogs toward us.

"Are y'all leaving?"

"Yeah." Aniston rustles his hair. He reaches out and hugs her.

When they break away, he sticks his hand toward my waist. I stare at him a moment before realizing he's offering to shake my hand. I give him a firm shake as he says, "Take care of her, Dr. Easton."

"Yes, sir." I cut my eyes toward Aniston, who presses her lips tightly. I'm certain she's doing her best to hold back any amused or admiring sound.

Yep. As soon as we're in my truck, she puts her hands on her cheeks and gushes, "That was so sweet of him!"

I laugh. He will be a great man one day. "If only Morgan could've acted so maturely."

Aniston rolls her eyes. "Ha. Not a chance."

I admire her delicate features before focusing on the road and backing out of the parking lot. The lowering sun shines on her golden hair and highlights her profile. It takes more strength than I want to keep my eyes on the road and drive toward the interstate.

If I weren't expected to speak at this event, I'd drive us back to my place for a quiet evening by the pond.

But it will be a pleasant change to have someone like Aniston on my arm, in particular someone who *is* Aniston. I'll save the pond date for later. She's too fancy to smell like fish guts and bug spray tonight.

Riding with her makes me wish even more that we didn't have to go to an event. This is the longest time we've been alone, and I'm enjoying the small talk. We alternate between usual talk about work, school, the kids, and everyone else in Apple Cart and asking one another questions. Nothing life changing, but common questions of curiosity.

"Your turn," Aniston demands after sharing that she eats just about anything. She'd asked my favorite food, which is steak, so now it's my turn to come up with a question.

"Uh, your favorite color?"

"Yellow."

I nod. "That's cheery."

"It's in a lot of nature. People think of blues and greens with nature, but yellow is underrated. It's in a lot of leaves and sands and mountains. It's also in the sky whenever the sun reflects on clouds."

"Very true." I'd never given it much thought.

"And yours?"

I open my mouth to spout out "red," my preference for most non-neutral color items. Before the word leaves my mouth, I glance at Aniston with the sun shimmering across her face and shoulders as it peeks through the trees into the window.

"Whatever color you're wearing."

She tilts her head toward me and lifts the corners of her mouth. I lift my own lips into a slight grin before turning back to the road. That came out way cheesier than I had planned. Especially since I didn't plan on it coming out at all.

What's wrong with red?

Nothing's wrong with red, except that Aniston isn't wearing red today. She's wearing purple. If her dress were turkey-turd brown, that would be my new favorite color.

We sit in silence for a moment, with me wondering if my answer flattered her or she gave me a grin out of pity. When I can't take the silence any longer, I say, "Your turn."

"What am I tonight?"

I laugh and run a hand over my hair. Luckily, it's too short to mess up. "What are you?"

"Yeah, like to you?"

I scratch the side of my neck. With the heat rising up my chest, my tie may as well be a boa constrictor. How did we go from favorite food and color to a question like this?

I'd much prefer it if she answered first, since my answer will be based on her opinion. What I want us to be and what she thinks we should be might not align.

After giving it way too much thought, I notice Aniston staring at me. She nods, as if encouraging me to answer.

"Tell them whatever makes you comfortable. You can be my neighbor, my friend, my hay-baling client . . . or my date."

The last part comes out in almost a whisper. I don't want to pressure her into claiming me in front of hundreds of strangers if she's not ready for that. Although I'd be honored.

The heat in my neck has now risen to my face. I flip my air vent so it's blowing directly on me. I'm so lost in my anxious mind that it catches me off guard when Aniston finally says something.

"I don't usually go through this much trouble to get ready for something that isn't a date."

My lips curve into a slight smile, but I force myself to keep my eyes on the road. We're now in Tuscaloosa traffic, and I don't care for her to see my blushing face.

Aniston places a hand above my knee and leaves it there. I drop one hand from the wheel and wrap it around hers.

So it's settled. We're on an actual date—alone.

Aniston

I've never cared much for traditional sports, only outdoor-adventure-type activities like kayaking, skydiving, and mountain climbing. However, it's impossible to grow up within a hundred miles of Tuscaloosa, Alabama, and not get immersed in football culture.

From Jennifer cheering for the Apple Cart Armadillos to my dad watching every Bama game on Saturday, I'm fully aware that football is a big deal to most people. We all know the sport brings in bank, which is why The University is more than happy to offer top-notch sports facilities.

That's why when Easton parks near Bryant-Denny Stadium, I have a suspicion this "ball" cost a pretty penny.

We lock up the truck and go to a part of the stadium I've never seen in person—The Zone. This is where Nick Saban's daughter supposedly had her wedding reception.

Tonight's event might not top that, but it's clear they spared no expense, from the tux-tailed waitstaff to rows of buffet tables.

"So this is a ball?"

"Apparently," Easton answers as he runs a finger under his collar.

"Wait, you've been to one before, right?"

He shakes his head. "I go to things like this only when I have to. I try and avoid fancy events."

"Then why come to this one?"

"I have to talk."

I raise one brow and scan the vast room filled with fancy folks before turning back to Easton. "Well, how special."

His face reddens, but not nearly as much as mine beneath my makeup mask. "I didn't want to do it, but some people talked me into it."

"Some people?"

"Other doctors and stuff, you know."

I lift my chin in a half-nod, even though I don't know. He's the only doctor I know on a first-name basis. Unless you count weird old Bessy McCain, who is a self-proclaimed holistic doctor. People would call her to cure their warts. She'd pray over their warts, and they'd shrivel up in a few days.

I didn't believe it until I witnessed it happen to Kyle Tolbert's hands in third grade.

Bessy lives in Wisteria and mostly keeps to herself. She lives off her own land as much as possible and never wears shoes. One time as a kid, I spotted her in Piggly Wiggly when they had a huge meat sale. Her hair stood on end, and she was barefoot. She was buying up a bunch of bacon, complaining that someone had killed her wild hogs.

I was scared of her until middle school. Then some of us decided to roll her yard. She met us with a shotgun, solidifying my terror of her to this day.

"You all right?"

"Hmm?" I face Easton.

"You're awfully quiet."

"Yeah, I'm just thinking."

"About what?"

"This crazy old woman who never wears shoes and tried to shoot us once."

"What?" Easton laughs, and I realize how insane that sounds.

"Nothing, my mind wanders."

"I'll say. Want to go ahead and get some dinner before everything starts?"

"Sure."

I follow Easton through the buffet lines. There's so much food, it's like the elaborate version of a church potluck. Instead of chicken and dumplings and a million green bean casseroles, they have scallops and steak.

We fill our plates and find a seat at a small table near the corner. Glasses of water and silverware are already placed on the table.

I unfold the cloth napkin and lay it across my lap. My eyes land on the feet of a group standing nearby. All of their shoes combined must cost a fortune. I suddenly feel like Bessy barefoot in the Pig with my Belk's sale-rack stilettos.

There's probably more money in this room than in all of Apple Cart County combined, even counting the bank.

"Have you been here before?" I ask Easton in between bites of some of the best food I've ever eaten.

And that's saying something. Although my wardrobe consists of mostly lounging and outdoor attire, I've eaten some top-notch meals. One of the many perks to traveling for several years straight.

"Once. There was a celebration-type thing for the med school. The room seemed bigger, but there weren't as many people then."

"What's the deal tonight?"

"A medical organization I belong to is working with the Nick's Kids Foundation."

"Oh, that's nice."

Easton nods with a mouthful of steak. "I suspect half the people in this room came hoping for a Saban spotting."

I roll my eyes. "That's the problem with Alabama. We don't have real celebrities."

"Are you saying Saban's not a real celebrity?" Easton smirks and his words come out sarcastically. Still, he said them loud enough to turn a few heads.

This town takes Saban seriously. Very seriously.

We exchange a glance, then laugh and go back to eating. I'm fully aware of a few older, overly dressed people giving us the stink eye.

Somehow I manage to tune out the thousand or so people mingling around, along with the instrumental music and clatter of silverware against porcelain plates. Easton and I are in our own little world, holding down the corner table for two.

Of course, all good things must come to an end. As I'm basking in my fairy tale, a lady in feathers and puffy sleeves comes and taps Easton on the shoulder. Either she's really into bringing back the early nineties, or she thought this was a costume party.

Then again, I guess once you reach a certain level of wealth, you can wear whatever the heck you want. Or you can be like Bessy and do it anyway.

"Easton, it's time." Her words come out in a songlike rhythm.

Maybe she's here as entertainment? I've heard rich people are into odd entertainment. Aside from football, of course. I stab a bite of pork with my fork as Easton excuses himself and follows the feathered woman. Good ole football and barbecue—the great social equalizers of the South.

They disappear into the crowd, so I can no longer locate the feathers. I finish my water and take this opportunity to go to the restroom.

When I exit the stall, a horde of half-a-dozen women stand shoulder to shoulder checking their appearance in the mirror. I slide in when one leaves to wash my hands. A quick glance assures me Adrianne's voodoo magic is still working. She wouldn't allow me to pay her for the help, so I need to review her on Yelp or something.

On my way back into the mob, a butler—or waiter dressed like a butler—offers me a glass of sparkling champagne. It's been a while since I've had something stronger than cookie crack, so I take it.

A few sips can't hurt. Plus, I just visited the restroom, which should alleviate the wardrobe malfunction that happened the last time I went out with Easton.

I'm sipping my champagne, elbowing my way through the crowd, when a large man backs up from the buffet table with a plate full of crab legs. He loses his balance and fumbles around to juggle the plate and keep all the crab legs intact.

While he's successful at saving his food, he bumps into me. Champagne sloshes my face. I rush to a nearby table and set the glass on it. The only napkin I see is one folded across a woman's lap. I snatch it and march off, blotting my face and neck before the liquid falls to the dress.

The woman spouts off something behind me, but I don't care at this point. I cannot soil another dress.

As I'm retreating toward our table in the corner, someone speaks into a microphone, greeting the crowd.

Everyone around me stands still and turns toward the center of the room, so I do the same. The man says some sort of corny joke I don't get, then mentions Saban. People cheer, clap, and go a little wild. Who knew such a tightly buttoned group could get so rowdy?

The announcer mentions Easton and congratulates him on all his help with a charity. He had mentioned speaking tonight, but I didn't understand the magnitude of his role until now.

Easton blushes a bit as he gets the microphone and thanks everyone, then highlights some of the efforts he's helped with when it comes to the medical field. "And I'd like to thank my date, Aniston, for joining me."

I shrink my shoulders in as all eyes turn on me. Thank goodness, I dried the champagne from my face. However, the woman whose napkin I stole now knows my name. Just great.

A few people whisper, then turn back to those being awarded. The announcer mentions other people standing near Easton, and one by one, they speak.

I'm content lingering until Easton is released from this ceremony portion. That is, until I hear one woman whisper to another, "It's so sweet of Dr. West to bring a woman with a skin disease."

Skin disease? What the flip is she talking about?

Easton is lined up with the other participants, holding a

plaque. While he's still occupied, I decide to check on what might make a woman decide I have a skin disease.

Maybe the lady whose napkin I snatched started a rumor?

I make a beeline back to the restroom, which is now vacant. I assume the rush earlier was due to everyone checking makeup in case Saban showed up.

That's when I get a glimpse of my appearance. Ugh. That champagne all but melted my makeup. Now my face is dotted with red splotches peeking through Adrianne's makeover perfection.

Perfect. I could pass for a circus performer.

I close my eyes and sigh. I could deal with hiding a pee stain on the back of my dress, but how the heck do I hide my face?

When I open my eyes, I spot the reflection of a fan on the side wall. Not a ceiling fan, but one of those foldout fans used in Asian dancing.

A light bulb figuratively sparks above my head and I pull the fan from the wall. It's a decorative piece beside some fancy frames. And it was well attached. A piece of drywall trickles down and hits the floor. Oops. The fan is stiff and doesn't fold in like an accordion, which is fine since I need it open.

I face the mirror and hold it in front of the lower half of my face. Perfect.

Okay . . . so nothing in this scenario is perfect. However, it does cover up all the red splotches on my cheeks, chin, and nose.

I leave the restroom with my new shield conveniently placed just under my eyes, where all the damage is. As I weave through the crowd, I fan a time or two to try and act natural. Why else would I have a giant Crimson fan in front of my face?

The crowd has scattered, leaving only Easton and the others in the center. A photographer snaps photos of them with their plaques. I hang back near a column and wait for the photographer to finish.

When they break, Easton cranes his neck and scans the room. I lift my arm and wave when he faces my direction. He narrows his eyes, then smiles and comes toward me.

"Hey, I'm done with all my duties now."

"Great." My response comes out muffled behind the giant fan.

Easton frowns. "Why are you holding a fan in front of your face?" His eyes bug, and he places his hand on my forehead. "Are you overheating again?"

I giggle behind my makeshift shield. "No. I had an accident."

"You peed again?" he whispers.

A nervous laugh bursts out of me, and I shake my head behind the fan.

He lifts his eyebrows. "What happened?"

I sigh. "It's a long story. The CliffsNotes version is I had a reaction to skin cream, ended up at Adrianne's for help covering it up, then someone bumped into me and got champagne on my face, making it worse again."

I lower the fan slower than molasses running out of a Mason jar. Once it's below my chin, I stare at Easton, anticipating his reaction.

Nothing.

"See what I mean?"

He shrugs. "Your face is red, so what?"

I balk. "Adrianne and Morgan worked all afternoon to cover it up." I glance around, then lower my voice. "While you were getting the award, I heard one woman say how sweet it was for Dr. West to bring a date with a skin disease." I raise my voice again. "Skin disease!"

Several people turn our direction, which makes me actually blush. I lift the fan again, not wanting to imagine how red I am at this moment.

Easton crosses his arms over his chest and around his plaque. "Aniston, this is crazy. You're beautiful."

"Maybe before the splotches," I comment sarcastically. "You won an award from Nick Saban. You don't want to be seen with me."

Easton sets his plaque on the nearest table and snatches the fan from me. Before I can protest, he sets it down too. Then he reaches for my face and pulls it into his.

He holds my head a few inches from his. "You're always beautiful. At the salon, when I first saw you at your door, and now."

I blink up at him as he pulls me an inch closer.

"Do your lips hurt?"

"No, why?"

I barely get the word "why" out before his lips are on mine. His hands leave my face, and he cradles my head with one. The other wraps around my shoulder and brings me closer to him.

He kisses me like we're the only two in the room. After a few seconds, it starts to feel that way. The voices and music surrounding us fades, and if it weren't for my uncomfortable shoes, I'd forget where we were.

His lips and hands send shivers through my nerves until my entire body is tingling. As I'm deciding whether I should bake the man a pan of cookie crack or ask him to marry me—maybe both—he pulls back.

My lips sting. Not from the face-product trauma, as my lips and eyelids were the only parts of my face not affected. They sting from Easton withdrawals.

"Let's get out of here," he whispers. He picks his plaque up and takes my hand.

When we start through the crowd, my self-consciousness gets the best of me, and I snatch the plaque from him. I hold it up to my face.

He jerks it down. "Seriously?"

We're almost to the door when I answer, "Those people were staring at us. It's my face."

He laughs. "They're staring because we just made out like two teenagers at prom."

I grin and giggle, also like a teenager at prom.

Easton leads me out of the building and down the steps. "How about we go get ice cream on the way home, and you can tell me the full story."

I start to decline, not wanting to spill my guts on yet another embarrassment. Do I really want Easton to know this all started because I wanted to remove facial hair? Then again, I did confess to peeing on myself the last time we went out.

"Sounds great." I smile as we get in his truck.

There's no holding back now. Either this man will embrace my crazy and love me in spite of it, or cut and run for the hills.

CHAPTER 16

Easton

I find myself whistling on the way to church. Although I'm happy to spend the morning in a place of worship, that's not the reason for my extra-cheerful mood.

It's Aniston.

Last night went better than I could've hoped. I'm not the type to kiss someone in public, especially a kiss like that. But when I found out why she had that stupid fan in front of her face, I had to prove I found her just as beautiful as ever.

While we shared a bucket of Bluebell, she relayed in detail the events leading up to her hiding behind the fan. I choked a few times from laughing so hard. Then I got a little nerdy, explaining that everyone has some facial hair, except for people with a condition called alopecia universalis. After Aniston zoned out a bit, I kissed her again.

That woke her up, and she seemed to enjoy my chocolate-flavored kiss.

We talked and laughed as long as we could before it was

time to get back to the kids. Probably for the best, as I didn't need the temptation of a whole night alone with Aniston.

I take a huge breath and park my truck. Not what I should have on my mind as I pull into church, but I'm only human.

At this stage in my life, I'm just happy to think long term about a woman. The last few years have been a revolving door of blind dates and setups in between women showing up at my door with a covered dish or faking an illness to see me in the clinic.

Worst of all, I'm sure most of them only want to date a doctor. It might help a little that I'm still youngish and not overweight. But for the most part, it has nothing to do with me as a person.

Aniston is more impressed by me fixing the side mirror on her truck or taking Carter fishing. That's the kind of woman I want to date.

I nod and greet several people on my way to the porch steps. Morgan should already be taking her place in the choir, so I don't have to worry about an interrogation.

When I dropped Aniston off last night, Morgan was pulling up with the kids. She sat in the van and stared at us until we decided to walk in the house together and shut the door. I kissed Aniston good night in the hallway, away from the windows.

So I'm certain she got the third degree from Morgan after I left.

Thanks to people like Morgan, the main thing I miss about Tuscaloosa is privacy. Aside from upscale restaurants and movie theaters, of course. I guess there's not enough going on in Apple Cart for people to focus solely on their own lives. Although, the nosiness does die down some once football season gets into full swing.

I sit in a pew near the middle as usual, and Morgan catches my eye from the choir. She makes a contorted face, which lets me know she's trying to communicate something.

I reach for a bulletin left on the pew from first service and study that in favor of ignoring Morgan. It's actually from two weeks prior, according to the date, but still a nice distraction.

Apparently, I missed the monthly fish fry—again.

"Excuse me, is anyone sitting here?" I turn to a woman's voice.

"No, ma'am." I slide to the end of the pew so her family can spread out.

I'm now sandwiched between a family of five and an older couple. By the time I've scanned the back of the old bulletin, the preacher has finished his welcome.

The piano player strikes the first few keys, and everyone stands to sing. I abandon my bulletin and stand with the rest of the congregation. Morgan smirks at me a few times, so I drop my gaze.

From the corner of my eye, I watch the family to my left. The kids are older than Carter and Willow, most likely teenagers. My mind wanders to years down the road, sitting in church with Aniston and her kids.

Of course, we're a long way from that, as I haven't even gotten her to go to church with me.

When the last song ends, everyone in the choir retreats to the pews. I sit and study the older couple on my right. The man reaches for the woman's hand, and she takes it. They have to be at least mid-seventies. That's a great goal to have.

Not until the man pushes his glasses up the bridge of his nose and stares back at me do I realize I've looked too long. I open my Bible and try to focus on what the preacher is saying rather than dreaming up life stages with Aniston.

I spend the next hour drifting between listening to the sermon and daydreaming. When church lets out, I'm one of the first to make it out the door. Not because I want to avoid Morgan and other nosy people—though that is an added bonus. All these families and couples have made me want to spend time with Aniston and the kids.

I call Big Butts on my way to the truck and order enough barbecue and wings for four, along with some fixings. Maybe they haven't had lunch yet. If they have, then I'll have my lunch covered for the next few days.

Several people stand in front of the food trailer when I park to pick up lunch. During the week, a bunch of city workers crowd the large picnic table nearby. Today it's filled with people waiting on to-go orders.

As I climb out of my truck, Billy Bob pokes his head through the window and calls out a name. A man in khakis stands from the table and collects his order.

"Hey, Doc," Bradley greets me from beside the trailer. His sheriff's badge catches the sunlight and almost blinds me.

"Hey, Bradley. How have you been?"

Bradley bites off a rib and chews it slowly before answering. "Can't complain. Where's your new friend?"

I don't even have to ask who he's referring to. In four words, Bradley proved my theory that news of Aniston and me has traveled through town. Billy Bob saves me from an interrogation by yelling my name.

"That's my order. Good talking to you, Bradley."

"Yeah," he mutters around a mouthful of rib. His eyes narrow as I exchange money for my food.

Without saying another word, I get in my truck and drive home. No doubt keeping quiet will fuel just as many rumors as having answered him.

During my time in Apple Cart, I've learned that if someone doesn't know something, they'll just fill in the blanks—with whatever they see fit.

Random scenarios play in my mind on my drive home. By the time I turn into the drive leading to my house and Aniston's, I'm prepared for any random old person to come by the clinic tomorrow and congratulate me on my engagement. Or even marriage, depending on which old person it is.

Maybe I should cut to the chase and propose right now over a plate of pulled pork?

I stop in Aniston's driveway and glance at the food bags on my passenger seat. Nah. I'm no super romantic, but the last thing I want is to become another cliché Apple Cart proposal story.

Over the past year, I've heard my fair share of them. Everything from hiding an egg in a chicken coop to plowing "Will You Marry Me?" in a corn field. My favorite is the spray-painted water tower. Not for the lack of creativity, but because the guy was drunk when he climbed the tower . . . and the girl said "no."

I climb out of the truck and gather the bags. Voices come from the backyard, so I walk that way instead of the front. Willow floats in the pool as Carter bobs to the top with a pair of goggles covering most of his face.

He lifts a ring high for Willow to see, then spots me. "Hey, Dr. Easton."

I nod since my hands are tied up with food. "Hey, y'all eaten lunch yet?"

He shrugs. "We slept late and ate cereal."

"No, sir," Willow answers.

"Want some barbecue?"

"Always." Carter grins. He climbs out the side, and Willow swims to the ladder.

After drying off, Willow takes one of the bags from me, and Carter opens the door. We enter through the back and set everything on the kitchen counter.

I suck in the cool air. "Is your aunt here?"

"She's in her room," Willow answers.

"Oh." I'm deciding whether to ask one of them to get her or let her be for now when Willow interrupts me.

"You can go get her."

"Okay." I clear my throat and start walking, then stop when I reach the hallway. "Which room is hers?"

"Upstairs. The last door on the right," Willow instructs.

"Thanks." I take my time going upstairs. Even though they told me to, I'd hate for a rumor to start about this.

I can hear the gossip train now. *Easton was upstairs alone with Aniston. In her own house, while the kids were there. Heard he bribed them with pulled pork.*

I stop at the top of the stairs and run a hand through my hair. Maybe this is a bad idea.

Her door is open. I take that as a metaphorical sign to go in. After knocking, of course.

I knock on the side of the half-open door. No answer, so I knock louder. Still no answer. I step in front of the opening and peek inside.

Aniston is spread across the bed sideways, her arm over the edge of the bed, and one leg hanging out of the cover.

I start to turn away, but something pulls me toward her. Against my better judgment, I step inside the room. She snores loudly, and I follow her bellows like a sailor after a ship siren.

The snores grow louder and more nasally the closer I get. Sounds like a deviated septum. I make a mental note to refer her to an ENT.

It's hard to decide if she's sleeping soundly or just sleeping noisily. Either way, it's now a good bit past noon and I'm hungry. I reach down and shake her shoulder gently. She flinches, but lets out another whale song.

I shake her again, and she flips over under the cover. One more try, then I might as well abandon my mission and eat with the kids. I shake her other shoulder faster than the first two times. She rolls to the corner of the bed and takes the cover with her.

Bright red panties flash. I cover my eyes and start backing away. This was a bad idea. A very bad idea.

Forget the rumor mill. This scene is worthy of the *Apple Cart Weekly.* Our only saving hope at not making the front page is that they have a special story on the upcoming ball season.

I continue backing out of the room until I run into a chest of drawers. Seething, I bend and grab my throbbing leg. "Son of a—"

"Easton?"

I hop back and lift my head to Aniston sitting up in her bed.

"I'm so sorry. I'm not being creepy, I just tried to wake you up." *Way to go, Easton. That didn't sound creepy at all.*

Aniston fans the covers over her and folds her arms across her chest.

"I didn't know you weren't wearing pants."

"Or a bra," she adds, tightening her arms against her chest.

The hand not holding my calf goes up in surrender. "I swear, the kids said I could come get you. I brought lunch. It's from Big Butts. If you want to sleep again, I can feed them and act like this never happened."

Not that I could ever forget something as humiliating as this. To my relief, Aniston laughs so hard, she snorts.

I straighten and lean against the wall so I can relax my hurt leg. "I'm sorry."

"It's fine. I don't think you're creepy." It takes her a while to get the words out since she's laughing so hard.

I blink. The relief I should feel with her saying she doesn't find me creepy is clouded by shock. Even I creeped myself out by trying to wake a half-naked woman. Although I had no idea what was under the covers when I started the mission.

"Why are you laughing?"

Aniston coughs and pats her chest, then quickly recrosses her arms when she realizes she's without a chest protector. "You're the last person I'd find creepy."

"Really?" I'm flattered and, in an odd way, a little offended.

"Yes, the perfect gentleman. Now if you'd be so kind as to step into the hallway for me to properly dress, then I can accompany you to lunch."

I shake my head and exit the room, stepping lightly on my hurt leg. Anniston cackles out behind me. I close the door and stand against the wall.

A few minutes later, the door opens, and Aniston slides out wearing the blue dress she wore the night we ate in Tuscaloosa.

"Wow, fancy for Big Butts."

She does a little turn, then shrugs. "Maybe I like the way you look at me when I wear this."

I raise my chin and smile. "Do you?"

She blushes and nods. I pull her close to me and lean down to kiss her. Before our lips meet, she covers her mouth with her hand. She holds up a finger on her other hand, signaling me to wait. Then she backs up and heads toward the bathroom.

"Hold that thought. I need to brush my sleep breath."

I laugh. "Fine, but I expect no more interruptions. So go ahead and pee while you're in there."

"Haha," she yells from inside the bathroom. A few minutes later, I hear a toilet flush.

I laugh. Maybe proposing over pulled pork isn't so farfetched for us? She's already dressed for the occasion.

Aniston

"It's been almost thirty-six hours, and my skin is nearly back to normal." I lean toward my camera to get a close-up of my face.

I'm recording a vlog about my first official parent's night out—my date to the ball with Easton. Of course, I had to explain my hair-remover mishap. If I can't travel, the biggest draw to my posts is my brutal honesty.

After recording the recap, I shut down my computer to get everyone to school. I'm dressed decent and wearing makeup, since I have to also go into Carter's class and deliver cupcakes.

Today is Student Appreciation Day.

I get Teachers' Appreciation Day, Principal's, Custodian's, Lunch Ladies', whatever. But students? Those little jokers are appreciated enough. Every other day is about them.

Dress like your favorite zoo animal. Wear your favorite character. Blah, blah, blah. We've been in school not even a month, and Carter's had like ten of these. The first full week of school, he had to wear a different color every day. One day I forgot the color and put about five on him. He looked like a rapper from the 1990s.

Willow's room is empty when I walk by, and Carter is making his bed. I stop in his doorway and smile. They're good kids. I doubt they'd be this responsible if I'd had them from birth. My sister laid good groundwork.

"You hungry?" I ask when he's done with his bed.

Carter yawns and nods. When he gets to the doorway, I wrap an arm around his shoulder, and we walk downstairs. Willow is standing at the kitchen counter, putting Pop-Tarts in the toaster.

"Are you going somewhere today?"

Smart girl, wording that politely. What she's really asking is why I'm fully dressed and wearing makeup, with my hair not thrown in a bun.

"I have to take cupcakes to Carter's class."

She glances at the plastic container on the countertop. "Good thing I didn't eat one."

"If there's any left, I'll bring them back for y'all."

She smiles. "Thanks."

The Pop-Tarts pop, and Willow sets them on a paper plate. She offers one to Carter, who reaches for it with sloth-like speed. He's never fully awake until we get to school. Some days, I suspect he sleepwalks to class.

I go through the checklist of backpacks, lunch boxes, etc., ending with the carton of cupcakes. A weird déjà vu wipes over me, as not too long ago, I did the same thing with cameras, hiking gear, and my own snacks.

We load everything in the truck, and I grab a Coke on the way out. Caffeine is a must any time I walk into a room with multiple kids under age ten. Both kids grab a Gatorade for the ride.

Aside from a few yawns, we make the trip to school in silence while waiting on our energy to kick in. The car line curves back into the main road. My fault. Had I not taken so long recording my vlog, we'd have made our five-minute window.

I've learned there's an art to the car line. There's a five-minute window I can hit where we miss the early-morning rushers, but swoop in before the last-minute arrivals. That window is now closed.

So we wait.

Once Willow is out the door, I decide to go ahead and park. "You can walk in with me to save time," I tell Carter.

He nods and yawns, per his usual response this early. We park close as possible, while avoiding one of Georgia's off-limit spaces. I've parked in enough so far to recall where most of them are. So we're close to the dumpster, but not close enough to get dumped on—I hope.

Carter and I get out and walk across the dew-covered grass to the front of the school. Georgia opens car doors for kids as we pass. I keep my head forward as if I don't notice her. It must work because she doesn't speak.

Georgia is a lot of things, but quiet isn't one of them. She always has something to say, usually negative.

"Go on to class. I have to sign in," I tell Carter when we enter.

"Okay." He yawns once more and heads down the hallway while I stop in front of the office.

I shuffle the cupcakes to one side and sign my name. Then I glance back at the door. Georgia isn't there. I let out the breath I didn't realize I was holding. With my head held high, I turn toward Mrs. Pebbleton's room. I strut inside the doorway and hold the cupcakes high.

Little faces beam at me. I'm the hero for bringing cupcakes. Good cupcakes—the kind with buttercream frosting and plastic rings on top they can keep.

"Happy Student Appreciation Day." I smile at the kids and raise the cupcake container. My eyes widen when it floats from my hand.

Nope, it didn't float. Georgia is behind me, holding the box and shaking her head.

"Aniston, the special-day section of the room-mom handbook clearly states that all special treats must be homemade. This includes edible treats."

I raise a brow and take a deep breath as I try to come up with a clever response. Instead, I say, "How do you know it wasn't homemade?"

Georgia picks at the edge of the container with her mauve nail and peels off a sticker. She holds up a Piggly Wiggly price tag.

Steam rushes from my nostrils as I narrow my eyes on the evidence. "One would think store bought is best because you can read all the ingredients in case of food allergies."

Georgia rolls the price tag between her fingertips. "One

would know homemade means more, and the only ingredient that can't be bought is love."

Isn't that the truth?! I've never seen a "love for Georgia" pill on the market, and that's what it would take to make me love her.

As I'm silently plotting a revenge dessert to bake Georgia, she continues. "You have a list of any and all allergies for the kids in your room. It shouldn't be too hard to follow. After all, it's all in your handbook."

That settles it. I was dreaming up a dessert that would simply put her out for a spell. Now I'm contemplating one that may convict me of murder.

Death by chocolate. How's that for a headline in the *Apple Cart Weekly*?

"I'm sorry. I had a busy week, and all I know how to make is cookie crack."

Georgia blinks at the word "crack."

"Pardon?"

I give her my best fake smile. "It's a family recipe."

Like a proverbial mic drop, Georgia loosens her grip and drops the cupcakes into a trash can by the door. Then she nods toward a cart in the hallway. "Good thing I woke up early and made extra. I'm sure you were too busy with your neighbor to bother."

She struts to the rolling cart and pulls a tray from the top. "Oh look, just enough for your class. What a coincidence."

"How convenient," I mutter through clinched teeth.

Georgia shrugs and passes me with the tray. I follow her to the back of the room, where she lays it on a table. "Do you need any plates?"

"I think I have that covered." I open the cabinet door stocked with paper supplies and pull out plates and napkins.

"Just checking," Georgia sings as she struts past me into the hallway.

I wait until I can no longer hear the cart rolling before I

turn around. Then I place the cupcakes on plates and pass them out. Bad as I hate to admit it, her cupcakes are beautiful. Each one is piped to perfection, and they're all the same size.

Whenever I've attempted to make cupcakes, some come out larger than the others, at least half are lopsided, and the frosting doesn't spread evenly. If I find out she secretly bought these and put them on a platter, I'll sue.

The room mom across the hall is busy flipping pancakes. I step toward the door for a better look. They have tons of toppings for their pancakes and even bacon. She also has one of those brown paper signs with "Rise and Shine" scripted neatly across it. The word "Shine" has sun rays around it. If that weren't enough, she's decorated the entire room in sunshines and clouds.

Stick a fork in me, I'm done.

I pass out the remaining cupcakes to my room and watch the kids chow down. One kid eats his from the top, frosting first. He now has a cupcake goatee from taking a huge bite.

Mrs. Pebbleton smiles at the students, and I focus on her rather than their gross little faces. "Do you need anything else, Mrs. Pebbleton?"

"No, thank you, Aniston." She grins at me.

I give her a pleasant face, or at least I try. Who knows what comes through after my encounter with Georgia.

On my way out, I glance at the cupcakes sitting sideways in the small trash can. I ease my hand down and pull them out.

Sure, they're turned on their side and most of the frosting is stuck to the container. But they're still good cupcakes. Nothing was in the trash can besides papers, anyway. I double-check. Well, there's one tissue. But who's to say it's used? Besides, the cupcakes are shielded by their box.

A kid at the table closest to me whisper-yells, "Did she just get cupcakes from the garbage can?"

Why yes, I did.

I slip out and shut the door behind me. No need to give these youngsters a front row seat to the pancake festival across the hall.

Most every door is open on my way toward the front of the building. I peek inside to find everything from full breakfast buffets to luaus to a taco bar. Seriously? It's like nine. Who eats tacos at nine in the morning?

Okay, so I do—or did. However, that was before I moved back to a small town and became a parent. Especially before I became a room mom.

Seeing the amount of effort everyone else put forth makes my skin crawl. I flip the cupcake box over and open the lid. I pull the least messy one from the container, but still end up with a fistful of frosting.

This is why I could never play the board game Operation. My hand-eye coordination at maneuvering objects is nonexistent, especially when I'm stressed.

One bite of the cupcake makes me forget how messy I am for a moment, and I moan loud enough to gain a few stares from the people in the office.

TikTok Tami sashays through the front door wearing darkened sunglasses and high heels. Those accessories catch my eye first, as there isn't a lot else in between. For that reason, I focus on her sunglasses. She stops in front of the office window.

I polish off the last of my cupcake and slide past her to the door. Paul, who runs the General Store, rolls some kind of book cart up the catwalk. He stops when he spots me.

"Hey there, where'd you get those cupcakes?"

I almost say the trash but catch myself. "There's more inside." That's the safer answer, as I'm sure Georgia has more up her sleeve somewhere.

"Mind if I have one?"

Before I can admit they're trash cupcakes, he grabs an

extra messy one from the middle. He licks some frosting and tips it toward me. "Thanks."

"You're welcome." I sprint in the direction of my truck and reach for my second cupcake, not caring to monitor its messiness.

I've devoured half of it by the time I'm on the main road headed for home. Then I chase it with two more.

Once I park in front of my house, I've had four trash cupcakes and accomplished nothing besides humiliation and a huge tummy ache.

I hop out of the truck and take the remaining cupcakes inside. When I make it to the kitchen, I step on the trash-can pedal to open the lid. I hover the cupcakes over the open lid for a second, debating grabbing one more.

Nah, I've had more than enough. I already unbuttoned my jeans on the ride home to get some relief.

I loosen my grip and let the cupcakes fall in the can. My chest tightens when I remember promising Willow I'd bring home any left over.

For the second time in an hour, I dig cupcakes out of the garbage. They truly are trash cupcakes, especially with the spaghetti sauce dripping down the side of the container.

Good thing they stayed inside the container. I hold it eye level and survey the damage. I'd better put them in some-thing better.

I rummage through the cabinets and find a long, rectangular Tupperware with a lid. One by one, I transfer the remaining cupcakes from the store box to the Tupperware. I try and straighten the frosting best I can, which is near impos-sible since I chunked the box upside down this time.

In my defense, I never intended on digging out second-time-trashed cupcakes. But here I am. This could make a great metaphor for my experience with school so far.

My encounters with Georgia play in the back of my mind, and I hum that nineties song by a band named Chumbawamba. *I get knocked down, but I get up again. Hmm, hmm, hmm, hmm, hmm.*

I remember about as much of that song as I remember about nineties pop culture. My mom loved that era and seemed stuck in it with her choice of words and entertainment. Had she lived longer, I'm sure I'd know more too.

The biggest tidbit I recall is her love for a show called *Friends*. She even named us after one of the actors. Being the second child, I got stuck with the last name. Whenever I complained about my name being too unique, she'd argue that I should be thankful her favorite wasn't Lisa Kudrow—whatever that means.

Done. I prop one hand on my hip and assess my work. Not too shabby for what I had to work with. I straighten one of the cupcakes that's touching the side of the plastic, then lick some rogue frosting off my finger. *Man, that's good.*

There's plenty left for the kids, so I grab one more. About halfway through it, my stomach starts to churn. I unzip my pants to give my unbuttoned button some company. That doesn't help.

Stupid cupcakes. I need to hide these from myself.

Holding my stomach, I scan the room for a place I won't find them. Microwave and refrigerator are off limits, and they'll get lost in the cabinets. I snap my fingers. Perfect. The oven.

I've used it all of twice since moving in. Both times to cook bacon. And we're currently out of bacon, so that will be perfect.

I cover the cupcakes and bow over before crossing the kitchen to the oven. It's time to visit the bathroom. I jerk open the oven, then grab my stomach as I toss the container inside and shut the door with my foot.

Then I hurry to the nearest toilet. Maybe I'll be done before it's time to pick up the kids. I have a hunch it will take a while to drop these other kids off at the pool.

CHAPTER 17

Easton

"Really?" I lean back in my chair and stare at the computer.

A representative from the children's foundation is on my cell phone line with "exciting news."

"Yes, that's the third donor today who mentioned hearing about us on a parenting vlog. I suspect the uptick in other donations is due to it as well."

I smile. "That's great. Thanks for letting me know."

"Please send thanks to the woman behind the post."

"I will. Have a good afternoon." I hang up the call and slide my phone to the edge of my desk.

I click my web browser and find Aniston's vlog. I laugh as she describes her skin mishap, then perk up when she mentions me without mentioning my name. My insides heat up as she describes our night out in her own colorful way that only Aniston can.

She ends the vlog by naming the nonprofit and shares a

link where viewers can check it out and make donations if they wish. There's over a million views on this one video.

No wonder we saw a surge in donations today. I knew she made a living off videos, but had no idea how popular they were. This is a whole different world to me.

I simply went to medical school, show up to work, and help people get better.

The amount of influence she has by using a camera and her storytelling skills amazes me. Even more so when I consider how she easily transitioned from posting about traveling to her life as an instant parent.

It's that kind of determination that makes me like her that much more.

When the video ends, I click off the browser and continue checking charts for my upcoming patients. I make a mental note to go by and thank her on my way home this evening. Although I'm certain I don't need a reminder to visit Aniston.

The more I'm with her, the more I'm drawn to her. She's like an elusive drug I just discovered and keep chasing down for one more fix.

I do my best to put her in the back of my mind as I finish the last few hours of the workday. I've learned the hard way to put her in the back of my mind when I'm busy. Putting her out of my mind completely was a huge failure, so I finally quit trying.

When the last patient leaves and my office assistant locks the door, I gather my things with an extra pep in my step. I hum on my way to the truck and continue humming to the radio on the ride home.

If I were in a cartoon, my heart would beat in a literal heart shape inside my shirt while little birds floated around my head. Yeah, I've got it bad.

I turn down our road to a different kind of bad—smoke.

Hopefully the pasture didn't catch fire again. Sometimes the people who live across the pine trees thin out their land

and don't watch it well enough. One time part of the pasture caught fire, and Luke and I had to put it out. As dry and hot as it's been, it could happen again.

I speed up, gravel slinging from my tires. The pasture looks fine, but there's definitely a cloud of smoke. It's puffing above Aniston's back porch and pool.

I slide in her driveway on two wheels and barely put the truck in park before I jump out. Rolling up my sleeves, I rush toward the back. When I get to the house, I hear panicked voices.

Willow spots me and opens the door off the patio. I dart inside and stare at Aniston, who's dumping pitchers of water on the fire.

"That's making it worse. Do you have a fire extinguisher?" I ask.

She dives into my arms, sloshing a half pitcher of water as she collapses against me. "I don't know. We called the fire department."

I rub her back and swallow my nerves. My instinct is to comfort her, but I can't until the fire is out. "Willow check the closets," I command. I stroke Aniston's hair one more time, then let her go to help with the fire.

The upside to literally dealing with life and death on the job is that I tend to remain calm in these situations. I jerk my head in search of something to smother the fire. Most of the firefighters are volunteers, so I'm not sure how quickly they can arrive.

Willow still hasn't returned from searching for a fire extinguisher, and the flames are growing. My eyes land on a large pan of sand right outside the door. "Help me, Aniston."

She shakes out of her trance when I say her name, and we rush out the kitchen door. Together, we lift the heavy pan and take it inside.

"On three, dump this on the fire."

Her eyes widen with fear, confusion, or maybe both. But she nods.

"One, two, three." We toss the sand—pan included—toward the oven, dumping some on us and the countertops in the process.

The flames fizzle out when the sand smothers them. Aniston backs up to the refrigerator and sits on the floor. She sighs heavily and wipes her sweaty brow. I sit beside her and slide my arm around her waist.

She leans her head on my shoulder, and we stare at the mess in silence for a brief second. Then Willow rushes in with the extinguisher. Her beaming face goes downcast when she realizes we've resorted to other measures.

Carter comes in crying. "It's all my fault. I put the oven on to cook a pizza."

"You don't know how to cook a pizza," Willow scolds.

"I can read the box now," he wails.

Aniston stands and pulls him in her arms. "Shh, it's okay. It's my fault. I'm the one who hid a plastic thing of cupcakes in the oven."

I want to ask why she hid cupcakes in the oven, or hid cupcakes period, but decide now isn't the time. A siren yelps outside, and I stand. "I'll talk to them."

A fire truck and Bradley's police car are in the driveway with their lights going bonkers. I wave a hand. "Fire's out, but the smoke made a good bit of damage to the kitchen."

Bradley puts his hands on his hips, as he often does to assert his authority. I walk over and cut the engine on my truck and shut the door. In all the panic, I did neither before.

"Everyone's okay, just shook up," I add, as Bradley and two firemen follow me to the back door.

We step inside the kitchen, and I take a look at the real damage for the first time, not just the mess we made with the sandbox. Smoke stains run across the entire back wall of the kitchen, and some of the cabinets are scorched. It's safe to say the oven and stove combo are ruined, too.

Bradley steps toward Aniston and rests a hand on her shoulder. Even though he's doing his job, my primal instincts stir up jealously. He's a good-looking, successful guy and a little closer to her age. He's also flirty.

The hairs on my neck lower when he bends down to console Carter. Like a dog who's been given a treat, I drop my defenses.

Carter cries as he explains through hiccups what happened. Aniston rubs his back, and Bradley assures him that things like this happen all the time.

"Consider yourself lucky, Big Dog. You're better off to learn the importance of checking inside an oven at your age than waiting until you're at a frat house and decide to cook a pork roast for twenty guys after you're four beers in and forgot your roommate uses the oven to hide Skoal cans and bad movies from his girlfriend."

I blink at Bradley's analogy. "Wow, that's . . ."

"Specific." Aniston finishes my thought as we exchange glares over Carter's head.

Bradley pats Carter's head, then straightens. "Happens more than you'd think."

Most people would laugh and call his bluff, but working in the medical field has taught me to expect nothing aside from the unexpected. And living in Apple Cart has taught me that nothing is unexpected.

Willow sets the fire extinguisher on the island and sighs. I don't think she's moved until now. "What do we do about this?" Her young face wrinkles with concern.

Bradley stares at what's left of the oven. "File it on home-owner's insurance, get quotes, and get it fixed. Y'all will need a new oven for sure."

"Eh, we didn't use it much anyway," Aniston says. Her attempt at sarcasm is laced with a hint of panic.

I reach over and wrap my arm around her shoulder.

Bradley snickers and shakes his head. "Too bad y'all picked today to use it."

Aniston shoots darts at him with her crystal eyes. "Too soon, Bradley, too soon."

He tips his hat her direction and winces. "I apologize, ma'am."

I fight back a laugh and relax my grip on her shoulder. That comment diminished any concerns I might've had about Bradley having a shot with her.

Aniston gives me a tired grin, then turns to the firefighters. They've made their way toward the oven and are checking out the damage. "Would either of you like something to drink?"

"No, ma'am," one of them answers. The other shakes his head.

They check out the walls and discuss what might need to be done. The good news is we got the fire out before it really spread. The bad news is the smoke was so heavy that it did a number on everything around the oven.

After Bradley and the men leave, we all take a seat at the kitchen table.

"Y'all can eat with me until the kitchen is remodeled." I nod toward the patio. "And we can grill too."

Aniston smiles at me, then at the kids. She takes my hand and gives it a squeeze. A string of electricity flashes through my veins. Funny how she's the one giving me comfort in this situation. "I'm glad you showed up when you did."

I stroke the back of her hand with my thumb. "Me too. I wish I'd come sooner. I wanted to give you some exciting news as soon as I got home."

Her eyebrows raise. "More exciting than this?"

I laugh. "No, but good exciting."

She waves her free hand before returning it to her lap. "Please, do tell."

"Thanks to your vlog, the foundation has seen a major uptick in donations."

"Really?" Her jaw drops. "How do you know it's from my vlog?"

"Some of the donors mentioned seeing it today."

Aniston wiggles in her seat and giggles. "That's awesome. I had no idea that would work."

I shrug. "You're a woman of great influence."

She smiles, and so does Willow. Even Carter perks up the tiniest bit.

"Hey, how about we go eat someplace tonight? Since . . ." I let my voice trail off and nod toward the oven.

Aniston drops her shoulders and lets out a large breath. "Good idea." She turns to the kids. "What do you guys want for dinner?"

The color returns to Carter's face and he lifts his head. "I was thinking pizza."

We all start laughing, even Carter.

"I think that can be arranged. We can get some cupcakes too." I cut my eyes to Aniston. "Unless Aunt Ani doesn't want to fight temptation."

She gives me a flirty grin. "I fight temptation every day by living across from you."

My mouth goes dry and I tighten my hand around hers. Then I grab the edge of the table with my other hand to hold myself back from playing out the scene in my head. The one where I shove the salt, pepper, and napkins on the floor, then dip her across the table and kiss her until she's unconscious.

"Aunt Ani, were those the trash cupcakes?"

Aniston and I break from our seductive stares when Carter speaks. I clear my throat and remind myself that we have an audience. An underage audience at that. No throwing her across the table and kissing her senseless. At least, not for now.

"Trash cupcakes?" Willow wrinkles her nose.

Aniston lets go of my hand and scratches the back of her head. She laughs nervously. "It's actually a funny story. How about I tell y'all on the way to get pizza?"

Willow shrugs, and we stand to leave. *Trash cupcakes?* I'm intrigued too. Only Aniston.

Aniston

Every week, I discover yet another part of the room-mom handbook I forgot to read. I'm convinced Georgia knows the thing by heart, or else she wouldn't be so quick to call out my faults.

Her memory must be impeccable. I bet she can still name all the presidents. I do good to remember what I wore the day before, and if what I'm currently wearing is clean.

For once, I get to wear sweats to school and not feel underdressed. We're at a workday that's apparently mandatory for room moms.

Forget the fact that Willow has a football game later in the day, or that it's the weekend. Georgia doesn't care.

I yawn and pull my hair into a ponytail as the doorbell rings. "I'll get it."

I shuffle down the stairs and smile when I see Easton's truck through the window. He insisted on helping us since Georgia stressed the importance of having men there to do the heavy lifting. I think what really made him want to help was me explaining how Georgia raved about her husband, then mentioned she was aware not all of us had men in our lives who could help.

That made Easton roll his eyes back in his head and scowl.

So pretty much the same reaction I had when Georgia said it in our monthly room-mom meeting.

I open the door, and Easton holds up a mug. I clap my hands and bounce on my toes before taking it from him.

"Thank you." I down a huge gulp of coffee.

The coffee maker in our kitchen went down in the fire, which means I have to make coffee in the RV. Most days I just settle for a soda, or forget about the RV kitchen altogether. I'm visiting it less and less these days, as Jennifer's home is starting to feel more like my home.

Maybe one day, I'll work up the nerve to sleep in the big bedroom.

"Are the kids ready?"

I crane my neck toward the stairwell. "Haven't checked yet. I just got ready." I yawn and take another sip of coffee.

Easton smiles. "It's not *that* early."

"It is for a Saturday."

He shrugs and follows me inside. I stand on the bottom step and yell, "Kids!"

They appear at the top of the stairs and slog down. Carter has his usual zombified look, but Willow is wide awake.

"What will we be doing?" she asks.

I clench my teeth and look at Easton, then back at her. "I'm not totally sure. Probably whatever Georgia tells us to do."

"Is that the mean lady?" Carter asks in between yawns.

"Don't call her mean, Carter."

"Well, isn't she?"

I grit my teeth again and waver my head. "Let's go. We don't want to be late."

"I'll drive since the supplies are in my truck," Easton offers.

"Supplies?"

"Yeah. I brought some equipment that might help."

I smile. Anything that might tip me toward Georgia's good side is welcome. "Sounds great." I motion for everyone to go out in front of me, then lock the door behind us.

Once we're halfway down the driveway, I turn to see what's making such a loud racket in the bed of the truck. The end of a weed-eater flaps whenever we hit a bump.

"What all did you bring?"

Easton raises a hand nonchalantly. "You know, the usual. Weed-eater, shovels, rakes, a chainsaw or two."

I arch my brow, then face forward. In my line of work, a chainsaw is never usual, but I haven't done yard work since . . . well, ever. The dead flowers on my front porch are evidence of that.

When we get to the main road, the so-called usual supplies calm down. Either that, or we're now talking loud enough to drown them out.

The sun almost blinds me as we turn onto the road leading to the schools. I shade my eyes with my hands, as I didn't think to grab my sunglasses. I was too focused on my coffee mug. Besides, it should be illegal to come to school this early on the weekend.

Maybe I should suggest that as an amendment to the room-mom handbook?

Easton parks the truck, and it takes all of two seconds for me to spot Georgia's tight ponytail. She's marching around with a clipboard, pointing. Before I can duck behind a pile of mulch, she makes eye contact with me. My heart skips a beat or two as she fixates on me, calling me to her with her secret voodoo powers. I approach her slowly like a deer in the wild, afraid any human might be a hunter.

Except in my case, I know Georgia's a hunter. She preys on naive victims like myself. One wrong move, and I could end up mounted on her living room wall.

I cock my head and watch her from a few feet back as she bosses a teenager for pulling a weed incorrectly. Anyone who's picky about weed pulling wouldn't stoop to mounting something in their living room. Nope. She'd so put me in the basement.

Georgia continues to hover over the kid, inspecting his weed pulling like her life depends on it. Even though my life might depend on it, I interrupt them.

"Georgia, I'm here for whatever you need." I cringe as the words leave my mouth, but they take her attention off the young guy.

He glances back at me and sighs. I give him a quick nod, then focus on Georgia before she's on to me.

Georgia loops her arm through mine, and my entire right side tingles like it's poisoned. Maybe I'm allergic to Georgia. How great would that be?

"Aniston, let's see what I need you to do." She lets go of me and waves at someone behind us. The heat returns to my body, confirming I do have a Georgia allergy. I turn to acknowledge whomever saved me.

Georgia turns back and asks, "Have you met my husband?"

I follow her eyes to the man whom I assumed was my savior a moment earlier. He steps over and extends a hand. "Carlton Jenkins."

I shake his hand. "Aniston Wilson." *Carlton Jenkins.* My eyes widen when I make the connection. He owns the town's only pharmacy aside from the hospital. It's housed in a small duplex downtown, with a bait-and-tackle store on the other side. A strange yet convenient combination for the elderly in Apple Cart.

If only a coffee shop would open up next door, half of the retired men could knock out their morning errands in one location.

Carlton releases my hand, and I take note of how he's dressed. He's an attractive man . . . if you're into eccentric. He's tall and fit, but thin, with the body of an avid runner. Given the glowing yellow of his tennis shoes, I assume he must run at night. He's wearing a flannel button-down similar to the lumberjack logo on paper towels, with cargo shorts and white socks pulled to his calves.

An odd combination even for slaving away on the elementary school grounds. Then again, should I expect anything different from the one person on the planet who vowed to spend his life with Georgia?

I swallow a hint of vomit forming in my throat as I stare sympathetically at him.

Georgia snakes a thin arm around his waist and loops her fingers to one of the pockets on his shorts. He seems immune to her handsy-ness. Maybe he can write me some sort of prescription for the Georgia virus.

"Aniston, is your family joining us today?" Her commanding voice snaps me from imagining such a medical phenomenon as Georgia repellant.

"Yes, they're wandering around here somewhere." *As I tried to do before you spotted me.*

"I guess since your family unit doesn't include a man, we can put you guys on the sweeping and raking tasks." She smiles at Carlton and gives his side a squeeze. "The husbands and fathers will take care of the important tasks like trimming limbs."

Carlton presses his lips together, so I can't tell if he approves or disapproves of her backhanded comment on my singleness. Even worse, the fact that my kids no longer have a father.

My blood starts to boil, and I chew the inside of my jaw as I toss around appropriate—although snappy—responses to her dig. While I bounce comebacks in my brain like a boxer dancing in the corner of the ring before the next match, Easton's voice rings from behind me.

"I'll be more than happy to cut out anything unnecessary around here." He steps beside me with a large weed-eater in one hand and a chainsaw in the other.

My blood goes from boiling with rage to bubbling with excitement as I fight the urge to add, "In your face, Georgia!" Instead, I stand cemented by Easton and lift my head a little higher.

"How kind of you, Dr. West." Georgia loosens her grip from Carlton and nods to the equipment in Easton's hands. "You can help Carlton with the oak tree near our building."

Carlton nods to him and walks to a smaller chainsaw. He attempts to crank it a few times before Easton steps in and pulls the chain. It rumbles instantly. He nonchalantly hands it back to Carlton before cranking his own chainsaw on the first pull.

I smirk, amused that my guy beat Georgia's in a proverbial peeing contest.

"Aniston, follow me," she snaps in my ear.

I flinch and tuck tail as Georgia leads me to the pile of mulch I tried to seek refuge behind earlier.

"We need to work on this flower bed." She points a sharp red nail to the spot her teenage servants weeded earlier.

"You need me to spread mulch?"

She holds the same finger in front of me. "Not yet. First we need to fertilize the seeds planted last week by the women's club."

Georgia points to a nearby portable. "There's a wheelbarrow full of fertilizer that you need to spread before covering it with mulch."

"Got it." I even add a small salute.

One corner of her lip plays with a smile, then straightens. "I'll have your kids help with raking leaves."

I widen my eyes to silently ask if she's done barking out orders. She pats my shoulder. "Carry on." Then she walks away with a huge smile plastered across her face.

I glance over my shoulder, then to both sides to make sure nobody else is nearby. Nope. Georgia smiled at me . . . on purpose.

Several reasons for this impromptu sign of camaraderie plague my thoughts on the way to the portable. Then I smell the answer even before I see it.

Flies and gnats circle my face as I get closer to the wheelbarrow. The stench is almost too potent to bear, especially in Alabama humidity.

Yep, Georgia has assigned me the task of spreading manure. Of all the literally crappy things for her to do.

No wonder she's smiling.

CHAPTER 18

Easton

Homecoming is to Apple Cart what Election Day is to larger cities. Everyone comes from miles around to show their support. The crowd in front of Piggly Wiggly is so thick that I question whether our population doubled over night.

According to Aniston, people "literally come out of the woodwork to watch a parade."

In the short time I've lived here, I've managed to avoid any Christmas or homecoming parades. However, Willow is riding on the Toybowl cheerleader float, which warranted my attendance.

Aniston puffs her cheeks and stands on her toes. She's decently tall, but still has trouble seeing above the crowd.

"Want to move by the church and stand behind the people in lawn chairs?"

She cranes her head toward First Baptist. "Good idea. Too many people standing and sitting on tailgates here."

I take her hand, and together we walk toward the church.

Eyes suck to our interlocked fingers like moths to a flame. At first, I fought any public sign of us being together. Then I went to the school workday and walked up on Georgia gloating about Aniston not having a guy in her life. That pretty much made me screw my ban on PG-PDA.

Carter is at his elementary school, where they were instructed to sit on the front lawn with their classmates who aren't in the parade. At least that's what Aniston had to send out to the class as part of her room-mom announcements. Parents were specifically advised to keep their distance and let the teachers monitor their kids.

That's how we ended up at the Pig with ninety percent of the other adult population in town.

We stop behind a row of lawn chairs under an oak tree by the church parking lot. I greet several older ladies I recognize from their visits to the clinic. They smile at my hand holding Aniston's, and Ms. Ethel gives me a wink. Paul is beside Ms. Dot, looking a little too cozy. Maybe I should wink at him.

They must be pretty serious, or else he'd be in front of his store peddling cheap cowbells and plastic shakers. However, there is a very visible price tag on his lawn chair. Big surprise.

Engines rev up the road, and we all turn our attention to the parade making its way downtown. Leading the pack is the armadillo mascot standing on a lawnmower. I expected a side-by-side or maybe a four-wheeler, but not a lawnmower.

Apple Cart never ceases to amaze me.

Following the armadillo are several jacked-up pickups with bed sheets flying from the toolboxes. Armadillos are painted in red on the white sheets, converting them into massive flags. They flap, then flutter downward when the trucks slow behind the mascot. Football players hang out of the trucks' interiors and crowd the beds, waving and whistling to onlookers.

Ms. Ethel turns to the others. "That Harrison kid has really grown into a handsome young man."

The other women agree, and I bite back a laugh as Mrs. Maudy cleans the lens of her glasses with a handkerchief to get a better look before they pass.

We wait as cheerleaders and band members march behind the team. They're followed by class floats decked with chicken wire and tissue paper.

Once the high school floats end, a large John Deere pulling a flatbed heads our way. Girls' voices chant, and Aniston perks up from her bored stance.

"Here comes Willow's float." She grins as the bed comes into full view.

We both pull out our phones to snap photos. Willow waves at us momentarily before continuing to cheer.

An odd sense of comfort fills my chest as I smile at Willow, then turn to Aniston. She's still snapping photos, grinning wider than the armadillo mascot's head.

In this moment, sandwiched between old people and oak leaves, I don't feel like myself. For once, I'm more than simply a small-town doctor supporting the local school. I'm here for people I care about. I came with my girlfriend to watch her daughter.

"She was so cute, right?" Aniston elbows me and scrolls through the dozen or so photos she snapped while playing parental paparazzi.

"Yeah," I mutter, glancing at the phone screen.

I try and sound casual instead of giving away the sense that for the first time since I left for med school, I feel like I belong. Even when I dated Roxanne, it never felt like this.

Like family.

I'd experienced trickles of this same sensation now and again over the past several weeks. When I first met Aniston at her door, when we ended up in the pool, on the slide at the park, when we first kissed—and every kiss after that.

But when Willow floated by on the tractor trailer and Aniston beamed with delight, it hit me like a hurricane wave.

Aniston is now preoccupied with the homecoming court, seated in lawn chairs atop another tractor trailer. I half-listen to her commenting on their dresses, while I fight the urge to picture her in a wedding gown.

I've suspected I love Aniston, but today solidified that notion. Not only do I love her, but I love those kids too. I love all of us together.

My momentary daydream is interrupted by ear-bleeding bleats. Aniston's melodious laugh brings back a bit of bliss, but it's quickly drowned out by a pack of goats prancing down the asphalt. Daisy, the town's only massage therapist, is leading them on leashes. More like they're leading her.

I've referred several people to Daisy for back and neck pains, but I don't know much about her. Other than the fact that she also makes candles and apparently does something with goats.

Ms. Ethel waves a hand as she passes. "Daisy?"

Daisy cocks her head our direction and smiles.

"I'm coming to goat yoga soon as my doctor gives me the clear."

Daisy gives her a thumbs-up, then quickly fists the leashes tighter when the goats speed up.

Ms. Ethel tilts her head up and squints at me. "So, can I go?"

I frown. "I'm not even sure what goat yoga is. Besides, that bunch looks a little unsettled."

"Hmph." Ethel focuses back on the parade and folds her arms over her walker.

Not that I enjoy raining on anyone's parade—pun intended—but a woman nearing eighty with a walker has no business doing anything with a goat. Especially something that implies her flexing in athletic positions.

I make a mental note to speak with Daisy about giving Ethel a massage. Maybe we can convince her goat yoga is getting a massage with goats in the room. Wait, wouldn't that be goat massage . . . doesn't matter. My answer is still no.

The goats are almost out of view when one stops in front of Paul's store and takes a big poop in the street.

Paul shakes his head. "Dot, I knew we should've stayed at the store. This is the perfect opportunity to market my shovels."

I smirk at Aniston, who's biting her bottom lip to keep from laughing. Her cheeks shake when she faces me, so I turn back to the street.

Daisy's friend Adrianne runs out of her salon across the street with a broom and dustpan. She helps Daisy scoop the poop as the local politicians' vehicles start backing up behind the stalled goat herd.

When Adrianne starts toward her salon with the dustpan, the crowd cheers. Daisy blushes and waves as she hurries her goats out of the way. The cars start rolling once again. Behind our elected politicians rolls up the reigning county Applesauce Queen. She's on a John Deere tractor, which doesn't surprise me at all. What does surprise me is that she's driving it.

Paul points a shaky finger her way. "I sold her those boots the other day."

Pink leather boots peek out from her long blue dress as she steps on the pedal to make up for lost time after the goat incident. She tosses candy to the kids nearby and waves the usual pageant-girl wave.

I'm impressed by her ability to maneuver an antique tractor without power steering while wearing an evening gown and tossing candy. Then the fire truck behind her honks at some kids and startles her. She jerks forward, spilling half her candy and tilting her crown to one side of her head. But she readjusts quickly, keeping a professional composure.

A police siren belts next, though neither the beauty queen nor us onlookers are startled this time. Bradley's cop car flashes its lights as he brings up the rear behind a line of four-wheelers. I'm not sure what the four-wheelers have to do with the parade. At first, I assumed they were a Boy Scout troop. Then I spotted several adult men and females too. The group ranges in age from about five to seventy. None of them are dressed the same or have any apparent commonalities besides riding four-wheelers.

Apple Cart may have a four-wheeler club. I wouldn't put it past this town.

Bradley tips his hat as he passes. We all nod or wave in acknowledgement. A sticker on his rear bumper reads, "Follow the law, or the law will follow you."

One by one, the sounds fade. The band and cheerleaders, then the goats and sirens.

Paul mutters something to himself about shovels before standing and straightening his belt buckle. He rests his hand on Dot's shoulder. "Wait here and I'll pull around the pickup." He struts past the oak trees into the church parking lot.

Aniston checks her phone, then looks at me as the other older women start to stand. "According to Georgia's instructions, we're allowed to pick up Carter in ten minutes."

I chuckle. "We're about a ten-minute walk from the school. How convenient."

She twists her mouth. "Eh, best go back to Pig and get the truck. We'll have to get Willow too, and she comes with a lot of baggage."

I wrinkle my brow. "That's not nice."

"I mean like poms and backpacks and stuff, not like my kind of baggage."

She starts toward the grocery store, and I wrap an arm around her shoulder. "You don't have baggage."

"Uh, I inherited two kids and more property than I can handle, and my only skill set is making engaging videos."

I laugh. "First of all, your kids are great. Second, you have a kindhearted neighbor who's always willing to help with the property. And as for skills . . ." I arch a brow and lick my lips.

"Haha." She rolls her eyes, then blushes.

A big part of me wants to dip her in my arms and allow her to use her kissing skill set right here and now. But the more sensible part of me—diminishing by the minute—decides to play it cool in front of the entire town.

Aniston leans into me as we stroll down the sidewalk. The leaves rustle on the oak branches overhead, and people mill about, collecting loose candy and finding their vehicles. I choose to focus on the overall camaraderie of the day and ignore the guy bending over in front of us, revealing a thick patch of lower-back hair and a plumber's trademark where his pants are too low.

He picks up a sucker from the gutter, then grins at me. I force a smile and study his T-shirt. It's faded with grease stains, but I can still make out the words "Raised on Reagan" across the chest.

Aniston nudges closer to me as he brushes past us and cuts across the street, almost knocking us off the sidewalk. "Wonder where he's headed in such a hurry?" I ask.

"Hopefully to the General Store for a belt." Aniston's mouth tugs into a grin.

I burst out laughing. "So you noticed too?"

"How could I not?"

"What an encore to the parade."

"Yep, a real showstopper," she adds, smiling.

We laugh the rest of the way to my truck, gaining more than a few stares and whispers from the townsfolk. I unlock the truck and roll down the windows after we get in. Aniston buckles her seat belt, then swings her legs out the window.

"Make yourself at home."

"Don't mind if I do." She lifts the corner of her mouth playfully.

This somehow reignites my desire to kiss her. I lean

toward her, then meet eyes with Becky Douglas on the other side of my truck. She's the *Apple Cart Weekly* reporter. I clear my throat, and Aniston turns her head toward her feet.

Becky squeezes by Aniston's toes sticking out from her sandals. "Pardon me."

Aniston recoils her feet and folds them under herself, cross-legged. "Sorry, Becky."

"That's fine." Becky continues past the truck and through the row of cars in the Piggly Wiggly parking lot.

"Where to first?"

"The elementary school." Aniston shuffles in her seat like she's trying to get as comfortable as when her feet were out my window.

I back out of the parking lot and drive to the elementary school. Traffic moves steadily until the armadillo pulls in front of us. I lean back in my seat and idle behind the lawnmower.

He turns toward the middle school, and we continue to the elementary. I park near the front of the building and cut the engine.

After I unbuckle, I stare at Aniston, still buckled and picking at her nails.

"Aren't you coming?"

She sighs. "I'd rather not face Georgia for one day if possible."

"How am I going to get Carter?"

She twists toward me, tugging her legs behind her. "Just go to the office window and sign your name and ask for Carter."

"But I—"

She holds her finger to my lips to shush me. "They will allow it, trust me. You are now his emergency contact."

The familiar tingling sensation overtakes me again. Aniston added *me* as his emergency contact. So much for suppressing the feeling of family.

After a long pause, I open my mouth to speak. Instead, I kiss her finger, then move my way up her arm. Aniston giggles as I plant kisses along her arm, then shoulder, then neck. Her neck is a particularly ticklish spot, so I linger there a little longer.

Once I've had my fun, I make it to her mouth and enjoy her special kissing skills.

Several minutes later, we pull apart. Aniston leans her forehead against mine and takes a breath. "If you like that, I can sign you up for his room mom next year."

We both laugh so hard that Aniston falls on top of me, making me hit the horn. That earns us a few glares from a group of lunchroom ladies going to their cars.

I cough to clear my throat after laughing so hard and open the truck door. "Let me go get him before I cause any more trouble."

Aniston winks and props her feet out the window again. "I'll be here waiting."

Lucky me.

Easton

Aside from the pay, the only upside to working in the ER is it's never boring.

Larger towns see more injuries due to wrecks or possible violence, while Apple Cart County emergencies err more on the side of human error. Someone got drunk and did something stupid on a dare. Food poisoning from eating a random weed that came up in the garden. Standing too close to a homemade explosive while someone else shot at it.

Perhaps my favorite to date was the guy who came in because a beaver bit off his nipple. No kidding. He was trying to break up a beaver dam in a neighbor's pond, and the animal retaliated.

You really can't make this stuff up.

Regardless of the training and experience I've had both in bigger towns and Apple Cart, nothing could prepare me for tonight.

My phone beeps, along with all the other medical professionals' phones on the floor. We're alerted by text that a large charter bus wrecked a few miles out of Apple Cart. It was carrying a load of people back to Alabama from the casinos in Mississippi.

Since we're the nearest hospital and don't get that much traffic all at once, the first responders are sending all passengers our way.

Brooke frowns at her phone, then raises her eyes. "So much for a low-key night."

"Yeah, get all the X-ray techs and nurses to their stations for me. I'll meet the paramedics at the door and help direct everyone."

She nods. "Got it." Brooke slips her phone in her coat pocket and marches toward the kitchen area, where most everyone hangs out until something like this happens.

I head for the ER entrance to push through anyone too injured to worry with signing in at the desk. Since Apple Cart isn't a buzzing metropolis, they rotate the few doctors through the ER. That means it's my shift, and only my shift.

My phone rings, and I answer. "Hello?"

It's Donald, a nurse practitioner who works in the adjoining county. He got a call and is on his way to help.

I sigh as a hint of relief rises in me. "Thanks, Donald."

I'm the youngest doctor in town by some twenty years. When it's my ER rotation, the other two tend to go out of town for the weekend, since they're halfway to retirement already. Whether they were called first, I have no idea. I'm just thankful Donald is coming.

Once I hang up the phone, I hear ambulance sirens buzzing outside. I hurry to the back door and peer out the small window near the top.

Three ambulances pull up in unison. Apple Cart only has two, so the third may have come from Donald's county.

I run a hand through my hair and voice a silent prayer. The first ambulance door opens, and two men hop out with a stretcher. I recognize Bradley right away from his tan cowboy hat. The next door opens with another stretcher. I open the door and swallow. Why didn't I drink that second cup of coffee when I had the chance?

Oh yeah, because the coffee here is horrible, and I didn't anticipate treating a busload of gamblers.

Too late now. Bradley is leading the charge, reminding me —and everyone else—that he's also a trained paramedic.

I walk with Bradley as a nurse props open the door and waits for more to file in. He briefs me on what happened and how several people in the back took the brunt of the impact.

"According to the driver's report, he saw a large bull in the road. Tried to dodge it, got caught up in the puddles from the rain showers we've been having all day, and hydroplaned. Then he veered off the road and flipped down the ditch. The back end hit a pine tree."

"How's the driver?"

Bradley shakes his head. "Fine as frog hair best I can tell. These riding in the back took a beating from that pine tree." He nods toward the guy on the stretcher. "Especially this man here. He was on the can at the time."

I widen my eyes at the bruised man on the stretcher. By the way he smells, that wreck literally scared the crap out of him.

"I'll have Brooke run a CT scan to check for internal bleeding."

Bradley nods. "Thanks, Doc."

I text Brooke to meet us at the CT scan machine. Bradley briefs me on more details about the wreck as we hurry down the hall.

When we make it to the room, I have the men help move him to the machine. Then I walk out with Bradley to tend to other patients.

Donald rushes to me as we're taking another man to a triage room. I clap his shoulder like I'm congratulating him on winning the presidency. Aside from Aniston, I've never been so happy to see someone.

"Thanks for coming so quickly."

"Sure thing. Where do you need me?"

I send Donald with Bradley to get the next batch of people in rooms, while I go check on the patients already receiving care.

Most everyone I see is suffering from general soreness or something minor like a dislocated shoulder or arm. I correct what I can and prescribe rest, medication, or referrals for what needs more attention.

Brooke leads the charge among the radiology techs, scanning and running ultrasounds on anyone subject to a possible internal injury. I knock on the door to the X-ray room after splinting an injured finger.

She opens the door, and I enter.

"Everything still going well?"

Brooke blows a strand of hair from over her eye and nods. "Yes, sir."

A heavyset woman in a tank top sits on the X-ray table, complaining about her rib cage. I introduce myself and ask Brooke if there's anything I need to look over.

She points toward the room behind the wall that shields the technicians from radiation. "I have some scans ready to look over for broken bones. The patients are all resting in their rooms."

"Okay." I cross behind the wall and start examining the images.

Brooke adjusts the machine to the woman's chest level and instructs her when to hold her breath and when to breathe. Then she joins me behind the wall to take photos.

After a few snaps, Brooke and I exchange a glance. There's an extra bone showing above the woman's ribcage. If one of her ribs has broken in this position, she will need immediate attention.

Brooke raises her eyebrow at me, then she circles back to the main room. "This time, Miss Maller, I need you to raise your arms above your head so I can take a few photos under your arm."

The woman raises her arms like a bank robber caught in a heist. Brooke gasps and trails her eyes toward the floor. I stand, then come out from behind the wall when I can't get a good view through the window.

Two thick pork chops lie on the floor in front of the woman's bare feet. She wiggles her toes and grins sheepishly.

Brooke and I lock stares of bewilderment before turning to the patient. I start to ask if those are pork chops, but it seems like a rhetorical question at this point. Those are, without a doubt, pork chops.

Instead, I slant my eyes toward Brooke and say, "That explains the extra bone lodged under her arm."

Brooke nods, her mouth clamped shut. Either she's trying to hide amusement or still in shock. Probably both like me.

I pinch the bridge of my nose and channel the same emotionless demeanor I had when the guy waltzed in holding a dead beaver in one hand and his bit-off nipple in the other. Otherwise, I'll lose it.

"Miss Maller, where did these pork chops come from?"

"My bralette," she answers, calm and natural, as if I'd asked her name rather than where she'd gotten pork chops in the X-ray room.

I shake my head and bite the end of my tongue to not laugh. It doesn't entirely work, as a snicker escapes with my next words. "No, ma'am, where did you originally get the pork chops?"

"The buffet bar at Goldstrike. They don't hand out to-go bags. Stingy folks." She shakes her head and lowers her arms. "I mean, when you win a free buffet, it's supposed to be all you can eat, right?"

She glares at me, as if asking me to agree. I drop my gaze to the crusty pork chops. I've never been a fan of buffets, but I'm pretty sure that rule means all you can eat in one sitting.

"Miss Maller, I'm going to clean up these chops and let Brooke redo your X-rays while I read others."

"Okay." She shuffles back on the table, wiggling her toes when she does.

There's no sign of shoes in the room, so she may have lost them in the wreck. Or not worn any on the trip. I wouldn't put it past someone who smuggles pork chops in her bra to gamble barefoot.

I pull a pair of latex gloves from the back of the room and blow in them to puff them up, then pull them over my hands. Even though there's a medical-grade material barrier between my hand and the pork chops, I still pinch them with the ends of my fingers.

One in each hand, I step toward the trash can and dump them inside. Then I dispose of the gloves and make a mental note to have the trash taken out of this room ASAP.

Brooke smirks at me as I return to finish reading the scans. I make my notes in silence, not speaking until I'm done.

"I'm going to check on more patients. I'll take these results on the way."

"Thanks." She smiles wider, then giggles.

"Have fun," I say sarcastically as I leave the X-ray room.

I shut the door, happy to put that patient behind me—at least for now. For the next hour, I make rounds to all the rooms, checking on people and making sure they leave with what they need.

So far, only one person has needed to stay with us overnight—the guy sitting on the toilet when the bus hit the tree. Talk about being in a vulnerable situation. I think I'd rather have a beaver bite off my nipple.

Bradley follows Donald around all night, offering "help." I'm glad it's Donald and not me, as Bradley likes to try and take charge of every situation. That works great for him as the sheriff, but not so great in this situation.

The last patient I attend to is an elderly woman on an oxygen tank. Oddly enough, her breathing is fine. Well, except for the fact that she's on oxygen and admittedly smokes a pack of unfiltered Marlboros a day. She's in here because her knitting needle jabbed into her arm during the wreck.

I'm busy cleaning her wound and prepping her for stitches when Brooke comes in. "I can help. The nurses are all in other rooms, and I finished the last scan."

"Thanks, Brooke."

"Is this your girlfriend, Dr. West?" The older woman raises two eyebrows that aren't eyebrows at all. More like brown pencil markings.

"No, ma'am. This is Brooke, the head radiology tech."

"Hi." Brooke gives her a pleasant smile before preparing the tools needed for stitches.

"Oh." The woman lets out a raspy laugh, then coughs.

"Careful. Just relax, Miss . . ." I glance at Brooke, communicating that I don't have any papers with the woman's name.

"Ursula," Brooke says.

"Miss Ursula," I repeat.

"Well, that's a shame. You two would make a mighty handsome couple." She turns toward Brooke, who's bringing a tray of instruments our way. "And y'all would have some right handsome offspring too."

Brooke blushes. "Uh, thanks?"

"So was this your first trip to the casino, Miss Ursula?" Not that I care to know, but someone needs to steer her away from the topic of Brooke and me.

Instead of answering my question, she cocks her head. I rub ointment on her arm, then lift my own head to find her within inches of my face.

"You have lovely eyes. I have a step-great-niece who'd be perfect for you. Her divorce isn't final just yet, but I could line things up for y'all to meet soon as it is."

My jaw drops, and I have to pull it in before I can speak again. "Relax, please. This shouldn't take long. Your arm should be numb, so you shouldn't feel much pressure."

She snorts. "I've been kicked by a mule and flogged by a hen, and that was just last week. A little needle ain't gonna hurt me. Heck, that's what got me in this predicament." She coughs again, and I steady the needle until her arm quits shaking. "As I was saying about Clarabelle."

"Clarabelle?"

"My step-great-niece."

I clear my throat and try to ignore her chatter about how pretty Clarabelle is, especially since she got her hair extensions.

I'm almost done with the stitches when Brooke blurts out, "He has a girlfriend."

"Oh." Ursula sounds shocked. I cut the remaining string from the stitches and meet her gaze. She blinks. "You should've said something."

I turn to the tray, not caring to carry on this conversation. Ursula, however, is more interested than ever.

"What's her name?"

"Aniston," Brooke answers before I can politely state it doesn't matter.

"That's a peculiar name. Only one I know of is this gal whose parents died. She grew up around here."

"That's probably her," Brooke comments.

"Well, I hope she's settled down. She was quite the rambler back in the day. Always moving around like a bee on hot rock, never staying any place too long." Ursula lets out a raspy chuckle.

I take her uninjured arm and help her from the table. "I think you're all set. Take it easy on that arm for a week or so. It will be sore. Take some over the counter anti-inflammatories if you experience any pain, and don't hesitate to call if it gets worse."

Ursula straightens and starts rolling her oxygen tank away. "Thanks, Dr. West."

"Take care." I shut the door once Ursula and her tank are safely in the hallway. Then I lean against the door and sigh. "That woman's something else," I say to Brooke. "Do you know her?"

She laughs. "Know of her. Ursula is from Donald's hometown."

"Then why didn't he get her?"

Brooke raises her eyebrows and twists her mouth.

"Got it." I start straightening the room to busy my mind. It doesn't work. I turn to Brooke and frown. "What she said about Aniston . . ."

Brooke crosses her arms and shakes her head. "Dr. West, don't let a crazy old woman like that worry you. She doesn't know Aniston now."

I nod, feigning conviction. Brooke must see through the charade because she continues her case. "People in small towns like to judge us by our past. To some, I'll always be the girl who got pregnant in college. Others have moved past that and simply see me as a single mom. Aniston may have been flighty and unsettled for a time, but she's committed to a new life here with Carter and Willow." Brooke rests her hand on my arm and looks me in the eye. "And with you."

Only when I force a grin does Brooke leave my side and

start resetting the room. Everything in me wants to believe Aniston is settled in Apple Cart with the kids—with me.

But the pink RV parked in the yard is one big eyesore reminding me that she can strike out for greener pastures anytime.

Aniston

I hum to myself as I step onto the front porch. The air is a little crisp this morning, and the potted flowers have gone from dead to snapping off and decaying. That must mean fall weather is on the horizon at last.

A fog settles over the field, and I step onto the walkway to sneak a peek at Easton's house. My heart beats a little faster as I anticipate seeing him after we all do our work and school duties. Ever since the kitchen disaster, we've made it a habit of eating dinner together whenever possible. And ever since around that time, things have been going well between us.

So well that it scares me.

My bare feet grow cold against the concrete as I stand like a statue, staring at his house. A mixture of bliss and fear swirl inside my stomach until I'm almost nauseous.

That's it. Time for some caffeine.

I retreat inside my RV for coffee before making sure the kids are awake. It's Monday, so everyone's getting Pop-Tarts and soft drinks for breakfast.

If I've learned one thing taking kids to school the last two months, it's that Mondays are not for messing around. Don't waste time trying to cook eggs and bacon or assume everyone will drink apple juice and milk. Grab-and-go with a side of caffeine is just what the doctor ordered.

Doctor . . . I sigh like a teenage girl in a cheesy movie. Easton may as well appear in a cloud above my head, with cartoon hearts swirling around.

I down the rest of my coffee and head upstairs to round up the troops. I'm halfway up when I hear rumbling. Carter passes me on his way to the bathroom, and Willow steps out of her room fully dressed. A tinge of guilt hovers as I almost regret not making them eggs. Of course, that would involve waking up earlier and planning on my part.

"Y'all got up good today."

They don't answer, as Willow now has a toothbrush crammed in her mouth and Carter is in his usual morning zombie mode.

"I'll warm some Pop-Tarts. Y'all want chocolate or strawberry?"

Now they're vocal. Willow mouths "chocolate" around her toothbrush, and Carter yells "strawberry" before we hear the toilet flush.

"Got it." I leave them to get ready and head back to the RV to cook breakfast. The least I can do is throw the pastries in the toaster for a minute.

In about fifteen minutes, we're all in the truck, Pop-Tarts in hand, ready to start the day. Carter even brushed his hair. That's a sure sign it's going to be a good day . . . or maybe he's into girls now. Oh crap, do they like girls this early? I'm not ready for that.

I bite off a hunk of my own chocolate Pop-Tart as we turn onto the main road. Willow reminds me of what practices she has today as I'm dropping her off. When we're in line at the elementary school, I have Carter double-check his folder to make sure I didn't miss anything. I'm terrible about checking it over the weekend. Unless, of course, I have room-mom announcements from Georgia to stuff inside on Friday afternoons.

She's given me something to send out over the weekend no sooner than two on a Friday several times now. I should investigate whether she's waited until the midnight hour for other classes.

I jump at a loud knock on my window. "Well, speak of the devil." Georgia stares at me. I roll down the window and blink, as her reflective vest almost blinds me in the morning sunlight.

"What did you say?"

My face grows hot. *Did I make that devil statement out loud?* "I said, 'This road isn't level.'"

Georgia shakes her head. "I totally agree."

My eyes bug at hearing Georgia agree with me on something. Even if that something is a lie I made up on the fly.

"I've been trying to get the school board to approve us repaving it. When I get the okay, I'll get you out here to help."

And there it is. I sigh. Why couldn't I just keep my mouth shut? Or better yet, admit to pet-naming her "Devil Went Down to Georgia."

Someone opens Carter's door, and he climbs out. "Bye, buddy," I call as he walks toward the school.

We're still several yards from the entrance, thanks to Georgia stalling us. Someone honks a few cars behind. Georgia holds up her stop sign, and the honking ceases. Maybe I should invest in one of those. I bet Paul could find me one.

I pull up a few inches, and Georgia sticks the sign in my window, in my face. Since I can't see where I'm going thanks to the big stop in my face, I put the truck in park. Not because Georgia said so, but for safety reasons.

She lowers the sign when I stop. "The reason I stopped you is to give you this." She pulls a binder out of nowhere and tosses it in my lap.

I flinch when it hits my legs. Instead of the creepy school children cartoon that has plagued my nightmares for the past two months, grinning jack-o-lantern cartoons stare at me. These I can deal with.

"This is the playbook for the Fall Festival."

"Playbook?" I open it to a random page, half-expecting to find Xs and Os with arrows going in every direction.

Nope. It's another small how-to book by Georgia.

"Since you're my assistant on this, you need to study it. That will educate you on all the different departments. I also have notes on what you can help me collect."

"Collect?" I raise a brow, then glance in my rearview mirror at all the backed-up cars.

"Yes, consult the index for collections. They're broken down by grade level and class, so as to not overburden anyone."

There's an index? And what about overburdening *me*? I close my eyes to keep from rolling them. That doesn't work, but at least she can't see me rolling them behind my eyelids.

"Aniston, don't fall asleep. You're holding up traffic."

I grit my teeth and jerk the truck in drive. "Bye, Georgia." Then I gas off and hopefully leave a trail of smoke in her face.

CHAPTER 19

Aniston

I should be at my niece's volleyball game. Instead, I'm rushing around the Pig like a mad woman, in search of every paper towel roll I can find.

Everyone I meet gives me weird glances when I round another aisle with one buggy of groceries and another of paper towels. Even Paul looked at me strange. However, he did offer me a case of twenty paper towel rolls in exchange for some cookie crack after I told him my predicament.

Georgia failed to mention until today that it was my sole responsibility to have all the supplies in by tomorrow. So I spent all day at the school checking over the collection bins to find that we're really short on empty paper towel tubes. Maybe that's because it was up to Carter's class to bring them.

Well, excuse me for forgetting to send out one little notification on GroupMe.

That leaves me with trying to make a sow's ear into a silk purse at the last minute, per my usual time frame.

Let's see. I pull out my list. I found three paper towel rolls at home, a six-pack in the janitor's closet at school, one in the gas station bathroom. Add Paul's twenty he's delivering later. That leaves me with . . .

"Forty to go." I sigh and start counting all the rolls I have in my buggy. I still need seventeen rolls.

I make one more loop through the paper towel aisle to make sure I didn't miss one. An older lady is staring at the empty shelf I wiped out earlier, so I conveniently drop a four-pack of Brawny by her feet on my way to the cash register.

New total needed: twenty-one.

Morgan snickers when I finagle my buggies into her lane. I point a finger at her. "Don't you say a word."

She lifts her hands in surrender, but grins like a possum. She helps me unload my groceries and starts scanning them, when the most annoying voice calls my name.

"Aniston."

Georgia. I'd recognize her voice anywhere. School, here, the depths of hades.

I raise my eyes first to Morgan, who's face communicates that she will attack Georgia at my signal. That gives me the courage I need to peer over her head at Georgia.

"I just dropped in to get a few odds and ends for the festival." Georgia gestures toward my extra buggy. "Looks like you're doing the same."

I narrow my eyes and continue unloading paper towels onto the conveyer belt. Instead of taking my hint that this isn't the time or place to have such a conversation, Georgia sashays toward us.

Morgan raises her hand, and I'm afraid she's preparing to punch Georgia. Nope, she's reaching for her phone behind the register. Maybe she's preparing to call Bradley for backup.

"You know you can just order stuff in bulk off Amazon," Georgia quips.

I nearly bite a hole in my tongue as I prepare a response that won't land me in jail. "Even Amazon requires a two-day shipping notice, unlike some sources that wait until the last minute."

"Like you?" Georgia's perfect teeth slide into a satisfied grin. And maybe it's the crappy florescent lighting of the Pig, but I swear a small sparkle glistens on her left front tooth.

That's it. I slam the last paper towel pack on the belt and prop my hand on my hip. "I was referring to, I don't know, maybe someone who waits until the last hour to tell people things need to go in folders or be delivered to the school."

Georgia folds her arms and her smile slumps. "Every instruction I've given you at the last minute was to keep you from failing at your job."

Steam rises from my feet to my head. If I get any hotter, I'll have to unroll some paper towels to mop my sweat off the floor. Or Georgia's blood—depending on what move she makes next.

"Aniston, everything is in the handbooks. Why do you think I go through the trouble of making them?"

I throw my arms in the air. When I bring them down, one lands on the register, startling Morgan. Up until now, she's had her eyes glued on us like a TV season finale. She even opened a bag of M&M's to snack on while she enjoys the show.

"I don't know, Georgia. Maybe to make the rest of us look bad?"

"Now why would I ever want to do a thing like that?" Her voice is the perfect mixture of sweet and sour, like my favorite dish at that Chinese place in the Tuscaloosa mall.

"That's it, I'm done." I reach in my purse and slap my card on the belt.

Morgan snaps out of her trance to ring up my groceries and à la carte.

A receipt about as long as my leg shoots out the register. The dozen or so rolls of paper towels are to blame for that. Apparently, when you buy multiple brands and quantities, they don't all go on the same line.

With one hand on each buggy, I march toward the automatic doors, ignoring Georgia as I pass. In record time, I manage to unload all the groceries in the back seat, along with all the paper towels I can fit. The rest have to go in the front with me.

When I get in and turn my head to back up, all I see are puffy white rolls . . . and a few Brawny guys smiling back at me. I roll my eyes at the flannel eye candy and roll down the window. Hanging my head out like Ace Ventura, I drive down the road to Dollar General.

Twenty-one paper towel rolls, then I can go home.

I park and don't bother locking the doors or rolling up the window. If someone wants to steal paper towels, then they have more problems than me.

As soon as I enter Dollar General, I scan the store like I'm preparing to swipe whatever I can in a post-apocalyptic raid. If Georgia keeps calling the shots, it may come to that. Better to prepare now.

A row of laundry detergent on a top shelf catches my eye. I grab a buggy and make a beeline for that aisle. Sure enough, the paper towels are close to the laundry detergent. I snatch everything I can, mentally taking note of how many are in a pack.

If my calculations are correct, counting the twenty Paul owes me, I will have two extra. Perfect, my household can keep some. Win-win.

Just when I think I've conquered all odds, I turn and run smack into someone. I drop the paper towels and bend to pick them up. Another woman's hand reaches down and gets them for me.

I'd recognize those pointy fingernails anywhere.

I straighten and take the paper towels from Georgia. "Thanks," I mutter. My throat burns when the word creeps out. It would've been easier for me to break up the asphalt in the car line for repaving—with my teeth.

I drop the pack in my buggy on top of the others, then speed walk to the register. A young girl slouches over the counter, filing her black fingernails. When I set a roll of paper towels in front of her, she blows pink bangs out of her eyes and stares at me.

There's a ring through both her nostrils, and I get the sudden urge to scratch my nose. Sneezing has to be complicated with that thing.

She slowly lifts her elbows off the counter and glances at my buggy. "Uh, this line is twenty items only."

I don't see a sign indicating that, and the other registers are backed up with customers. I narrow my eyes and smile. "Yes, and I have only one item, paper towels."

The girl tosses the fingernail file in a bucket by the register with other files for sale and rolls her eyes. "Fine."

I smile at my small victory and start unloading my loot. Five minutes later, I'm back at the truck, unloading yet another haul of paper towels. This bunch I have to put in the bed of the truck, since there's barely enough room inside for me to shift gears.

"Aniston."

Come on! I lift my head toward heaven in a desperate plea to catch a break. Then I lower my head to catch Georgia rushing toward me, waving a bouquet of yellow flowers.

What the . . . ?

She jogs up to me as I'm unloading the last of the paper towels. "I bought you something."

"Paper towels? Because it's a little too late for that. Although, I will accept a reimbursement."

Georgia shakes her head and smiles. "No, these." She lifts the roses, wrapped in cellophane, with the words "Happy Fall, Ya'll!" across it.

I force myself not to comment on the misspelling of "y'all" and assume these were imported from someplace above the Mason-Dixon line.

"I bought you these." Georgia beams like a kindergartner who's picked weeds on the playground for his teacher.

"Why?" That's the only response I can come up with. Well, there's others, but they all involve language more colorful than those roses.

"To make your day brighter."

I walk around to the front of my truck, climb in, and slam the door. As I'm driving off, Georgia literally runs me down. How, I'm not sure. She's wearing wedge sandals. But now she's pulling on my door.

I jerk the truck in park, causing her to jerk with it. Somehow, she stays on her feet and still has the roses in her hand. "I'm not leaving until you take my gift."

"Fine." I snatch the flowers from her hand and turn toward the parking lot exit.

Great. A big pack of paper towels flew out of the bed. I put the truck in park once more to go get them. A car backs over them with its left tire. I shake my head and wait for it to move before retrieving the paper towels.

Smooshed or not, I need every roll I bought.

Then I hurry back to the truck before Georgia tries to interrogate me again or buy me another DG pity present.

Aniston

. . .

I pull out of the parking lot and sit at the stop sign, waiting my turn. In small towns, we don't always follow the conventional driving rule of who arrived first goes first. There's usually a waving contest involved, where everyone parked at the stop sign tries to wave the other car to go ahead. Finally, someone gives in and goes first.

Today, I let everyone else engage in the battle of the waves while I read the tiny card Georgia attached to the flowers.

Aniston,

I can tell you're stressed. I think you may need some help. I'm here for you if you ever need any counseling or advice on parenting or just life in general.

-G

I crumple the note and toss it out the window. Of all the nerve! Who is *she* to offer *me* advice? If I needed advice—which I don't—I'd go to Easton, or Morgan, or Brooke, or even church. Not the devil!

Tears prick at the corners of my eyes when I realize what I really need is my sister. She'd know what to do in this situation—with school, the kids, Easton, and most of all, Georgia. Jennifer was a pro at relationships and family stuff. Why can't she be here when I need her most?

When all the cars have gone their ways, I turn on my blinker and head the opposite direction from my house.

My hands sweat as I grip the steering wheel and speed up. I haven't gone to this place since my sister died, and I didn't intend to for a while. But I need to talk to her—dead or alive.

My stomach buckles as I turn into the entrance to the town graveyard. It's on a lonely paved road, conveniently located near the hub of churches downtown. My parents are buried here, as are Jennifer and Luke.

A few dead leaves blow past me when I get out of the truck, setting the mood. I grab the bouquet of flowers and shut my door. It echoes in the otherwise quietness of this field full of tombstones.

My family name comes into view as I walk up the slight hill toward my parents' tombstone. A few feet from it is a much newer tombstone with name "Stevens." Tears creep down my face as I stare at the dates below Jennifer's and Luke's names. Both died in their mid-thirties, way too young.

While mom's span of years is only a few longer, it didn't seem so sudden. Maybe because she was sick or because when she died, I thought of thirty as ancient. Or maybe it's because Jennifer's and Luke's deaths are so fresh that enough time hasn't yet passed for grass to grow on their graves.

I sit on the bench between the two tombstones. Dad had it put there when Mom died so we could "visit" with her. Sadly, those visits grew less and less for me, until they didn't come at all.

Never in a million years did I expect to come here to visit with Jennifer. Yet here I am. I twist around to face her grave.

"Hi." As soon as I speak, I scan the area to make sure I'm alone. If anyone caught me talking alone in a graveyard, they might really think I need counseling.

After an awkward pause, because this is a one-way conversation, I decide to stand and give an impromptu monologue to catch Jennifer up on things.

I stand near what I think is her head. "First of all, thank you for giving me the kids. You could've given them to anyone, really. Morgan, Brooke, someone from your church. But you gave them to me. That means more than you know."

I sigh and pause a moment as I wipe the stray tears from my cheeks. My eyes gravitate to the flowers in my hand.

"Oh, and here are some flowers. I know they look crappy, and please ignore the misspelling of y'all. That bugs me too." I laugh through my tears.

"I got them from Georgia. You remember her? I'm sure you do. Or maybe not since they say no sad memories in heaven." I clear my throat and glance around to make sure once more that I'm alone. "Anyway, she's a handful, and I wish I had you here to help me know what to do. And I'm sorry for all the times that I teased you about just being a mom and PTSO person. It's way harder than you made it look. Way harder. So I just thought you needed to hear that. And that I love you."

I take a step back and slide my hands in my pockets. Then I turn toward the truck, but stop after a few feet. I look over my shoulder and add, "Oh, and thanks again for the kids. I need them more than they need me, but I think you knew that all along."

CHAPTER 20

Easton

When I drive up to Aniston's house with Carter and Willow, Paul's pickup is parked sideways by the garage. The kids look as confused as me. I park, and we all climb out of the truck. Paul stands by his tailgate with his hands on his slim hips.

"Evening, Easton. I got something for Aniston." He reaches into the bed of his truck and starts tossing out paper towels.

Aniston had called me earlier and asked if I could bring the kids home from Willow's game since she had to run last-minute errands for Georgia. However, she didn't mention anything about Paul unloading cleaning supplies.

After dumping a pile of paper towels in the driveway, Paul nods. "Tell her I like my crack extra crispy." Then he climbs back in his truck and drives off.

Willow and I exchange skeptical looks. "Okay, I'm sure your aunt knows what that means."

"Cookie crack," Carter comments.

"I'm certain, but . . ." I bend and start stacking paper towels in my arms. "Maybe she knows why he left these in the drive too."

Carter shrugs. "He's strange."

"Very." I laugh and hand both the kids a few rogue rolls until they're all off the ground.

We walk to the back door, and Willow drops a pack as she fumbles for her house key.

I kick the pack inside before I walk in. Still confused, we stack all the paper towels by the back door. Either Aniston is suddenly into extreme couponing, or this has something to do with room mom.

I sit at the kitchen table as the kids put down their backpacks and hurry to the pantry in search of snacks. Before I can consider finding something to start for dinner, I hear the gravel move on our road. I lean toward the window and spot Aniston's truck.

"Looks like Paul just missed her," I say to myself more than the kids, since they're preoccupied with comparing chip flavors.

Aniston parks in the garage, and I go to the door. As soon as I open it to greet her, she opens her truck door. Paper towels fall to the ground. What is up with the paper towels?

"More paper towels?"

Aniston gets out and frowns. "My errand for Georgia."

"Paul just dropped off a load too."

"Good." She nods and starts collecting what fell.

I walk over and help. "So . . . you got Paul in on some sort of weird pyramid scheme?"

She shakes her head. "He ran into me buying all the rolls at the Pig and offered what he had if I'd make him cookie crack." I take several larger packs from her.

"Oh, and by the way, he said he likes his crack extra crispy. Whatever that means."

"Not gooey in the middle."

"Ah." I follow her inside with the paper towels, then back to the truck.

She opens the back door to a mound of Piggly Wiggly bags. "I had to get groceries too, and there's more paper towels in the bed."

I turn toward the half-open door and call inside. "Willow and Carter, could you come help?"

The kids bounce into the garage, now hyped on junk food. Carter's mouth is laced with Cheetos dust.

Aniston leads them to the bed of the truck and hands them each an armful of paper towels while I gather grocery bags. I get all I can carry in one load, except for the bag with pork chops on top.

Too soon. I'm still squeamish after my encounter in the ER a few weeks back.

Aniston comes behind me and picks up the few bags I missed. We walk inside like an assembly line at a paper towel company. Aniston and I even manage to balance a pack each on our arms above the food, so we don't have to make another trip.

That is, until I realize nobody shut the truck door and jog back to do so. I come in to everyone unpacking grocery bags.

"You got ice cream!" Carter jerks the lid off the Bluebell excitedly. His face falls when it drips in a puddle onto the countertop.

Aniston drops the bananas she's holding and rakes her hands through her hair. "I knew I shouldn't have made that last stop."

She takes the dripping gallon from the counter and opens the door to the patio. Without saying anything, she tosses the ice cream out the door and continues unpacking groceries.

Shocked, I stare out the open door to Buster licking a stream of milky residue. "Aniston, I don't think he needs to be eating that."

"Calm down, Doc, it's not chocolate." She slams a can of green beans on the table and digs inside another bag.

Calm down, Doc? Who stuck a stick up her butt? I picked up the kids, helped unload all this, and dealt with Paul's weirdness. What is wrong?

"What's wrong?" There. I said it out loud.

Aniston sets down the box of rice she's holding and marches outside, slamming the patio door behind her.

I can deal with a lot. Pork chops falling out of bras, beaver-bitten nipples, and the list goes on. But I can't deal with her acting immature and snippy at me for no reason. I open the door and follow her out.

"Aniston, tell me what's wrong."

"I had a bad day, okay?"

"Want to talk about it?"

"No." She snorts and folds her arms.

Buster picks up the ice cream bucket in his mouth and starts to trot away. "I really don't think he needs that much ice cream, chocolate or not."

Aniston stomps over to Buster and jerks the bucket from his mouth. He doesn't give it up without a fight, growling and biting off a chunk of the paper container in the process. She scowls at me and tosses what's left of the ice cream toward the pool.

A stream of vanilla fans over the pool like white paint flying on a canvas. Then it rains over the water, clouding the crystal-clear surface.

I stare back at her, both confused and afraid. "Why would you do that?"

"I don't know." She throws her arms up. "Why would I buy up all the paper towels in Apple Cart or go talk to my dead sister?"

I blink. "You talked to your sister?"

"Yes!" she yells.

"Like in a dream or with a fortune teller?"

Aniston sighs and shakes her head. "No, at her grave."

I tilt my chin and take a step back.

"Why are you looking at me like that?"

I blink. Should I run? I don't want to be the next victim of an ice cream tantrum. I slant my eyes toward the murky water. We're gonna need a lot of chlorine to clear that up.

"Like what?" I finally find the courage—or stupidity—to respond.

"Like I'm crazy!" Aniston raises her voice and eyebrows simultaneously. Her pale blue eyes widen into a serial-killer stare. Not her best look, especially when trying to convince me she's *not* crazy.

"Sweetie, if you had a bad day, let's just talk about it."

She pouts and blows out a long breath. "That's just it, Easton. I'm done with talking, with buying up paper towel rolls, with planning every little stupid thing under the sun. I'm done trying to be something I'm not."

Something she's not? I shouldn't take that personally, but I do. My insides tumble like tennis shoes in a dryer. What does she mean by that? She didn't mention me or the kids, but is she done with us too?

I manage to lift one foot and take a step toward her. My body fights against it, as my legs go heavy. My mind screams "run." She narrows her eyes, and it's like I'm Chris Pratt approaching a baby raptor.

When I'm within a few inches of her, I reach out and touch her arm. Instead of the comfort I always get from touching her, I get nothing. Unless I count the stickiness from ice cream drippings, which I don't.

"Please, Aniston, whatever happened, talk to me."

Tears fill the corners of her eyes, and she shakes her head. "I need some time alone. That's all. I'll be fine later." She kisses me on the cheek.

But there's nothing in this kiss. No comfort, consolation, or care. It's more of a formality.

Without saying another word, she walks off the patio to her RV. Then she climbs inside and shuts the door behind her.

I understand her need to take some time for herself and be alone. But did she have to run in there? What's wrong with taking a walk by the pond or going to her room in the house? Even her sister's old room?

Instead, she chose that blasted RV.

Even though it might not have been intentional, when she shut that door behind her, I took it as her shutting the door on me.

I walk back inside. Willow and Carter glance at me sheepishly. I'm sure they heard every word of our argument. I rake my hand through my hair and look at them. "Your aunt has had a rough day. How about I grill us dinner?"

Willow nods. "We have pork chops."

I swallow and adjust the waist of my pants to try and ease the queasiness in my stomach. "What about burgers? I think I saw some hamburger meat in one of those bags."

Both kids agree and start shuffling for meat and buns. I can tolerate a lot, but if I grill pork chops tonight, I might need to hide in an RV.

Easton

Thank God, I'm not working the ER later. I'll do decent to make it through my regular office hours. I didn't sleep at all last night. Every hour, I'd toss and turn, worried about Aniston.

She wanted to be alone, which I can respect. We all need that. For that reason, I went home after eating with the kids and didn't call her. She was still in the RV when I left, and I can only hope it wasn't to avoid me.

A big part of me wanted to sneak back through the field after going home to see when she left the RV. If she walked out right after I left, that should mean she was avoiding me, right?

I may be paranoid, but I'm no stalker, so I kept my butt at home. I worked out, read, watched several episodes of *Stranger Things*, shopped for fishing lures on eBay. Anything to pass time and try to make myself sleepy. I even tried a warm shower followed by a glass of milk. My grandparents swore by that as the magic formula to send anyone to sleep.

But nothing worked.

Now I'm dragging myself into work like a sloth on sabbatical. I greet the people at the front of the clinic and walk down the hall to my office.

A few minutes into checking my messages, Brooke passes by my open door with files in her hands. I rise from my chair, then stop myself in midstance. I'm certain Brooke doesn't know anything more than I do right now. It's been half a day since I've seen Aniston. Then again, she may know the details to Aniston's bad day. That might help.

I stand fully. Then my conscience gets the best of me, and I decide it best to wait for Aniston to give me details. So I sit back in my chair. However, if I know the details, I can better understand what's bothering her. I start to stand again, then sit when I realize it's wrong to put Brooke in that situation. She shouldn't have to choose between her friend and boss.

What if I started a conversation about Aniston, though, and Brooke simply volunteered the information? I stand again.

"Are you okay, Dr. West?"

I jerk my head toward the door to find Brooke staring at me. "Yeah, why?" Total lie, but concerning work, I'm okay.

She wrinkles her forehead and points toward me. "Is your chair okay?"

I plop back in it, banging the headrest against the blinds on the window behind me. "Oh yeah." I ignore the clinking blinds and twist some, trying to play it cool. "Just stretching."

Brooke raises one eyebrow. "Yeah, well, your first patient is here if you're ready."

I nod. "I'm ready." Then I stand one last time and circle my desk like I'm eager for the day ahead.

Brooke gives me a sympathetic smile and continues down the hallway. I stop at the first patient room and pull the chart from the file holder on the door. A routine physical, so nothing weird so far.

My bet is by two o'clock, someone will come in with an allergic reaction or a self-inflicted cut or burn. People tend to take on strange hobbies during the lunch hour. Everything from forging knives to milking goats.

I knock on the door and wait until I hear a "come in."

As soon as I push the door open, I drop the file folder and jump back. A scrawny middle-aged guy is buck naked, except for a watch. What in the world?

Out of instinct, I cover my eyes. "Uh, sir, there's no need to dress down to . . . uh, you can wear clothes."

"I signed up for a full physical."

Yes, and we're not a brothel. "That's not how this works. Have you ever had a physical before?"

"Not a full one."

I laugh nervously, still covering my eyes. "I'm going to step out and give you a moment to redress. Okay?"

"Fine by me. Y'all keep it a little cool in here."

I backtrack toward the door and ease out, shutting it behind me. This will definitely rank up there with pork chops in the bra. Maybe even outrank it.

I shuffle nervously in the hallway for an appropriate amount of time needed for someone to get dressed. Then I tack on a few more minutes for safe measure before knocking again. There's already a vivid picture of the guy burned into my mind. No need to see the real thing for a second time.

As luck would have it, he's wearing everything but socks and shoes when I open the door again. "Good deal. It looks like I gave you time for everything but your shoes."

He shakes his head. "Nope. I didn't wear none."

I shrug. "All right, then, let's get started."

Someone who doesn't wear shoes shouldn't complain about the temperature of the room. And why do so many people in this county choose to not wear shoes? I scratch the side of my head and pick up his chart.

Regardless of the awkwardness, naked guy did give me a small window of relief from pining over Aniston.

The rest of the patients aren't quite as flamboyant. Even the woman who brings in a basket full of kittens because she "don't trust the vet with my babies" doesn't offer enough distraction from my relationship.

By the time the day ends, I'm determined to do something. I'd talked myself out of calling, sending her a text, or stopping in after work. Best to give her time to get over whatever it is and let her come to me. Still, I need to let her know I care, if for no other reason than to ease my mind.

On my way out, I stop by the pharmacy/gift shop at the hospital. Odd as it seems, this is the best place in town to buy flowers. And often the only place.

To my surprise, they have a bouquet of yellow flowers. They look like small sunflowers or something. Yellow is Aniston's favorite color, so that will be perfect. I can leave them with a note on my way home.

That should show I'm thinking of her without me invading her space. I hope.

As the cashier rings me up, I pull the card attached to the wrapper on the bouquet. It's small, which is great encouragement for me to not say too much. I jot a quick note.

. . .

Aniston,

I'm here whenever you want to talk.
If you want to talk.

I'm tempted to write more, but shove it inside quickly. I've said what needs to be said and no more. I fist the flowers and walk out of the hospital to my truck.

The whole drive home, I worry myself with how Aniston's day has gone. Has it been better? Has she resolved whatever went wrong yesterday? Did she get a good night's rest, or stay in her RV all night making crack?

At last, I turn down our gravel road. My truck creeps slower the closer I get to her house. The goal is to leave the flowers and drive away.

I don't see any sight of their truck, so I pull up to the front and sneak to the porch. Buster comes around the side of the house, wagging his tail. I pet him and thank him for reminding me not to set the flowers too low. Last thing I need is him dragging off my heartfelt gesture.

The front windows are decently high, and Buster's decently lazy. I set the flowers on the windowsill closest to the front door. If she doesn't notice them, one of the kids will for sure.

Then I tiptoe back to my truck and go home.

Aniston

. . .

Yesterday was one for the books. I spent half the night moping around in my RV, then remembered that I no longer live alone in an RV.

That led me inside, where I found the kids had already eaten, Easton had left, and my kitchen was infested with packs of paper towels. The kids had finished their homework, so I sent them to take showers while I started unrolling the paper towels . . . one roll at a time.

Willow helped some before bed, but it still took me half the night to get the seventy empty paper towel rolls I needed.

Sometime in the wee morning hours, I finally fall into bed.

The next thing I see is Georgia standing over me, waving paper towels like flags. "If you'd planned ahead, you could've slept more tonight. Or if you'd just told everyone as planned, it wouldn't take much to gather seventy paper towel rolls from the entire class."

I shoot up in bed, my body shaking in a cold sweat. I reach for the lamp on my nightstand and almost knock it over as I fumble to turn it on. My eyes scan the room. Nobody's here. It was a silly dream—no, a scary dream.

I wipe my hands down my face and shake my head. My body starts to recover from the fright, but I'm soaked in sweat. Good excuse to finally take a shower.

Funny how having ice cream drip across my arm or routine hygiene weren't enough to convince me I needed to shower. Seeing Georgia in my dreams? I need an extra-cold shower with lots of soap to wash off that one.

Partly from exhaustion and partly from necessity, I take my time in the shower. Then I decide to go all out with blow-drying my hair and putting on makeup. Since I'm dressed, I make a quick video about the stresses of doing random tasks like unrolling paper towels to meet a cardboard-roll quota.

I don't share it just yet, since Georgia expects me to stay

and help with something at school today. Tonight is the Fall Festival, and I can only imagine all the tasks she's dreamed up for us to complete before then. If I wait a bit, I'm sure I'll have more to add to my vlog.

By the time the kids get up, I've given myself an amateur makeover, videoed a segment for the vlog, and cleaned the kitchen. Carter comes down first and opens the refrigerator. My heart pings. How selfish of me to wake up at five and not cook breakfast.

"Hey, buddy, if y'all get ready a little earlier, we can stop and get a biscuit."

He blinks sleepily. "From the gas station?"

"Yeah." I smile. In the past few months, I've learned that gas stations are to seven-year-old boys what Target is to sorority girls.

He grins and gets a juice box before shutting the door. Willow comes down next. She pours herself a cup of orange juice, and some drips on the counter.

She glances around the room, then at me. "Aunt Ani, where are the paper towels?"

"In the pantry."

Even though I had a few extra rolls, some were squished from the car running over them at DG. So I went ahead and unrolled them all in case Georgia deems some unusable.

Willow opens the pantry door. "Whoa." She takes a step back, and I snicker at the folded paper towels stacked in the corner. There are three stacks almost as tall as her.

She picks one off the top, and the whole stack starts to tumble forward. I rush toward them and open my arms to brace them. Then I slowly step toward the pantry, pushing them back in place.

When I move back, she gives me a concerned stare.

"It's okay, I'll work on a better stacking system later." I grin and clasp my hands together as if I've just come up with a solution to save the planet.

"Are you okay?"

I prop one arm on the counter and shrug as she wipes her spilled juice. "Yeah, I didn't sleep much, but you know. Guess it's all the excitement about the festival." I giggle a little hysterically, then grab my second cup of coffee.

Or is that the third?

"Go ahead and gather your things, so we can get a biscuit. I'll take out the trash." I exit through the garage and pull the large trash can toward the road.

When I'm walking back from the end of the drive, I notice something bright yellow on the front windowsill. I jog over to see what it is.

My blood pressure shoots sky high when I notice yellow petals. That snake in the grass Georgia. I leap on the porch, missing two steps, and snatch the flowers.

Of all the low-level tricks. Did she really think upping her game with real flowers would work?

My hands shake as I open the card. Her annoying voice echoes in my head as I read the words. Why is she still offering me advice?

I squeeze my fist around the flowers and march toward the truck. "Kids, ready to go?"

Carter is already feeding Buster by the garage, and Willow comes out the back door. I toss the flowers on the console and wait for them to get in before peeling out of the drive.

"What are those?" Carter asks when he climbs in the back.

"Nothing." I slow down when we get to the trash can and park. Then I get out and slam the flowers on top of the can before driving toward town.

I must've scared the kids, because they say nothing until we're at the Quick Stop ordering biscuits.

I order a dozen extra sausage biscuits for the minions I'm sure Georgia has lined up to help. It's too late for me, but I refuse to let her suck all the joy out of some other poor souls.

For myself, I buy a candy bar. A biscuit won't do today.

CHAPTER 21

Aniston

I tug at my shirt, which says prominently in Comic Sans font, "Fall Festival Princess." Cheesy grinning pumpkins are printed beneath it, giving me more reason to put on a coat even though it's a balmy sixty-nine degrees outside.

Georgia had one of her minions make us all matching shirts. Well, most of us. Her shirt says, "Fall Festival Queen."

I lock the truck after the kids barrel out and start walking toward the school. Even though we're here early, Georgia gave exact instructions on where workers are to park. She even assigned us all spots in a replica of the parking lot. And yes, it was in my Fall Festival manual.

It could be worse. Maribelle had to park by the trash cans, where they're bringing in a dunking booth. I'd rather walk a country mile any day than deal with that.

We walk through the overgrown grass on the side of the road, dodging cars coming from both directions. Food trucks come into view, as do the few fair rides.

When we reach the school, I dig in my jeans pockets for the cash I set aside to give the kids. I'm halfway through my lecture of staying with people they know while I'm busy when Morgan walks up with a corn dog on a stick as long as my list of duties for tonight.

"What's up, Fall Festival Princess?" She laughs, then takes another bite of her corn dog.

I roll my eyes and zip my jacket.

"You know you'll burn up in that."

"Worth it," I say.

Morgan points the end of her corn dog at me, coming dangerously close to smearing mustard on my face. "Hey, don't repeat the sweater incident that landed you in the hospital."

"Fine." I unzip my jacket, feeling a little more defeated with every inch of my shirt that shows. With my jacket no longer doing the job I intended, I pull it off and tie it around my waist.

At least Georgia didn't have the same thing printed on the back of the shirts. That space was reserved for the word "Staff," as if we're nightclub bouncers or people checking seats in a stadium.

Both of which I prefer to being here.

My kids start walking with Morgan's, and I yell at them to remember what I said. Morgan fans her corn dog and says, "Ah, they'll be fine. Why don't you come with me to get a funnel cake?"

"Can't."

"Why? Surely you're not on a sugar fast?"

I shake my head and point to my shirt. "I've got to report to the queen for my royal duties."

Morgan balks. "Oh, forget her. I've got the whole paper towel scene between you two on my phone. You can use it for a vlog, or blackmail . . . or both."

I shake my head. "You filmed that?"

"Of course! I'm always recording things that I might can send to *America's Funniest Home Videos.*" Morgan licks mustard from her finger. "Although, this one seems more fitting for *Cops.*"

"Whatever, I gotta work. Catch you later."

Morgan waves at me with her corn dog as I walk off. "Whatever, I'm getting cheese fries."

Oh, Morgan. I shove my hands in my pockets and walk the green mile to the designated planning area—aka the gym office.

Georgia isn't hard to spot among the crowd, as she's wearing a tutu and crown. So that's what a Fall Festival queen looks like.

Maribelle finds me and grabs my arm. "Thank God, you're here!"

I frown. "That bad already?"

Maribelle sighs. "Half the workers are home sick. Something about getting food poisoning from a biscuit."

My jaw drops. I'm the one who brought in biscuits this morning. "But my kids aren't sick."

"What?"

"Nothing." I shake my head and feign a dumb look, as if this is all news to me. The sick part actually is—just not the biscuits.

My sleuthing sense engages, and I recall what we all ate. The kids got bacon, egg and cheese biscuits, and I got a King Size Reese's. Hmm, it must be the sausage.

"I'm glad I didn't come earlier. I never turn down a free biscuit," Maribelle comments.

I laugh nervously.

"There you are." The queen herself has spotted me. She rushes over with Gretchen Wieners, who has somehow managed to make her princess shirt look decently cute.

Georgia wields a clipboard like a battle axe. "We have got to work double-time. Everyone but us four are at home hugging their toilets." She strokes Gretchen's thin arm. "Thank God, Mindy was on a Keto fast at the time."

Mindy. Why can't I ever remember that girl's name?

"Apparently we're the only three who didn't eat one of those gas station biscuits." Somehow she makes "gas station" sound like a curse word, then side-eyes Maribelle. "And of course, not all of us could make it."

Maribelle looks in the opposite direction. Whether to avoid Georgia's glare or check if she's alluding to someone else, I'm not sure. It's pretty apparent to me she means Maribelle.

Georgia starts walking. Mindy follows her, and Maribelle and I fall into place like little ducks in a row. Although I'm pretty sure I'm the goose in this scenario.

As we walk past tables, Georgia checks off a list and barks orders. "I will man the tables in here, checking on all our vendors and helping them find their spots. Then I'll check the outside games and entertainment. Mindy will take up tickets and check armbands." Georgia pulls a money bag from a table and hands it to her. When Georgia points toward the door, Mindy breaks off and heads for the front of the school.

We continue walking. "Maribelle, you can help direct parking." Georgia snatches a reflective vest off a hook and hands it to her. She points toward the parking lot, and Maribelle breaks off.

My stomach knots, as it's now apparent I'm the only princess in this grim fairy tale still stuck to Mother Goose. "Aniston." Georgia turns on her heels and faces me.

I stop in my tracks, almost accidentally chest bumping her.

"You are in charge of making sure the outdoor games all have a space." She focuses on my hands and twists her lips. "I see you didn't bother to bring your manual, so you can borrow a page from mine." She flips open her binder and pops the rings open, then hands me a map of the game area outside.

"Won't you need this?" I wave the map, giving her a chance to take it back. I'd rather be accused of forgetting something else later than of stealing her map.

She smiles and shakes her head, then taps the side of her tight hair with a bright orange fingernail. "It's all up here."

Ah, so that's what fills the small space between a ballerina side sweep. I feign a smile and give the map a gentle shake. "Got it."

Before she can give any further instructions, I head out the door toward the open field that's usually a playground. Tonight, it's the main grounds for the outdoor events. I grab a pen from a 4-H booth and decide to start there.

Several local farms have their animals set up as a petting zoo of sorts. I talk with everyone and make sure they have the space they need before moving on. Easy enough.

The games start where the animals end. There's apple bobbing, followed by knocking over cans with Nerf guns. Near the center of the games is Bradley, marching back from a pyramid of hay with one of those speed guns.

I check my sheet, as I'm not sure what this is or how much room he needs. "Hey, Bradley. What's this?"

He holds up the gun and grins, then he dips his head toward a bucket of baseballs. "Kids, or adults . . ." He grins at me before continuing. "Can pitch a baseball at the hay and I'll tell 'em how fast they throw."

I nod. "Neat idea."

He tilts his head. "You've never seen this before?"

"I've never been to a Fall Festival before."

He props a hand on his hip and frowns. "Seriously? You grew up here."

"Yeah . . . I didn't do much."

He shrugs. "Wanna give it a go?"

"Maybe later. I have stuff to do." I wave the paper, then walk off.

"See ya," he calls as I pass.

I continue checking off spaces and making sure everyone has a spot until I'm back where I started. That's when I find Georgia waiting for me by the animals.

"Aniston."

"I just finished."

She points to the apple-bobbing bucket a few feet away. "What is this?"

"Uh, a bucket of apples." I chuckle. "I thought that was obvious."

"Duh, but what is it doing here?"

"It's a booth. Bobbing for apples. Ever heard of it?"

"Yeah, in the twentieth century, before hand sanitizer was invented."

I'm no genius, but I believe hand sanitizer has been around more than two decades. Instead of correcting her, I go with sarcasm. "Now that we have it, wouldn't that make it safer?"

Georgia exhales heavily through her nose. Her whole face moves, but her crown doesn't shift a centimeter. Must be that tight hair holding it in place.

"Aniston, we cannot have people dunking their heads in the same buckets and biting the same apples."

I chunk my hand in the bucket and pull out an apple. Not caring that water is streaming down my arm, I shove it to my mouth and take a bite.

Georgia's face reddens until it resembles an apple. She huffs and squats behind the bucket, then shoves it. Apples wash over the grass like a rising creek. The water soaks into the ground, and the apples roll a few feet near the petting zoo cages. A rogue goat jumps the fence and starts eating one.

I raise a brow at Georgia, who sets the bucket upright as if she didn't just do that on purpose. One of the farmers comes to get his goat.

"Oopsy." Georgia giggles and steps to the side, pulling me along with her.

I turn back to assess the damage as she marches me across the field. "You're just gonna leave that mess there?"

"The animals will eat it. Besides, water and apples disintegrate."

I bite my lip and contemplate that. First the hand sanitizer comment, now this. I'm not sure where Georgia went to college, but I'm not sending my kids there.

"You can help me with the ninja course."

"Ninja course?"

She nods enthusiastically as we stop in the center of the field. "Yes. Brittany was supposed to help, but as we all know, she was poisoned by biscuits someone brought."

I roll my eyes. "You got me. My whole plan is to poison the world so that I can be the last room mom standing. That's why I advocated for the apple bucket."

Georgia wrinkles her nose. "You're very sarcastic."

"What can I say? You bring out the best in me."

She scrunches her brow into an evil stare and lets go of my arm. Kids are starting to line up at the front of the obstacle course. Excuse me, "ninja" course. Funny, as I always assumed ninjas used nunchucks and sticks, not monkey bars and bouncy houses.

There's caution tape across the front of the monkey bars, which starts the obstacles. That doesn't look promising. Georgia turns to the group of kids gathering and the teenager taking up tickets.

"Welcome to our main event. Your parents must sign a waiver if you're under sixteen for you to participate." She presses an orange nail on a clipboard in front of the teen worker. Then she picks up the pen beside it and slams it on top. She smiles mischievously. "Only two at a time, as this is a race. My assistant and I will demonstrate."

"Wait, what?"

Georgia glares holes through me. "Don't act like you don't want this." Then she adjusts her crown—which still hasn't moved—and stretches her arms overhead before jerking down the tape.

"Go!"

I stand in shock for a few seconds as Georgia leaps to the monkey bars like, well, a monkey.

"Get 'er, Ani!"

I turn to Morgan cheering me on, an ear of buttered corn in one hand and her phone in the other. If she's making a run for *AFV*, I may as well do her a solid.

I kick off my sandals and take the monkey bars two at a time to make up for lost time. After dodging a few puddles and hopscotching through tires, I catch up with Georgia on the small rock climbing wall.

Her choice of attire makes up for my late start. When she swings one leg over the top, her tutu catches on one of the pegs. I ease over as she's trying to unhook the netting of her skirt.

Once I rappel down, I dart toward the next obstacle. My heart pounds so hard, I expect it to show through my shirt. Most likely a combination of my weird eating habits these past few months . . . and being around Georgia these past few months.

Endorphins kick in, and I climb the knotted rope that leads to a short slide. Morgan is within earshot, cheering me on. More people start chanting my name, giving me strength to go on.

I've got to win this thing. Not just for me, but for everyone.

At last, I make it to the final obstacle. A bouncy house? I haven't gone in one of these since junior high, and it didn't end well. For all my extreme sports, I tend to stay away from inflatables. They're unstable and just plain awkward.

No sooner than I enter the small opening, something pulls me back. I land on my back with a tiny bounce and stare up at Georgia. How did she catch up so quickly? I must really be out of shape.

She's wearing the queen shirt and leggings, no tutu. I guess that's how. She abandoned it as a casualty of war. The crown is still intact, as I suspected. And that's the first thing I go for.

I wiggle out from under her, stand, and jerk the crown from her head. She balks and shoves me like we're five. I shove her back, and she falls on her butt.

As I start to run past her, she grabs my ankle and pulls me down. That's all it takes for us to full-on wrestle.

I'd be lying if I said I hadn't dreamed of wrestling Georgia in a one-on-one fight. However, even my wildest dreams didn't include us rolling in a bouncy house, with a metal crown poking in my back.

We continue rolling around, me on top, then her. One time I get her in a head lock, but she bites—hard. The more we wrestle, the more unstable the surface is beneath us. Maybe we're pushing harder as we go. Just when I manage to pin her down in the corner, I feel the ground under my hands, and the roof falls on our heads. We're deflated!

I roll off of Georgia and fight my way out of the rubble. When I make it to the exit hole, I come face to face with Easton.

Easton

Shock, hurt, anger. Those emotions only scratch the surface of what's rushing through my mind. Shock at Aniston fighting with Georgia in an inflatable. Hurt at Aniston tossing out my flowers. Anger at her putting them *on* the trash rather than *in* the trash to make sure I saw them.

Nothing says "screw you" quite like tossing my bouquet of flowers to the curb.

Her pale eyes stare at me with a hollowness. It's as if she's looking straight through me. This all but confirms my suspicion that she wants nothing more to do with me.

I step back from the inflatable and walk away. I came here to give us a chance at a normal night after everything. To give her a chance to undo trashing my flowers. Instead, I find her wrestling another grown woman. And it's not even hot wrestling, like in mud or an above-ground pool filled with Jell-O. No, it had to be in a kid's blow-up house.

"Easton!" Aniston calls behind me.

I take a few more steps, then stop. The desperation in her voice, paired with my delight in hearing her say my name for the first time in days, does something to me. My mind screams *walk*, but my body begs *stay*. I'm a reasonable man, but when it comes to Aniston, all reason flies out the window.

My shoulders tense as she stops behind me. "Easton, can we talk?"

She's close enough for her breath to brush against my neck. I turn slow as a sloth pouring molasses. We're a few inches apart, and my heart burns like the time I ate those nachos from the Quick Stop.

"I'd love to talk, Aniston, but . . ." I scratch my head, debating how to play this. "I said so on my flowers."

Maybe that didn't sound too condemning. It's hard not to sound that way when I pull my trash can to the road and find the flowers are sitting on top of hers.

"Your flowers?" Aniston scrunches her forehead.

"Yes, I left a bouquet of flowers on your windowsill so Buster couldn't reach them. Yellow, your favorite color."

Aniston's eyes widen, and she blushes. "You left those? I thought they were from Georgia."

"The woman you just brawled with in an inflatable?"

She must've heard her name, because at that moment, Georgia falls out of the deflated castle, plops a bent crown on her head, and stumbles toward us. She looks like a drunken tooth fairy as she almost tumbles over a little kid.

The boy clings to the adult next to him, and a group of kids nearby run away. I don't blame them. From her pulled hair, broken crown, and scowling face, Georgia has managed to scare just about everyone around. Except for maybe Aniston.

"Yes," Aniston answers.

"Why?"

"She bought me these fake roses."

I wrinkle my brow. That doesn't sound like Georgia. "Are you sure it was her?"

"Yes! She ran me down in the Dollar General parking lot to give them to me."

I shake my head, confused by why either Georgia would do something so out of character or why Aniston would lie to me. Then again, she did trash my flowers.

She turns slowly as Georgia creeps behind her, breathing harder than a charismatic evangelist on the last leg of a revival tour. "Tell him, Georgia."

Georgia sucks in air and catches her breath before propping her hands on her hips to try and steady herself. She straightens the crown on her head, or at least tries, and stares at me.

"This woman is crazy. First, she attacks me in a bounce house, then she lies about me."

Aniston throws her arms up and lets out a hysterical laugh. "What in the world? You struck first in there." She points to the deflated pile of plastic. "And it was your idea for us to compete in the first place." She turns to me. "She did give me fake flowers. If you don't believe me, go to Jennifer's grave. I left them there when I went to see her."

Georgia stares at the ground and bites her lip. Then she reaches out for Aniston's arm. "Aniston, I really think you should see someone. Seeing dead people isn't normal."

Aniston jerks her arm free from Georgia. She steps toward me, tears brimming her eyelids. "Easton, you've got to believe me. This is all her fault. I never would've thrown away your flowers had I known."

I sigh. My body aches as my mind wrestles between believing her or not. It all sounds a little crazy. Even if it is true, I'm not sure I'm cut out for her constant warring with Georgia.

"Aniston, I care about you, a lot. But I'm not sure what to believe anymore." I glance between her and Georgia. "You two are obsessed with outdoing each other, and it's getting old."

I turn back to Aniston and put my hands on her shoulders. My arms tingle at touching her for the first time in days. "All I ever wanted was to be with you and take care of you. But I can't do that if you won't let me."

"Take care of me?" Tears drip from her eyes, but her face communicates that they're tears of anger more than sadness. I immediately regret my choice of words when she pushes my hands off her and stomps. "I don't need you to take care of me. I'm a capable adult." She wavers her head. "Aside from medical emergencies, I don't need you to take care of me. So you best shop elsewhere for a potential trophy wife."

One of my biggest faults is putting my foot in my mouth. I think before I speak, but I don't always consider how someone might interpret what I say before I say it. I never meant to insult Aniston or have her think I assumed she needed me. Whether Aniston wanted to hurt me back, she did. Her words cut deep, and our time together plays out in my head like a highlight reel.

Cutting the hay, fixing her mirror, cooking dinner, keeping the kids. Did she think I did all that because I assumed she couldn't? I didn't. I did it because I love her.

Something I would've told her had this conversation not taken a turn for the worst. Now saying "I love you" would look like a Hail Mary to salvage any relationship we might have left.

"Some trophy," Georgia mutters behind us. I'd forgotten she was standing there.

Aniston's angry eyes and Georgia standing beside her in their matching shirts pushes me over the edge. I can't deal with whatever crap is going on right now. It's apparent I'm not as important to Aniston as she is to me. I do something out of character, but what I feel is right.

I turn and walk away.

CHAPTER 22

Aniston

Some trophy. My ears burn with those words from Georgia as I stand planted in the soggy field, staring at the back of Easton's head. For every step he takes, another piece of my heart breaks.

I've got to go after him. But first . . .

I reach down and grab a handful of mud near my shoe and sling it at Georgia. She flinches and squeals like a five-year-old girl would at a spider. I lift my chin in momentary victory, then wipe my muddy hand down the front of my princess shirt.

Easton is now near the end of the field, all the way to the food trucks. I take off jogging after him. My eyes fixate on his jeans as I weave around the crowd of people. I've stared at his butt a lot the past few months, but always out of want rather than need. Now I'm zeroed in on the Wrangler logo so I don't lose him in plain sight.

I'm gaining ground when a group of teenagers stop in

front of me to take a selfie. I shuffle around them, losing sight of him for a second. When I locate my target again, his butt has gained a few yards more ahead of me.

I stumble around a couple carrying a large teddy bear and break off toward the food trucks. Easton heads for the parking area. If I can make it past the trucks, I can break into a run and catch him.

There's a small shuttle where people can donate blood right beside the Big Butts truck. I cover my mouth at the thought of people donating blood and barbecue smoking within inches of one another. Nobody else seems to mind, given the line to both places.

My eyes land on a small opening between the food truck and bloodmobile. If I can just make it there, I'll be free. As I squeeze between the lines toward the opening, one of those tube-man blow-ups dances in my face. I push it aside, only for it to follow me. Bear hugging it, I tilt my head to the side and try to shuffle past.

Once I'm free, I hear a truck crank. Sure enough, Easton's truck lights up. *No, no, no.* "No!" That time it comes out audibly.

I race down the hill and run toward his truck. He's parked a good piece down the road, not too far from our truck. My heart sinks when he starts to back out. I kick it in overdrive, running fast as possible and flailing my arms like an Auburn fan at the Iron Bowl.

"Easton!" I scream at the top of my lungs as his truck pulls into the road. His brake lights shine like a glimmer of hope. A beacon on a lighthouse, promising rescue from a wave of storms.

I scream his name once more and come within a few yards of his tailgate as the brake lights go out. My last shred of hope goes out with them as he drives away.

Catching my breath, I slump my shoulders and inch toward the edge of the road. The last thing I need is for someone to run me over. Then again, it would put me out of my misery.

In a daze, I walk along the side of the road. The glow of the fair rides behind me leaves just enough light for me to see where I'm going. Not that it matters, since I'm not sure where I'm going. Home? Back to the festival? To visit Jennifer again?

I stare up at the stars and let out a laborious sigh. No use going back to the graveyard. I know my sister isn't actually there. The Big Dipper catches my eye, and I fixate on it a second. I wonder how far heaven is above that? Could Jennifer and Luke and my parents see people on Earth?

If so, how would they feel about me right now? Would they sympathize with me? Scold me? Be embarrassed?

I drop my head and walk a few feet farther. If only I had a sign to let me know I'm doing all right at life.

"Moooooooo!"

I jump about three feet and land on my butt in the ditch. My heart jumps higher than that and lands in my stomach. When I manage to stand, I'm facing a giant bull only a fence away from me. A fence I pray is electric and well maintained.

Breathing in and out slowly helps regulate my heartbeat to a normal enough pace for me to continue walking. If that's my sign, I'm not sure how to interpret it.

Even though the fair only officially started about an hour ago, I decide it's best if I go home. First, I need the kids. Time to eat crow and head back to the field.

I turn around and walk closer to the road than the pasture, in case my bull friend tries anything sketchy. However, given the choice between the bull and Georgia, I'd take my chances with the wild beast. By that, I mean the bull.

My feet tense as I step onto the concrete walkway leading to the school. Then the rest of me tenses when a hand rests on my back. Georgia? Easton?

"Morgan?"

She frowns. "I was worried about you. I saw you fighting that balloon guy when I was giving blood."

"You give blood at these things?" I noticed the long line, but it never occurred to me to actually do it.

"Yeah, I give whenever I can. Sometimes plasma too . . . for the money."

I blink. There's got to be better ways to make extra cash.

"You should give sometime. Blood is a natural way to donate."

My stomach churns at the idea of it. Just seeing the IV in my arm during that night in the hospital was enough to make me squirm. "Oh, I don't know. There's so much sugar running through my veins that my donation might send someone into a diabetic coma."

She laughs. "Anyway, I watched you run and holler for Easton out the window of the bloodmobile. As soon as they unhooked me, I came for you." She shakes a hand dismissively. "Don't worry, Isabella and Willow are with the younger kids."

I nod. "Thanks, Morgan."

She reaches inside the neck of her shirt and pulls her phone from her bra. "I also got the whole Georgia fight on video if you ever need it."

I close my eyes and pinch the bridge of my nose.

"Don't worry. I stopped videoing when Easton came up."

I puff up my cheeks and kick a loose pebble in front of me. Then I let out a breath and stare at Morgan. "I've never embarrassed myself so badly."

"I think Georgia should be embarrassed, not you."

I wince, not convinced.

Morgan nods and grins. "She lost her skirt, was wearing that stupid crown, and you were on top when the bouncy collapsed."

I shake my head. "How did that even happen?"

"One of the carnies working the Tilt-A-Whirl came over to

check. Turns out, a piece of Georgia's crown broke off and punctured the side."

"Great, I'm sure we'll have to have some sort of stupid fundraiser to reimburse the inflatable company."

Morgan shrugs and holds up her phone. "I bet if we post this on social, we could make enough to cover the cost, plus take all our kids to Dollywood for fall break."

I burst out laughing and so does Morgan. Once we recover enough to walk, we start toward the field.

"Just say the word, and it's done." Morgan wiggles her eyebrows and lifts the phone once more before tucking it safely behind her boobs.

I shake my head. "I'm not that desperate . . . yet."

She nods and drapes an arm around my shoulder. We stroll around the side of the school, then I freeze at the sight of Georgia.

She's still wearing that broken crown and has her tutu back on, even with half of it ripped. TikTok Tami stands beside her with her belly poked out, painted like a pumpkin.

"Is that?"

"I can get the kids if you don't want to walk past her."

"Thanks." I smile at Morgan. "But is that Tami with her?"

"Yep, I see she's doing the whole 'pumpkin in the patch' look again."

"Huh?"

Morgan rolls her eyes. "She likes to paint her stomach when she's pregnant this time of year."

"I couldn't even tell until now."

"She's good at hiding it until she needs to. Word around town is that whenever her boyfriend threatens to leave, she gets pregnant."

My eyes widen. "Yeah, I'm gonna just head toward the truck."

"Meet you there in ten." Morgan pats my shoulder, then removes her arm and struts toward the odd pair.

I choose not to care what Georgia and Tami are talking about and continue in the opposite direction. I walk across the road from the truck until necessary just in case the bull tries to greet me again.

To top off the night I'm having, the truck won't crank. I dig in the toolbox for jumper cables, but only find actual tools. By the time Morgan gets back with all the kids, I'm digging under the back seat.

"What are you doing?" she asks.

I hold up a pair of volleyball kneepads in desperate need of washing and add them to the pile of empty Pop-Tart wrappers, used napkins, and dirty clothes I found. "Hunting jumper cables but finding everything else."

"Will the truck not crank?"

I shake my head. "Do you have any cables in your van?"

"No, but odds are with the number of rednecks per capita in this town, somebody here does."

"As long as it's not Georgia." I point to the pasture beside us. "I'll ride that bull home before I have her jump us off."

"I can ask around."

I prop my hands on my hips and glance around at all the cars. "Let me just get our things and lock up for now."

Morgan nods, then helps me gather what we need from the truck. Willow transfers what we should throw away to the bed until I can get a trash bag.

Five minutes later, we're walking down the road with backpacks, volleyball gear, pom-poms, and purses like an ill-equipped motley crew on a post-apocalyptic mission.

Maybe Easton was right. I do need him to survive—or at least to adult.

Blue lights come into view as we get closer to Morgan's van. Just great. Bradley stops and rolls down his window.

"We'll get out of the middle of the road," I say.

"What's going on?"

"My truck won't start."

"Want me to drive y'all home and have Kyle drive the truck to your house?" He lifts a radio. "One call, and he can be here."

I smile. "That would be great, but we can ride home with Morgan."

The only thing holding me together right now is the fact that I'm *not* in the back of a cop car.

Bradley turns off his blue lights—finally. Though the damage is done, as a dozen or so people walked by while he talked to us. I'm certain at least two people took photos with their phones.

"Suit yourself. Hand me your key, and I'll have that truck delivered ASAP." Bradley lifts a hand through the open window.

I pull my keys from my jeans pocket and fumble with the ring until I manage to detach the truck key. Then I hand it to him. "I'm parked a little ways back there to the left."

Bradley squints out his windshield. "Up there by Mason's pasture?"

"Yep." More like by his bull.

"Thank ya, ma'am." Bradley tips his cowboy hat and drives toward my truck.

The rest of us stumble down the side of the road toward Morgan's van, then pile inside.

"I don't have a seat belt." Carter is sandwiched between two of Morgan's kids in the back.

"It's okay this time, Carter. Just sit still." That shouldn't be a problem, since he has no room to move.

Halfway out of town, the scent of sewage fills the air.

"Ewww, Ethan!" Sophia coughs and rolls her eyes back in her head, grabbing her neck to mock choking.

Ethan grins, then glances at Willow across the middle seat from him. "It wasn't me, I swear."

Isabella scrunches her nose as Morgan rolls down the

windows and adds, "Ethan, we all know it was you. Silent but violent. That's your game."

Ethan blushes and slumps down in his seat. Willow smirks and holds back a laugh as everyone else laughs, gags, or a little of both.

That fart cuts some of the tension until we turn down my drive and Easton's house is visible in the distance. He's so close, yet so far.

I hold my stomach as Morgan's van bounces us down the gravel road and stops in front of my house. The back van door opens with the push of a button, and kids bolt out in every direction.

We sit in silence for a second with the windows down, then Morgan cuts the engine. "Wanna talk about it, Ani?"

I unclench my stomach and stare out the window. "I think I blew it with Easton."

"No, you didn't."

I jerk my head toward Morgan and give her a serious stare.

"Okay, so maybe you did some damage, but nothing that can't be buffed out. Not a total destruction, more like a fender bender."

"Yeah, my whole life is one fender bender after another. I keep holding my breath and riding on one wheel, waiting for someone to tell me it's totaled."

She pats my shoulder and sighs. "You know, when Ken left me, I didn't see it coming. I mean, looking back, there were signs, but I didn't see them until it was too late. The fact that you can recognize the fender benders says something. You have more control of your life than me." Morgan slaps her steering wheel and laughs. "I was cruising along on autopilot. In my mind, we were headed to the beach in a Maserati, when all along I was running carpool in the minivan. Sometimes we need to just look at our life for what it is and do the best we can from there."

I wipe my hands down my face, then regret it when I smell them. "For once, I'd just like to have the kind of life Jennifer did. You'd think that wouldn't be so hard with her house, kids, and dog. I mean, she all but handed me her perfect life on a silver platter."

Morgan balks. "You think Jenn had it that good?"

I nod. "Yeah, I do."

"No, honey. She was cute and had a great marriage, sure, but she wasn't without problems. The school depended on her for a lot. She quit working and put all her dreams aside so her kids could still do their activities since Luke had to travel so much. She was at the church lots of times helping with stuff nobody even knew about, and she never took any time for herself. That trip they left on was the first time her and Luke had time to themselves since I don't know when."

"Really?"

Morgan nods, her face going sad. "I offered to keep the kids and encouraged her to take it. Not a day goes by that I don't regret that. If they hadn't—" Her voice chokes.

I reach across the console and wrap my arms around her. "Morgan, we all think those things. It's nobody's fault."

"I know," she squeaks.

We sit in silence, hugging, sharing a moment, until someone screams. Instantly, we break apart and jump out of our respective van doors.

Morgan's youngest has jumped in the pool in his underwear. She rolls her eyes before yelling, "Andrew!"

He turns around to both of us standing, hands on hips, at the edge of the pool. As soon as he makes eye contact with his mother, he swims toward the steps.

"I swear, these kids don't give you time to get upset." Morgan glares at Andrew, dripping as he climbs out in his Spider-Man underwear. "At least not about yourself."

We both burst out laughing. Willow announces she'll get a

towel, and I sit down and dangle my legs in the pool, not caring that my shoes are still on.

That makes Morgan laugh even harder. She lies down beside me on the concrete, and Buster comes by to sniff her.

"Quit it, Buster." She pushes him away from her face, then leans on her elbow and pets him.

Ethan comes over and strokes Buster's back. "Mama, why can't we get a dog?"

"We don't need a dog. We have your brother." Morgan nods toward the patio, where Andrew is shaking his hair out while he waits on a towel.

Laughing so much that my side now hurts, I lay my head back too, and stare up at the stars. That view never grows old, no matter where I am. If it weren't for our friends and the kids' activities, I'd load up the RV and start homeschooling them tomorrow.

My eyes trail until I find the Big Dipper. This time, it points directly toward Easton's house. Yeah, that's just one more reason to stay—or leave.

I haven't decided yet.

CHAPTER 23

Easton

I've fished more the past few weeks than I have in all my years post medical school combined. With everything else in my life, I viewed sitting by the pond, waiting on a fish to bite, as a waste of my time.

Then Carter asked me to fish.

I hesitated before agreeing, given the weirdness between Aniston and me right now. However, Carter can't help whatever's going on between us. So I agreed, and I'm glad I did.

For the past few weeks, we've met at the pond on Saturday mornings and sometimes on Sunday afternoons. I'm not sure whether he was the same way before his parents died, but Carter is an old soul and wise beyond his years.

I first discovered that when he brought up topics like gas prices and the Alabama quarterback. Most kids his age want to discuss toys and superheroes. Although, Alabama football players are superheroes to some people around here.

A few leaves blow from the trees outlining the pasture. I

zip my jacket and recast my reel, while Carter fumbles with his bait. We're using crickets that I uncovered when I moved a tarp off a hay disc.

My eyes follow the fishing line as it flies across the water and lands in the center of the pond. I notice Aniston at the edge of her house and try to ignore her. Too bad I can't cast the line a little farther and reel her in.

But what good would it do if I caught her?

I assume she's fine with me having a relationship with Carter, but she hasn't acknowledged my existence in weeks. And with her kitchen remodel now finished, I can't use the excuse of inviting them to dinner. The last time we spoke was the Fall Festival. She didn't even come to my door when Carter stopped by trick-or-treating.

On Halloween, I saw them loading into the truck, with Carter dressed like a hunter. I showered and changed out of my work clothes in case they came by here. They did, but *she* didn't come to the door.

All I got was a straight-lipped smile from her when our eyes met for a second. At least, it looked like a smile from behind her windshield. That's what I choose to believe.

"Do you like fishing, Dr. Easton?"

Carter's question catches me off guard. I quit staring at Aniston's house and turn to him. "Of course I do. Don't you?"

"Yes, sir. You just seem a little off today."

I laugh. "Because I haven't caught anything in the ten minutes we've been out here?"

"No, sir. You keep staring off at the field."

Sure, *that's* what I'm staring at. I choose not to let him think otherwise. Instead, I turn the conversation to him.

"Do you like fishing?"

Carter nods. "It's my favorite. I also like archery, and I used to play baseball and football some with Daddy." His voice creaks at the word "Daddy."

I reach over and squeeze his shoulder. "It's good to remember those times. I fished a lot with my grandpa and love those memories. We also worked together, and he taught me everything I know about tractors."

Carter grins at me with a missing front tooth. "I think Daddy would be happy I'm still fishing."

"Me too." I choke back my own emotions. Not so much about my grandpa, but more about my current situation.

My lease for the carriage house is up when the year ends. Since it technically belongs to the kids now, with Aniston overseeing it, I'm not sure if I'll renew it—or if that's even an option. It just occurred to me that she may send me packing. Just because she allows me to hang out with her nephew doesn't mean she wants me living in her backyard.

We fish in silence for a few minutes, and I'm reminded of why I quit fishing so often. I'm not patient enough to sit and wait on the fish to bite. For me, fishing was all social. A way to spend time with my grandpa. I enjoy being with Carter too, except for the parts where there's no talking or catching fish. That gives me too much time in my head.

The way I work, I don't get a lot of downtime to dwell on my own life. Most of my thinking comes when I'm in the tractor. Thanks to the grass dying off with the changing season, I don't do that near as much lately. Staring at Aniston is forcing my suppressed feelings to the surface.

Thank God, it's too cool for her to be prowling around in a bikini.

I recast my line to have something to do, then check out what Carter's got going on. He's hooking a new cricket after losing his bait in the water. Then he meets my gaze.

"You're in love with my aunt, right?"

My body goes numb, and my hands no longer have grip. The fishing pole hits the ground, and I blink at Carter. I can't decide if I'm more shocked that he'd think that or ask that. I guess he really is wise beyond his years.

Carter blushes. "I'm sorry. That's personal." Then he faces the pond and recasts his line.

The easy way out would be to leave it at that. If only I weren't so desperate to talk to someone about this. I didn't want to call my dad. He's never met Aniston, and I don't exactly ask him for love advice all the time. So doing so all of a sudden in my early thirties about a girl he's never met wouldn't make much sense. Of course, neither does talking to a second grader.

"Yes, Carter, I do."

There, I got that out of the way. I admitted my love for Aniston as I'd planned on doing weeks ago. Only I'd planned on telling her and not her seven-year-old nephew.

Carter raises an eyebrow at me and smirks. "Then what are you going to do about it?"

"Excuse me?" I'm not used to many people talking to me this way, especially kids.

Aniston's one of the few people who speaks to me like I'm not all-knowing because I went to medical school. That's one of the things I miss most about her. Maybe Carter has some of that in him.

"You can't just stand here staring at her across the pond. You need to go to my house and talk to her."

I sit on the dried grass and lean back on my hands. "Carter, it's not that simple."

"How come?"

Good question. It should be that simple, but it isn't. "Your aunt is unlike anyone I've ever known. That's part of what attracted me to her. It's also why I don't know how to act toward her in certain situations. She's going through a lot right now with raising y'all and adjusting to a new life. The last thing she needs is adding me to the mix to confuse her further."

Carter shakes his head. "If you're waiting on her to talk

first, you may be staring across this pond for forever. She is stubborn."

I cackle out laughing and fall back on my elbows. "Carter, you are a wise young man."

Carter isn't laughing. His face is serious as stone. "Please, Dr. Easton. Don't wait too long to talk to her."

"I won't." I say this more to end the conversation than as a promise.

I'm tempted to run across the field and knock on her door. But after all Aniston has been through—and is still going through—I can't blindly show up without thinking this through. I need a plan—or better yet, a sign from her.

When I talk to her again, I need to make it count. The last thing I want to do is scare her off for good.

Aniston

I wiggle my toes in the balmy water, then set my feet on the towel above the pedicure tub. Thanks to the sensation of hot water jetting up my legs, I have the sudden urge to pee.

I turn to Morgan, who is glued to a *People* magazine. "Do you know where the bathroom is?"

She points to the right without lifting her head.

"Thanks." I wipe my feet best I can, then shimmy barefoot across the linoleum floor, praying I don't slip and bust my butt.

Morgan talked me into letting the kids go to the basketball game at school with her mom and Adrianne so we could have a girls' night. She and Brooke agreed that a pedicure was the perfect way to relax. According to Brooke, "It's the second most relaxing thing next to a massage, but we can be beside each other and talk, unlike massages."

I would've been fine watching *Steel Magnolias* and eating junk food, but as Morgan pointed out, I do that enough. Their goal was to get me out of the house. Since I'm staring at a golden Buddha statue while sitting on the toilet, I'd say they succeeded.

As I'm washing my hands, I take a good look at my face. My eyes are droopy and bloodshot from lack of sleep. Despite my effort to put on makeup and fix my hair, it's apparent that what's inside doesn't match the packaging. I'm miserable, and it shows.

I jerk off a paper towel and dry my hands. It's nice to pull a paper towel and not have forty-seven more fall out with it. If for no other reason, that makes it worth leaving the house.

When I get back to the massage chairs, Morgan is flipping through a different magazine, and Brooke is studying a clip full of fake fingernails in different colors. I sit between them and stare at the fake nails in Brooke's hand.

"Are you getting fake nails on your toes?"

She laughs. "No, silly. This is just for picking colors."

I nod.

Morgan lowers her magazine. "Ani, have you never had a pedicure?"

I shake my head as I dip my feet back into the water. "Clearly, if I had, I would've peed before I came."

Morgan shrugs. "So let's talk about Easton."

"So . . . let's not." I face forward and turn my chair's massage feature to the highest setting before closing my eyes.

"You have to talk. Come on, Aniston, why do you think we took you out?"

I peek one eye open to Brooke. "Not me. I wouldn't pry. I just liked the idea of eating at a chain restaurant that isn't fast food."

"Thank you, Brooke." I emphasize her name as I scowl at Morgan.

Morgan rolls her eyes. "Well, excuse me for worrying about your HEA."

"My what?"

"HEA: happily ever after."

I face forward again and concentrate on the rows of polish on the back wall. The colors are organized in a pattern of light to dark, and I find it mildly soothing. Unlike Morgan's accusations in my ear.

Besides, I'm not sure I believe in happily ever afters. If anyone was headed for an HEA it would be my sister, and we see how that panned out. You'd think Morgan wouldn't still be buying into fairy-tale bull herself. She reads way too many celebrity gossip stories. They've corrupted her brain.

"Ignore me all you want, as long as you stop ignoring Easton."

I snap my head toward her. "I'm not ignoring Easton."

"Oh really. So you don't time taking out the trash and checking the mail around his usual schedule?"

"I—" I can't deny waiting until he's at work to venture past my front lawn. "Wait, how do you know that?"

"A little birdy," Morgan gloats. I cross my arms and give her a death glare until she elaborates. "Okay, Willow told Isabella, and she told me."

"That little snitch!"

Morgan grabs my arm with such force that the tiny Asian woman at my feet cowers down. "Don't you punish that precious child. She's concerned about you, that's all."

I shake my head, mulling over snippy comments to Morgan in my mind. I'm about to lead with the mother of all sarcasm when Brooke speaks.

"I'm worried about you too, Aniston."

"You are?"

She nods. "It's none of my business what you do about Easton, but I want you to be happy. You don't look happy."

I swallow. *Thank you, Captain Obvious.* Of what I observed in the golden restroom mirror, my face screams anything but happy.

"For what it's worth, Easton doesn't look happy either," Brooke adds. Then she smiles at the guy working on her feet and hands him the clip of colors, holding up the bright red.

My eyes widen as I imagine Easton at work. Has he been moping? Is he quieter than usual? Has he refrained from telling corny jokes? Okay, so that last one would be a welcome change.

Obviously reading my mind, Brooke continues. "He's been moping around the office, and I caught him talking to himself the other day."

I laugh. "Probably going through his to-do list."

Brooke shakes her head. "I heard your name."

Morgan grins. "Maybe you're on his to-do list."

I reach back and smack her. She rubs the side of her chest, as the little nail lady scoots her stool back a few inches.

"Ouch, my boob." Morgan narrows her eyes.

"Sorry, I was aiming for your arm." I point a finger in her face. "But that was inappropriate and inconsiderate."

She folds her arms over her chest. "Point taken."

I turn back to Brooke, who is capable of having an adult conversation and not scaring off little nail ladies. "Has he said anything to you?"

"No, you know how Easton isn't one to talk about his life. And I haven't pried. I'm pretty sure it's frowned upon to grill the boss about his love life."

I waver my head. "I know y'all are right, and I miss him like crazy." I sigh. "I just wish I had some sort of sign that things would work out, you know?" I glance at both of them, but neither answers. "What if we decide we're just too different? Now, or six months from now, or, God forbid, after we get married one day?"

Brooke grins when I mention marriage. Clearly, she's still hanging on for her own HEA.

Morgan pats my hand. "You don't get to know. Had you told me when I started dating Ken in high school that he'd leave me one day, it would've ruined everything."

"You never would've dated him, would you?"

Morgan moves her hand from mine and laughs. "More like I would've laughed in your face and dated him anyway. I think life has a way of letting us see what we need to see when we need to see it, and nothing more. That's why we don't know when or how we'll die. None of us can predict the next year or even tomorrow. That's part of what makes life exciting. Even with the nasty divorce, I would do it all again, because I remember the good times and how I now have four beautiful kids. A little crazy and wild, but still beautiful."

We all laugh until we start to cry. Not unlike the women in *Steel Magnolias*, which we'd be at home watching right now if I weren't scared of Morgan.

The nail people put the finishing touches on our polish and stick thin rubber flip-flops on our feet.

"These are to wear until they dry," Morgan explains. Then she stands, grabs her purse and boots, and goes to the register.

"Do we not need to stay for them to dry?" I stand after Brooke, a little confused why we're taking off so quickly.

"We usually walk down the block for ice cream and let them air out."

I arch my brows at my bright purple toes against the pink sandals. "You wear these out?"

Morgan nods. "Yeah, who cares?"

I shrug and dig in my wallet after Brooke pays for her nails. The tiny woman who worked on Morgan's feet rings me up. She's barely visible above the register.

She thanks me for her tip with a smile and nod. Then, she surprises me by speaking English for the first time. "A tip for you, my dear. Love is always worth it."

"Thanks, that's profound. So you speak from experience?" She's got to be nearly seventy. I imagine her and a cute little man strolling arm-in-arm around the park.

"No, fortune cookie." She grins.

I half-smile, then follow my friends out the door in our paper-thin throwaway shoes. Regardless of where she found her wisdom, it's still good advice.

CHAPTER 24

Aniston

I pour a cup of coffee and dig in my purse for the truck key. Ever since Bradley brought it home from the festival, I've been meaning to put it back on my key ring. Instead, it's lived in the bottom of my purse.

After searching long enough to need a second cup of coffee, I retreat to the laundry room for the spare keys. I refuse to let something like this make us late.

When I open the key box, the van key catches my eye. Should I? Could I? It's not as invasive as sleeping in Jennifer's bed, which I still haven't done. However, I have raided her closet a few times and enjoyed her extra-deep bathtub. The van was left for our use like everything else.

Before I talk myself out of it, I snatch the van key and slam the box shut. With the key in one hand and a coffee mug in the other, I climb the stairs to make sure the kids are awake.

Willow is already brushing her teeth, but I find Carter still in bed. I slide the key into the pocket of my flannel pajama pants and sit at the edge of his bed. "Carter," I whisper near his ear. I nudge his shoulder and give it a gentle shake before saying his name louder.

His eyes blink open as he yawns. After a little more coaxing, he climbs out of bed. I sympathize with him. Mondays are my least favorite day of the week. Although Saturday and Sunday weren't so special this week either.

After our Friday night excursion to Applebee's, the nail salon, and the ice cream parlor, I spent a lot of time analyzing my situation with Easton. Brooke confirmed that he was working the ER that weekend, which gave me an excuse not to run to his house and have *the* conversation.

The one where I'm not sure what to say or how it will go. The one I've dreaded ever since he walked away from me at the Fall Festival.

Once Carter is coherent enough to brush his teeth, I go downstairs to fix breakfast. By that, I mean pour cereal.

We have a full gallon of milk and we're actually up in time to eat at home, so it seems senseless to waste this opportunity on Pop-Tarts. I'll save those for when we're out of milk and running late, which could come early as tomorrow.

The kids sit at the island and start scooping cereal. I stand by the sink to eat mine, peering out the front window. Fall has always been one of my favorite seasons, with the cooler weather and beautiful colors. I glance at the kids. My heart warms in anticipation of spending the holidays with them.

It will be hard, no doubt. The first of many without their parents. For me, however, it will be the first of many where I'm not alone, blowing through for Thanksgiving and Christmas dinner before darting off on my next adventure.

The only thing missing now is Easton.

I sigh and raise my bowl to my mouth to drink the remaining milk. Unladylike, yes, but a convenient habit I developed living alone.

The kids bring their bowls to the sink, and according to the microwave clock, we might just be early today.

"Y'all ready?"

"Yes," Willow answers. Carter halfway nods in his zombie-like state.

"Let's go." I make sure everyone has their backpacks and that Carter has his lunch box. I'm proud to say I've been faithfully packing his lunch the past few weeks. It's the one area of my life that's actually improved.

The kids walk to the truck and open their respective doors. I go to the van and pull the key from my pocket. "Want to take the van?"

"Really?" Carter perks up for the first time since waking.

"If y'all are comfortable with it."

They shut the truck doors and rush over like we're headed to the beach rather than school. "Okay, then." I climb inside the driver's seat and shut the door.

My chest tightens when I adjust my seat. It's too close to the steering wheel, and I know that's because my sister sat here last. I move it back a few inches and take a deep breath. Then I back out of the garage and stare at the controls.

By the time we get to school, I've decided I like minivans. This one has all the cool features Morgan's does, plus it's a ton cleaner and doesn't smell like farts—yet.

I may as well get over the whole cool factor. Why not embrace the van life? There's a good chance I'll end up a spinster anyway.

We drop Willow off and turn toward the elementary school. Carter is happy to have his sliding door back instead of having to shove the truck door open. I like it too since it shuts itself.

Once the door closes, I hear a loud knock at my window. I roll it down to none other than Georgia. Just great.

The last few weeks, she's left me alone. Easton leaving me alone has sucked, but Georgia leaving me alone has been a welcomed break. Like when it rains for days on end, then the sun suddenly makes an appearance.

The absence of Georgia has been a ray of sunshine in my life. Now it appears we're headed for bad weather.

"Aniston, I need you to park and come in the office with me."

I stare down at my flannel pajamas and gulp. "Uh, I'm not really dressed for that."

Georgia peeks over my open window. "You're wearing pants."

"Yeah, pajama pants."

"So? It won't be the first time someone's come in the office like that."

"Yeah, but—"

"Pull over and park, you're holding up the line." Georgia lowers the stop sign she's holding and slaps the hood of my van.

I'm stuck in a moral dilemma between fight or flight. Do I go inside and fight with her over whatever this is, or do I hightail it home?

The car behind me honks, and I make the split decision to veer to the side of the building and park. I climb out of the van and shrug my purse on my arm. Maybe if I pretend I'm not wearing pajamas, nobody will notice. Who's to say plaid fleece pants and leopard-print house shoes aren't in this season?

Georgia is waiting on me at the school entrance. Why should I feel ashamed when she's wearing that reflective vest and tight ponytail?

When I walk in the door, she grabs my arm and leads me past the office window.

"Don't I need to sign in?"

Instead of answering, she continues leading me to an office behind "the office." Principal Dingle sits behind a large cherrywood desk.

"Have a seat, ladies." His voice is clipped, and I'm having a hard time reading his mood. He stands and shuts the door as we take the two chairs across from him.

I smile nervously. It's been a hot minute since I was called into the principal's office. That was eleventh grade, for skipping school. I knew what I was in for . . . and I had on actual pants.

Dingle sits in his chair and frowns at Georgia. Then he turns his computer screen toward us. Chills cover my entire body when I see my vlog site.

"Georgia brought this site to my attention. She sent me a few links and said she was upset about some of the content."

My neck itches, and I wonder if it's splotchy to match the heat rising in it. Either my nerves have gotten the best of me, or I'm coming down with the flu. Maybe pajamas weren't such a bad choice after all. Just in case I end up in the hospital again.

Georgia smirks my way and sits a bit straighter in her chair. My worst nightmare starts rolling before me as he hits play on the episode where I rant about the PTSO. This is it. I've sealed my fate. We may have to skip town and homeschool.

My whole life flashes before me as I relive the vlog from the other POV. The one that isn't me making the video. I scratch my neck and curse myself for not taking it down when I realized my mistake. This vlog was my personal rant, never meant to go public. But when it did, it went viral.

Then I got greedy and made more. Now I'm paying the price for making money in such a frivolous way, like reality stars and people who sue over spilled coffee. I lower my head in preparation for my punishment.

"Now you see what kind of backlash I've been dealing with all year," Georgia quips.

I close my eyes and mentally prepare for the principal's response like a kid anticipating a shot at the doctor.

"Actually, Georgia, that's what I wanted to address."

Here we go. May as well pack up the RV if I make it out of here alive.

"I watched a lot of these, and Aniston brings up some good points."

I perk up. Did he just compliment me?

"Some of these videos are very positive about the PTSO." He clicks on one where I recapped the workday and another where I showed decorations for the Fall Festival, urging everyone to come out.

"But that still doesn't cancel out what she said about the room-mom duties."

Principal Dingle removes his glasses and rubs the bridge of his nose. "Georgia, are you really making these moms do some of this? Do you really have a two-hundred-page manual?"

Georgia wrinkles her nose, looks at me, then back at him. Either she's confused, or my body's so numb that I farted without feeling it. After a long pause, she nods slowly.

"Georgia, I warned you not to let this get out of hand. These ladies are volunteering their time to help the school."

Georgia shrinks back in her seat. This makes the first time I've seen her powerless. Well, except for those glorious twenty seconds when I had her pinned on her back in the bouncy house.

Principal Dingle turns to me. "Aniston, I'm sorry for all the stress this has caused you, and other moms. We appreciate all you do. I'll be looking into this room-mom manual, as well as all other PTSO manuals Georgia has created in the absence of your sister. I also apologize for pulling you from your car this morning. I'll let you get on to work . . ." He cocks his head and notices my pajama pants. "Or whatever it is you plan on doing."

I stand. "Thank you. I vlog in this." I smile, and we share a quick laugh.

He shakes my hand, and I open the door to leave. Georgia stands behind me, but stops when he calls her name.

"Georgia, if I could speak with just you another moment, and please close the door."

I exit the building, a huge weight lifted from my shoulders. I don't know what he'll say to Georgia after I leave, and I honestly don't care. For once in my life, I'm the kid who gets to leave early instead of the one staying back for punishment.

Easton

I'm under the tractor working on the hydraulics when my phone rings. I almost drop it when I see the name across the screen. *Aniston.* I fumble the phone before I manage to answer and hold it to my ear.

"Hello?" I wince at the nervousness in my voice.

"Easton?"

"Yeah?"

"I hate to bother you, but I need your help."

My heart rises, then sinks. I wanted to hear "I need you" without the help part, but I'll take what I can get at this point.

"Sure, what is it?"

"Could you possibly watch the kids for a bit? I've been called to an emergency PTSO meeting, and Principal Dingle said it's vital we all attend."

"Okay, send them over."

"Thanks, we'll swing by soon. I owe you one."

Hmm . . . I'll have to remember that.

Before I can comment, she hangs up. I stare at my phone a second before putting it back in my pocket. Then I glance down at my dirty jeans and shirt. I need to run to the house and shower before they come over.

I jog to the house, not taking the time to kick off my muddy boots until I make it to the bathroom. There, I leave my dirty clothes and boots in a pile and jump into the shower. I wash in record time and run a towel over my damp hair before wrapping it around my waist.

Then I decide its best I shave. I've never been fond of myself with facial hair, but haven't kept my face cleanly shaven the last few weeks. Even if Aniston stays in her vehicle, I don't want to chance her seeing me like this.

My hand shakes with nerves as I quickly run the razor over my face. I'm almost done when the doorbell rings. I shave the last patch of my chin, nicking it at the corner. For a tiny cut, it bleeds like a stuck hog.

I grab a square of toilet paper and hold it to the cut, then hurry for the door. When I open it, Aniston stares at me and her eyes widen.

I touch my chin as my face heats up. "Oh, I cut myself." I move the paper from my face, then glance down to realize I'm wearing a towel and nothing more.

Worried the towel might slip, because that's my luck, I hold tightly to the knot on the side. Aniston reaches toward my face and applies slight pressure to my chin with her thumb. My Adam's apple bulges at her soft touch. I've missed her hands, her face, her lips.

I stare at her like a stalker until she starts to blush. "Oh, sorry." I glance at my towel. "I'll get dressed. Bring the kids on in."

She half-smiles and follows me inside. I notice a trail of dirt from my boots on my way to my room. "And sorry about the mess."

Aniston doesn't answer. I shut the door behind me and slip into clean clothes. I don't bother checking my face. Maybe if I'm still bleeding, she'll touch me again. Wow, I'm *that* pathetic.

When I return to the living room, Carter and Willow are on the couch. Aniston is in the doorway, literally one foot out the door.

"Thanks again, Easton. I'll be back as soon as it's over." She steps onto the porch, closing the door behind her.

I turn to the kids so I won't watch her drive off like the lonely man I've become. "You kids hungry?"

Willow sighs. "I told her I could watch us, but she insisted we stay with an adult."

I laugh. "I'm sure you could, but I don't mind. Say, how would y'all like to get something to eat at Mary's?"

They agree in unison. Then Carter jumps from the couch, commenting how he's been craving a cheeseburger from there.

"Let's go, then." I swipe my hand toward the door. "Uh, in a second." I wiggle my bare toes and realize I still haven't put on socks or shoes.

I duck into my room and reappear a minute later wearing boots. Clean boots. That reminds me of my mess, so I hold up a finger. "One more minute."

After collecting the boot debris with a broom and dustpan, we can leave. I open the door and motion for them to head out. Carter shoots me a look that communicates "finally."

We climb in the truck and head for town. Nobody says much until Willow comments, "You're bleeding."

"Oh." I touch my chin and blood dots my fingertip. I grab a napkin out of the door and hold it to my face.

Carter informs me of how many school days they have until Thanksgiving break. "What are you doing for Thanksgiving?"

I grip the steering wheel tighter. "I guess going to my parents' house."

"You guess? You don't know?" Carter raises his brows.

"Yeah. What about y'all?"

Willow and Carter exchange a look that makes me wish I hadn't asked. They're quiet for a few minutes as I turn into the parking lot at Mary's.

At last, Willow answers, "It's not for sure, but Aunt Ani said we may take a trip."

"Huh, well that sounds like fun." I swallow the lump in my throat and attempt to swallow my emotions with it. I hope this isn't a trip where they don't plan on coming back. Who knows with Aniston.

I cut the truck engine, and we go inside the restaurant. There's a decent-sized crowd for a weeknight, but it is the most popular place to eat in the county.

Mary waves from behind the counter when she notices us. We find a booth near the back and settle in. A minute later, a young waitress brings our menus and leaves with our drink orders.

Carter closes his menu and folds his hands on the table. "So, about what we talked about last week."

I sit like a statue, feigning ignorance. By talking, he means that he interrogated me about Aniston and told me to talk to her. Since I almost dropped my phone in tractor grease at the sight of her name, it's clear I haven't held up my end of the bargain.

"I know you remember." Carter sticks a straw in the Styrofoam drink the waitress sets in front of him. Then he orders a cheeseburger with ketchup only, all while never taking his eyes off me.

If he weren't four-foot tall with a few missing teeth, I might be intimidated.

"What did you guys talk about?" Willow turns from me to Carter and back to me.

I sip my tea to stall answering. But there's no need, as Carter does it for me. "I told him to talk to Aunt Ani."

"Oh." Willow presses her lips together.

"No, Carter. Other than to say I'd watch you two, we haven't talked yet."

"Well, why not?" His face contorts, and I can't decide if he's angry, upset, or both.

I'm not used to a seven-year-old interrogating me. But this is not your average seven-year-old.

"Carter, son." I rub my temples. How do I explain this? "It's complicated."

"Not to me. You like her, she likes you. That means you should be together."

"I—" I stumble on my words and take a sip of tea to clear my voice. "It's not always that simple."

"It should be."

I cut my eyes toward Willow, who's leaning against the wall, taking it all in. "What do you think?"

She sighs. "No offense, but I have to side with Carter on this one."

"Excuse me. I need to visit the restroom." I dart toward the single-stall restroom and sigh once I lock the door behind me. I take a few minutes to breathe and prepare myself for whatever Carter asks next.

As I'm returning to the booth, the waitress brings our plates. We all play nice as she sets them in front of us and grants Carter's request for an extra bottle of ketchup.

I debate asking her to join us and volunteering to tip her whatever money she'd forfeit by doing so. Anything to keep these kids off my case. Instead, I let her walk away as I pop a fry in my mouth.

"You should talk to her tonight," Carter comments before biting into his burger.

"Fine. I will when she picks you guys up."

"No, Easton, this can't wait. You need to do it now. That would be romantic." Willow's eyes go dreamy as she talks.

"You really think so?" I wipe the corner of my mouth with my napkin, not sure if it's blood or ketchup on my chin. At this point, I don't care. I have more important concerns, like why I'm taking love advice from babies.

"Yes, sir. Like in the movies," Willow adds.

"She's got that thing at the school," I say.

"We can go there!" Carter gets a little too excited, gaining us a few stares from across the room. "Sorry," he whispers.

"You really think she'd think it's romantic . . . and not get mad?" I can't believe I'm even having this conversation.

"Of course." Willow grins.

I pick up another fry and hold it midair. "Can I at least finish my food first?"

Willow grins wider. Carter nods. "Do you think I'd suggest we leave before I finish my burger?" he asks.

We all laugh a minute, then continue eating. I try and enjoy my steak sandwich best I can, but it's hard to eat in anticipation of what will come next.

CHAPTER 25

Aniston

I haven't heard anything from Georgia since our meeting in the principal's office. She's avoided eye contact with me at all costs in the car line. That's fine by me. Plus, it offered some entertainment the day she nearly stumbled into traffic to avoid looking my way.

I've enjoyed having momentary silence until all the holiday events come into play. I suspect that's what this meeting is about. Maybe Principal Dingle called me on behalf of Georgia. Maybe she's afraid of me. That would be convenient.

Maribelle sits beside me holding a tiny plate stacked high with cookies. She smiles and greets others as they shuffle past us. I wonder what made everyone suddenly leave the refreshments table and hurry to find a seat?

Principal Dingle strides toward a microphone set up beneath the basketball hoop. So that's why.

I sit straighter and survey the room. No sign of Georgia.

Unless she's observing us from upstairs like a sniper, she's not here.

"Good evening, parents." Dingle adjusts his glasses on his thin nose. "Most of you probably assume this meeting is to start planning the Christmas fundraisers. Well, it's not."

A few audible gasps and whispers fill the room before he continues.

"We'll have time for that when we come back from Thanksgiving break. No need to plan so much so far in advance like we've done recently." He clears his throat. "I called you here tonight to announce that Georgia Jenkins will no longer serve as PTSO president after the end of the year. This holiday season will be her last to lead us."

More gasps come from the crowd, including from me. Maribelle almost chokes on an Oreo, and Mindy tears up.

"I felt this change was best moving forward. What I need from all of you tonight is a vote for the next president. Since Georgia was our original VP, we have nobody next in line. Please write your choice from those in this room to serve as the next PTSO president, effective in January."

He picks up a stack of paper slips and a cup of pens from a nearby table. Then he hands them to Mindy, who takes one of each before passing them to her left.

Since I'm in the back, I have time to scan the room for viable candidates. Who should I vote for? My eyes land on Maribelle, who's playing Jenga with a stack of Oreos. No, she doesn't want this. I can't do that to her.

I consider Mindy or her friend, but decide either would be sitting ducks for Georgia to puppet master from behind the scenes.

Who else is in here . . . TikTok Tami stands near the gym entrance. Did she become a room mom? I don't think she could pull it off. Besides, she looks very pregnant now.

Morgan and Brooke know better than to be in here, but I may write one of their names anyway. They're pretty common names. I'm sure there's another Morgan or Brooke in here someplace.

The woman beside me shoves the cup of pens my way. I take one, along with a paper, then pass them to Maribelle. My hand sweats around the pen as I debate one last time before folding the paper.

Dingle steps back behind the mic. "When you have cast your vote, please bring your paper to me." He lifts another cup from the table and holds it out to collect votes.

The woman at the very end of our row takes the cup of pens and extra papers up as well. One by one, people drop slips of paper into the cup. Maribelle and I take ours once she manages to remove her plate from her lap without messing up her cookie castle.

"Has everyone turned in a slip?" Dingle holds up the cup, scanning the room for acknowledgment.

People nod and mumble "yes." Then he nods and stands behind the table. We whisper among ourselves as he unfolds the papers one at a time. It doesn't take him long, and then he returns to the mic.

"Okay, this is easier than I expected. It looks like we have a landslide vote. One person got all the votes except three. There's two for Mindy . . ." Mindy smiles back at everyone from her front row seat. "Someone left one blank. Very funny." I lick my lips and lower my head. No way I'm fessing up. "And the rest are for Aniston Wilson."

Wait . . . did he say?

Maribelle shakes my arm. "Congratulations."

No! "Can I decline?" I say this more to myself than Maribelle.

She snorts and swats at my knee. "No, silly. This is awesome. You're a voice of reason for us normal people."

I cock my head her way. As much as I want to run for the hills and never look back, I know she's right. I have to do this.

Someone in the center of the room makes eye contact with

me and starts a slow clap. It catches on until even Mindy is clapping. TikTok Tami yells, "Speech!"

Again, what is she doing here?

The clapping continues, and Dingle points to the mic, smiling. I stand slowly and make my way to the front. I've never given a speech, unless you count talking into my computer mic, alone, for a vlog—which I don't count.

I stare straight ahead as I make my way up front. All eyes are on me. My entire body burns like a thousand lasers are shooting through it.

Principal Dingle steps aside when I step up to the mic. I bend it down, since he's basically a skinnier Will Ferrell. It squeaks in my ear, and I wince.

"Hi, uh, thanks for voting for me?"

A few rogue claps come from the back. I clear my throat and continue.

"I've never given a public speech before, so bear with me. Truth is, I don't even want this job." I laugh nervously, and Mindy shoots me a jealous look. I ignore her. "What I want is to make PTSO good for everyone involved—parents, teachers, students. We can't do that if we're always stressed and not having a good time."

"Preach it, girl!" A woman in the middle of the room pumps her fist in the air.

"Thanks." I grin at her. "As I was saying, we had all these micromanaging rules. It's as if they put us in charge of things but didn't trust us to be capable adults—"

I stop midsentence when all eyes turn toward the door. TikTok Tami smiles crazily as Easton walks past her. Carter and Willow stand by her in the doorway. I shrug to them, but they only smile in return. At least that assures me nothing tragic happened.

"What's wrong?" I ask Easton when he's within a few feet of me.

He doesn't answer me with words, but he does use his

mouth. Before I can blink, he cups my face in his hands and kisses me. Right there in front of everyone. Principal Dingle, the PTSO moms, my kids, TikTok Tami. And wait, is that the janitor I see out of the corner of my eye?

Ah, who cares. I close my eyes and wrap my arms around him. We kiss like nobody's in the room. Maybe that will spur the principal to fire me from this newly elected job I never wanted.

Once we pull back, Easton grins at me and says, "Nothing's wrong now."

I narrow my eyes, then smile back at him as his face beams. I'm not sure what he's been going through the past month, but it's clear he has missed me. He moves his hands from my face to my shoulders and stares deep into my eyes. "I love you, Aniston."

My eyes start to water as I whisper back, "I love you too." I give him a kiss on the cheek, lingering only a few seconds as I remember our audience.

Easton gently squeezes my shoulders, then raises a hand toward the crowd. Blushing, he says, "Sorry, ladies, and principal." He turns toward the door. "And Coach."

I follow his gaze. Apparently that was Coach and not the janitor. He waves a hand, then TikTok Tami grabs him and kisses him. He pushes her off, and she runs out.

Coach hooks a thumb toward her and stares at Dingle. "Can you do something about that now?"

Dingle nods. "I'll have her banned from the gym and playground first thing tomorrow morning."

"Thank you." Coach wipes his mouth with the back of his hand and continues sweeping around the doorway.

Easton and I lock eyes. "I didn't mean to rush in and interrupt, but the kids insisted I not waste any more time."

"I'm glad you did." I rub my thumb across the small cut starting to mend on his chin. Then I turn to Dingle. "Sir, if you need me to step down due to this PDA, I understand."

He flaps a skinny finger toward my face. "You're not getting off that easy, Ms. Wilson. I expect you ready to report for duty first thing after the holiday week."

"Yes, sir."

Everyone cheers again, and even Mindy comes by to congratulate me. She tears up when she hugs me tight. I catch my breath, surprised at how someone so small can squeeze me like a tube of toothpaste.

Principal Dingle bangs a plastic cup against the table and yells, "Meeting adjourned."

Women scatter in various directions, chattering as they leave. I wrap my arms around Easton's neck again and stare into his dark eyes. The kids make their way toward us, and I open my arms to include them.

I never expected to have my own family, especially in the way it happened. But these three people mean the world to me, and no matter where I am or what's going on, I'm never letting go of them.

Aniston

Easton shoves one more bag into the RV and shuts the door. Morgan adjusts her sunglasses and takes inventory of her kids. "Andrew, get out here. We're leaving!"

Andrew barrels around the side of my house, barefoot. Morgan props her hands on her hips. "Where are your shoes?"

He points to the pool, which has been winterized and is not heated. I'm certain he'd be swimming by now had Morgan not yelled for him.

"Go get them." She snaps and points toward the backyard.

Andrew races off as the rest of her kids settle into my RV. I surprised Morgan by letting her borrow it for fall break. She's taking her kids to Dollywood over Thanksgiving. This will make their first family trip without her ex or her parents.

For that reason, I hid Tylenol in both the kitchen area and glove box. I'll text her that after they've been on the road a few hours. It should make for an even better surprise than the RV.

"Any final instructions?" Morgan asks as Andrew returns with his shoes. He's holding them, rather than wearing them, and climbs in the RV in his sock feet.

"Just fight the urge to fill her with cheap gas. Any final instructions for me?"

Morgan nods. "If you want the pecans a little crispy, put the casserole on broil for about two minutes at the end. And I wouldn't pull out the banana pudding until it's time for dessert."

"Got it." I smile.

Morgan asked if there was anything she could do for me since I lent her the RV free of charge. I halfway joked that she could cook my Thanksgiving meal. She agreed on the spot to prep everything and leave me heating instructions. How could I turn that down?

Easton meets us by the driver's door. "All your bags are inside. There's also plenty of snacks still in the pantry."

"Shhh." I pinch my lips and nod back toward my kids. Then I turn to Morgan and Easton. "Don't let your kids tell my kids that's where I keep my secret stash."

They both laugh. "You're secret's safe with me." Morgan makes a zipping motion over her mouth. "Any souvenir requests?"

Easton's eyes light up like a kid at Christmas. "Some of those caramel Moon Pies. You can't find that flavor around here."

"Got it. Ani?"

I twist my lips and stare at the sky before facing Morgan. "Hmm . . . I'm not much of a souvenir person, but if you get to meet Dolly, an autograph would be nice."

Morgan grins. "It would be a lot easier if you wanted a candy apple or T-shirt or something, but I'll try."

I grin. "Thanks."

Before I can say anything else, Morgan grabs me in a tight bear hug. I stand limp for a second, then my arms regain enough feeling to hug her back.

"I'm gonna miss you, girl," she mumbles into my neck.

"We'll miss you too, and think of you with every bite of Thursday's dinner."

Morgan pulls back and laughs, then opens her door and steps inside. She hangs her arm out the open window and adjusts the rearview mirror. "Next stop, Dollywood!"

Her kids clap and cheer from the back. Morgan leans out the window and whispers to me, "Just kidding, y'all know I'm so gonna stop at Buc-ee's."

Easton wraps an arm around my waist and gives me a gentle squeeze. I bite back a laugh. Morgan is the biggest sucker for tourist traps.

"See y'all next week." She winces at the morning sun and pulls the visor down, then backs out of the driveway.

We watch her head down the road, waving as she honks the horn.

It's odd seeing my RV's taillights. The only time that's happened is when I got stuck on a mountain in north Georgia and paid a hippie college kid hiking nearby to pull it out. I held his "medicinal marijuana" for collateral so he wouldn't take off with my home.

"Do you miss her?"

I look at Easton and scrunch my nose. "Morgan?"

"No, the RV."

I narrow my eyes toward the dust flying off the gravel road from Morgan's departure. "Nah."

"It's understandable if you do. You lived in it for years, and had it here as a snack-time refuge." He squeezes my side until I laugh.

"Quit making fun of me hiding snacks. I'm told a lot of moms do that."

"I'm sure they do. I'd say you got the upper hand this week, trading Morgan's sweet potato casserole for Cheez-Its and snack cakes."

"True. But we still need a turkey before Thursday."

"I've got it covered."

"Do you?"

"Yeah, my mom's bringing it."

I nod. "Well played, Dr. West, well played."

"I told her we would have everything else, which seemed to impress her."

The blood drains from my face. "So you let her believe I can cook all that? What happens at Christmas, and any time after that? I can't live up to a Morgan meal."

He laughs and turns me toward him. "No, silly. She knows we outsourced all the fixings. And I might have mentioned how you're not really a cook, including the kitchen fire."

I pop his arm. "Easton. What else did you tell her about me?"

He wraps both arms around me and pulls me close. "Just normal stuff. Like how you're a good mom and funny and make the best crack I've ever tasted."

"Easton!" My eyes widen as I imagine his mom's response to me making "crack" and Easton having tried multiple kinds of crack.

"Don't worry, I explained that it's made of cookies and legal sugar. I told her how it played a role in the day we met."

"You didn't mention my attire, did you?"

"Just that you're the most naturally beautiful woman I've ever laid eyes on."

"Stop." I swat his arm.

He grins. "I can go on if you want."

I shrug. "May as well."

His face goes serious. "Then I told her you're the only woman I could imagine spending the rest of my life with."

My heart swells and a tingling sensation courses through my limbs. "You told her that?"

He nods. "I sure did. I meant every word of it too. That's why I hope you'll renew my lease next month, because I plan on staying in Apple Cart . . . if that's what you want."

I hug my arms around his neck and snuggle into his chest. "That's what I want more than anything. To stay here with you and the kids." I nuzzle against his neck before lifting my head. "Besides, Morgan took off with my backup house."

He rolls his eyes. "Very funny."

We share a quick laugh, then I kiss him. He holds me tighter and kisses me in a way that says this is the beginning of forever.

One thing I've learned is that there's no guarantee how long our forevers will last. However long I have left on this Earth, I'm thrilled to spend it with these kids and this man. We may not be the perfect family, but we're perfect for each other.

EPILOGUE

Three Months Later

Aniston

I straighten the banner above the gym entrance. This is my first official event as head of the PTSO.

Since I skipped prom and homecoming dances growing up, I had to call in some reinforcements. Brooke helped head up the decorations, and Mindy stayed on board to brief me on everything from last year's Daddy-Daughter Dance.

I cut back on a lot of the decorations. Apparently, Georgia ran up quite a bill at Hobby Lobby last year. I decided to use half that money and order pizzas and float the rest toward something else. Like, I don't know, maybe actually helping the school.

Speaking of Georgia . . . I freeze halfway down the ladder

when I notice her talking to Mindy. By the time I make it to the floor, she's by my side.

Easton comes over from hanging the last of the balloons. "Georgia, how are you?" He glares at her in a way that communicates, "Don't mess with my girlfriend."

I put my hand on his arm. "It's okay."

He half-smiles at me. "If you need me, I'll be with the balloons."

"Okay." I give him a pleasant face and he returns to the center of the gym, glancing back a time or two on his way. I cross my arms and turn to Georgia.

"I just wanted to say I think you're doing a good job with this."

My shoulders slump a bit as I loosen my defenses. She sounds and looks sincere. "Thank you, I appreciate you saying that."

Georgia peers around me into the gym. "Of course, I'd have gone with a Valentine's Day color scheme since it is February."

I bite my bottom lip. We have red and white everywhere, which are the school colors. Is that not Valentine's enough? I didn't want to toss in a ton of pink since we're inviting dads too. However, this is not the hill I want to die on. I raise my eyebrows and force myself to keep my mouth shut.

"Anyway, good luck with everything." Georgia glances back at me, her eyes like a puppy at the pound that's been passed over one too many times. She turns, drops her head, and starts toward the parking lot.

I could easily go back into the gym and help the others finish decorating. I've made peace with Georgia and have nothing more to fight over. However, an aching sensation inside won't allow me to let this one go.

"Georgia?"

She turns at her name.

I swallow, already regretting the words I'm about to say. "Would you like to help?"

Her face lights up like a Vegas billboard. "Could I?" She hurries back to me.

I'm already cursing myself in my head, even though I know this was the right thing to do. "Yeah, but you know I'm in charge, right?"

"Absolutely." She smiles and follows me as I enter the gym. "I can help with whatever you need, and I'm happy to offer suggestions if you need it and—"

"No suggestions, please. Unless I ask."

She nods enthusiastically. "Got it." Then she leaps at me and squeezes me tightly.

I stand petrified, partly out of shock and partly out of pain.

"This is going to be so much fun." Georgia sways back and forth a few times, moving me with her, before releasing me.

I let out a deep breath like I've had a metal corset unhooked from my middle. She's way stronger than she looks. Though I should know this thanks to our ninja battle at the festival.

"Uh, you can help Mindy and Brooke hang the lights."

Georgia claps and practically skips toward the bleachers where the women are setting up a photo booth. Easton comes over and squeezes my shoulder. I flinch, as I'm still a little tense from Georgia's chokehold.

"Are you still okay?"

I sigh as Georgia untangles lights for Mindy and Brooke, then look at Easton. "Yeah, I think I am."

"That was nice of you to let her help."

I grit my teeth. "Yeah . . . we'll see how it goes."

He chuckles. "You know, I was thinking about the dance again last night. Are you sure it's fine for me to go with Willow since I'm not technically in her family?"

My jaw drops. "Of course, Easton. You're the closest thing to a daddy she's known since Luke passed. Why would you even say a thing like that?"

"I don't know, maybe because it might mean more if I was officially in her family."

I tilt my head, confused at what he means. Before I can ask, he's on one knee, holding a diamond ring. My eyes bug when I realize what's happening. He's proposing.

"Wait, are you for real?"

He nods and laughs. "Uh, yes."

"And you're not just doing this so she'll have a stepdaddy at the dance?"

He stands and holds the ring between us. "Now, come on. That's a little extreme, don't you think?"

I waver my head. "Eh." My eyes dart between him and the ring, as I still need reassurance this is real. "You're really proposing, to me, now?"

He lowers the ring, his face saddening. "I mean, if it's okay. I wanted to do something cool like take you on a trip or at least out to eat first."

I shake my head, tears filling my eyes. "No, this is perfect. No more trips, at least for now. I've traveled enough. And yes."

He grins and picks me up, then swings me around. We kiss until I'm dizzy. Then I pull back and stare into his eyes.

"Do you want the ring now?"

I laugh. "Oh yeah, the ring." I hold out my left hand.

He slides it up my finger. "At least I know you didn't say yes for the diamond."

I laugh harder and wipe away tears with my right hand. It's a beautiful ring, but he's right—that doesn't even matter. We stand embraced, laughing and admiring the ring.

"Sorry to interrupt."

I turn to Brooke a few feet away, holding a paper lantern.

She notices my hand on Easton's chest. "Holy cow, that's gorgeous."

I beam. "Easton just proposed."

"Wait, like right now?"

We both nod.

"Oh my gosh, you guys need a picture." She pulls her phone from her back pocket. "Say cheese."

We smile and strike several poses, including some kissing and some showing off my ring. Before long, Mindy and Georgia find their way to us and spot the ring.

"Eek!" Georgia jumps and claps. "How exciting. Aniston, I can so plan your wedding."

"No!" Easton and I shout in unison.

Georgia stops celebrating and clenches her teeth. Hurt washes over her face.

"No thanks, I mean, no thanks." I smile at her until a bit of pink returns to her cheeks. "We don't need a big wedding is all."

"Nope," Easton agrees. "We already have everything we need." Then he spins me around one more time, making me laugh until I cry again.

This is one dance I'm not going to skip.

ACKNOWLEDGMENTS

First, I'd like to thank God for giving me creative ideas and placing the right people in my path to help see them to fruition.

My husband, Blake, gets credit next for always supporting my writing endeavors, even if he finds my stories a little too "girly and Hallmarkish." Of course, this book kind of broke the mold when it comes to that.

I also want to thank my readers and ARC team for their support. It means the world to me that busy people would give of their time to read early, post reviews, and share the news of my books with their friends. I couldn't do this without y'all!

As always, I'd like to thank my editor, Joanne. She's always a pleasure to work with and polishes my books to help them shine.

ABOUT THE AUTHOR

Kaci Lane is a journalist turned fiction writer who believes all stories should have a happy ending. While unsuccessfully trying to learn Spanish for a decade, she has become fluent in sarcasm, Southern belle and movie quotes. She is married to a Southern Gentleman and has two young children who help keep her humility in check. Connect with her on kacilane.com or Facebook.

BOOKS BY KACI LANE

Bama Boys Series*

Hunting for Love

Chicken about Love

Hammered by Love

Cutting out Love

Geared for Love

Guilty of Love (coming soon)

Apple Cart County Christmas*

Christmas in Dixie

Crazy Rich Rednecks

Queen of My Double-Wide Trailer (coming soon)

Schooled on Love Series

Taco Truck Takedown

Side Hustle

Buggy List

Off-Season

Books in Shared Series with Other Authors

No Time for Traditions

A Perfect Match in Silver Leaf Falls

*If you enjoyed spending time in Apple Cart County, revisit the quirky community with the Bama Boys series or Apple Cart County Christmas series. Both include secondary characters from the Single Southern Mamas series.